ALSO BY KIMBERLY KING PARSONS

Black Light

WE WERE
 THE
UNIVERSE

WE WERE
THE
UNIVERSE

A Novel

Kimberly King Parsons

ALFRED A. KNOPF

New York

THIS IS A BORZOI BOOK
PUBLISHED BY ALFRED A. KNOPF

www.aaknopf.com

Knopf, Borzoi Books, and the colophon are registered trademarks
of Penguin Random House LLC.

Library of Congress Cataloging-in-Publication Data
Names: Parsons, Kimberly King, author.
Title: We were the universe : a novel / Kimberly King Parsons.
Description: First edition. | New York : Alfred A. Knopf, 2024.
Identifiers: LCCN 2023028841 (print) | LCCN 2023028842 (ebook) |
ISBN 9780525521853 (hardcover) | ISBN 9780525563525 (paperback) |
ISBN 9780525521860 (ebook)
Subjects: GSAFD: Black humor. | Novels.
Classification: LCC PS3616.A78265 W49 2024 (print) |
LCC PS3616.A78265 (ebook) | DDC 813/.6—dc23/eng/20230623
LC record available at https://lccn.loc.gov/2023028841
LC ebook record available at https://lccn.loc.gov/2023028842

Jacket illustrations by Maria Ramos
Jacket design by Janet Hansen

Manufactured in the United States of America
First Edition

For my mother

No matter where we are

We're always touching by underground wires

Of Montreal, "The Past Is a Grotesque Animal"

Part One

TINY
TOADS

M Y DAUGHTER IS BACKLIT BY THE SUN, WAVING AND calling to me, but I'm split—half of me is here on the playground with her, half is in the past with the girl who taught me about negative space.

Gilda shouts, "Watch, Mama! Mama, watch!"

We're at Hidden Wonder Park—Gilda's favorite—and she's found a new friend, one of these helpless kids she drags around and calls sister. Lit this way, they could be twins, though today's sister is younger than Gilda and smaller: not much more than a toddler. They both have wild hair and skinny arms, plus the same unearthly beauty all children share. That eerie, opalescent skin, those unformed, boneless noses. Two fused girls, holding hands. They make a single shadow.

One of Gilda's shoes is gone. You bring a kid to Hidden Wonder specifically to get a moment of peace, but she'll keep sucking you in. Bring a book and you'll never open it. Start tapping on your phone and this is the precise moment your child will fracture her tibia, poke some newborn in the eyeball.

I should stand up and look for Gilda's sandal. I should. My body may be on this park bench, but astrally I've hurled myself back to freshman art class—Intro to Whatever, Whatever 101—my whole soul pulsing in that paint-spangled studio. The art girl was a wry genius with a heap of curly hair—she worked the easel next to mine. If you looked close, you'd notice this girl was always spattered, sparks dotting her forearms and cheeks, smears on her fingers, little fans of color on her neck. God knows where else the paint got to. I spent a lot of time imagining a tub of faintly rainbowed bathwater, the art girl stepping out of it.

"You watching me?" Gilda yells.

"Definitely," I shout.

The studio was in the unrenovated part of campus, in a corrugated metal building we called the Art Barn. It was full of natural light but poorly ventilated. There was a constant, delicious reek of oils and solvents and dangerous glue—that semester, a bunch of us kept getting nosebleeds. Whatever carcinogens I likely sucked from the air, whatever sick, slow-growing seed may be lodged in my lungs, it was worth it. The art girl wore these concert T-shirts with the sleeves cut out huge—when she lifted her paintbrush, you could see all down the side of her. For weeks she quietly watched me struggle with some assigned still life—a bowl of fruit maybe, a chair. One day she touched the paint-speckled notch at her throat, made a sound there, turned her canvas toward mine.

There's a bank of plastic spring-mounted animals near the playground gate. Gilda hops like a rabbit toward the fake rabbits, jerking the girl along. "Gentle," I trill, hoping to god this sister's arm stays in socket. She'll wise up and escape soon, they always do, but for now she belongs to Gilda. "Remember we are *gentle*," I say again for the adults, hoping nobody has noticed Gilda's dirty foot. I beat being a teen mom by just a couple years, not that I look especially young anymore. I've always had to work hard to seem convincing.

The playground tug is such a bitch. It's too hot today, too crowded. Even the qualified caregivers seem on edge. Out here, we're all stars in the theater of parenthood. Each playground misstep requires a verbal assessment, correction, and redirection given to your child in patient, loving tones. One-liners delivered by parents, for parents. The kids don't hear a thing. I shade my eyes and act like I'm looking close at my daughter.

The art girl gently explained light and dark to me. She tilted her head, brought her long hand to hover close to my failure. She said, "Can I?" and in my notebook she flipped to the first blank page, pinched a nub of charcoal. She made her case with a sketch of those famous, about-to-kiss vase people, and I let my heart go wild with the thought that something might happen between us.

"See, Mama?"

Gilda and her captive mount their rabbits and rock on them. The sister copies Gilda—one hand up to twirl a slow, invisible lasso.

"See us?"

Lord, Gilda, yes. I remind myself that all this neediness is just a phase, and a flattering one too. Like without me to confirm it for her, nothing in the world exists.

The art girl was super straight, but I ached for her that entire semester, always slow with hard truths. We became friends, a form of torture. She had an off-campus apartment, a bad spine and an oxy script, an inherited family parrot in her living room. She would play records and sit on her couch while I danced, not *for* her exactly, but if you walked into the art girl's place at the right moment, you might have gotten the wrong idea.

"Are you seeing this, Mama?" Gilda yells. She and the sister stand up on their rabbits, prepare to make the short leap to Astroturf.

The art girl's bird watched me dance too, jerked its slick head, cranked open and shut the pupils of its white eyes. It ate raw hamburger as a treat, and it would rip the shit out of your hair if you danced too close to its perch. You had to be calm, not get hysterical, while the art girl helped extricate you. "They live to be a hundred," she told me once, grimly unhooking my braid from beak and claw.

"Are you seeing us *up in the air*?" Gilda shouts.

"I see the air," I say.

Gilda's too worried about me, too busy making sure I'm riveted, and that's when the sister bounds off, breaks free. "Bye, fren!" Gilda's girl screams. She shoots across the playground and hides behind another dark-haired girl, her real sister maybe.

"Mamaaaah," Gilda says, and runs to me, mournful. "She left. Did you see she left me?"

I palm her hot head. "I saw, Gilly. Deep breaths," I say. I take a few of those too, jerk myself from my pining, pigmented past, reassemble here in the heartbreaking now. Poor Gilda. Loss is the lesson life teaches, ready or not.

Thank god she's amped on fruit leathers, fully tweaked from corn syrup, and it doesn't take her long to move on. She runs from me, full force to the play structure.

The art girl's creepy parrot—the way its eyes would dilate and contract, dilate and contract. It never said a word, but because it could have, you got the feeling it was planning something vile.

I USED TO HAVE a better brain. Clean and organized, the wires soldered just so. A headline I read this morning, ungodly understatement, "Motherhood Not Best Thing for Women's Mental Health." I have a scrolling list like everybody: oat milk, milk-milk, butter, make that dentist appointment, pay my sliding-scale therapist. That's all fine, but I've got these memory hemorrhages too, Technicolor scenes that barge into my thoughts.

"We go *down* the slide," I yell to Gilda, but she presses on, scrambles up hot metal, ruins the flow for a glum boy waiting at the top. She crawls around him, pushes down the ladder, shoves against the line of pissed-off kids. I say what I have to say, and Gilda does exactly what Gilda wants: our contract.

"I didn't do that," she shouts, waving her hand like a wand at where she's been, what she's done. I can't tell if she's simpler or more complex than other three-year-olds. She tells these tremendous lies, no shame. She has her own room, but she's always slept with Jad and me, and sometimes in the mornings we'll wake up damp in her little puddle. She'll rub her eyes, her hair all crazy.

"That's not pee," she'll say. "That's champagne."

Co-sleeping is what my attachment parenting message boards call this lifestyle—family slumber, family bed. As Gilda's gotten bigger, *bed wrestling* is maybe a more apt term, *slumber struggling.*

"Help," she calls, now low in the slack loop of a swing. Not the goddamn swings. I come here to sit, not push. What I want to do is not get up for a good long while. I want to drink this iced coffee, the one I bought but can't afford, my daily middle-class lie.

"Mama, push," whines Gilda, pitifully pumping her soft legs. I shake the ice in my cup, pretend not to hear. I give her a thumbs-up and wait it out.

Eventually, she runs to a group of kids playing under the slide. She says something I can't hear, and they turn and squint up at her. I can tell she's being an asshole by the cock of her head. She's recently learned the word *stupid,* and I have to fake surprise every time it falls from her tiny mouth. What *is* surprising, and a relief, frankly, is that she hasn't learned the complete phrase yet. *Stupid-butthole-bitch* is a thing I say to myself, maybe louder than I realize. An incantation—I do it snapped to a beat. *Stupid-butthole-bitch* when I lock myself out and Jad has to come home and let us in. *Stupid-butthole-bitch* when I burn Gilda's macaroni. I hate the word *butthole* above all else. It's a punishment to say it.

There it is—Gilda's gleeful voice: "You soupid rats." I don't want to intervene, but now I have to stand up, make an effort.

"No thank you. No, ma'am," I loudly say, like *Look how very shocked I am.* The good parents are watching.

A boy from the underslide crew glares at me, then at Gilda. He's shorter than she is but sturdier, with inflamed cheeks and a big round head.

"Shoe," I sing, pointing to the dusty, flipped-over sandal I've spotted near the fence. "We wear shoes in the park." This is partially a distraction and partially an act of ass covering, a lesson I learned when Gilda was tiny and the world at large seemed compelled to point out her messy hair and unsocked feet to me all day long.

Gilda runs off, but the underslide kid goes too. He intercepts the shoe, holds it out of reach. Gilda sets her jaw, shows her tiny bottom teeth. I'm grateful again for how bald her anger is, thankful I can so clearly see when rage gathers in her.

"Gilly, remember we are kind," I say, but the boy is *wielding* the shoe now, has it cocked above his head.

"Hey!" I say, and clap three times to break the spell. Gilda is too close to this maniac, too far from me. "Hey, *kid*!" I yell. I'm not performing anymore, smile gone from my voice. I give a wet, two-fingered whistle that scatters the chirping grackles and stuns everyone—children and parents alike. Time stutters. People turn their heads, look to see who has made such a vulgar sound. The kid drops the shoe, runs fast to the big vacant rabbits.

I stand there feeling obscene with my hand at my mouth, then wipe my fingers on my sleeve. My mother used to call us home with that whistle, her terrifying trick, a whipcrack my sister and I couldn't help but run toward.

"Kind," I say, soft. Gilda doesn't even pick up the sandal, just leaves and goes to grab at the hanging rings, not because of what I've done but because she's Gilly, wild and vibrating, utterly disobedient, wanting to be everywhere at once.

I sit down, heart thudding, and roll through all the ways I'd die for her. I'll throw myself on that trash can over there if it turns out to be an explosive device. I'll shield her with my body if poison rain starts spewing from the sky, eating everybody's flesh. It's too horrifying to imagine something real.

When Mom was pregnant with Julie, my parents had me pose for a picture on a tricycle they'd gotten at a garage sale. Mom held the camera—also secondhand, same sale—and my dad was the one telling me to smile. Just as the flash popped, I was aloft, tricycle and all, wheels spinning, high over my dad's head. He'd seen what my mother missed, a rattlesnake in the scrub behind me. The photo is marred by his blurred pink hands, the long streak of his arms. I'm smiling in the frame, unaware, no threat in the shot. At this point in my life, I have no way to tell pure memory apart from the image itself—the photo has shellacked my experience. This is the type of story I'd fact-check with Julie, but she hadn't arrived yet.

"I was dead then, Kit," is something she used to say about those pictures from my early childhood, before she was born. "Not dead," I'd say, "unalive," which is a very different thing. Of course now *dead* really is the right word for what she is.

Something else I don't actually remember: the snake was a baby. My mom snipped it in two with a pair of garden shears and my dad pulled off its young rattle. He put it on a string, and I wore it around my neck all summer, the tiny thing so new it didn't make a sound.

After Dad left, he stayed on in our small town, not because he wanted to be near Julie and me, but because it was easier to be somewhere familiar, driving the same roads, shopping at Flip Mart, listening to the same bugsong every night. He mostly managed to avoid us while we were growing up, which was some feat—the smallness of Wink, Texas, can't be overstated—but then our mom mostly avoided us too, and she was the one raising us. Even the laziest, most unfit parents can hustle when they perceive danger, is my point. It's not heroic—it's biology.

Rattles are good luck, silent or not. I'm sure my mom still has the thing somewhere, in one of her filthy coffee cans or rotten shoeboxes, and I wonder how it might look around Gilda's neck. Then I think, *That's a choking hazard, you absolute butthole.*

There was a boy in my high school with a pet python called Monty. What a dork this boy was! He had burgundy bedsheets, a misstep by a well-meaning mother, I realize now, an attempt to hide stains. Instead, the boy's whitish streaks proudly crusted. The bed stayed unmade, begging for bodies, though the dork never invited any of us girls into it. Curious, I would have climbed right in, stains or no. I would have let the dork do whatever he wanted to me—this is the way I've always been. Instead, he played it cool, and my friends and Julie and I smoked his dirt weed. He'd open Monty's glass tank and all the other girls would scream and scatter. Not me. I fed on their fear. I let the dork drape me with Monty, let the creature coil his way under my T-shirt, tight around my waist, hungry for heat.

"Isn't that dangerous?" Julie asked, flustered and innocent, barely pubescent. But I knew exactly what I was doing. I was okay sitting besnaked in a beanbag chair, trying to look like a girl who knew how to fuck. On the dork's wall there was a poster of a porny model, fake blond and naked with a snake belting her hips. My mentor.

Bleach, we need more of it at home. Jad's oat milk, the milk-milk, the butter.

Gilda zips past, alone and quiet. Other children screech together, sonics blistering the pavement. Their screams are joyous, like the chorus of Julie's favorite psychedelic pop song. An infectious, happy track about being sad, begging the feel-good hormones to flood your depressed brain. She used to play it over and over.

"C'mon, chemicals!" shrieks the singer.

Pete, my best friend and easily one of the smartest people I know, says when he sits still and listens there is only silence lapping at the sides of his mind. He says it's blank and black and soft in there, the dark foam rubber of nothing, a squishy mat like the ones he and I used to stand on together in restaurant kitchens. I wanted to punch him when he told me that—I was so envious.

"Everything moves right through me," he said, "that's how stupid I am," and I said, "No, not at all, you've got the whole game figured out."

Come on, brain. Come on, chemicals.

I'M FAKING ASTONISHMENT at Gilda's monkey bar prowess when I notice a woman sitting beside me. How long has she been here? Like me, she has a book resting face down in her lap. Like me, there's a huge coffee on the bench next to her. By the way she scans the shriek-ing bodies, I can tell she's got a child in her charge. Occasionally she stands for a better look, then slowly lowers herself down.

"Bit of a crowd," she says in a British accent so strong it would stand out anywhere, especially here.

I say, "Sure is," and there's an extra southern lilt in my voice, a full-blown drawl, like my body wants to assert its origins too.

There's a big, curved gem hanging from a slim chain around this woman's neck. It's rippled like water, milky. It's sea glass or Lucite, maybe aquamarine. I have no idea if the thing is manufactured or organic, if it's heavy or featherlight, solid or hollow. I'm not sure if it's expensive or something her kid made, but the color—I'm certain because it's *my* color, as much as a shade can belong to a person—is celadon, greatest green. I want to put this woman's charm in my mouth, suck it like candy.

She sees me looking and touches it, smiles shyly. Celadon and I begin to have the sort of conversation I'm used to having with other moms, the kind where you don't quite hear each other, don't exactly turn your head, where you speak noncommittally about whatever is directly in front of you.

"I'm surprised so many are here today," she says. "It's quite hot."

"Humid," I say, and Celadon stands, shields her eyes.

She's a lot older than me, and so much more stylish. She's wearing cropped, high-waisted pants, navy blue, and they look formal and anachronistic, faded and moth-eaten, like something a *Titanic* deck-hand drowned in. *Gaucho,* I think, but I'm not sure that's right. Her white T-shirt is threadbare, inside out and too big, knotted at the waist. It's her husband's, is my guess, and it's sexy as hell on her. Her arms are strong and tan, and she's curvy—bedecked, as my mother would say—and clearly not wearing a bra. The unexpected, absolute certainty of this undoes me, always. How do people get on with their lives when bralessness is near? There are brass buttons on the hips of her pants, nonfunctional, I suspect, because I see a side zipper, the true point of entry. Her pants make me think of fucking on a yacht on open water. I bet Celadon fucks in the sea, not the boring old ocean.

Nearby, a baby is learning to walk, lurching away from its mother. What a creep I am, lusty in front of all these kids, these nice, normal people under the full sun.

When Celadon stands again, some small piece of paper—a receipt maybe, or something more important—falls to the ground and skips into the wind.

"Oh," I say, "your—"

We watch the scrap roll over the Astroturf, tornado itself toward a trashy little tree. I consider running after it, diving for it, but Celadon only squints into the sun and says, "Doesn't matter." She feels around in her pockets. "No idea what that was," she says, not looking at me. "Gone now." She's careless, carefree.

She sits, balls her fists, presses them to her closed eyes. "I have *such* a headache," she says. "Little shits are brutal today."

I laugh at how blunt she is, how refreshing. Moms in Hidden Wonder don't generally refer to children as shits, not out loud anyway, not to strangers. This isn't Shady Park out by the bus stop, where some of the moms smoke and the kids are wild and trampling, the seesaw murderous. You take your kids to Shady Park to toughen them up, get their asses kicked a little. Hidden Wonder is a different place.

There's a small gold hoop high in the cartilage of Celadon's ear, same glint as the buttons on her pants. Some women have this ability to look cool and put together, no matter the circumstance. Clothes and accessories are "pieces" on them.

There's a masala stain in the shape of a marlin on the ass of the overalls I'm wearing. I recall the meal, though I don't remember sitting in it. By the time I noticed the fish, he was forever. I see him every time I wear these, yet I keep wearing them. I don't like spending money on clothes, and the stain feels like part of me now, fated and deserved, a gross mystery for the unfortunate people in my wake.

I'm not trying to impress anyone, and Jad has never complained. "Ooh, I like when you wear these," he said just this morning. He was hugging me in our dim bedroom, chin resting on top of my head. He moved his big hands around my ribs, under my T-shirt, down to cup my ass in grubby underwear. "I can get all the way *in there*," he said breathlessly, but instead of turning me on, this made me feel sexless: a big, baggy pocket, personified.

A pocket sums me up, pretty much. I'm done with the diaper bag, and yet I still have to carry all the bullshit that was in it. In the bib of my overalls: my phone, a spare fruit leather, a pouch of organic apple mash, Gilda's EpiPen. Wasp sensitivity runs in Jad's family and I've become obsessed and paranoid, annoying and sad, like the peanut moms. In my actual pockets are crayons, my keys and wallet, and a chocolate kiss for bribing, melted probably, hot as it is. I'm not a Kleenex carrier. In my family, we were against them. They make you sickly, was my mom's idea. The body is an efficient machine—it knows what it can get away with. Buy a pack and your nose starts dripping, she claimed. Same with ChapStick, which causes your lips to stop producing their own gunk. What we carry around determines what we need.

Celadon stands again, glares at the springy animals. I'm thrilled to see there's a stain on her pants too, her gauchos, if they are gauchos. It's a black streak on the thigh, could be a handprint. You try to wear something cute and your kids use you for a napkin. She sits and turns to me, leans close.

"I felt my menstrual cup," she says. "Just then."

"Oh," I say, putting the words together.

"*Inside,*" she says, a stage whisper. Her breath moves my hair. "Do you use one?"

It's an unusual question, though not as unusual as you might think among women who have had children. Once you've been slit open by a surgeon or taken a shit in a birthing tub, a whole glittering world of conversational topics emerges.

"What?" I say. "Oh, no. I should, though."

"The environment," she says.

"Cheaper," I say. "You like it?"

"I'm getting used to it," she says. "You can really see what's coming out of you. I like that quite a lot."

She draws both hands together to make a bowl, stares into it, and grimaces. Her hair is black and thick, cut blunt. I'm relieved to see it's very unwashed, like mine. I want to make a bodily confession too. I could mention that my uterus swells when I walk upstairs, how it feels like it's going to fall right out of me. Just as I'm formulating this as a question—has Celadon experienced this same terrible blooming?—Nancy comes through the gate with bratty Riley, who is crying like always. She unbuckles him from his stroller, lets him loose to be annoying in a new setting. She gives me a big wave, walks to the bench. She's wearing overalls too, goddamn it.

Nancy and I met almost four years ago in Attached at the Heart, a community program for new moms. I left those classes feeling terrified, the stakes suddenly sky-high. Instead of getting a failing grade, something I had a lot of experience with, I could potentially fail a whole-ass person. But Nancy finished the course reeking with new-found confidence, and in my bleak postpartum fog, I clung to her. Did she want to go for a walk while our children napped in their slings? Did she want to come over for a cup of coffee, maybe listen to some records? The babies would take turns bawling while Nancy tried, for months, to lure me into her essential oil cult. Our friendship never really cemented.

She and Celadon glance at each other, give tight, unfamiliar smiles. The menstrual cup, full of blood, falls away, gone to the place where all promising playground conversations go to die.

Nancy stops right in front of me, looming, blocking my view of Gilda. She is giddy to talk about the package thieves in our neighborhood.

"Out of control," she says, shaking her head. "They go right behind the delivery guys. They *stalk* the trucks." She pulls a tube of cream from her fat diaper bag, some cloying floral, and gums up her hands with it.

We live in Pivot, a suburban mid-city between Dallas and Fort Worth. Most of the real crime happens in those real cities, but any time we get a car burglary or a spritz of graffiti, Nancy starts slavering.

"They don't even care what they take. They stole diapers from my neighbor," she says.

Riley has stopped crying. He sits in the shade next to Gilda, who is turned away from him, making a pile of dirt. Does this qualify as parallel play, which is developmentally appropriate, or is this Gilda being weird? Either way, I can't blame her for ignoring Riley—his snot-chapped face, his grabby hands.

"A baby was printed on the side of the box. Like, clearly, it was Pampers," Nancy says. "Who would do that?"

"I don't know, somebody with a kid?" I say. "Diapers aren't cheap."

"Exactly," Nancy says, missing the point.

Celadon drinks deeply from her coffee, and I calmly state that a package thief isn't the same type of person who breaks into your house and slits your throat while you're sleeping. Nancy cringes at the gash I've made, the gore I've brought to the playground. Does Celadon notice that her blood has jumped to my mouth, to this new conversation?

"Yuck," Nancy says. "Yuck! That's not what I mean. But it's a continuum, you know?" Nancy aims this question mostly at Celadon, who says nothing.

Nancy wants our block to teach the package thief a lesson. She says we should get together and box up something horrible. "I mean really bad," she hints. "Like what?" I keep asking, but I can't get her to say shit or piss or jizz, no matter how hard I try. I'm messing with Nancy for Celadon's benefit, showing off. Then Gilda is screaming because there's a bug in the dirt, and Riley is screaming because screaming is his very favorite thing to do. Nancy and I lope over to them, no real choice.

There's a jolt at my chest—the phone vibrates in the bib of my overalls. I suspect it's Jad, calling to see why there's a lull in my incessant stream of Gilda photos, but it's my mother, a hard pass. She has a bunch of greasy cats, all with the same name: Friend. I know they're swirling slick around her legs as she calls from her sticky kitchen, her sweatpants coated in fur. When it's time for the Friends to eat, she tosses great handfuls of kibble onto the linoleum like chicken feed. Out her window is Wink, spiteful little town, people driving by, judging the rusted car parts or paint cans or whatever-the-fucks she keeps stacked out there, a pile of used kitty litter growing like a great pyramid in the side yard.

I decline the call and deal with Gilda—"We don't break anything we can't make," I say about the June bug she begs me to smash—and when I turn around, Celadon is gone. I'm sorry I didn't get to say goodbye, sorry I didn't get a good full-body look at her as she walked away.

I sit on the bench, and Nancy takes Celadon's seat. The vibe gets chaste.

"Who was that?" Nancy asks. "What's her deal?"

Her deal is she's hot and interesting, I want to say, *unlike some people.* "No clue," I say. "I thought you knew all the moms."

Nancy beams like it's a compliment. "Not *every* mom," she says. She sighs, drums her fingers on the bench. "You know, something like glitter would be good," she says—again with the fucking package trap. "Confetti! Or that invisible ink the banks use."

"Invisible," I say. Gilda is spinning in circles with her arms out. When Julie and I used to do that, Mom told us we'd get worms. Same with chewing with our mouths open or staying in the bath too long. Anything we did that annoyed our mother: worms.

"Not invisible," Nancy says, trying for the word. "Permanent." I feel a half-assed tenderness for her, annoying as she is. We moms are all so tired, so scattered. "I want these thieves to know who they're dealing with," she says.

"Oh, they know," I say.

Riley is spinning now too, but when Gilda notices, she stops, runs away. "They're so cute together," Nancy says. She says she and Brad are thinking of having another kid, asks if we are too. Motherhood is dementia—Nancy and I have had this exact conversation before. She's like those people at lunch who talk about dinner. Isn't this enough? Our hands are full.

"Longest relationship of your life," she says. "Everyone should have a sibling."

"Totally," I say. I open my mouth and pop my jaw, stare right at her, cruel.

Nancy takes a quick breath. My story, my *deal*, sweeps across her face. "Oh, god," she squeaks, "I'm sorry."

"Don't be," I say.

She blinks fast, touches my knee.

The dark part of me keeps going. "Listen, I'm agreeing with you. I loved having a sister."

This is fine. *Sister* doesn't touch the person under the word. To say *sister* to a damp-eyed acquaintance, that's not about Julie. Nancy being sorry—anybody being sorry—that's not my business. These peripheral condolence-givers don't know what they don't know, and now they never will: the specific chip in Julie's front tooth, the way she pronounced the word *penguin*—"peen-gwun," for the record.

"I'm just . . . ," Nancy says. "I'm sorry for your loss."

"Thanks," I say, and I'm grateful for that, truly. "Sorry for your loss" is the car that drives you back to civilization, away from where you're stranded. We cruise past the awkwardness, and I lob Nancy a fat, soft question.

"Y'all got a busy day today? We sure do," I say. "Gymnastics."

"Soccer and the library," she says. "Busy, busy."

"Groceries," I say.

We lean hard into pleasantries. We talk about the heat index, bad, and the air quality, worse. I tell Nancy I'm going out of town for the weekend, sans Gilda, for the first time ever. She seems to judge me for that but doesn't say anything, just smears sunscreen on Riley while he screams. Gilda goes down the slide, looks over at me like she deserves a prize.

I check my phone. "We're fixing to leave soon."

"All right, woman, y'all go on," Nancy says, relieved, though we both know there is no soon at Hidden Wonder, no timely exit even when you need one. It will take me a good half hour to wrangle Gilda, to coax and bribe her away. Nancy still has time to hard-sell me a copper aromatherapy locket—"Carry peace everywhere you go," she says, trying her oily pyramid scheme again.

Nancy, with her serious, sad-cow eyes, is wearing her frizzy hair in a low braid like me. Her overalls are a darker denim with wider legs, but our sneakers are the same brand. Neither of us wear socks. It must look like we're farmers or painters or like we're on some sort of team, second stringers, sitting on this bench. The visual appeal of overalls on a grown woman, if there is one, is the potential to make the wearer look adorable. I was adorable in college—I could sit on any cute girl's lap without crushing her, boys used to toss me into swimming pools. For a while I was petite, which is what you are when you age out of adorable. Now I'm just short. Unadorable, unadored. Loved of course, but that's a different thing. As a fashion statement, overalls say, "No comment." They're great for tamping down your desire, for neutralizing the entire situation of your body. I got mine on sale.

IT'S NOT THAT I want to masturbate in the vestibule of the Tiny Toads gymnastics class, specifically. There's nothing particularly erotic about the clown-colored interior and the frigid air-conditioning, the dead-eyed caregivers sitting in folding chairs, scrolling on their phones. The vibe is institutional, bureaucratic, like an auto-body repair shop or the DMV, only there's a bunch of friendly amphibians painted on the walls, children screaming in the background, the faint aroma of shitty diapers. This isn't my precise kink or anything, it's just that Tiny Toads is where, twice a week, I come a little bit alive, in this hour where Gilda is fully occupied, when I'm not responsible for anybody but myself.

One wall of the room is a huge two-way mirror, tiny gymnasts contained on the other side of it. I'm invisible to Gilda and she's content behind glass, touching her toes, flailing in the ball pit, standing in line for the froggy hop. My focus shifts to the pissed-off mom pacing in front of me, chewing gum and yelling into her phone. She's wearing acid-washed jean shorts, and a deodorant ghost haunts the belly of her black T-shirt. "I did call y'all during business hours," she smacks. "It rang and rang and rang and rang and rang." Those many rings charm me. She's even younger than I am—maybe a true teen mom—but like the rest of us, she looks exhausted. "Send somebody's ass out here to fix it," she says. "*Now.*" I love how loud she is, the unselfconscious way she stalks the lobby.

I cross my legs, squirm in my seat. Jad once told me he looks around every room he's in to see who he can take in a fight. It's not because he's violent—he never even raises his voice—he says it's just that people always try to mess with the tall guy.

"I've never noticed you doing that," I told him.

"Why would you?" he said. "It's a seconds-long calculation between me and me."

What a pair the two of us are in our own minds, me trying to fuck every room, him trying to kill it.

From the gym I hear Miss Jasmine's bouncy words of encouragement. Jazzy, as the children call her, is cheering, helping them tackle the balance beam. She's gorgeous in the two-way mirror, light and movement, heat and sound, neon against the backdrop of cadaverous lobby dwellers. Jazzy is not the type who snorts powders or pops pills—she is high on her sole purpose. She trampolines her worries away. She's leaping across the gym mat of life, streamers trailing. I'll never have the energy of Jazzy again—I never had it. I only want to feel her hum, her life force. When I fantasize about her, I fixate on the two of us naked, comparing skin. "This is what pregnancy does," I'd murmur, opening my arms for her. "These are my blown-out elastin fibers." I want to be stretch-marked all over her, draped across that tight body.

I touch my phone—tiny porn machine—but keep it tucked in the bib of my overalls, obviously. I uncross my legs, cross them again. When Jad comes home tonight I'll sneak off to the bathroom. Shower or sink running, I'll hide from my family and tap out my highly specific, highly disgusting search terms.

The porn I've been watching too much of, is, well, porn. Jad knows about it, he once claimed to be into it—how hot, his horny wife— but lately it feels like something I should downplay. I don't want him worrying about the mother of his child behind some locked door, the oven timer going off, something burning on the stove. Even when I'm alone, I watch my selections without sound, in case a participant says something accidentally hilarious or genuinely disturbing. Catchy as a TV jingle, a snippet of dialogue from an early, formative scene haunts me still: "All right, boys," said one gangbanger to his brethren, "let's get in those guts and bust some nuts." Now I'm a muter for life. Women and women and men and men, every sweaty permutation in absolute silence. Grainy amateurs, slick professionals. All the jiggling and bulging, the stretched magic, angles going from good to great. People clumped together in my hot, filthy brain. Action rising, tapping and more tapping, windows opening on the little screen, the same phone I use to talk to my mother and pay my electric bill. Scenes popping up unbidden, triggers I've touched by mistake, links leading me to spectacular, accidental worlds. A rush, my flexing feet, then the absurd reality of the tiny tits and asses in my palm, sexy people no bigger than my thumb. The fun ends with a swift maternal urge to check every performer's ID, make sure they're all legal, well paid, and hydrated.

I'd never watch porn in public, but when a delivery guy comes through the door of Tiny Toads, bell clanging behind him, I imagine he's here for Jazzy, that my fantasy has bled into the real world. He's wearing his all-brown garb, the summer version, with the little shorts. He's got those tan, muscular calves they all have. He drops a package on the front desk, scans it with his plastic gun, belches, and clangs back out. Jad could take him, I decide.

The thought of a distant, bloody-minded, fucked-with Jad—it does something for me. Feeling generous, I invite him into the vestibule, a replacement for the delivery guy. A threesome, I fantasize about it constantly—men and women, one of each, just men, just women, Jad and not Jad, etc.—but I'd never have the nerve. To be naked with the person inside of you, I can handle that, but to be so blatantly seen, nobody blinded by tits and proximity—no thank you. Being caught from across a room or even the length of a bed, it scares me. This is probably why I can't stop thinking about it.

"Tuck, friends! Tuck! Let your knees say hello to your belly," Jazzy chirps.

Maybe together, Jad and I could pull the exuberance out of Jazzy, could suck *her* out of her, steal it away. If I were brave, I could bring her home and we'd do all the things people do to each other, even silly things. Like could Jad somehow stack us? Do me, then her, then me, then her? I've seen it done—though I'm not sure about the setup. In porn they're never helpful, always leaving out the mechanics, the prep. Why not show the recipe for the dish too? Not just a picture of the half-eaten thing, gaping on a plate?

I close my eyes. Now Jad is nowhere and Jazzy is replaced by Eddie, the line cook at my first restaurant job. He pushed me against the wall like a cop, my ponytail wrapped around his fist. I'm moving around in my vault, picking up the past and looking at it. There's the Kristy or Kristen or Christine who slid her underwear off at a campus dive bar, kicked it onto the dark floor. That redhead in the changing room at the public pool last week—Jad's type—who locked eyes with me, then swept her sundress up and over her head. There's Celadon, my new friend, her green charm a pendulum in the air as she sways over me, head tipped back. Look at the cool white underside of her jaw, a soft spot to hook your finger.

A tiny toad, not mine, breaks free from the trampoline line and pounds on the two-way mirror, pinning me back to the bleak room. He cups his eyes and tries to see into the waiting area, which of course he can't. "Git, Josiah!" barks True Teen Mom, who has ended her phone call and is now flipping through a Honda repair manual. She speaks to her kid with such contempt, I don't think I could love her after all.

Gilda's often so close to me I can't get a good look at her, but there she is now, moving in the framed glass. She's uncoordinated but enthusiastic. Her favorite part of gymnastics is the gold leotard—"leo turd," she says—that she wears over sparkly silver tights. This outfit is pilled and baggy because I wash it so much. Unlike my wardrobe, I keep Gilda's clothes spotless. Our landlord pays for water, and I get a euphoric throb when I have one big load in the washer and another in the dryer—for me, midwash even beats the feeling of clean and folded and put away. When Julie and I were kids, everything was dingy and we barely noticed. I don't remember Mom ever changing our bedsheets, though she must have. The first time I spent the night at a friend's house, I buried my nose in her pillow, inhaled the powdery, angelic scent, said, "What *is* that?" She put her face where mine had been. "I don't smell anything," she said. "Just clean, I guess."

Gilda's taller and skinnier than the other kids, her black hair tangled and wild, her brows intense. When we're at home or outside, she is kinetic and zipping, but enclosed with other children, she turns inward. Sometimes, in line for the tumble mat or the uneven bars, she zones out in her metallic uniform, chews on her lips. Back straight, face placid, she's odd and silent, a beautiful, terrifying robot. Other kids, short and shouting, whiz around her, indifferent.

I lean back in my chair, look up at the industrial ceiling tiles. Directly above my head, a dead tube light flickers, blinks itself awake. It hums, dims to almost nothing, then glows brightly at me, the boldest bulb in the room. All through the tadpole circle and the goodbye song, I feel interrogated, spotlit. It's a relief when the gym doors open and the kids start rushing out. Gilda comes last, Jazzy leading her by the hand.

"Kit—quick question," Jazzy says. She's wearing peach leg warmers, sweet god.

Gilda runs to me and I pick her up. She puts her face into my hair and hides.

Jazzy glistens—that skin! Her plump cheeks are pink and there's a cleft in her chin, marvel of collagen. Before I can get too excited about what she might say, she asks again if I've had a chance to pay this month.

"I'll check tonight," I say, like I have some accountant at home, a team of financial advisors to consult.

"No problem," she says, chipper. *Great, then I'll just keep my eighty dollars,* I think. Tiny Toads gets paid after Jad does on the fifteenth, not a second sooner. Jazzy grabs her high ponytail with both hands, splits it to pull the elastic tight. There's something written on her palm in purple marker. When I make out the word, it gives me a hot, lusty stab. It's my name, blocky and upside down, but it doesn't mean anything—just a reminder.

"Thank you so much!" Jazzy says, and smiles. "Bye, my love," she says to Gilda, who is hiding still, one hand down the neck hole of my shirt.

"Thank *you*," I say.

In another life I'm on my back, Jazzy's inky hand pressed on my sternum, pigment sweating off.

IF ANYBODY WANTS to see me in person, they have to meld into my ridiculous day, Gilda's rigid routine. Pete joins us on our afternoon walk. He talks and talks as I push Gil in the stroller. She's getting too big for it. If she doesn't sit with her knees bent, her feet skim the sidewalk. She folds herself in, gangly. When she wants me to stop, she skids her glittery plastic sandals on the ground like brakes.

"You packed yet?" Pete asks.

"Not yet," I say. "I'll do it when you-know-who goes to bed."

Two months ago, Pete's longtime boyfriend, Brian, dumped him. Pete was shocked, then devastated, then hell-bent on healing. He busied himself planning a heartbreak trip, and he's insisting I join him too. "I'll pay your way," he begged. "You know I need my moral support bitch," he said, though really I'm just a shelter dog with heartworms and a skin condition, my own complicated problems.

Not many people in my neighborhood like to leave their air-conditioning—the few we pass on the sidewalk glance down at my smooshed daughter and judge me.

She's very tall for her age, I hope my face says.

I'm caffeinated already, but we stop by Splits so Pete can grab a coffee too. When we come through the doors, Christian, my favorite barista, says, "Little Bit! Back again?"

Gilda beams at him, then pulls the stroller shade down to hide her flattered face. Christian gets busy with a hemp milk latte, and I watch Pete silently redesign the gaudy menu fonts, the outdated décor. The aesthetic is even worse than he knows. Splits has a double life. In the evenings, it skews—they dim the overhead lights and turn on colored gels, take away the pastries and start pushing cocktails. The baristas slip into these white lab coats and a terrible DJ shows up to spin spirit-crushing dance hits. The theme is confused—a disco crossed with an urgent care. Splits is so close to my house, none of this bothers me at all. They could play nothing but ska and do actual colonoscopies in the back and I'd still come here all the time.

Pete pays and Christian asks if he can give Gil a treat on the house: a cookie the size of her head. Sugar is a bad idea but I give in, hoping it will keep her occupied while Pete and I talk.

Back outside, I scan the wilds of Pivot for anything of interest. The stunted, crispy trees on my street, a sea of soft black asphalt, a deranged red squirrel chittering from a power line. I keep interrupting Pete to name everything in turn, point out shapes and numbers, any glint of gold we happen across—Gilda's favorite. This counts as quality parenting, but walks are right up there with the playground for me, the tiniest bit of a break. Usually I keep the ride rough, jerk Gil around a little, cheerfully yell her name—if she falls asleep this late in the afternoon, I'm fucked—but today she's focused and alert.

Pete's indifference to Gilda means she is, of course, obsessed with him. She calls him Hair, like that's his name, because before he got his fancy job he used to dye his brown waves wild colors. Pete and I met just a few miles from here, in college. We were both waiters at Easy Cheesy, this ridiculous fondue place near campus. I instantly recognized in him the things I saw in myself—here was somebody with a mighty death drive, somebody bighearted who was also kind of a fuckup, someone who was not exactly overflowing with impulse control. We've changed a lot since then. Now Pete writes pharmaceutical copy, and despite not having a background in science—when I met him, he was a theater major—he's apparently very good at it. "I sell drugs," he sometimes tells guys in bars. Now I have Gilda and do nothing dangerous or interesting with my days.

Pete and Brian used to throw these beautiful dinner parties, and once, Jad out of town and no babysitter free, Pete said it would be fine if Gilda came with me. I spent the night pulling her away from blown glass and gaping electrical outlets, keeping her from climbing up Pete's leg. She mauled a sushi boat while well-dressed people watched. She put her little fist in Pete's whiskey and he handed her the crystal tumbler like she'd earned it, then went off to pour himself another.

"Blue truck, Gilly. Look at the blue, blue truck," I say.

"I want Hair to push me," she whines, and Pete says, "Noted," and puts one finger on the sticky plastic handlebar.

"How are you holding up?" I say.

"Biggest mistake of his life," he says, shoulders back. He's had time to metabolize. When he first told me about Brian ending things, Pete was so racked with sobs I could barely make the words out. It was three a.m. but I picked up his call anyway. I was already awake, staring at the ceiling, racked with guilt. Nobody ever gets racked with anything good. I'd slid out from under Gilda, who was damp and gummy in a pair of these awful flame-retardant pajamas my mom keeps sending her. I had to pommel-horse over Jad, longest husband, and step out into the hallway.

"Oh, babe," I whispered to Pete in the dark, "what an absolute shithead," but then Gilda was crying too, wailing from the bed, saying, "Mama, come back to me. Mama, where did you go?"

Pete steps over a smear of dog shit. "Huge mistake, a hundred percent," I say. "Who does he think he is?"

"Did I ever tell you he loves cops?" Pete says. "Loves them! If the kids next door had a party, or their music was too loud, or if one of their cars was blocking our driveway, he'd call the cops. Or, like, if somebody stood on our street too long, he'd call the cops! 'People stop to return text messages,' I said. 'People look at directions!'"

"Jesus," I say. "You didn't tell me that."

"Plus his taste in clothes. And the fact that we'd exhausted all topics of conversation. He doesn't have interests. You have to be into something, you know? Even if it's, like, fly fishing or, I don't know, zydeco."

I only knew Brian filtered through Pete, just as Pete only knows Jad filtered through me. On rare occasions when Brian and I were left alone in a room together—say, if Pete got up to clear the table at their place—the two of us would get smiley and quiet. We'd look out the window or competitively stroke the dog's head.

I'd talk directly to Brian's border collie. "Hello, sweetheart! You like that? You like the ears most of all!" Or I'd ask some drab random question, like "Have you ever been to Hawaii?," and Brian would look confused. Had we been talking about travel before? We had not. "I'm shy of them" is something Gilda says about certain people, even if they are old friends, even if they are family.

"I mean," I say, "he was always so boring." As soon as I say it, I know it's too much.

"Yeah," Pete says, blinking away hurt. "Exactly. Whatever the fuck, just, Jesus, have something to say." He pulls at the neck of his sweaty T-shirt. "It's boring *here*. I'm ready for some fun," he says.

My enthusiasm for this trip is mostly theoretical. Pete plus me plus a plane ride away—all the arrangements I've had to make for Gilda—it hasn't been fun accounting for each disrupted bath and nap and bedtime, the ripple of these variations, what a monster she'll be when I get her back. I kept wanting to tell Pete no, absolutely not, let's try again in a few years, but he firmly made his case—our case—a long, long list of things to escape. For example, humidity. For example, annoying, well-meaning Jad and shithead motherfucker Brian. A mom who never calls—Pete's—and a mom who won't stop calling—mine. My weird message boards and the constant scroll of Pete's social media accounts. His memes and trolls, family bigots blocked and forgiven, unforgiven, reblocked.

"You're part of my healing journey," he whined, though Pete and I don't exactly have a legacy of wellness together. Not so long ago, we were bad influences. We'd tug out each other's vicious inner teenagers, drive them around town, unleash them at parties and bars, hold stall doors closed while they got high. Once, just before I got pregnant, Pete dropped me at home blackout drunk, bleeding from the mouth. That's when Jad *grounded* me from Pete, said we weren't allowed to play together for a while.

"Isn't it kind of neat?" I tried the next day, Jad throwing open our bedroom shades to the satanic morning light. "How alcohol thins the blood? How a tongue can be so bleedy?" He'd brought me a cup of coffee, but it was scalding, too brutal to drink, and he'd set it on the nightstand just out of reach, some dirty interrogation trick.

"What the hell happened?" Jad asked, but I was possibly the least qualified person in the world to answer that. "It was all Pete's idea," I said, mystery solved, Pete squashed under the bus. My half of the story was lost forever, puked out in taco-laced ribbons down the side of Pete's Volvo, but Jad needed me to know his side. A loud, spooky version of me at two a.m., red mouth dripping, not understanding how doors work, that a knob is something you turn. Jad rubbing his socked feet around on the porch to sop up my blood.

I thought I'd have to finesse the fuck out of it, but Jad was fine with the trip.

"You sure Gilda won't be too much?" I asked, giving him an easy out.

"Not at all," he said, cheerful. "You should go! We'll both benefit." Jad says time away lets you appreciate all the good in your life. I didn't say that leaving also lets you more clearly see the daily frustrations that grind us to dust, grievances vast and insignificant, overlapping and separate, petty and stupid, conscious and buried.

A hatchback crawls down the street, young country blaring. "Can't wait to unplug from work," Pete says.

I'm plugged into nothing. I have no deadlines, no personal ambition, no professional goals of any kind. I'm dedicated to aimlessness and my adorable, needy family. Pinning Gilda down, brushing her tiny teeth, slicking her hair into disobedient pigtails. Endless, invisible, critical labor. Dishes. Laundry. So much mopping.

Pete says he won't miss negotiating our dumb metroplex—the noise and poison, miles of highway between where he is and where he needs to be—but I barely drive the shitty Kia Jad and I share. I loathe the car seat, strapping Gilda in. The screaming, negotiating. Unstrapping, adjusting, restrapping. When Julie and I were kids, we used to flop around loose in the back seat. We'd beg Mom to take turns fast and she'd actually do it. She'd stop short and fling us to the floorboards for the thrill. That's the kind of mother we had.

Pivot is a car town that doesn't like to be walked in. Every day when I push Gilda around in the stroller, drivers stare at me like something's wrong, like I'm a criminal or the victim of a fresh crime.

"Grackle," I sing to Gilda. "Two grackles and some stepped-on gum."

Gilda doesn't want grackles, she wants help. Her button hurts, she says. "Why is this button?" she says, pulling at her waistband.

I bend down, unsnap her little shorts.

Fulfilling tiny needs—that's what I'm good at. Gilda has finished her cookie and will be thirsty soon, so I fish under the stroller and hand her the sparkly gold water bottle.

"Sip," I say.

"No thank you," she says.

"Please hold it," I say.

"I'm ready to get out of this punishing heat! And all this ugliness. The tech parks and the strip malls and the drive-thrus, all of this . . . blight," Pete says.

"My body is crowded," Gilda says. "I said no to you."

"Blight," I repeat. "Hold on to the bottle. Please, Gil."

"Yeah," Pete says. "Look around. These tract houses are damaging the world." He gestures to the evil houses around us, exactly like the evil house up the block where I live my life. I don't say anything about Pete's nightmare condo, a soulless hunk of metal squatting on the tollway. Brian gave him the place in the breakup, then went and bought himself a faux Victorian by the golf course.

Gilda holds her sparkly bottle out to Pete. "Here," she says. "Have this, please."

"Nope," Pete says.

The bottle sails and clanks, rolls down the sidewalk, off the curb. I put on the voice I use to keep from losing my shit.

"Oops! We dropped it," I say, wobbling and crouching, swiping under a Prius.

I put the contaminated bottle under the stroller and hand Gilda the backup, also gold. Now she's thirsty, as I predicted, and she guzzles as we glide on.

"The allergies, my god," Pete says, rubbing his eyes.

Ragweed and mold and mountain cedar pollen bother Pete. Dust is my problem, plus these flowering Texas shrubs that smell like cum.

"Stop sign," I say. "How many sides do we see?"

Gilda says, "Don't want sides." She wants applesauce. "Are you hearing me?" she asks, tipping her head back.

Pete steers while I unscrew the foil pouch. Gilda grabs it and is quiet, slurping hidden spinach, secret kale.

There's plenty Pete doesn't have to say. How he sits propped in bed, bathed in blue light, his narcotic television streaming, streaming. Competitive baking shows, competitive pet grooming and decorating and glassblowing. Psychological experiments where young, dumb hotties let their young, dumb lives be surveilled, vote other hotties off the show. His very favorite program: an actual dermatologist lances actual boils on camera. Pete refers to his TV people by their first names, gets offended when I don't instantly know who he's talking about. Time collapses and dissolves on his huge flat-screen, where he can witness his chosen family's pores and goose bumps in HD.

Aren't we so artful in our distractions? This is something my sliding-scale therapist always says. He's on board with this trip too, says everybody needs a break.

Brian ended things brutally, no explanation. All of Pivot has been tarnished, draped in something Pete calls the Shroud. He says he's reminded of Brian at every corner store, every bar. Pete's been lighting special candles and seeing a psychic, a woman named Esmerelda who shares signage with the Planned Parenthood. On their first meeting, she went groping for the source of his pain—the man or woman or child or animal or city that did him wrong. "I'm getting an R?" Esmerelda tried. "I'm getting S? No? T? Really? Starts with a *vowel*? Not a vowel, right?" Pete knows she's a fraud. He doesn't care.

"I want to be rid of Brian," he said when I pressed him. Esmerelda pulls cards until Pete's fortune comes out how he likes it. "I'll pay anybody who can make him disappear."

I let the money part go. Pete has lots of it now, and it bothers me. This is something I'm working on, and I don't need a psychic or a sliding-scale therapist to explain that. Money is random and meaningless, and I want some more of it. It's not like Pete isn't generous. When we're together and a bill comes, I make a halfhearted move for my wallet, but it's all show, a pretend reach for the Door Open button when somebody rushes at your departing elevator.

Rich people travel when they get depressed, but there are much cheaper solutions. My coping mechanisms used to be psychedelics and/or sex with strangers, though marriage and motherhood have wrenched those from me. Pete says fucking doesn't work like that for him, but new, inconsequential sex used to snap me right out of a dark place. It was best when it was a little bit scary. Maybe with a guy I didn't know anything about except that he worked at the window-tinting place where I took my car. Maybe slow sex with somebody's wild wife in a house with an obscene number of lit candles and a huge, slobbery dog. Was the husband going to bust through the door? Was the dog going to knock over those candles and incinerate us? I could step out of those people's lives and feel brand-new. It was the same with psychedelics, a trip you take in your bedroom to solve all your problems. But Pete's never been a fan—"I would absolutely come unraveled," he's said.

Pete is struggling, the weight of his life buzzing vivid and cruel, humming electric. Now that Brian's gone, he's dealing with feelings of crushing loneliness and unlovability. Maybe he's worried about dying alone, mail piling up, nosy neighbors smelling something off, making a sick discovery of him.

"You're excited about going, right?" Pete says, a tinge of worry in his voice.

"Go where?" Gilda says.

"Nowhere," I say. "I'm excited," I assure him. It'll be fine—to have an adult conversation without a child hanging from my neck, drink an adult beverage, talk about Pete's adult problems.

" 'Cause we're going to the grocery store?" Gilda says.

"Exactly," I say.

Pete pushed hard for nature, which surprised me. He's so urban, so indoorsy, I forget he grew up in the Piney Woods, that he knows the good snakes from the bad and which berries will make you die.

He thought of the West during one of his weekly massages. Usually, these sessions end with a whipping of eucalyptus branches, but this time he'd opted for a hot-rock component. Sweating, spine pinned, Pete decided he needed mountains and vistas and deep quiet, time in the wild to refresh and revitalize. He researched and came up with Plunge, Montana, and its Boiling River, which he says is pretty much what it sounds like. He says that for hundreds of years the bewildered and unbalanced, the wounded and the fed up, have traveled there to soak in the purifying waters.

"I'm excited, too," Pete says.

"Hey, Hair," Gilda says, skinny arm stretching. "Hold hands."

"You don't have to," I say.

"It's fine," Pete says, cheerful. He lets Gilda squeeze his finger. "I booked a cute hotel."

I say at this point I'd settle for a Jacuzzi tub in an Econo Lodge, so long as a certain demanding small person isn't invited.

IN THE TOWN where I grew up, there's not a proper grocery store, just the little family-owned Flip Mart and a vending machine behind the post office, a sun-bleached car wash bay where a nice lady sells tamales from her trunk. Wink isn't known for its conveniences or cuisine—it's famous for Roy Orbison and two sinkholes. Like me, the Soul of Rock and Roll left as fast as he could, but the sinkholes are so big they had to put them on the map, mark them forever. Scientists come out to measure every year, worried that soon the holes will gang up and become one solitary, disastrous sink. Slow ribbons of grit turn in the sky, and the whole place descends, flatter than flat.

Pivot isn't exactly a cultural hub, but at least there's a supermarket in our neighborhood, a nice one with fake milks and uncaged, free-range everything, a bunch of assorted nut gunk. Gilda rides in the baby seat, enormous, her stroller collapsed in the bottom of the cart.

We turn in to the cereal aisle and there he is: it's Bad Dad, an unshaven vision in a Sub Pop T-shirt, down on one knee like he's about to propose to some oatmeal. I try to push past him without stopping, but Gilda's too quick.

"We know you," she says accusingly.

"Sure do," he says, looking up at us. "Who am I?" he teases, hand on his chest. Gilda regards him coolly.

"Benji's dad," she says.

I fumble with the rubber band on my braid, pull it off, and slip it around my wrist.

"Bingo," Bad Dad says. He stands, steps close to me. "Hey, you," he says. Whenever I forget about Bad Dad, there he is, showing up to toy with me.

"Hello, hello," I say, my voice low and breathy. "Haven't seen you in a minute." I rake my fingers through my hair, wonder where his wife is. There aren't many stay-at-home dads in Pivot, so they stand out, plus none of them look like Bad Dad. He's bad for lots of reasons—he lets his kid ride a scooter without a helmet, encourages him to piss on the grass like a wino and pet strange dogs, tied up and left alone—but mostly Bad Dad is bad because he's so hot he makes you want to demolish your marriage, walk away from your family, blazing. One cloudy day in Hidden Wonder, Nancy gave me the lowdown, told me Bad Dad's mom killed herself with her car when he was young, that he was the one who found her. This sealed my fascination. Something I heard on a murder show: asphyxiation turns the skin cherry red. Could it be true? Every time I see Bad Dad, I fixate on that color, the garage of my thoughts cursed by this crimson woman, her toxic tailpipe.

All my other crushes are harmless, unreciprocated and safely fenced in my pervert mind, but Bad Dad roams, dangerous. We once sat in the same booth at a toddler birthday party, eating pizza and watching budget clowns botch our kids' face paint. Under the table our thighs touched and burned. He has a way of keeping eye contact across a room, a library full of greedy story-time kids between us. There was a big block party last summer with a keg and a parade. They'd set out cones to close the street, and Bad Dad and I stood against a fence, as alone as two people can be in a crowd. We were preternaturally aware of our spouses—Bad Dad's wife and son waving sparklers on a close strip of grass, Jad down the street a bit, oblivious, giving Gilda a piggyback ride.

"You were the singer?" Bad Dad asked, thrilled, after his huge, veiny pheromones had overwhelmed me, forced me to mention—no, to *brag*—about the band I was in as a teenager.

"Yep—I was the lead singer, played guitar," I said, a lie.

"I can totally see that," he said, and closed his eyes, a film of some false me flitting onstage in his brain. "I was in a band too," he said. "But we were so stupid. Just screaming."

"Screaming is underrated," I said. "Screaming is *smart*."

Bad Dad turned then, put his hand flat on the fence behind me. He leaned in and said, "I wish I knew you before."

"Before what?" I said, playing dumb. I ducked under that miraculous arm, said, "Oh, I think my . . . ," and walked off, not even bothering with the rest. I fortified myself against him, went home and furiously reimagined an alternate ending.

Weeks later, I sat close to him on the floor at Little Drummers, a dozen kids percussing in the middle of the room. "Sorry to crowd you," he said over the racket. He scooted a foot away, a test.

We've never been weak at the same time. My attraction to him seems tied to something primal. The position of the planets, my menstrual cycle. A slow rise in my body temperature, simmering in the dark with my sleeping family. An urge pulls me out of bed at night and I pace around, flexing my hands, wanting anyone, anything else. Then, like a switch, the moon waxes or wanes or whatever and my guts calm down. Recklessness recedes. I get under the covers, curl myself around my Gilly, shove my face into Jad's armpit. I'm a butthole bitch, an idiot—thank god I'm also a coward. The rest of the month is Jad's heavy head in my lap, scratching his flaky scalp while we watch TV. It's slow cooker recipes and rinsing out recyclables, setting up a discovery zone for Gilda to discover when she wakes in the morning.

Gilda—her reach impressive—is pulling things we don't need off the shelves, tossing them into the grocery cart. I'm letting her do it, pretending not to notice.

"Where *is* Benji?" she asks, suspicious.

"He's here, with his mama somewhere," Bad Dad says.

His wife is pregnant again, due any day now, and from what I know of her she seems nice, like somebody I'd be friends with if things were different. Still, I struggle to fully unthorn Bad Dad. Certain people, their precise chemical makeup—you writhe against it. I know I'm not the only one. I suspect he plays this game with many moms, that if we cross-checked our stories, we'd all end up in tears.

Bad Dad shakes a box of cereal, makes a joke about the knockoffs he buys since Benji can't tell the difference, these shameless generics with their rip-off names: Lucky Elves, Colonel Crunch. He smiles at me in his knowing Bad Dad way. He drags his gaze down my neck, across my chest, back to my eyes. He wants me to know he's looking. I don't often feel sexy anymore but I'm still young, which for some men is the same thing. I look at his hands, think about how he might help me take my life apart.

"How does Benji feel about Frosted Fakes?" I say, rolling with the cheap cereal bit. Bad Dad laughs, and I arch my back a little.

"What's wrong with your voice?" Gilda says then, a box of Pop-Tarts in her hand. She's right here, of course, listening, watching. "I have to pee, you know," she says.

"I didn't know that," I say, my voice back in my flat daily register. "Can you wait?"

She looks at Bad Dad, then back at me. She frowns, searches my face.

"I can hold it," she says finally, but it sounds like a threat.

Gilda has blocked the cock, I can tell by Bad Dad's expression. He looks down the aisle, maybe worried his wife will be looking back at us. I crash from my tiny little high. He says, "Well, it sure was good to see you." His demeanor shifts, though he's not quite as slick as he thinks he is, sliding from horny to neighborly.

"You too," I say. "We've gotta run."

"See ya, dude," he says, and goes to high-five Gilda, but she only blinks at him, leaves him hanging.

"She's a tough crowd," I say, and he laughs. The hug we don't give is there, hot in the space between us.

I STALL IN the family planning aisle, hoping to god we don't run into Bad Dad again, his pregnant wife and his feral kid. I'm light-headed, trembling a little because Texas respects air-conditioning above all else. Gilda pulls a floral box of panty liners off the shelf and tosses it into the cart. Not my brand but it's fine.

"Do we need that?" She points out a distant vat of lube.

Our cart is full, and there are so many things still on my list. Eventually I make a break for it, take us quickly to the milk and butter and eggs and cheese, then the vegan equivalents for Jad, all the food the two of them will need for a weekend without me.

A harried woman reaches past me for a tub of soy yogurt. In her cart there's a towheaded baby girl, strapped in and gumming on a cracker. She twists in her seat, her green eyes huge with wonder, taking everything in. She coos and beams, waves a dimpled hand at us as she's wheeled away.

My vision goes cloudy, sudden floaters set loose. I'm having trouble seeing, but these places are all the same, the frigid dairy aisles of my life. I pull from the case and the products feel odd in my hands. Too light, like they're empties and we're on the set of a grocery store, a soundstage of a life.

"I have to pee," Gilda says again.

"Almost done." My teeth chatter—so damn cold.

Remember being little, when you'd get to take a sudden emergency bathroom trip at the store, peek into the guts of the operation? Mothers don't do this now, send their girls off alone to grungy back rooms.

In Wink, the Flip Mart didn't have a public restroom, just a toilet in the back for Kenny Flip and his huge, grunting son. When a customer asked, the Flips would suggest the gigantic, glowering truck stop down the farm road. "More comfortable out there," Kenny claimed, though everybody knew about the endless stalls and scummy bank of showers, that it was a place where faceless long-haulers, masturbators, and unashamed shitters came and went. The Flips made an exception for children—not too crazy about the idea of a kid pissing herself in the aisles maybe, some mom abandoning her cart to deal with it.

Gilda and I move to the front of the checkout line, our list finally complete, and a sluggish, sunburned clerk begins her slow scan. I lift Gilda out of the too-small baby seat—she has to stand up to get her long legs free—and I take her stroller out from under the cart and unfold it. "Sit, baby," I say.

I remember breaking away from Mom on Mr. Flip's reluctant

okay, hands on my crotch, shouldering through the clear flaps into the belly of the back room. This was the place where the grunting son's hairy hands came from, startling me when he'd move gallons of milk around in the dairy case. I made my rush to the small bathroom, complete with the secret mop bucket and its private gray water, something no customer was supposed to see. Dribbles of pee on the toilet seat, two distinct yellows, one lemony and one a deep gold. The hidden griminess of it all, the sink and the cracked tiles and the slanted floor, the dank space in such contrast to the tidy aisles and orderly pyramids of produce.

The ridiculous snacks I've let Gilda pick out—Kool-Aid and pudding and a bag of pure cane sugar—snail along the conveyor belt. The brand names are tilted and strange, the colors and fonts slightly off, everything looking fake as fuck.

At Flip's, the instant relief of peeing in the dingy, half-lit room, skipping the sink because it seemed like washing there would only make me dirtier. I came back to the safe fluorescence of the store, looked down the aisles for Mom and Julie, who was in the cart, her little baby head swiveling, green eyes scanning, looking for me too.

The past stutters here, pins me down. The way Julie peered around Mom as I ran to them, her tiny front tooth like a white seed, wet finger in her mouth. How she grinned at me.

"Everything come out okay?" Mom joked, and I nodded, serious, a grown-up doing grown-up things, all by myself.

"I went away, but now I'm back," I told Julie. I walked alongside the shopping cart, begging Mom for treats. I whined, got denied, then gently scolded, pacing the aisles at the speed of her slow-rolling cart. Holding my sister's fat baby leg in my hand. Julie, alive.

If you have to think about breathing, I've noticed, there's a good chance you're not doing it. Whatever is about to happen, it can't happen here. I fight off a full-body retch. I stop lining the conveyor belt with Gilda's bad choices.

"Sorry," I rasp to the cashier. I mash myself around the cart. "Sorry."

I grab the handles of Gilda's stroller and lunge toward the exit, leaving everything behind. "Wait," calls the cashier, still scanning a pack of veggie dogs. "Ma'am!" *Listen,* I want to say. *The extinction of my sister—the cosmos will not recover.*

"Excuse me," I'm yelling at the sudden people everywhere, all of them walking exactly where I want to walk. "Move. Jesus, move!" The universe is fucked, now and forever, that's all.

Another undeniable fact, suddenly so clear: nobody knows me. Not my sliding-scale therapist, though it's his job to pretend he does, not the people who love me. Especially not them. If anybody really knew the real me—I'm certain—they wouldn't want to.

Gilda gets glimpses. She has an all-access pass, first because she was literally inside me, then strapped to my chest for months—the fourth trimester, they call it—and now she's with me always, hanging out, quietly observing. She wraps her sticky fingers in my hair, scowls equally at everyone. Of course Gilda never even met Julie—still, sometimes she gets this very somber look and says, "Is your sister dead like a shadow? Is she dead like that pile of leaves on the floor?" That's the thing—Gilda doesn't get it. She's young enough to confuse ground and floor, no matter how often Jad or I gently correct her. The old brown carpet in our living room or our cracked driveway or our patchy lawn—to Gilda, all the world is floor.

Nobody knows me, but they still need me, all of them. Nobody wants a mother too sad to make a sandwich, a wife too crazy to fuck, a friend who sounds insane. They need me in the grocery store, in the bedroom, at brunch. They need me to be available and so I am, or my body is. The body goes around fulfilling my obligations. The body makes grilled cheese and gives blow jobs and gets ready to fly off to god knows where with her brokenhearted best friend.

Gilda grips the sides of the stroller and I dash for the automatic doors. There's our wavering reflection—the unhinged woman, the confused child—and I am grateful when the glass splits apart, releases us into the swelter.

Gilda is stunned. She doesn't start crying until I stop running, blocks away. "My snacks," she wails.

"YOU YELLED," Gilda says as I struggle with the front door. She's stopped crying but her eyes are pink. My vision is scalloped now, perforated by lacy white lights. My dumb lungs seem sticky, useless.

"Not at you," I say, trying another key. Another. I'm sweating through my very worst underwear.

"No," Gilda agrees. We left so quickly I didn't even strap her into the stroller. Noticing this, she crawls out and stands next to me on the porch, grabs her crotch. "But at people."

"I know," I say.

I shake past keys that aren't even for doors—one for an old bike lock, one for a register at the restaurant where I worked before Gilda was born, so huge it's like a joke key, a toy. Every day, every single day, I mean to take the strays off this ring.

This is me not punching wood paneling, not wailing. I am quiet, focused. I try the first key again, but this time I infuse my hand with fake confidence. I will my heart to slow its wobble. The key turns and the dead bolt glides in its groove.

Gilda and I are met by a muggy microclime in the dim front hall. I help her with her sandals, softly step out of my sneakers. I undo her shorts and she rushes off to pee.

"Flush," I say. "Hands. For real." Sometimes she stands on her little stool and runs water into the sink. She holds her dirty hands close to but not in the stream, an act of defiance that takes exactly as long as the requested act. I carefully line up our shoes on the tray by the door. I walk to the thermostat and tap it awake. Household management always soothes me.

The toilet flushes, water runs. "Smell," Gilda says, trotting back to me, holding out her hands.

"No thanks," I say, buttoning her shorts again.

She stalks me while I part the drapes, let the bright day in. "You made us run," she says. "We went so fast."

"I know," I say. "I had to leave."

My living room, unlike my person, is clean and orderly, spotless because nobody has been here all day. My best work is invisible—the miniblinds I soak monthly in the bathtub, the top sides of fan blades I climb a ladder to dust.

Gilda goes to the basket in the corner and yanks out animals and blocks, all the plastic crap my mom sends. I hope we've gotten past the grocery store incident, but she darkens at the empty basket.

"You left all my foods," she says.

"I'm sorry, Gil," I say. "We'll get more."

"My choices," she says. "You *left* them." She clenches her fists in the hot living room.

I read somewhere that the force of a child's tantrum predicts their adult perseverance. One day Gilda will bring the poor world to its knees. She is rigid and furious, stomping her feet. I hesitate to say her outbursts trigger me, but it's the truth. They remind me of my father and one bad, early boyfriend. Those men acted like children, my child acts like a child, and all of them have me covering my ears, closing my eyes, wanting to be away.

Our father once threw a fit and put his foot through a wicker laundry hamper. The top wouldn't stay on, the side was crushed, but Mom kept it, this broken reminder of violence everyone in our family had to touch each day.

"His lesson to live with," she told me. But our dad didn't have to live with the ruined thing—he moved out soon after. Mom probably still has it, somewhere in her mess.

I know kids save their worst behavior for those they trust. Still, it doesn't take long for Gilda's screaming to crumple me.

"We go back!"

I sit on the floor in front of her and unhook my overalls, pull up my shirt. This'll work. Her screaming dissolves and she scoots to me, shuddering.

The fact that I'm still breastfeeding an almost-four-year-old is either my greatest accomplishment or my secret shame, depending on the company. Some of my crunchy message-board moms seem to think this is just fine, ideal even. Gilda calls breast milk good-good, says, "I need good-good because my heart gets thirsty."

I only nurse her before bed or first thing in the morning, or, like now, when she gets hurt or scared and needs quick comfort. The body takes care of Gilda when the mind is elsewhere. There used to be a sort of rush, a blissed-out hormonal thing that happened. The happy feeling is supposedly caused by the same chemicals that rinse your brain when you get to the chorus of your favorite song—meted-out dopamine sweeping through, carrying you to the next verse. Nursing is a shortcut, I know, but I don't understand the problem with shortcuts, so long as something nice is on the other side. My high school guidance counselor called me "pleasure-seeking," and I still don't understand what's so bad about that. Beats the alternative. But I haven't felt the happy feeling in a very long time. Lately, my skin crawls when Gilda latches.

"Finally," my friend Yesenia said when I called to confess this. "Time to cut that shit out."

Yesenia still lives in Wink, has three kids and another on the way. She was the drummer in the band Julie and I started in high school— You Are the Universe—and once at a show in Abilene she puked in her lap and kept playing, a divine demonstration of never missing a beat. For years I had a little crush on her that she politely refused to acknowledge. Senior year she met Joe at midnight mass and they got married right after graduation to sanction their fucking. They immediately started a family, and amazingly, this has all been precisely the right path for Yes. Now she homeschools and cans jam, the picture of maternal grace and competence, a childcare oracle I consult almost daily. Julie and I weren't exactly parented, so it's Yes I turn to for advice, though we have different approaches. I got deep into attachment parenting early on, charmed by message boards with names like Merciful Mamas and Empathy Wins. They snared me in their bright, loving net, their warm dogma about as far from my mother's beliefs as any I could find. Bedsharing—capital B—is one of the foundational tenets lauded by this bunch, along with Being Responsive and, of course, Breastfeeding.

"Bullshit," Yes said. "If they're old enough to ask for it, they're too old to get it," which is this thing people say about nursing when they're trying to be cute, everyone thinking they're the only one to say it. But Gilda talked so early, too early, even. She could ask for things well before she was out of the socially acceptable nursing window. The first time she spoke I was convinced I imagined it, her first word not one but two. She was sleeping on my side of the bed, between the wall and me, Jad snoring with his back to us. One night I woke to see her viper-black eyes watching me by moonlight.

"Hey," she said. "Hi." No repeated consonantal nonsense, no *mama* or *dada*. A greeting as clear and familiar as any old friend, calm and direct. She tugged my tank top down, didn't have to say any more about what she wanted from me. *Hey. Hi.*

"Use your mom voice and say no," Yes instructed.

"What's mom voice?" I had to ask, a genuine question.

I keep nursing because it's the path of least resistance, not because I like it.

Gilda unlatches and smiles at me. "Bath time," I say, and jump up before she can ask or remember anything else about the grocery store. This is a tactic from my otherwise useless father, a singular flash of parenting brilliance I recall from early childhood: "If they're acting crabby, throw 'em in the water."

Gilda's chipper, cheerful. That's the disarming thing about tantrums, how fleeting or everlasting they can be. "Mimi sent you a present," I sing, holding a ripped-open FedEx box, enticing her to the tub.

"I have to be naked to get it, right?" she asks, stripping out of her shirt as she runs to the bathroom.

"Yep," I say, thinking, *Please, please never repeat that out of context. Please don't make some sad, lifelong association.*

I follow Gilda down the hall. The bathroom light—I swear it comes on a full second before I touch the switch. I stop in the doorway, take a deep breath. I decide to ignore the tingling in my fingertips, the blood beating in my ears.

Gilda waits in the tub, and I twist on the taps and let the water thunder. We're out of bubble bath—it was in the cart—so I sneak some hand soap into the stream.

My mother has sent little capsule animals in the mail. Gilda soaks in the warm, melon-scented water and watches the gelcaps split apart, squeals as the creatures break free.

I am vigilant from my perch on the closed toilet lid—well, vigilant-ish. Instead of paying the overdue electric bill or using the meditation app Jad made me download, I read DMT message boards on my phone while Gilda is occupied. This is the psychedelic the young people are doing these days, or maybe they've been doing it forever, but I've only just heard about it. It's a naturally occurring compound, a so-called spirit molecule that's already present in the body. When taken at high doses, it triggers a ten-minute trip that feels like twelve hours. It sounds like my kind of party: self-transforming fractal elves come around to speak in cogs and wheels instead of words, plus soothing, Plasticine sounds—like your head is inside bubble wrap, but nice—impossible colors, talking to the dead, et cetera. I've come to think of DMT like it's a tropical vacation or skydiving—something for the bucket list. All the insight with none of the headache. Lose your shit, melt into a silver pool of self, and then—bam—sober, back home with your kid and a soft, fleeting dream. The ideal psychedelic for a busy mom.

"How much do you love me?" Gilda asks, now a perfect angel.

"All the way to the top," I say, imagining the look on her face tomorrow when she realizes I'm not here.

I'd rather do DMT than go to Montana.

For me, psychedelics have always been beneficial, therapeutic—and I'm referring to fully obliterative *macro*doses, not these barely-feel-it micro-tinctures people blab about on public radio. Before Gilda, I used to text the word *spaceship* to a kid named Lloyd. He'd meet me at the doughnut place, and I'd leave with a glassine envelope, soft paper squares tucked inside. Dropping acid was this magnificent clearing, a long white hand swiping layers of chalk from the blackboard of my brain. I could do it and come back clean, focused.

Psychedelics squash shame and guilt, help you make sense of things that make no sense. A trip is a story with a clear beginning, middle, and end—a narrative that unfolds perfectly, a plot tailored for you, telling you exactly what you need to hear.

I worry I'll never have an internal supernova again because I'll never be in the right mindset until Gilda is, what, grown? Away at some future hypothetical sleepaway camp? Even then, the stakes are too high. She's ruined my fun with her unconditional love. Nobody wants an LSD mom. Nobody wants to *be* the LSD mom. Could I take LSD to get over my fear of taking LSD? During the trip, could I make peace with my multitudes, come down confident that a mother does not have to fit a specific set of criteria to be good? Then—*then*—could I take LSD again later, for real? It'll never happen. Jad would never approve. He truly believes the present moment is a gift, that the desire for chemical escapism is a sign of maladjustment.

"Isn't that taking the easy way out?" he once asked me. "Leaving your body like that?"

Oh, man, I didn't say. *Is it ever!*

For Jad, drugs are remnants of youth, like video games or skateboarding. He checks out library books about meditation for me. He bought me a gift certificate for a float tank—a sweet, useless gesture we couldn't afford. Hanging out in that dark vat didn't work. Like bobbing in a warm, wet coffin. I felt nothing, not even fear, and I'm very claustrophobic. I don't love elevators, and once when I was a kid Julie had to cut me out of a too-small turtleneck. They don't tell you that the tank people dissolve tons of salt in the water to make you float, that any tiny cut or scrape gets irritated. You think you know your body, whether it has cuts or scrapes, but you don't really know until you're in that faux cosmic soup. Hangnails on every finger, chapped lips, weird genital stinging. All the parts we do daily, tiny damage to, never noticing.

The tiled walls force Gilda's happy voice into echo. In the many, many DMT testimonials I've read on message boards, users reach a point in the telling that defies description, a kind of narrative black hole. There are no words, but some try anyway: protected enclosure, rapturous containment, something gleaming otherworldly on the ceiling above.

"Yo, it's def a CLEAR GLIMPSE of the unitary absolute RADI-ANCE," says AffectionateFerret52. "The visual field is a hoaxxx," says Mrshroomie_in_the_mesosphere.

In the tub, Gilda does that thing I hate where she shifts from front to back, rocking and sloshing, making a household tidal wave. It's time to fish her out. I drain the tub and towel her off. I'm buttoning her into her pajamas when I realize she's somehow managed to keep her head totally dry. Her face is dirty, her hair sticky and sweaty. Oh well.

The sun is still up, but I'm angling to shut down the show. A sudden ecstatic sense of possibility comes over me. The sooner it's tomorrow, the sooner I'll be with Pete, out of town, free. I pull the blackout shades, close the curtains. One thing you can do as a parent is manipulate time. Kids trust you to tell them when a day is over, and sometimes that has nothing to do with the sun. Never mind if the birds are still singing, if there are teenagers throwing Frisbees in the cul-de-sac. I worry that my influence in Gilda's sphere, as her mother, is massive. Our spheres are almost entirely our mothers' doing, for better or worse.

"Dinnertime," I say, but it isn't.

Gilda wants chicken nuggets. "The pretty ones," she commands. There are a few still in the freezer, thank god, the fresh box left behind in the grocery store melee. These are not the hormone-free, cage-free ones she keeps refusing to eat—I've finally dropped that charade. These are made from drugged, deformed chickens crushed and shotgunned through metal screens, their pink slurry molded and shaped just so. Pretty. I'm not vegan like Jad, but I've stopped trying to tell Gilda that her favorites are, you know, poison.

"My mouth loves 'em," she says. I cut up the carrots and broccoli she never eats, a little wish on every plate. I microwave the organic, thick-cut fries she uses solely as ketchup transport, the fries themselves always left behind in limp pink piles. I arrange everything artfully on the partitioned tray. She gets water instead of milk and I hope she doesn't notice there are no raisins today.

"You come here," she says, and scowls. She likes to sit in my lap at the table, make me into her flesh-and-blood booster seat. This is not my favorite thing, to be so close to someone else's mastication, clamped in place, but resistance only makes the meal take longer.

"Why does she do this?" I asked Yes.

"Because you let her," she said.

My arms belt around Gilda's waist, and soon the scent of her head gets to me. Warm euphoria spreads—the drug of her.

"Chew," I say, relieved she doesn't require much dinner conversation, that we don't have to go beyond the actual mechanics of eating, the number of bites she's taken, the number of bites yet to take.

She smacks and I clear a neon scab of mustard from the plastic bottle. I line up the salt and pepper shakers, sweep her crumbs into my hand the second they fall.

"Nuggets is chicken and chicken is birds," she explains.

"Swallow," I remind her. I take another hit of her dirty hair. "You're right," I say. "It's birds."

She doesn't finish her food, she never does. She slides off my lap and goes to play with her dolls under the Christmas tree she won't let us take down. It's been there almost two years, plastic and flocked all to hell with industrial foam, listing to one side, winking with secular rainbow lights and nondenominational glass spheres. I'm not a believer—my mom dated a string of Pentecostals and later dragged us through a fervent Southern Baptist phase, but nothing ever stuck—and Jad isn't religious either. Still, we agreed that decorating a tree seemed like something we should do, festive and important with a kid in the house. We weren't sure if Gilda would remember our first effort—if her tape was running yet, as Jad put it—but we were covering our bases. She fell in love with the thing and now it's a permanent fixture in our living room.

"That baby runs your house," Yes says, so right.

I take Gilda's plate away, duck into the pantry, and sneak into my stash of gas station candy bars, cookies, hand pies, and more. These are pure trans fats and artificial dyes, things I hide from Gilda and Jad. I let a slow, toxic bite sit in my mouth. I move to the sink, charmed by lard and refined sugar, and then I spit straight into the whirring garbage disposal.

It's like all the times I don't come during sex—I still love having it. It's possible that nothing makes me want sex more than *not* coming during it. I used to love making strangers come, coming close myself. That was enough. I could go home and get myself off hours or days later, thinking about the person who'd failed me. Burning, unconsummated lust. Elongated ecstasy. Now I do this with doughnut holes. I'll buy a dozen different flavors, one bite each, then stand at the sink and ascend my body. When I finally let myself swallow one, which I eventually do, it's heaven.

Gilda comes to the table with the cut-rate Barbie my mother sent her. She strips the doll of its floral dress, its petticoat, gloves, and plastic shoes. She slowly discovers that this doll has no hands or feet, just nubs.

"Her gloves *are* her hands," she says, worried. I prepare myself for another tantrum, but Gilda keeps looking inside the little gloves, tipping over the tiny shoes, amazed. I could bring this up the next time I talk to my mother, a nice dig. "Bizarre," I might say. "And a miracle she didn't swallow them."

I scour the sink, disinfect the counters, polish every surface in the kitchen.

It really is close to Gilda's bedtime when Jad comes through the door, sweaty and spent from his run. Every day after work he changes into sneakers and shorts and sprints around his office park. He's always been athletic, but he started serious training right after Gilda was born—not in hopes of a race or anything, just for something to do. It's interesting timing, but I never give him hell for it. It's a bright spot in what I take to be an otherwise depressing work life. He's an undervalued and underpaid customer service rep for a discount home hospice supply company. All day he fields calls from pissed-off caretakers in their bleakest moments. It's not enough that these people's homes have been taken over by their loved ones' hard dying, they have to deal with cheap shower chairs and defective rubber sheets too. Since I insist on staying home with Gilda—she may grow up to hate me but she'll know I was a good mother, I was *there*, at least on paper—Jad's miserable job is our bread and butter. He's been reduced to apologizing for leaky bottles of barrier cream. If for a few hours a week he wants to pretend to be the Usain Bolt of parking lots, he's earned the right.

Gilda squeals and runs to him. He picks her up and steps into the hall, where I'm waiting, smiling wildly, blocking his path. Adult company! He pretends to eat Gilda's stomach and she shrieks. He puts her down and moves to hug me, but I'm smiling tighter now, looking at his feet.

"Sorry," he says, stepping out of his sneakers.

"Oh yeah," I say, like it wasn't killing me to see him standing on the carpet, the microscopic chaos of spit and dog shit he's tracked in.

I follow him into the bathroom and download Gilda's whole day while he pisses—what she ate and didn't eat, how she played so nice at the park. I can see the stress of listening in Jad's face, but I can't stop my childcare litany.

He washes and dries his hands, strolls to the living room. I trail Jad and Gilda trails me.

"Guess who did great at Tiny Toads today?" I gush.

"I did," Gilda says. "I did great at the balance bean."

"Balance *bean*," I say, raising my eyebrows at Jad, who sits on the couch. "And how was your day?"

"Fine," he says. "Good." He covers a yawn. "Work was whatever. Ate lunch out by myself. Pretty solid run."

"Cool," I say, fine with everything but maybe the lunch, the quiet booth and the likely bread basket, the bottomless sweet tea. Hearing about Jad's day always irritates me, not because he's done anything wrong, just because he gets to live a life outside of this house, doesn't have to bear daily witness to Gilda eating mustard with a spoon like it's a side dish. But I can't be mad, not this time, because tomorrow I'm the one who's leaving, for once.

Gilda crawls into Jad's lap. She traces the lion's head tattooed on his neck, the capital G behind his ear. "Guess what? At the grocery store," she singsongs, watching me close, such a snitch. "All our food? Mom didn't buy it."

"Oh yeah?" Jad says. She pets the damp neck hair that peeks out of his T-shirt. Now they're both looking at me.

"Yeah!" Gilda says. "She left the cart. She *yelled*. At *people*."

This announcement has all the spectacle of a classic Gilda lie. I could deny it, gaslight her, but she's looking at me for help, like I'm the only one who can translate her murky child version, say it so Jad understands.

"Yeah," I say slowly. "I did do that."

Jad doesn't say anything, just gently removes Gilda's pinching fingers from a mole on his face.

"Yeah," I say again, and flash my palms, laugh a little, like—*You got me!*

"For real?" Jad says.

"Those are true things that happened," I say slowly. "It's like a whole—it was this whole—" I laugh again and shake my head. "I didn't buy the stuff," I say, hands still up—guilty as charged!

"Huh," he says, grim, like I've shown him the beginnings of a fever blister on my lip or a fat spider on the ceiling.

"So there's no new foods to eat," Gilda adds with a dramatic shrug, satisfied.

I SHOULD BE packing for tomorrow, but Thursday night is date night and it's mandatory, mediocre therapist's orders. Jad showers while I nurse Gilda to sleep. I put on my date dress—a sacky green tunic that has seen better days—and April from next door sneaks in to sit on our couch. I love April because she's sixteen and self-assured, teeming with new beliefs. She and her high school friends are always holding rallies, protesting, walking out, sitting in, getting shit done. Tonight she's wearing a T-shirt that says, "Brains Are the New Tits." Gilda has no idea Jad and I go on dates—she'd never stand for it—but I hope some of April's spirit will seep into her while she sleeps.

We never have to suffer through small talk with April. We leave in a rush, like she might dissolve into thin air or change her mind, like Gilda might sense our plan and wake up screaming. April waves us away, smiles with her tiny dolphin teeth, everything under control.

Splits is in night mode, awash with colored lights and bad music, the coffee replaced by booze. Christian's shift is over and I'm relieved—being seen here three times in one day seems excessive even for me.

We order our usual—a club soda for me, Jad's light beer—and the lab-coated waitress slinks off to tell the bartender.

"Don't bother with the lime," I yell after her, not sure she can hear me over the DJ's throb. "Bacteria," I mumble, though Jad knows this all too well, that I can't abide bar fruit. He's quiet, tapping his fingers to the beat. We're not supposed to talk about Gilda on our dates, and I doubt Jad wants to hear about my new friend Celadon or the glorious assemblage of porn folk I visited in the bathroom earlier tonight. This leaves me grasping at the smallest talk.

"Why is everybody always pushing limes?" I say.

"Huh?" Jad says, scanning a laminated menu. "Are you hungry? Should we order food?"

"I'm still full from dinner," I say. "Bartenders, I mean. Who decides what gets to be garnish?" I think of Gilda down the road, asleep alone in our big bed.

"The people decide," Jad muses, reading the list of appetizers. "Nothing sounds good," he says, flipping over the menu and resting it on the table. He fidgets with his wedding ring.

"Lime industrial complex," I say.

"People just like citrus," Jad says. He takes a deep breath, and I know what's coming. "Do we want to talk about the grocery store thing?" he asks.

"We do not," I say, and his worried face makes me add, "Not right now. We want to talk about what you're wearing." I eye his maroon button-down and darker, differently maroon, pants. "How come I've never seen this"—I wave my hand around his entirety—"getup?"

"I've had these," he says, rubbing his palms on the pants. "And you bought me this shirt."

"But as a *combo*," I say.

"Bad?" Jad says, and laughs.

"It's a look," I say, something my mother says. Jad's outfit seems especially odd in the wash of red light aimed at our table.

"Well, it's too late now," he says. "We have to live with it."

Because he is the nice one, Jad doesn't dare say anything about my hair, which I fucked up right before April came. She was running a few minutes late, and I was left to stare too long in the mirror. I had a lot of feedback for myself, all of it mean. I decided to trim my bangs, even knowing that, historically, this ends badly for me. One side came out too short and I tried to even it out, then the other was too short, and so on. Afterward, my eyes looked sort of bald, so I'd tried a thick wing with my eyeliner, but I got that wrong too, with one eye much larger seeming than the other. Because my hair is so blond it's basically clear, so limp and fine it's basically cobwebs, a bunch of the tiny, invisible cut bangs got trapped in my sticky black makeup. A sharp, caked hair made its way into my eye—the smaller-seeming one—and sitting here with Jad, I try to ignore it, but I feel it precisely, wet and spiky, scraping around.

The waitress drops off our drinks. We wait until she's gone to laugh at the huge lime, smashed and sunken, fizzing at the bottom of my glass.

"Oh man," Jad says.

"The lime lobby," I say, poking the thing with my straw.

"Want me to get you another one?"

"It's fine," I say. I take a drink. "Tonight, I'll make an exception."

Jad sips at his foamy beer, gets quiet again.

"At nap time today? It was so hard to get her down," I finally say, rejecting date-night directives, giving in to my Gilda impulse. "She fought it and fought it. Finally, she fell asleep right on top of me so I couldn't move. She started sweating and jerking her legs, talking in her sleep. Know what she said? She said, 'I'll egg the house.' Where do you think she got that?"

"Who knows," Jad says, and smiles, distracted. "Kids pick stuff up."

"*Egg* as a verb! And who is she going after? Somebody pissed off the wrong girl."

I want Jad to joke with me, to imagine the houses Gilda might be egging in her sleep, our dreamy little delinquent, but instead he leans back in his chair, breathes in deep. "How 'bout we talk about it now?" he says.

"Eh," I say. "What's there to say?"

"You call your boy?" Jad asks, and I love that, the way he calls the discount therapist my boy, like he's my drug dealer.

"Nah," I say. "I see him Monday anyway. We'll talk when I'm home." Since I'm at the ass end of the sliding scale, I don't like to be a bother between appointments. He never calls me back anyway.

Jad looks so tired, so preoccupied.

The waitress floats by with a rack of radiant test tubes.

"Could we get one of those when you get a sec?" I call out.

"Sure thing," she says, and Jad looks at me, confused.

"You're drinking?" he says. I can't drink and nurse—Gilda might wake up in the night and need me.

"A shot," I say. "For you."

"Why?"

"Why not?" I say, and a twitch of annoyance drifts across his face, followed by a ripple of relief. He drains his beer. All we won't say tonight recedes into the terrible, blaring music.

Soon the waitress is back, dropping off the luminous concoction.

"What even is it?" Jad asks, sniffing the glowing tube. He sips a little, grimaces.

"An experiment," I say.

"Coconut," he says, choking the rest down.

"Nice work," I say.

Jad gets up and drags his stool to my side of the table. He puts his hand on my thigh, and I sink into him. The DJ plays obnoxious four-on-the-floor hits and Jad nods his head like it's good music. We watch a wasted lady do a slow spin in front of the empty pastry case.

"I'm glad you're getting a little break," Jad says. "You excited? Gil and I will have so much fun."

They won't. Gilda's meltdowns have been especially demonic lately, and she's about to completely drop her nap, but if fun is Jad's story, I'll let him stick to it. He's taking a vacation day to cover for me, but he doesn't have my same solo-parenting skill set, doesn't know about all the ways to slack while you're on the clock. Gilda and I have been playing a lot of Brush, the game where Mommy lies face down on the floor and Gilda puts barrettes and clips and rubber bands in my hair. We play Married, where I doze on the couch and she flips through our wedding album, entranced, curious, and ultimately enraged. The cake cutting always pushes her over the edge. "Where's *me?*" she asks, irate, tilting the book, trying to spot herself somewhere out of frame.

Jad unbuttons his cuffs, shoves his shirtsleeves up. He waves the waitress over, orders an explicitly lime-free club soda and another terrible test tube.

"You packed?" he asks.

He's a featherweight, drunk and sweating already. His good mood seeps into me.

"It'll get done," I say.

When our round comes, Jad checks to see if April has called or texted, but she hasn't. He notes the time.

"Goddamn it," I say. "Feels like we just got here."

My eye is still bothering me, so I ask Jad to shine his phone light into my face. He can't see anything the matter.

"Just seems regular," he says.

"Hurts," I say, rolling my finger over my lash line. "Be right back."

In the bathroom I lean toward the mirror, but the lights are red and dim in here too. I wish there were a way to take the eye out of my head and rinse it, take both of them out for a good wash. If my eyes were out of my head, down in the sink, would it feel like *I* was in the sink? I feel tipsy from Jad's drinks, drunk by osmosis.

Back at our tall table, Jad's gone. Because he's a superb problem solver, for a second I think he must be peering into *his* eye in the men's room, trying to somehow fish out my irritant for me. I wish him luck and wonder where my club soda went. I check my phone—no texts or calls from April. I slowly realize I've sat at the wrong table, that my bag, Jad's keys, and Jad are sitting several feet to my left. I'm clutching somebody else's damp napkin—these empty glasses aren't ours.

I stay where I am and watch Jad. Skinny, broad-shouldered, he scrolls through his phone. We look nothing alike—I'm short and puffy and pink, he's tall and sinewy and olive—but when I look at the people I love, I see them as I see myself, which is to say I don't see them at all.

"It's just me" is the first thing my mother says every time she calls, when I finally decide to pick up. That's my general feeling when I encounter any member of my small circle: *It's just you.*

But seeing Jad from here, the way he asks for the bill, the half smile he gives to the waitress—I size him up in the moment. I know each of his mannerisms, am frankly bored by them, but in the forced disco of the coffee shop, rubbing up against the terrible music, he is expanding, unfolding in front of me.

Mine, I think.

I've shredded the stranger's napkin in my hand without realizing. A different woman comes out of the bathroom. Jad double-takes, turns his head, scans the room. I never feel more loved than when I catch a loved one looking for me. Baby Julie in the shopping cart, her concerned, searching face—I shake out the thought, rub my eye fast and hard with my fist. "Don't rub your eyes!" says everyone, but I say go for it. It always feels incredible.

Jad sees me then, watching from my new spot. He smiles his full, real smile. His dimple—what a failure that word is, inadequate term for such a glory—makes its appearance.

I go back to our table, lean up against him. The check comes and Jad does careful math, signs with a little flourish. He folds his copy of the bill, slides it safely into his wallet. People will show you everything you need to know about them by the way they do something ordinary. I drop a few dollars on top of Jad's perfectly decent tip—a holdover from my waitressing days, solidarity in the searing hatred of customers—though we don't have the money to do it, don't really have the money to be going out at all.

It's unusually cool outside, and the contrast between the damp heat of Splits and the night air is enough that I need Jad's gangly arms around me. We walk like that, with me in front of him, but it's slow going. On the street, we stumble past two men, and they smile at each other. One says, "Get her home safe," and the other one laughs. Date rape, always hilarious. *I'm the one who got* him *drunk,* I want to yell at them.

Jad and I turn down our block and a streetlight switches on—the only dark one in a long row of those already illuminated. It casts us in soft green tones. With the sudden light comes a popping, chemical fizz in the sky. We stop and stare up at the sound.

"That's been happening," I say. "Lights turning on for me. Does it happen to you?"

"Really?" Jad says. "No, I don't think so. Not to me. Someone lovely lights your way," he slurs.

"Huh?" I say.

"Somebody lovely. Someone."

"Are you quoting something?" I say.

"No, just saying," he says. "Quoting me, myself. Right now."

This lodges in me, a sticky thought, a person lighting my way, something new to derange me. I see how Jad and I might look from on high: two people in love on a street corner, caught in a dome of light. Someone lovely.

I turn myself to Jad—give them the body when the mind is elsewhere—and touch him through his pants. He holds my face and kisses me. He puts his head in my hair and inhales.

"When we get home," he says into my ear, "I'm gonna fuck you up."

He bites my neck, hard, and the heat behind it is genuine frustration, the first honest expression of the night. This roughness is exactly what I need, and I tug myself away from the luminous green pool. "Oh, hell yes," I say. My cheap shoes and the liquor in Jad's system keep us from running home.

I count out bills in the kitchen for April. Jad hides his boner in the living room, goes off to close the blinds and curtains, unplug Gilda's tree. "She's a doll. Slept the whole time," April is saying, and that's when there's a crash from the living room. I run in to see globes shattered and rolling, the tree slammed on its side. Gilda wails from our bed.

"Oh my fucking god, Jad!" I whisper, and crouch next to him by the flickering mess. His hand is over his mouth, his shocked face appearing and disappearing in the flash. Sex is no longer a possibility, but now we are laughing on the floor, Jad totally wasted, April watching confused from the hall. A perfect night, in other words.

"I LOST CONTROL," Jad whispers in bed. He's embarrassed, sobering up. We've vacuumed all the tinsel and microscopic shards, have spent an hour getting Gilda back to sleep.

"You didn't!" I say.

He touches the huge purple mark he's left on my neck.

"I bruised you," he says, stroking the splotch with his thumb. "I can see my teeth."

"Not bruised," I say. "It's a hickey."

"I hate that word," he says. "You've been mauled—I mauled you."

"And I loved it," I say. "I'll put a cold spoon on it. There's tricks."

"The tree," he says.

"It's all cleaned up. Gil's asleep now and everything's fine." *That wasn't shit*, I don't say. *That was* fun.

Some girls grow up and marry their daddies—not me. Though I've called Jad Dad a dozen times on accident, he's nothing like my father—I blame the rhyme. Dad was destabilizing, quick to explode. He told himself the world had an intense personal hatred for him, then went looking everywhere for proof. On one of our few weekends with him, a burger worker gave a little chuckle at the way Dad said *onion rings,* then parroted it back to him, loud. "Large onion *rangs,* coming right up." When the order came, Dad held eye contact with the guy, threw the rangs in the trash, untouched. Julie and I ate, and Dad sat there psycho-quiet on his side of the booth. In the car he unleashed, punched his steering wheel so hard he broke the horn. It honked on its own all the way to Mom's house, honked back down the road as he drove out of our lives again. It's not that Jad doesn't have strong feelings—he's sensitive in general, attuned to injustices. Rage flares in him from time to time, but unlike my dad, Jad conquers it, kills it. He doesn't push anger down but deals with it, processes it right there in the moment. It's the sexiest thing—someone handling their shit, feeling every bit of it, then telling it who's in charge.

I put my hand under the pillow, scratch Jad's head until he falls asleep. I still haven't packed but I'm trapped now, hot under the covers, while Gilda snores softly beside me. I lie there watching not-porn on my phone, volume low. There's a video about a bunch of sisters born with really crooked fingers, some human-interest story. There's a live audience, people asking does it hurt, do the fingers affect the sisters' daily activities? Can they type? How do they put on their makeup? Each sister has her own specific finger issue. They're twisted and bent, thick or very skinny. But these sisters have nice lives. One of them is a renowned chef. One is a social worker.

The video breaks for an advertisement selling leg makeup. These legs—I know exactly which worn-out rut my mind is about to take. This ad and those finger girls—neither of them is innocuous. The leg makeup especially is meant to entice, to work its way into your brain. I don't know if I want to fuck those legs or have those legs.

I part knees in my mind. Real people and fantasies collide. A pizza guy jerking off, hat on backward, eyes closed. Two girls on a gingham blanket. I think about one of those parties where somebody gets you naked, ties you up, carries you around like a present and lets everybody touch.

I'm not touching myself, but still I'm getting myself so close. It's this rare thing I can sometimes do—my imagination so tremendous, hormones so out of whack. From the outside it looks like nothing, and that's my favorite part—how secret. In these moments I don't need anyone, not even myself.

I think of Celadon again. She's got on black latex gloves. She's saying, "This will be intense, okay?" Her hair is glossy, she's wearing her beautiful, strange clothes and I'm wearing nothing. She's saying, "I need you to relax for me, love." We are inside that charm she wears around her neck, bathed in pale green light. We are panting together in the cool room, the curved ceiling overhead. "Oh, darling," she says, her slick hands holding me apart. "Can I?" Now her charm is our craft, a vessel floating on water. We're in the sea, not the ocean. What sea is it? I make a lazy turn through the globe in my mind, looking for water.

Part Two

THE
WATER
WITCH

A T THE BAGGAGE CLAIM, PETE CHECKS HIS FUCK APP to see about Montana meat.

"Just to get an idea," he says. This isn't a meat trip, he assures me, something I hadn't considered until he said it. On nights long past, before Pete fell in love, before I got pregnant, he would go up to the bar to get us a round and get sidetracked by some hot stranger, a beautiful bear with thick lashes and strong forearms. Pete has a type and his type is himself. He and his distraction would drink both drinks and then, remembering me at last, Pete would drop a con-solation shot on the table as he and his twin streamed past, leaving, saying, "Want me to call you a car?"

"Is totally, totally fine," I'd slur, and mean it. I'd down my free booze, melt happily into the worn vinyl booth.

But this is a different, heartbroken Pete, one who mopes and holds my hand and won't even look at a hot stranger, let alone ditch me for one. A meat trip! Would that it were so, for his sake.

The loudspeaker says a fishing pole has been left at the security desk. "Please retrieve your rod," the voice says.

"Did you hear that?" I say, but Pete is lost in his little screen. He flashes me a picture of a penis, a beer can next to it for scale.

"It's fifty miles away," he says, and I imagine the dick out there drunk and alone, living a life in the mountains.

We stand with people from our flight, waiting for our luggage, and a silver-haired woman creeps through the crowd. She wears huge wraparound sunglasses and a sheer fluorescent skirt so indecent and stained it seems to transmit her mental state. She clears her throat and stands at the head of the empty, spinning conveyor belt. Everybody listens to her shouted pitch, no choice in the matter.

"Good evening, sirs and madams. You are about to hear a story of great import," she begins, cementing the fact that absolutely nothing important is coming. I look for her home base—maybe a setup with an old Casio and some maracas, a stack of Bibles or a couple marionettes with human hair. People avoid eye contact with her and each other, keep tapping on their phones, but I'm compelled.

This is exactly the type of person my sister would have paid attention to. Julie talked to everyone. She was in love with the overheard, the random, the incidental. She collected strangers—regular, boring people like cashiers and delivery drivers and somebody out walking their dog, but she especially loved the touched: oddballs and yellers, the paranoid, the very religious. People like this elderly, scantily clad storyteller. She loved their bizarre logic and glaring blind spots, their abysmal advice. They'd hook her with a gesture or phrase, and she'd begin to live in their damaged lives with them. This tendency was a byproduct of Julie's worst choices—she dredged up bad characters with a social net cast as wide as her addictions—but there was something sweet about it too, how tender and attentive she could be to those in trouble.

The loud woman weaves through the crowd, her story full of odd ideas and impossible dates, precise weather.

"Low cloud cover," she says. "Winds southeasterly and we're born with only one fear—falling." Her cadence, her looping insistence— she reminds me of my mother. "I hit a bit of a snag," the woman goes on. "We will never be contained as we were in utero, perfect and free from want."

This loose story culminates in an announcement: the woman is a clairvoyant water witch and she wants to read everybody's palms. There it is—the grift!

"Give me anything long and I can find water with it," she says. "Anything can divine. It's not about the stick. It's not!"

Even though we've heard most of her bit, by the time the Water Witch gets to Pete and me, I let her take it from the top. I know what it's like to be a waitress rattling off specials, wanting your customers to shut the fuck up. "Of the utmost import," she barks. She goes on about the exquisite embryos, the wind and the clouds, August fifty-second. Then she hits her snag—back to the womb we go.

"Guess what?" is my mother's favorite refrain, an indication that what follows is a total waste, something I would never have the capacity or desire to guess, a cue that now would be a great time to mentally check out, spend a few minutes examining my cuticles, maybe try to recall the B-sides of some of my favorite records.

"Guess what? Chimineas are better than fire pits," she called me early one morning to insist. "Who wants to sit on the smoky side of a fire? Nobody, that's who. With a chiminea, smoke goes straight up. Guess what you can burn in one? Birch or cedar or pine needles. Oak. You can get you a Skeeterlog. Can't burn plywood. You shouldn't burn chipboard." She was picking up speed. "Pinyon or applewood, fine. Not newspaper. Stained woods—bad. Hickory? Hickory's okay." She would have categorized the whole world like that if I'd let her: safe to burn or not.

The Water Witch has a similar narrative tic, projects it in a similar grating tone. The connection between divining water and reading palms is flimsy, but I'm not surprised when Pete puts his phone away and presents his hand to her. His fragile state has primed him for just this type of con. The Water Witch's mouth has the folds women's mouths get, folds like my mother's, my future folds.

There's a loud buzz and luggage rises and tumbles from a gap in the wall. I watch the circling bags, appreciate again my powerful choice of a bright duffel—hot green, I call it, there was no delicate celadon option at the thrift store—even though Jad and Pete and everybody who sees it says how god-awful it is.

"I've got this," I say, not that Pete makes a move anyway.

Off the track I jerk his boring black bag and my magnificent bag—"Gree!" a boy a little younger than Gilda exclaims—and toss them in a low arc. Traveling without a child is euphoric in its ease, even the annoying parts. Give me a slow security line. Give me a flight hung up on a tarmac where all I have to do is sit.

"Once, I was perfect," the Water Witch is saying. "And then I was born." *Same,* I think. The way she cradles Pete's hand—I'm not sure if she's disturbed or addicted or just lonely, not that those things can't all coexist.

"Spectacular," she quietly mutters, studying Pete's palm. We lean in to listen. "You got a lifeline longer and thicker than any I ever seen," she says. Pete gently bumps my hip with his. She says he will live to be ninety. He'll make money and then he'll make even more money. Of course he will.

"What a beautiful life you have ahead of you," she marvels. "What a beautiful line!"

Pete stares at his palm, maybe searching for some sign of Brian. A blood blister, a splinter. "Anything else?"

Pete claims he wants a Brian-free future, but a lot of his behavior feels like conjuring to me. Heartbreak isn't so different from falling in love, how you can't shut up about a person. You search for them everywhere, point them out in transparent obsession.

Pete once took me to a happy hour—a full hour in which he did not stop talking about his amazing new relationship—and when some violently caloric dessert was brought to our table, he exclaimed, like a profound reveal, "You know who loves chocolate? Brian!"

"How unusual," I said. "How absolutely noteworthy."

I was no better. In my early days with Jad, I passed a sweaty jogger on the street and had an erotic flash to that morning, Jad above me, panting open-mouthed while we fucked. *That guy breathes like my boyfriend,* I thought, labeling Jad as such for the first time, trying out the commitment in my mind. Ridiculous. What a rare and beautiful coincidence, another respirating creature, kindred being with a mouth hole.

"You should try a standing desk," the Water Witch says. "Sitting is ruining everybody's spines. Like you." She points at me. She mimics my bunched shoulders and caved-in chest. It's so mean and uncanny I instantly respect her. *Joke's on you,* I think. *I don't even* own *a desk.* She coughs and hocks, works a gob in her mouth.

A distracted man knocks into her with his rolling suitcase. "My bad," he says, friendly and unfazed, but the Water Witch glares at him as he glides away.

"You people," she says. She pushes out her tongue like she's tasted something terrible.

At this, Pete presses his hands together, gives the Water Witch a little bow, ready to be free of her. She asks gruffly why any of us are here. I don't know if she means Bozeman or the baggage claim, but Pete's already got his phone out again, is checking on our rental car. "Nature," he says, not looking up.

"Don't bother going down to Old Faithful," she tells us. "It used to be something." She says the pressure has been failing, we've missed the best of it by years. "Now it's just—" She squeezes her fist and pumps it at her crotch, a frantic little jerk-off, extra lewd because it takes place under her tie-dyed fanny pack. Pete bumps my hip again, harder this time. The Water Witch asks to read my palm next.

I take a step back, afraid of what she might say—my past, my future. There's no way Pete and I are both going to live beautiful, rich lives until we're ninety. She reaches for my hand, and I yank it away. I feel the blood in my feet, veins swelling.

"Don't want to," I say, too loud, fists balled at my sides, how Gilda would handle it.

The Water Witch cocks her head and looks at me as if for the first time. "Where have you been?" she says.

"I'm sorry, what?" I say.

"You left," she says. "You up and left."

Something like laughter swells in my chest. "I what?"

She covers her mouth then, opens her eyes wide at me. "Someone wants to speak with you," she rasps, and I stumble, trip on my bag, and grab Pete, my neck hot.

Pete's had enough. "Nope," he says to her, suddenly unfolding his wallet. "No, ma'am. Thank you for your service."

The Water Witch grunts and refuses his crisp ten, turns from us and plows through the revolving exit. "What a cuckoo bird," Pete says.

Through the glass we watch her scan the curb. There isn't a boom box or a grimy, spread-out blanket on the sidewalk, no fast-food containers of murky liquids—only a waiting car. The Witch climbs into the passenger seat and the driver leans to embrace her. She's somebody's person, beloved.

"I thought she wanted money," Pete says. He thinks everyone wants money.

"She didn't," I say.

A MEANINGFUL NATURE EXPERIENCE is a real thing you can read about on the internet, Pete tells me in the rental car. People point to the dolphin pod that saved their marriage, the tree that helped them stop pulling out their eyelashes.

"MNEs change lives," Pete says. "There's so much documentation."

We both know I'm not going to look it up. There is clarity, Pete says, often a feeling of rising, leaving the body.

I am not calm, but I am calmly running my fingers over the buttery leather upholstery. I'm performing tranquility, recalling the Water Witch's unsettling tongue. I'm playing with the deluxe stereo, the electric windows. After Pete's Volvo, this is the nicest car I've ever been in.

"The important thing is to go into nature with an open mind," Pete is saying.

I run a nub of lipstick on with help from the fancy flip mirror, but it makes me look even more pale. At a red light, Pete watches me pat concealer on my blotchy neck.

"Wait," he says, moving my hair. "Is that a—"

"Love bite," I say.

"Aw," he says. "Y'all are like tweens."

Pete merges onto the highway and I pinch my cheeks to pink them up, try to look cute, like somebody on vacation.

MNEs can be triggered by wildlife sightings or other organic phenomena like patterns, swirling colors, or strange textures. Sunsets. Waterfalls. Creeping vines. People describe how birdsong changed their life, Pete says, how the smell of a certain flower made them switch careers, how the northern lights helped them forgive their dickhead father.

I've never had a meaningful relationship with the natural world unless drugs were involved. I don't know what to call the vast, flat nothing where I grew up, but nature seems wrong. When Julie and I were kids, we'd catch horny toads—these dry, snub-nosed lizards—but there was nothing majestic about them. They were slow and stupid and we'd toss clumps of them into a big bucket. We had no real plans for them. They'd piss and piss until they were floating—eventually we tipped them over so they wouldn't drown.

When I try to imagine what an MNE is like, I hope for something with the bliss and edge of a psychedelic. A memory glitters in the folds of my brain: that very first acid trip at our friend Big Large's trailer, his mother out of town.

Julie and I met Big Large one summer night at Oasis Cinema in Kermit. Mom had forgotten to pick us up after our movie, and Big Large circled the dark parking lot looking worried, eventually offering us a ride. Walking was impossible, and who knew how long we'd be waiting around? In the cab of Big Large's truck I had my house key poking through my fist, ready to take out his eye if he touched us. He was eighteen, just two years older than me, but I was suspicious of this guy who had already graduated and had a real job with the county, a guy who was a man, kind of. On the drive to Wink, Julie warmed all the way up to him. It took me a while to see what she saw, that he was a purehearted kid in there, inside his big, soft body—a gentle late bloomer. He spoke with a slow, true twang, loud and friendly as hell. He drove us around all the time after that, spent many nights taking Yes and Julie and me to distant towns for pizza or to go bowling, out to the faraway Walmart, where we'd just walk the aisles together. We'd always end up back at his house, where his mom was hardly ever home.

On the night of our first trip, Big Large was tripping too, but it was a party and he was in host mode, taking care of things. Julie, Yes, and I had just started to feel the gleam when it tilted into something ominous. There were no other girls there, and a bunch of boys were being obnoxious, one of them playing *Texas Chainsaw Massacre* on the TV, thinking it was funny. Some guys were fake wrestling, throwing real elbows, and they spilled a drink all over the pink rug in the living room. Big Large rushed off to get a dishrag. He came back and dabbed at the mess, and some new guy came into the trailer and said, "Dude, is that blood?"

Big Large laughed and said, "Not blood, y'all, it's wine cooler," but it was too late for Julie and Yes and me, the party had plunged into hellscape. Blood was on the TV and the pretty pink rug. Yes was disappearing, becoming part of the couch. Julie was gone too, now just a glowing orb in the corner. I ran over there, took the orb's hand like she was four instead of fourteen. I tied the orb's sneakers, led the orb outside, past some dogs fighting in the kitchen. Outside was better, cold and starry. Full gulps, deep, frigid breaths. We heard Big Large kicking everybody out then, saying a mad neighbor called the constable. It wasn't true. "Not y'all," he whispered as the boys streamed past, his forearm out to protect us.

"Constable ain't got shit on us," one guy said, and spat, but he left with the rest of the rowdy crew. They got into their trucks and bounced down the dusty road, mean dogs barking and spinning in the flatbeds.

"It's not a bad trip, just a bad curve," said the orb, my brilliant little sister. Big Large brought us back inside, poured us orange juice because he'd heard it counteracted strychnine. Yes had reappeared on the pink shearling rug, which was softly undulating. The four of us sat together on those damp and sticky synthetic fibers, waited to belong to the world again. Then Big Large—who could handle driving, no matter what—got us all home safe.

Yes slipped into her bedroom window, and Julie and I beat Mom back from a third shift. We were snug and faking sleep in our twin beds, letting the freaky comedown cartoon play out on the backs of our eyelids, when Mom clomped through the front door. "Babies!" she called, tossing her keys down right on the floor. "Come and eat with me?" In the history of third shift, we'd never been asked to break-fast. Julie and I sat up and looked at each other, stunned. No choice, we came out of our room and sat at the table. Mom didn't ask why we were fully dressed, why Julie had glitter on her cheekbones, why both of us were wearing such heavy eyeliner. The plastic place mats stared back at us, floppy and wise. The wood grain in the table swam to life, all drifting visuals: swirling faces, constellations. Our mother's hands, always tiny and delicate, were not usually covered in a layer of fine white fur. She boiled water and talked about having to give a sponge bath to some blackhearted patient.

Julie and I found each other's sweaty feet under the table, tried not to look at each other's full-blown pupils. We managed to swallow some of the odd breakfast Mom set out: the gleaming hard-boiled eggs, incandescent macaroni. How we shivered when she pulled a rare treat from a paper bag. Strawberry shortcake from the Flip Mart, the plastic clamshell an open miracle in the center of the table, stabbed with a single fork. We needed to look grateful. Julie gazed at Mom's downy hands, saw what I saw. Mom worked her busy little paws together, watched as we ate.

Behind our dramatic approximation of chewing, our egos were beautifully obliterated. It was like an open door between adjoining rooms. I flowed into Julie's space, and she flowed into mine.

We waited until Mom was asleep—until she was in her room at least, tucked in bed with a Bud Light—and our appetites came back. We sat on the screened-in porch and let our identities touch. We comingled and passed the dessert between us, understanding that whipped cream was a gift from a cow, that strawberries were magic, something to hold in your hand, contemplate, and savor, every seed a different rainbow color.

"Look at that," Julie said, fruit balanced on the fork. She didn't have to say what we both saw—the pulse of it, how the thing was breathing.

IN OUR GROUND-FLOOR hotel room, Pete reclines on the bed closest to the door—the murder bed, he calls it—and reads aloud from the trifold brochure he grabbed from the lobby. Plunge, Montana, is in the Paradise Valley, on the northern border of Yellowstone. The city limits hold a post office, a barbecue place called Follow Yer Nose, and not much else.

"Fishing, hiking. A bowling alley in the next town. A dive bar, but it's giving me real queerhunter vibes." He holds up the pamphlet to show me, but I can't see from across the room. I'm lying on my stomach on the other bed—the survivor bed—which Pete made a big deal of giving to me.

"I believe you," I say.

Earlier, I texted Jad to say we'd made it to the room safe and sound. He told me bath time was horrific, that Gilda pooped in the tub.

That's a new one, I texted. What a treat, when we thought we'd made it to the comfortable stages of potty training—*comfortable* meaning near-daily piss accidents but only occasionally dealing with shit. Parenthood makes urine seem positively clean. With Gilda, it's about will, not ability. I wasn't sure if I was annoyed that Jad thought I needed or wanted to know about the bathtub turd—I spare him every gory detail when he misses bedtime—or glad Gilda was giving him some much-needed hands-on experience with her bullshit.

What sort of mediocre bedtime story would he tell her? Gilda's hard to please. She's a believer in the oral tradition, the more spontaneous and meandering the better. She encourages this by throwing out suggestions midway, like it's improv. "People teeth," she'll say. "Mucus. Long dogs!" Then she pokes holes in your plot, makes you try a different tack when she loses interest, or worse, she riffs on what you've given her and takes over, her own version an endless spiral, her last fight before falling asleep. Probably he'll let her stare at cartoons on his phone until she drops. But none of this is my problem, for once.

My phone buzzes, and I worry I've conjured them with my brief, gleeful freedom, but no, it's my mom. I reject the call into my open suitcase.

Pete walks around the room in his boxer shorts and driving moccasins. He leaves the bathroom door open even while he pisses. He takes a long shower and does his complicated skin-care routine: the layering of serums, the targeted creams. I'm too tired for any of it. I stew in my gross airplane germs, flip down the burnt orange coverlet, and get under the sheets fully clothed. Tomorrow I'll take a shower, slather myself in Pete's expensive stuff, dump a bunch of it down the drain.

It's Gilda's bedtime, which is usually my bedtime too.

I can't believe I'm the only person in this bed, that I get to sleep here by myself, that Gilda will not somehow crush the fifteen hundred miles between us with pure willpower.

This is only my second attempt at being away overnight. The first was a failure. It was supposed to be a sleeping trip at a hotel not far from our house in Pivot. Gilda was so little, and her nocturnal crises—colic, cluster feeds, teething, sleep regression—seemed to cycle, overlap, and synergize. I was delirious. I'd turn my head and see shadow dogs lunging. People made of smoke walked in front of me, dissolved around corners. We couldn't really afford it, but I was desperate, exhausted, so I planned to get full use of a room, span check-in to checkout, with sleep and a bath and some peace. I pumped a ton of milk, packed myself an overnight bag.

"Go," Jad said. "We'll be fine."

Jad and I had only recently started having sex again, and the sex we were having was sweet but perfunctory, lukewarm and rushed. Immediately upon my arrival to the hotel, lust lurched in me, like I'd somehow left it in that room, waiting. I closed the thick floral curtains, thumbed my phone, and turned the place into a dim masturbatorium. I scrolled through what felt like a pressurized backlog, reams of urgent porn I'd missed since the birth of my daughter, seemingly curated just for me: guys with scrunchies in their hair, women in ankle socks, women with sex machines, sex machines with sex machines, women letting coned ice cream melt all down their hands.

At first this felt almost chaste, like that summer after fifth grade when everybody started hugging each other in greeting, boys and girls stepping forward, pressing their whole bodies into you, something that had been unthinkable or unremarkable just the year before, now not only thrilling but socially acceptable, happening under the watchful eye of teachers and parents. What I was doing felt healthy and free from lewd descriptors, like I was a person experiencing the delights of the body for the first time, not a new mom jerking it in the hotel room her husband locked in at a promo rate.

Eventually I wore myself out, or I thought I had. I put my phone away and finally tried to sleep, but in bed my favorite fantasies washed over me. The vault of ex-boyfriends and -girlfriends. Dusk in a cow pasture, my first love looking back at me over her naked shoulder, her silk dress a chartreuse puddle in the dirt. The cross-country runner with blue eyes and black gunk under his fingernails, how he'd toss me around his dorm room, both beds, his poor roommate out in the hall with a textbook in his lap. I moved on to long shots: the half-dozen or so technically innocent but artfully erotic friendships I've maintained for most of my adult life—a waitress, a good friend's older brother, people from college I never fucked but should have. I progressed to sheer imagination, which is often better than the remembered because it is a longing perfectly cast, not recast, repurposed, or rearticulated, forced out of context. The cow pasture girlfriend's mouth, for example, free of her appalling politics and creationist beliefs. Some one-night stand's blameless torso, minus his silver chain and too-small head. Let's edit out that chain—let's crop that head. The circle widened: A girl in a gum disease commercial. Sunlight on thick thighs. A threadbare calico dress. The irate crosswalk guy who called me a bitch and spat on the hood of my car. These scenarios mutable, and, to borrow an unsexy word—possibly the least sexy word ever—bespoke for me. I fell into a hormonal swirl not unlike puberty, only with a freshly wrecked vulva, breasts leaking, my actions punctured by the periodic, unnerving, and imagined sound of my baby crying.

Soon I felt overstimulated and sick, unable to harness the desire. Even the imagined was too much, maybe especially too much—the blank bodies were starting to torment. I'd catch them climbing faceless up the walls, see them hovering on the ceiling.

These apparitions, the porn—all of it, of course, a distraction from the unthinkable, constant thought.

Tween Julie in a gigantic T-shirt in front of an open refrigerator, eating sliced ham, standing on one leg. Gap-toothed, pigtailed Julie in the back seat of Mom's Buick, fogging up the window with her breath. She used the side of her hand to make baby footprints, the tips of her fingers to make baby toes. She marched them across the glass like that. Grown Julie unwashed, diminished, behind a closed bathroom door, arms bruised and talking to nobody, hair matted on her head. "C'mere and help me get this knot?" Latchkey Julie on the honor roll, packing her backpack every night, laying out tomorrow's clothes for both of us. Julie, near the end, reaching for my hand when I tell her I'm pregnant. Things so tense between us, I don't even remember what we're fighting about, but the possibility of a baby—a Gilda—disarmed us. We sat holding hands in the car she would die in, squeezing *sorry*s back and forth.

And that's when I felt her come into my hotel room, as real and regular as anybody opening a door, slipping their shoes off, sitting at the foot of your bed. I let her settle, then reached over to turn on the bedside lamp. The bulb sputtered and popped, the filament blindingly spent.

"Um," I said to the dark.

That was the first time I realized she was maybe not finished with me. I sat there in the room and listened for what she might say. A whirring safe in the closet clicked softly, repeatedly, its internal mechanism opening or closing, opening or closing, I didn't know.

"What?" I said, wanting her to spit it out. I waited but nothing came, no message aside from the threat of a message. The charge in the air drained or I killed it or both. It was only a room again and I was alone.

I'd called Jad and convinced him to come get me. It wasn't even dinnertime yet. He was surprised but so relieved. Gilda had been crying since I left, he admitted. He was about to put in earplugs, try to power through it, anything to give me a night of peace.

"I miss you guys" was the excuse I gave.

THIS MONTANA ROOM is nicer than that other one, likely the nicest hotel in Plunge, and Pete probably searched those exact internet terms to get us here. We lie in our beds and watch the show he likes where makeup artists turn models into classic movie monsters.

"This is very much about contouring," the TV says.

It's the finale from last season, and Pete already knows how it ends. A group of pretty girls in bald caps sits in front of a bank of lighted mirrors.

"Who's your favorite makeup artist?" I ask, and Pete yawns and says, "All of them."

"You have to make bones where there aren't any," the TV says. The sound cuts to static and the picture flickers, a rainbow fritz. The screen ripples, rights itself.

Someone in the room next door is taking a shower, but this place is so poorly insulated it sounds like they're here with us. I keep thinking some new person is about to come out of the bathroom, one of the bald models maybe. A half ghoul wrapped in a fluffy towel.

"You're asleep," Pete says, and this is true and then it isn't. I still don't know what beasts the girls on TV are supposed to be. They're on the other side of their transformations now, makeup mostly removed, remnants of swampy paint around their mouths and nostrils.

"Did the makeup artist win?" I ask, bleary.

"Sure did," Pete says.

He turns off the TV and we say good night. This is, of course, my cue to be acutely awake.

Even though I'm always secretly or not-so-secretly wanting to fuck almost everyone, Pete is safely set apart, excluded from my filthy scroll, not even a tiny cameo. His presence is blessedly neutral. A platonic relationship, such a rarity for me.

I spin in the sheets in the quiet room. I'm too cold without the covers but too hot with them. I hear Gilda not crying, not curled up and breathing behind me, feel her soft little feet not pressing on the backs of my thighs.

At my periodic thrashing Pete says, "What's up? You're spazzing."

"Too tired to sleep," I say.

He flips on the lamp, fumbles around in his toiletry kit, gives me a large gray capsule. Like any number of pills Pete has handed me over the years, I swallow it dry—this is a talent I have—and then, just like in footloose, pill-eating days of yore, I realize I don't know what it is I've taken.

"In high doses it's an antipsychotic, but at this dose it's like a sleeping pill," Pete explains. He flips the light off again, tosses a pillow on the floor.

"It's *like* a sleeping pill," I repeat.

"It is one. It can be. Let's say it is."

Pete is scratching his shins under the covers, long, hard scrapes. I know it's his shins he's scratching because I know the sounds Pete makes in the night, even though it's been a while since I've slept in a room with him. You don't forget some people's night sounds. Julie, next to me in our childhood bedroom, would swipe her feet over each other in the dark. I'd know she was passed out when she made a little sound, a kind of "oh" in the back of her mouth, like she was surprised to find herself asleep.

"It is one," I say to Pete, and then we're both very quiet.

My ear, flattened to the pillow, begins to sing. Is some small, abandoned person desperately missing me right now? Is her body sending my body a signal? I feel guilty but I remember ears do this on their own, emit tests when they aren't being used, play little ear solos for fun. Maybe my body is sending my body a message and the message is just: your ears work.

I say, "Who has you taking antipsychotics?"

"Nobody," Pete says. "Myself. Just grabbed a sample pack from work, for sleep. Nothing knocks me out. I'm a supermetabolizer," he says, full of pride. "*Antipsychotic* sounds bad, but it's just a scary word."

There's not even a glint of the psychotic to Pete, nothing about this trip puts me in the slightest bit of peril. Not that peril is so bad. Peril is when endorphins kick in, make everything sparkle.

"Not so scary," I say. "It's not *decapitate*."

"*Menstruate*," Pete says. Then, softer, "You could get a prescription for something too, you know," he says. "It's not at all unreasonable."

Loud ice empties into a bucket somewhere outside. Quiet seeps and swells in the aftermath. I can feel starch on the sheets. I touch the wall in the dark room, let the remembered pattern of the burnt ochre wallpaper colonize my thoughts. I stick one hot leg out of the covers—my regulator leg, Jad calls it—and, ridiculously, I miss the feeling of Gilda at my back, how she clings and repositions, threads her toes through mine, puts her damp little hand between my breasts. How she connects, asserts herself with my every move, completes the circuit of us even while we sleep.

"Maybe when I'm finished nursing," I say, knowing this is a realm where Pete won't venture an opinion, that he'll drop the subject.

Pete's breathing deepens and my center softens, that syrupy, falling feeling that comes when a slow-mo drug kicks in. A past version of me would have relaxed, stripped out of my clothes, and curled up in the scratchy hotel duvet. Present me stays on edge, awake, worried, and sweating long after Pete has drifted off, afraid if I go to sleep I'll die. Not only am I borrowing a friend's prescription, that friend also has no prescription, just access and marketing copy he makes up. Who's to say these samples have even been through the gauntlet of testing, that they've made it out of the monkey stage? I will die in this hotel room and Jad, grief-stricken, tear-blind, will crash the car on the way to retrieve my body, leave Gilda screaming in a crunch of metal and glass. Dead mom, dead dad, no chance. No family lasts forever. Off she'll go to live with her mimi and the cats, in a house of rancid dairy and broken, scummy fish tanks. I remind myself again to list Yes as Gilda's disaster guardian on the paperwork. Why haven't I already taken care of this important detail? I consider getting up and making a note on hotel stationery, but no, it's too late, I'll definitely die tonight, and Gilda will grow up in a junkyard. Pregnant at sixteen, she'll get her driver's license and go out hoarding in the Buick my mom now refuses to drive. She'll learn how to scour garage sales, and my mom will put her in charge of gathering chairs. She'll come home with every variety—upholstered, stacking, folding, lawn—every genre of chair.

Then the chairs in my mind, so terribly many of them, are gone. Something happens that hasn't happened in years: I have a dream about Julie.

That's not exactly right. This dream is not *about* Julie, more like it belongs to her, like she's having it from wherever the dead dream. I'm here to lap it up and interpret, though it's more montage than story—a peek into the garbage disposal of her lived life: her stage fright, the men she liked, the dogs she loved, the scraps of paper she was always chewing. This dream is stylish, like Julie. It's beautifully shot. It is eerily cinematic and perfectly composed, the colors super-saturated. There are friends of hers running through machinations I don't understand. There are loud cars streaking midnight highways, high beams on, joyous.

This next part of the dream is all me, a souped-up version of a familiar terror: I'm moving down a dark road, a soaking-wet girl at my side. She is a skeletal trope, a ghostly cliché bleeding from the mouth. I've dreamed this girl before, but this time her feet are gone, a first. She walks directly on her shinbones, and that new detail—the white of the bones, the chalky sound they scrape out on the asphalt—it's a novel and vicious twist.

On the shoulder of the road, impossible luggage is scraping, too, trapped in a metal loop. A loudspeaker voice booms from the black sky, incomprehensible. My soaked, footless, bloody-mouthed girl has shifted. She's older now, in a lurid skirt. It's the Water Witch, of course. Like some annoying operator, she has crossed my wires with Julie's, has both of us dreaming the same thing from different sides.

"Kit," Pete says, and the haunted soundtrack Julie has chosen—lush atmospheric stuff, all swells and spooky, blended voices—cuts off quick, like when you walk too close to an orchestra of crickets.

"Kit," Pete says, "you're screaming." This is true and then it isn't. I sit up. The institutional ambiance of the hotel room rushes in, the facts of my real life, Montana, the faint tap-tap of coolant in the AC unit.

Alone in the weird bed, I do not think, *Where's Gilda?* but *Where's my mama?* This is such a ridiculous panicked-mammal thought, proof that even the most heavy-handed, nonsensical nightmare can turn you right back into a child.

Heart thundering in a strange place, I reach for Pete, more hoped for than seen, in the dark. He's here, my Pete, leaning over and taking me by the shoulders, gently shaking out my worst thoughts. I touch his face, lace my fingers through his beard.

"Am I?" I say.

PETE'S NOT IN the room when I wake up the next day. Maybe my night terror has made him turn this into a meat trip after all. Maybe he's decided to visit the lonely beer-can dick over yonder mountain.

It's quiet. Mornings, Gilda's chirpy voice is a tiny knife in the brain, but waking up without it feels wrong. I stretch out in the cool sheets and try to imagine a life where she's grown up. It is unfathomable that she will one day wipe her own ass and avoid my phone calls, that she'll come home to visit twice a year. I want her to stay with me forever, but I want her gone too. It's on purpose, this ambivalence, some ingrained magic. It's the reason teenagers are so impossible, why they grow to hate you so much. Otherwise they'd never leave us, and we'd never want them to.

No child around means no child-rearing questions for Yes. I text her just because.

I miss my dumb baby, I say.

Normal, she texts back. *But don't be an asshole. Enjoy it!*

What are you up to?

Joe got the kids an ant farm. Watching ants. Jealous?

But I am, truly. The way Yes plays and listens and parents. She loves it, knows what to do, takes pride. The children's desks set up in her living room, the color-coded hooks and cubbies, the daily schedule posted and cherished.

I scroll through pictures on my phone. Jad holding Gilda upside down, their faces matched in identical glee. Gilda with a metal bowl on her head. Gilda throwing absolute side-eye, furious with me for something.

Her lightness, how long and hollow she feels in my arms, a straw girl. How I carry her up and down the stairs like a broom. "Pick me!" she says in that little voice, arms stretched up. How she is always configuring my proximity to her, whether I'm emptying the dishwasher or cooking dinner or peeing. *Where's Mom?* her face says, such relief when I appear. It's a trick, this sudden longing for her. Chemicals in the brain, same as the ones that drive her to hound me. How she sits on my lap and strokes my face, touches every mole and freckle, asks about each of them.

"What's this one, Mama?" she'll say, right in my ear, loud and high. I'm always reminding her to use her inside voice, but I know one day I'll miss this precise tone, her young pitch.

My milk drops, hot and tingling. Jesus. My phone rings. I see my mother's name and, overstimulated, I panic-answer.

"Key-it!" she drawls, the only person in the world who can pull apart my name like that. Her twang comes with volume too.

"Hey there," I say, cheerful and upbeat, like it's me who's been calling her all week. It's a numbers game—she's been trying me for days, knowing with each small rejection I am becoming incrementally ready to deal with her bullshit. "We've been playing phone tag," I say.

"I know it," she says, both of us happy to forget even the most basic rules of that game. The relief in her voice shames me every time I pick up.

"Oh, sugar," she says, shocked when I tell her that, no, I'm not home, I'm in Montana. She's hurt. "Oh, Key-it! Who's taking care of my baby?" she asks. "Why didn't you bring her out here to me?"

Ringworm, I don't say. *Botulism and black mold. Generations of silverfish in an unused dishwasher.*

"It's just a long weekend," I say.

"Who's keeping her?"

"Who do you think?" I say.

"Can he," she says, ". . . handle that?"

"Of course he can," I snap.

I can't blame my mom for being suspicious of husbands and fathers. After all, my father, her husband, turned out to be a real asshole, as her father was, and his father before him. Asshole dads spanning eons, which is nothing rare. Still, she knows Jad is different.

"Must be nice," she says. I don't respond, both because I'm irritated and because Pete texts me a picture at that precise moment. I hold out the phone to look at the golden mountain range, the whipped orange sky. It's more Montana propaganda.

My mother says, "Are you pissed at me?" and it's like one of the mountains is saying it.

I hear her struggling with a cigarette, the metal scrape of the lighter. Her hands are bad.

"You on the porch?" I don't even have to ask. It's her wine porch, her smoking porch, the screened-in center of her life. She and Julie used to sit out there in twin rocking chairs, wasting their days.

"Yep," she says. Then, "Don't throw out any bottle with a neck!" she's yelling, agitated.

"Mom, who are you talking to?"

"The county. Did I already say that?"

"The who? They're there now?"

"Condemners are out here *crunching* my stuff," she says. "Guess somebody didn't like how the yard looked. DNS got called again," she says. "Jesus lord," she yells. "Stop crunching my stuff!"

"What are they doing?" I ask.

"Condemning!" she says. "Stomping around, taking pictures. Gary's here. These bastards."

"Don't be mean to Gary," I say.

This isn't the first time we've dealt with neighborhood services. Gary is a kind, shiny-faced man from Wickett. He's divorced, her same age, and they've known each other forever. Their high school football teams were rivals. I tried to get them to go on a date once, if only for the cute story, but Mom wasn't into it. Gary seemed game.

"Oh, Tammy, why the hell not?" he said. "We actually have a lot in common."

"Yep," she said, still so beautiful, standing in her ruined home. "We're both gonna die alone."

DNS visits always go the same way: some concerned citizen calls the county and they come out and look at the material, which is what they call my mom's mess. "Ten pounds of shit in a five-pound bag," Gary calmly explained to me that first time, my mom defending herself to his colleague. I'd had to drive out from Pivot to help, newborn Gilda sleeping in the sling.

"I do want it cleaned up," Mom told them. "But I need to look after my investments. I'm a ubercollector," she bragged. She gave them the tour. All of us watched her put a gun catalog on a pile of black garbage bags. "Stay," she said, "stay," one hand up as she backed away. She told them about her armadillo room.

"Y'all hear about the armadillo room?" she said, proud. "Go see the 'dillas!"

"We heard about the armadillo room," Gary said, as calmly and neutrally as one could say so.

She'd always loved the creatures, even when we were little. Julie and I gave her versions of them on every birthday and special occasion: cookie jars and Christmas ornaments and a magazine holder from the thrift shop, beach towels we bought on sale. Once you turned on your 'dilla light they were everywhere in the dark world, waiting to be found. They made her happy, and she used to line everything up in a lit curio case. After years of this it seemed like she was maybe getting sick of them, growing weary with each gift. Armadillo pencils! An armadillo placard that said, "Keep It Weird!" But by then she'd committed to the lifestyle.

Out in the hallway, she explained the cat trees to Gary's team.

"The back one they play on. Well, they can't right now because of the laundry. But that's the one they use. These side ones I got for free but haven't had a chance to put together. The red one is broken and these carpeted ones are broken. But for parts," she said. "Backups. The broken ones I got for cheap. The white one didn't cost me a cent," she said, beaming.

Doubles, triples, backups.

"Everything has a use. That could be a planter," she said about a solo rain boot. "Planters," she said about a stack of rusty buckets.

"Tamm, can you find me something," Gary said, gently, "that's *not* a planter?"

"It's pointless, Gary," I said. "Throw it out! Take this shit away!"

"Wasteful!" my mom is saying now, to this new, similar group of agents. "Y'all should be ashamed." She goes inside. The screen door slams.

"Hello?" I say. I can't handle a DNS visit. "Did I lose you?"

"Kit?" she says. "I'm here."

"Sorry, Mom. You're cutting out. Pete and I are out on a very long hike right now," I say. "Reception's bad."

To truly complete a phone call with my mother, I have to imagine her house, my childhood home, engulfed in flames, her inside it. She burns and I regress, become a vile, hateful daughter, and that's how I know the final stage—deep, personal shame—is close. Today, I get there quick. Full circle, I ask her about the diseased Friends, a gesture of goodwill.

"How's the one-eyed one?" I say, and her eager response peels her down to the person she is, a mother who has lost a child.

"Oh, he's my baby," she says. "A real stinker."

I turn tender for the gross cats: her company.

There aren't all that many hoarders in the general population, but in nursing homes and memory care facilities, like the one where my mother worked for years, the percentages soar. These people quite literally pick up and hold things to remind them who they used to be. They turn these contemplation objects over in their hands, a hazy life remembered. My mother saw this every day. She'd come home and complain about it—the woman with a collection of apple cores, to contemplate what? An apple she'd eaten as recently as lunch? Mom knew about these people and their disordered thinking, and still, after Julie, she fell into it.

The second I think about Julie, the connection on the phone really does glitch. That delicate animal response when someone stares at your back from across a room. The rush of pulse, tingling spine. A remnant from when we used to get eaten by tigers, maybe, when we'd be drawing on a cave wall and turn to see glowing eyes. It's like that, a full-body acuity, but instead of inducing terror, it's comforting, a cocoon of static. A buzzy, protected feeling. I'm sleepy maybe, or it's the residual effects of the borrowed antipsychotic.

"Hello?" I say.

There is static and a delay. My words break apart, chase each other, repeat a second after I say them. The air changes, is charged. The echo isn't me, the voice lower, a richer tone, lush. I close my eyes to listen hard. There is no more heavenly instrument than my sister's voice.

It's Julie, I'm sure of it. Unmistakable.

We sang together as soon as she could talk. Both of us had an ear, but Julie's voice was a thrum, a squeeze. My soprano was clear but too obvious. Thirsty. I belted like a child actor. Julie's alto came through rich and husked, raw, a voice that triggered devotion. There's an old recording of the two of us fighting about something, where she sustains a note to tune me out. She meant it to annoy, but it was magic. That voice so warm and alive—she couldn't make a wrong sound. She couldn't even read music. She'd sit in front of the piano, pick up a violin, fuck with a synth. She'd dick around until she found her way in. You could feel it atmospherically, a shift.

"Nothing special," she'd say, but these songs were catchy and unsettling at the exact same time. They were *hers*. Devil music, truly, because once she dragged a melody into the light, you'd be stuck with it, looping, looping, even when you were trying to sleep. Her mouth was a rip in the scrim of her body, light spilling. Grit in her tone already, even as a little kid. Sand and need and want in her.

She didn't hold it over me that she was the one with the real talent. She'd listen to some dumb track I'd made and say, "Kit, this is so strong."

I could harmonize with her, my one true offering to the band. Our voices worked together, offshoots of the same voice—Mom's. I'd fumble through the ladder of notes, different fills until I found her register. Together, we made a third voice. When things hit just right, we'd turn our heads and almost expect to see some new, blended girl in the room with us.

She's here, on the line now. Singing.

"What is that?" I say to my mom.

Eyes still closed, flat on my back, I feel Julie's weight on the hotel bed. *Stay,* I think.

"Hold on," Mom says. She's distracted, bossing people around.

"Collectibles!" she yells.

"Mom? Do you hear that?" Tears stream, pool in my ears.

"Huh?" she says. "Oh, it's the cats. Or it's these motherfuckers."

"No," I say. "Do you hear voices in the phone? A voice."

She listens. "Just yours," she says.

The heat withdraws, the song gone. I open my eyes, sop off my face with the bleachy sheet.

"Okay," I say. "Okay."

One of the guys yells for her, asks if the propane tanks in a heap out front are empty or full.

"Both," she yells back, and then, "Get me Gary! I talk to Gary and Gary only."

The screen door slams again. Mom lights another cigarette. I hear her creak down in her rocker. She slurps her drink. In the empty chair next to her, Julie is clawing at scratch-offs, drinking red wine from that stupid goblet she got at the renaissance faire—"Such craftmanship," she used to say, willfully blind to the cheap glass, the factory-etched filigree from ye olde assembly line. She is playing lap solitaire all wrong, flipping cards over in rows on her hot thighs, arranging them at random to have something to do with her hands. She is the hot thigh and the goblet and the wine. She's the whole deck of cards, the box the deck comes in, the cut deck, a single card, face down on the floor. She's the game she's making up.

If Gilda were here, she could end this call for me. The whole time I talked she'd be whining, "I want to hold Mimi," and my mom would say, "Let me talk to that baby," and we'd all know what was coming. Gilda's got a massive vocabulary—she can appropriately use *debris* in a sentence—but like every kid, she's phone dumb. Any call ends soon after it starts, with her mashing the keypad, hitting the wrong buttons, dropping the thing or shouting into it, hanging up—letting all parties off the hook.

"Hey, Mom, there's a, like a stream thing we're walking up on? We have to cross it, okay? I need to hang up. I'll call you later."

She exhales, coughs. "Okay," Mom says. "I'll just be here getting my property tampered with," she says. "But you go on and roam."

JULIE AND I used to walk home from school together, harmonizing in the heat. Western swing, hippie music, standards, things we'd been listening to forever. Dad didn't do much for us, but he fed our well of song. Before we were born, he sprang for a decent stereo, and when he ran off he left his records behind. Julie would sing both parts to teach me, then I'd do the highs. Sweat ran down our sides. Mean birds looped in the sky, the plain so flat we could see our tiny gray house up ahead the whole time we were walking, torture.

I was in charge of us. I wore the key on a shoelace around my neck, Mom's only directive not to use the stove or answer the door. Otherwise, we were free. The memory care facility where she worked was all the way in Odessa, at a place called the Quarry, which sounded like a spot where kids went to get high. Mom always said she was a nurse, but it wasn't true—she was a medical assistant, not that Julie and I knew the difference. She liked her job—wearing scrubs afforded her a level of respect she'd never had in her life.

I'd dead-bolt the door and we'd throw our bags down, cool off in front of the box fan. I'd make snacks—peanut butter and crackers for Julie, peanut butter on a spoon for me—and remind us to wash our hands first.

The television was on whether we were paying attention or not, adult voices in the house to fill the lonely space between school and the late sound of Mom's car crunching up the drive. I'd watch my favorite show, a popular series where children—not actors, normal kids like me—went to a scientist's house to do experiments. The point was to use household items, maybe to re-create the experiments on your own later, though I was always too lazy to try. In one particular episode—the inciting episode, as I've come to think of it—the kitchen scientist sprinkled black pepper into a glass bowl of ordinary water. The pepper floated, suspended on the surface. The kitchen scientist showed the invited child—a girl with a boy's haircut and a blue windbreaker—how to coat the pad of her index finger with bar soap. He showed her how to place her soapy finger into the bowl, into the middle of the peppery galaxy. What happened next was magic, which was so often the case with things on this show: the pepper came to life and skittered to the far rim of the bowl. A thick black ring formed around the outside edge, flecked and dense like the iris of an eye. The center stayed perfectly clear, a swelling pupil.

There was a practical lesson to this trick, something about surface tension or acids and bases—I'm still not sure. Julie would have gotten the takeaway, whatever it was, but she wasn't watching with me that day. She never cared much for the TV shows I liked. She was ten years old but more advanced in many ways already, her handwriting so grown-up, her script so straight and stylish compared to mine. She was already taller than me and would stay that way. At school, nothing got past her. She listened with her eyes elsewhere, teachers setting traps for her, calling on her in class when it seemed her mind had left the room. She'd look up from whatever doodle—the famous invisible cube, the smiley face with the hanging tongue—and answer precisely, a little sigh before she spoke, elegant in her boredom. They'd been sending her to my grade for math for years, something that infuriated me, and at that very moment while I was watching TV, she was probably doing actual science at our kitchen table, looking at mayonnaise or a segmented bug leg or her own blood under the microscope she'd bought with her birthday money. We were still good girls then, this was before Yes and I got corrupted by cool kids and corrupted Julie too: the harsh music and the cigarettes, the makeup on her eyes.

I loved this pepper experiment—I loved the kitchen science guy, how kind he was to the kids he entertained, a grown-up man listening to a little girl, thrilled to show her the secrets of the world. I learned so many astonishing everyday things from his show: that sand is made up of a million tiny seashells and one day the sun will die, that babies have more bones than adults and certain animals screw themselves to reproduce. I had gotten used to soaking up the scientist's miracles, then going about my day.

That night when I was trying to sleep, Julie rubbed her feet over each other in the twin bed next to mine. The sound of the TV, on now for Mom's comfort, was coming through the thin walls, news show after news show and then infomercials, her need for adult voices as strong as ours had been in the latchkey span.

I sensed the nighttime contours of our dark bedroom—the coatrack that loomed in the corner like a hatted man, an ottoman like a friendly crouching animal. As I got sleepier, the low popcorn ceiling of our bedroom grew vast. On it, the film of my experiment unspooled. I was on the bottom of the kitchen scientist's bowl, looking up through tap water. Above me, pepper floated in a thick constellation. I waited for the roof to come off, a giant soapy finger to descend from the void. What I felt was not anxiety but delicious anticipation. The feeling was sexy but not sexual, a warmth, a thrum. Something thrilling was about to happen.

Suddenly, Julie sat up, snapped on the lamp between our beds.

"Hey!" I said, startled, blinking against the brilliant crack of light. "What are you doing?"

"What was that?" she said, fingering the lace on her coral pink nightgown.

"What was *what*?" I said, heart zooming. Our room was our room again, my science chased away by the bright bulb.

"All that stuff on the ceiling," she said. "Those black stars."

I opened and closed my mouth. "You could see it?" I finally said.

"Where'd they go?" she said, no fear in her voice.

"Not stars," I said. "Pepper." I tapped my temple. "It came from here." I told her everything—the TV show, the scientist, the bowl, and the soap, and Julie nodded, understanding as I did, accepting the impossible.

We'd experienced something private, a tiny rip in the universe. Julie had always been a sister who seemed to know what I was thinking, one who swam in my brain with me. We sometimes transmitted information the way you do in dreams—one of us would raise an eyebrow and an entire catalog of experience streamed. But this was something else—a reverberation between two records you play back-to-back, two novels from two different centuries you read in the same weekend. Words and notes overlaid, matched. Two girls, connected.

This is a moment that sits in our history, brightly lit. My history, since hers is gone.

I DON'T CARE how much Pete paid, the hotel bed suddenly seems garish and filthy, grit rising from it in the golden light. Even if the sheets are clean, they never wash the bedspreads in these places. There are sweat crescents under my tits—I can't seem to straighten my fingers. I need to do something normal, habitual, like when you get too high and you try to come down a little, tether yourself to the real world. Crack your knuckles, tie your shoes. A former me would have smoked a cigarette. I wish for a Twinkie to chew and spit into the trash can. My phone tingles in my hand, magically morphing into porn mode. I put the Do Not Disturb hanger outside the door to the room; then I chain the lock too, worried about Pete interrupting.

In the bathroom, I type with my thumbs and quickly find a tiny performer, her hair in a ponytail, her eyeliner impeccable. I take care of myself standing up, one foot on the toilet seat. It's over in seconds, a relief and quite possibly a personal record.

Calmer now, the faint pulse draining away, I turn on the shower, let the water warm up. Pete's shaving kit rests on the sink, and I dig through it while I brush my teeth. He's got a hateful pot of iridescent cream, outrageously expensive, no doubt. It's probably made from ground-up blood diamonds and the mineral-rich tears of mine-shaft kids—the label's French, so who knows. It could be for Pete's under-eye area or his ball sack—if anybody has silky, supple balls, it's Pete. I scoop out huge, sparkling furrows with my fingernails, spin my hands together, slick myself to the wrists. I spit my foam into the sink and grab a tooth-whitening strip and some placenta-infused lip balm. I use Pete's golden tweezers on my one chin hair and take a deep whiff of his smoky beard oil. I consider stealing a sheet mask. Even though I'm well rested for once, I look exhausted. Maybe this is just my face now. I'm too young for the sag at my jaw. The dark circles under my eyes, which once seemed interesting, sexy even, now make me seem hard and mean. The corners of my mouth turn down. I strip, leave my clothes where they fall. In the mirror, I see my mother's tits. The steam does its thing, erases me. "You'll drown the fish" was something Mom used to say when our showers went long. Julie and I always wondered what the hell that meant.

I text Jad, who has been up for hours with Gilda already, has sent pictures of her eating incorrectly made oatmeal, dressed in an outfit too small, too warm for the season. He's packed the wrong-colored water bottle for the stroller, and I'm pretty sure he's forgotten the fruit leathers. Oh, he'll find out soon enough—Gilda will let him know.

Good morning! I say. *We are out on a very long hike!*

I sit on the edge of the tub while the shower runs, the bleach strip on my teeth. I think about Bad Dad, his one twisted, ultra-white tooth, high up in the gum. I blame that tooth for everything. I noticed it the first time we officially met, at Choo-Choo Park over by the on-ramp, the dirtiest playground in Pivot. Choo-Choo's namesake is a faded plastic train car the kids climb on. Scattered in the bushes are milky condoms and human feces, but there are few things parents on the playground circuit won't do for a change of scenery. You work it in as a treat—*Guess where we're going today?* Choo-Choo is fully fenced, and you can see the entire park from any bench—a luxury. One day Gilda and I found a dead bird in the dirt. Bad Dad was standing there watching us, his son hiding in the train car. He'd been on my social periphery for months, the hot guy with the bleak past.

"Look at this bird," Gilda said. "It's asleep?"

"No," I said, "that bird is dead."

"Oh no," Gilda said. "Sorry, bird."

"You don't need to be sorry, Gilly," I said. "And, good lord, don't touch it."

She crouched over the thing, clenched her hands to keep them from reaching out.

"If I touch, it'll get more dead?" she asked.

"No. That's the thing about dead," I said. "Dead is dead."

Bad Dad laughed then, and I smiled up at him. His T-shirt was tight around his broad shoulders—one of his jean pockets showed the worn shadow of his wallet. There are rare times when I can be my whole, real self with Gilda. I wasn't saying these things for Bad Dad's benefit. He was just *a* dad then.

"I see a feather moving!" Gilda said. "It's a little bit alive?"

"Nope," I said. The thing was roiling and anty, baking in the sun. "Look closer."

Gilda studied the bird. Satisfied, she stood up. "Dead."

"Yep," I said.

"You're so honest," Bad Dad said.

"I try to tell her the truth, no matter how harsh." A judgmental mom might have crucified me for that, but Bad Dad understood just where I was coming from.

"I think it's great," he said. "The way you talk to her."

I basked in his unexpected, explicit approval, not realizing then that this was part of Bad Dad's game. How much of my attraction to him was based on being called a good parent? *You're doing a decent job,* he probably went around saying, making moms wet all over town.

"And the way you listen," he said.

"Listening is harder," I admitted. "Something I'm working on."

The way Bad Dad looked at me then had nothing to do with my parenting. He invited us over to his house for a playdate.

"Today?" he said. "Happy hour?"

"Five?" I said. "Six?"

"Whatever time is happy for you."

Bad Dad's wife—it occurred to me she might not be home.

The house wasn't far, but it was in a different subdivision near the farmer's market. Nice stone pavers, circular drives. Even the fire hydrants seemed classier. The landscaping at Bad Dad's was mature and beautiful, and off to one side was a huge backyard. He'd told me to come through the gate, and when I did I saw something like half a dozen other women already there with their kids. We looked at one another, realizing how wholesome this day had become. What suckers we were—some of us had washed our hair, put on lipstick. We sat on Bad Dad's stylish outdoor furniture. There was, incredibly, an inflatable bounce house staked in one corner of the yard. Inside it, the bigger kids thrashed and jumped while the babies—there were lots of babies—lay clumped together, rolling and babbling on an oriental rug, which looked too nice to be outside. Music played from speakers disguised as rocks. Some of the women were drinking Jamaican beer and all of them were laughing too loudly at Bad Dad's jokes—including me.

There was a lull in the music, then came a dirty beat. The song was something I had danced to so much before Gilda, a pulse so indelible and filthy it stays with you forever. Even nastier than the beat was the first line, which was coming fast. The musician is a woman who is not exactly subtle. She squats at the intersection of sexy and scary. The first line of this song is unfathomably vulgar, even for me. The other moms looked oblivious, but I saw Bad Dad draw a quick breath. He calmly, coolly stood up. All the while I was calculating the time he had to make it to his phone, which controlled the music. Three bars left. Two. *Oh my god, these women are going to lose their goddamn minds if they hear this.* One bar left, but he refused to alter his gait. It was a countdown to this singer extolling the virtue of her titties, her limitless desire. Bad Dad made it with a single beat to spare, serene and collected. He clicked ahead to that one fire truck song the kids like, his execution flawless. I finished my club soda and got the hell out of there. Gilda was incensed—how dare we leave paradise? Bouncy house or no, I needed to stay very, very far away from Bad Dad.

Vapor billows from the shower. I turn off the water—hygiene can wait—and grab my phone to conjure the tiny, sexy people again, let them do their tiny, sexy stuff.

My sliding-scale therapist brings everything back to the body. "If we let it, the body can help to metabolize the pain of the mind," he says. I doubt he means jerking off, but this is my tried and true.

"When you try to tell that story," he'll say, "when you talk about that person or place, where do you feel it inside? Where is it trapped?" He says the body remembers, but I'm not so sure. There are whole swaths of experience I've fully amputated, buried, tossed off a high bridge. Unless I'm on drugs, which I will likely never be again, or unless I am fucking or getting myself off, I can forget about my body entirely. I play along, because therapy is a game. I used to have the same feeling in church, about the commandments, wanting to turn to my mother and say, *But none of this is real, right?* It's the same feeling I'd get when I was faced by a professor with a deadline, or an employee handbook, or my marriage. Like there might be some wiggle room.

"I feel Julie's death in my shoulders," I'll try. "I feel my mother's hoarding in my . . . jaw? Is *mandible* a word?" I'll caress the side of my face. My therapist will gently nod. From inside a little chair in my skull I turn the body to face him, look out through its eyeholes. I lie about all kinds of things to add texture to our talks. He sits there calm and quiet, sun dappled in his leather chair.

"I've been training for a marathon," I told him once. "My sister and I had pet rabbits when we were kids."

I spent the session going on about the rabbit hutch, where we kept it in the backyard. The special insoles I needed because of my high arches. "French lops!" I said. "My time is improving!" The texture I wanted was sweat, fur. Another person's life.

When I confessed these little inconsequentials to Yes, she got so mad. "What is the damn point?" she asked. "It's like lying to a priest. It only hurts you."

But Pete understands why I say the things I do. "You have your own version of the truth," he's told me, a compliment.

"I embroider," I admit. "I get bored."

When Julie and I were kids, we actually had hamsters, accidental legions of them, because Precious and Fancy, our first pair, turned out to be male and female—husband and wife, we determined, not sisters like we originally thought. I could have told my therapist how they became frantic, sudden sex partners, how we pulled them apart too late. Precious had so many babies. Julie and I panicked and didn't do anything about it, especially not tell Mom. Instead, we moved the cage into our bathroom, ashamed of the mess we'd let our pets make of their lives. One morning Julie was blow-drying her impossibly long hair—something she spent a decent chunk of our childhood doing—when she glanced at the cage and saw Precious chomp a baby in half. I rushed toward Julie's screaming just in time to see the rest get swallowed: the half with the face. Precious licked her bald paws clean while Fancy looked on, horrified, we imagined, their cottony corner nest drenched in black glop. All the babies had been eaten. Julie blamed herself, believed her hair dryer had triggered some sick fear response.

Why didn't I tell this story, when my perfectly adequate therapist could have pulled it apart, so rich with symbolism and gore, so much fierce love and maternal bloodlust, endlessly more entertaining than running, or a pretend rabbit in its pretend hutch?

"You lie. So what?" Pete told me. "If this guy's any good at his job, he knows what he needs to know."

The scale slides sweetly for me, and I like the guy well enough.

"I've inseminated you with a lot of information" is something else he's always saying at the end of our sessions. He's not a creep, just bad with words.

PETE'S BACK, bamming on the hotel room door.

"You did the chain!" he's yelling.

"Sorry!" I pull a towel around me and run out of the bathroom.

"Why'd you do the chain?" Pete's fingers curl through the crack. "You did the chain."

"I'm afraid of maids," I say, opening the door.

"You're what?" Pete says. He busts in with breakfast and a tray of coffee. "I let you sleep," he says. "That gorilla pill got you. Your eyes were kind of open?" He makes a terrible face—me, I guess. "You were so gone. It was gross. I did a pre-hike. Did you get my text? There's no fucking hemp milk in this town." My greasy hands darken the paper bag he hands me. "I got four kinds," he says. "You like lox, right? Brian *loathes* it."

"This is perfect," I say, and peek inside, careful of my towel. "I was in the middle of a shower," I say. Pete looks at my dry hair. He stares at the bleach strip on my teeth and I close my mouth a little.

"Well, go take the rest of it," he says.

"I might have used some of your products," I say, trying to talk without moving my lips.

"Girl, I know," he says. "It smells like me in here." He breathes deep, then sits on the floor to pull off his pristine hiking boots. "I'll eat what you don't want," he says.

"You're being too nice to me," I say. "I'm the one who should be doing this stuff. This is your trip."

PETE AND I really do take a long hike in the hills. It's early September and still hot as hell back home, but here it's nice and cool and the trees are already inflamed: vivid reds and golds, violet sparks. Pete points to snowcapped peaks of the Absaroka and Beartooth ranges, though I can't tell which is which. Maybe it's one mountain range with two names. I have no idea where I'm supposed to be looking. Like so many other times in my life, a man is pointing out something I only pretend to see. I've learned that if you look at their finger, they'll leave you alone.

Montana has big sky, like they say, warm light falling all over. It amazes me that money can buy you a whole different setting, different air and elevations, how it can enlarge the world. I'm overwhelmed by freakish wildflowers, tiny and bright and everywhere, and a sick part of me relishes crushing them underfoot. I'm so used to crunchy lawns and stunted trees, the brown water they pump in to saturate the sad grasses of our metroplex. The colors here are insane, perhaps intensified by my druggy sleep or the years I've been pacing from room to room at home, entertaining Gilda. When we go outside together in Pivot, it's only for hot concrete walks to the tired parks and playgrounds in our perimeter. Outside also means I'm wholly consumed with Gilda's precise whereabouts, her safety, her sunscreen, handing her water or a snack, rushing to her if she falls. I can't believe this Montana beauty is natural, that it doesn't exist to entertain us, that it doesn't care about us at all. I have to shake the feeling that I'm walking through the work of some overzealous landscape architect.

Pete's pants are perfectly autumnal: goldenrod with a dark brown belt. He smells like a campfire, probably some custom cologne he's had mixed up to match the experience. Everything he's wearing is brand-new, bought for the occasion.

He winces when I say, "How's your writing coming?"

When he's not bullshitting pharmaceutical copy, Pete writes plays, or tries to. Lately he's been working on a forlorn drama about a failed relationship, no surprise there. Over the years Brian has bankrolled a few productions at a little theater. Pete's characters talk to each other through fake walls, sit in spotlights and write pretend letters, read aloud from them as their hands move. The dialogue is always too smart for me, banter like popcorn popping, references spanning time and genre, flying right over my head.

"Ask the bitch," he says.

He says Brian has wrecked his concentration, that the two of them are still deep in the Who-Gets-What. A relationship's worth of refurbished antiques, their books and clothes hopelessly enmeshed.

Once in the early days of Brian, when Pete and I were still waiters at Easy Cheesy, I watched over Pete's shoulder as the two of them exchanged texts. This is what it is to be friends with me, a curious, boundaryless person. We were at the drink station, and as I angrily waited for a pot of decaf to brew—every server loathes a decaf drinker—I hovered and watched the exchange with Brian unfurl.

> Brian: 9:30? Get ready
> Pete: What are you gonna do?
> Brian: tell me what you want
> Pete: Rip me up, brutalize me, etc.
> Brian: 😍
> Brian: 🔥

This went on, but I stopped reading, not out of loyalty or decency, but because Pete went off with a full pitcher to water his section.

These messages were proof that Pete was in fact in love, that Pete and Brian were aptly matched, and it made me envious. Not because I wanted to brutalize Pete, et cetera, or be brutalized, et cetera, by Pete—though who wouldn't be charmed by the way he'd phrased it?—but I admired the ease with which he'd asked for something and, presumably, would get it.

That night I drank too much and told Pete what I'd read. For better or worse, this is me too, incapable of keeping even my own secrets. Pete wasn't mad—is never mad at me. *Brutalize, et cetera* would go on to become a refrain.

"What do you want to do tonight?" he'd ask, and I'd say, "I don't know, see a movie, brutalize you, et cetera." But later, alone in the quiet corners of myself, I lingered on the phrase.

"How do you know what you want?" I finally asked Pete. I loved how clean and simple being brutalized seemed. I myself had a mess of shifting desires—I wanted only to be led around by lust, lovers of all sorts steps ahead, spooling out a long ribbon for me to swallow.

"You know when you know!" Pete said. "Bitch, you need to get *specific* with yourself."

"Maybe so, maybe so," I agreed. At the time, it seemed like I had years to figure things out—hundreds of lovers yet to come.

Now my desires, when I'm not too tired to have them, are an annoyance, a Cheerio crushed under a bare foot. Bad Dad, how the cord in his neck makes me think about sitting in his lap, ruining both our lives. Celadon's huge, knotted T-shirt, how there might be enough room for me to crawl inside it with her. I sit on my hands, wait until these impulses pass.

Ultimately, Brian brutalized Pete in a different way, the boring usual way where one person falls out of love with the other, not the fun kind of ripping apart.

Pete's demeanor has darkened, my fault, and we stomp along in silence. To cheer him, I ask if he thinks Yellowstone will explode one day.

"Definitely," he says, eyes glinting like it's the best gossip. "In like, seven hundred thousand years, give or take. This place is primed for a super eruption," he says.

"Saw one of those on Porncore the other day," I say.

"It's what they think ended the dinosaurs," he says, ignoring me.

"Gross," I say.

Hiking is just fancy walking, and with no small child to tend to, I feel oddly self-conscious of my gait. The Water Witch's impersonation of me: hunched, face pointing down, eyes looking up. I try to take longer strides, stand up taller.

I brought a straw cowboy hat with me on this trip, something sun colored I saw on a girl in a catalog. I'm an admittedly soft mark—I never know if I want what a model is wearing or if I just want her. The hat was a rare splurge—I used the credit card—and on the catalog girl it seemed glamorous, the epitome of western escape. Out here, in actual nature, I feel stupid even holding it in my hand.

PETE'S NEVER BEEN to Wink, and this is one of my favorite things about him. I haven't told him much about my mother's house, her stacks of moldering newspapers, the microwave full of old bread baggies and used cling film, her stacks of warped plastic cups.

At this very moment, Gary's men could be flattening a path through my mom's mess, making their way toward the bedroom Julie and I shared. It's become a rotting tribute now, but at least I know nothing has been thrown out. The closet still packed with Julie's dark floral dresses and ripped jeans, her many coral lipsticks and crumbling eye-shadow palettes and a bottle of sour perfume on the vanity, shelves piled high with our disintegrating notebooks.

Julie could copy anybody's handwriting—it was one of her gifts. Mom had this stack of sweetheart letters Dad wrote when they were young, and Julie could duplicate them exactly: Dad's sloppy, downward slope, all those loose ampersands. It was Julie who signed our report cards and permission slips—not because Mom cared how or what we were doing in school, just because she never liked to be bothered with that sort of thing. Even more impressive, Julie could mimic every *Playboy* Playmate's bubbly centerfold scrawl. We discovered this special talent when Mom's boyfriend Keith lived with us.

Keith came after some guy named Clyde but before Mom's brief brush with Christianity—she dumped them all eventually, Jesus too. I was fourteen and Julie was twelve and Keith was a guy in boxer shorts in our kitchen. He bought name-brand cereals and pulpy orange juice, which we appreciated, and he replaced the messed-up garbage disposal and refilled the wiper fluid in Mom's car, took care of our dusty yard.

"Tammy," he'd say through the screen door, shirtless, stinking of sweat, cut grass, gasoline. "Y'all got a nest of dirt daubers out here. Want me to torch 'em?"

Keith subscribed to *Playboy* but he wasn't a perv. He was afraid of the tampons we kept under the bathroom sink and the panties we handwashed and left dripping on shower rods and doorknobs. He unplugged the toaster when nobody was using it because he worried our cat, Yoko—a normal, solo cat, years before the Friends—might stick her paw in there and get zapped. Keith didn't last long, but we liked him. Later, our mother would hold him up as an example. Wasn't that nice, that she never brought any Very Bad men into our house?

"He never tried anything with you girls, not even once!"

"Sort of a low bar, Mom," Julie said.

Julie and I could hear Keith snoring at night, loud, like he was in the room with us, on the floor in between our beds. Julie hated this, but to me it was a safe, steady reminder that there was a world outside of us and our bedroom and our stupid house. It was a sound that soothed me, same as the tide of big rigs that rolled down the highway, on to better places.

Every month Keith's *Playboy* came in a black plastic bag, and every month Julie and I got to it first. Keith drove around in a van, cleaning people's carpets, and Mom was always picking up extra shifts. When they were working, we had full run of the house, including our postbox. We knew stealing mail was a federal offense. That's exactly why we did it—to break an easy law, to have something illegal to read. We'd listen for the mail truck, run barefoot down the hot asphalt to the bank of boxes on the post road.

Once you ripped apart the wrapper there was no going back. You had to be bold, all in. There was no surreptitious slitting of the bag, or maybe there was, but Julie and I weren't capable of that. Everything seemed to ruin so easy for us at that age, our actions done in a fervor, stuff always breaking or spilling or falling apart in our house because we couldn't be patient or careful.

We'd take the issue and study it. The centerfold was always the first place we flipped to, for the same reasons everybody does, but also because of the questionnaire there, filled out in the Playmate's handwriting. The girls' real faces were airbrushed away, bodies too, but the handwriting was achingly intimate: their personal loops and flattened vowels, the slanted, sometimes illegible scribbles, the occasional smiley face or inky smudge. They had the handwriting of a naked doctor, a naked babysitter, a naked teacher. You could imagine some naked girl's naked hand trailing across the very page you were holding. Impossible, but I remember the crisp smell of the ink, the hot press of words through the back of the paper.

Julie spent hours taking over the Playmate's hands in our notebooks, writing out the nastiest, most ridiculous things I could think of for them to say.

Dear Kit, I would crawl across broken glass to suck the dick that fucked you.

Dear Kit, Did you ever know that you're my hero?

I tried it too but I was never any good. I needed Julie—a devastating mimic, professional grade.

After we examined the Playmate, we'd loosen her staples, pull her out whole, and slip her under my mattress with her many flattened friends. We'd put the mangled magazine back on the table with the rest of the mail we didn't want. If Keith noticed his centerfold was missing—and how could he not?—we never heard about it. Around this same time Mom began subscribing to *Playgirl*. For revenge, we suspected later. A spite subscription.

The men in *Playgirl* were oiled and had mustaches and looked a lot like Keith, who looked a lot like our dad. *Playgirl* was not delivered in a black pouch, because the men in it weren't fully nude. They wore Speedos, like Dad and Keith. You didn't have to rip into it, which took away the fun. *Playgirl* was only good upon closer inspection. It had letters to the editor, I discovered, these outlandish, likely fake sexploits readers just couldn't wait to share. I'd read these aloud to Julie in stupid voices. We made fun of how silly they were. We'd flip through without any urgency, then put the magazine back under the bills and church flyers with their dove drawings and drippy religious fonts.

On a *Playboy* or a *Playgirl* day, after we pillaged the magazines, we'd split up, serious.

"I'm going to go lie down for a little while," one of us would say.

"Oh, that's cool, because I'm going to take a bath."

I suspected Julie was maybe doing the same thing I was, alone in the house wherever she was, though we never talked about it. Later, when my first girlfriend and I got together and I came out to Julie, I wondered if those dual subscriptions had anything to do with me being queer.

"No way," Julie said. "I always fantasized about the girls too, but I knew I was straight."

"How?"

"Because I wanted to be them," Julie said. "I wanted to be a woman getting done by a dude. Did you want to do the girls or be them? Or do the dudes or be the dudes?"

"Yes," I said. "All of it. Everything," and Julie nodded like it made perfect sense. I felt stupid for how nervous I'd been to tell her, how long it took me to do it.

Around the time of Keith and the magazines, I discovered Mom's back massager could be used for illicit purposes. It was gray, big as a hand mixer, and it plugged into the wall, loud as a blender. Sometimes Julie or I would take it with us to separate rooms and close the door.

The night before I left for college, we squeezed together in my bed and reminisced. Julie picked through those old notebooks and I asked her if she remembered that back massager, and didn't she think it was a little bit revolting.

"What?" she said. "Why?"

"We used the same vibrator Mom used! And each other."

"I never did that," she said, horrified. "I only used it to massage my back!"

Where did that thing end up? we wondered. Was it still in the house? After Keith moved out we never saw it, or him, again.

"Maybe he took it with him," I said, "maybe he was using it too," and Julie said, "Please, I don't need to hear any more of your sick family theories."

We turned those moldy pages together, lit up on pink wine. Lines and lines of longhand, a spectrum of ink. "Whose is that?" I asked.

"That one's me," she said, flipping, flipping. "Me as Mom. Me. Me. Look at this," she said, and held up a page.

"That's me," I said, confident.

"Nope," Julie said. "It's me being you."

PETE STEPS SOLIDLY on the path, assertive and certain. He says he sees trail maps in his mind. They are detailed and three-dimensional and he can spin them around, go behind mountains and up over the tree line. He's got alternate routes for his alternate routes. He antici- pates streams and vistas, tells me what I should be appreciating at any given moment.

"The only writing I'm doing is, like, origin stories to Brian over email," he's saying. "Proof of ownership. Sure, maybe he paid for the lamp, but who carried the lamp home? Who had the *idea* for the lamp?"

Even when I walk in the familiar gridded parts of Pivot, I'm always second-guessing myself. New buildings seem to appear at will, side- walks wider or narrower or strangely askew. Painted houses seem to shift the pitches of their roofs, tweak the colors of their siding. I'm always having to recalibrate myself at traffic lights. Was I going this way or that way? I often feel as though I've been placed on a random corner by some giant, unseen claw.

I defer to other people for whole swaths of experience. Jad handles car stuff, the sickly lawn. He deals with our meager finances because my mother raised me to believe money is like good weather or sud- den diarrhea—entirely beyond your control. Julie was in charge of bands, new releases, old side projects, classics I missed—she filled in the gaps. Now my musical taste has stalled. I can go backward with my opinions but never forward—it's a forever-fractured discography I listen to narcotically, no real joy in it. Julie was also the one who kept up with fashion, styling You Are the Universe to look like Mormons or the Manson daughters—straight, loose hair, long floral dresses, matching ankle boots. In photos, she commanded us to be vacant and haunted, but mostly we just looked stoned. Pete tells me what's worth reading and what's not. "The prose is wretched but you'll probably like it," he'll say, running through some plot blow by blow. I try to take his suggestions, but I gravitate toward garbage books, fictional- ized accounts of real-life mistakes and large-scale disasters: crashed oil tankers, Chernobyl, people getting deep into debt and then getting killed for it. I like the slow unfolding of ruined lives. I want to look up from what I'm reading and feel better about my failures. At least I didn't scorch the earth and kill thousands of people with my bad decisions. At least my kneecaps aren't about to be broken by a mob boss. But even these books I never finish, too unmotivated or tired to see the tragedies through.

"Brian used to be so supportive of your work," I say, wondering if Pete can sense the irritation under this comment. Money begets money—rich people are magnetized, finding each other. There will likely be someone even wealthier next. Rich guys all the way up the ladder, Pete and some new person owning cities and continents and the moon and souls—the whole interstellar sweep in their wallets.

Out here with Pete, I pretend to be a person who is used to being somewhere besides the shitty place she left and the shitty place where she ended up.

As soon as puberty hit, I wanted out of Wink. I tied this feeling to no conceivable future geography, just a neon idea about where I needed to be: elsewhere. Julie and Yes and I spent many nights playing music and getting high, making predictions, getting ready for our lives to begin. It was a child's plan: One day You Are the Universe would get famous. Julie and Yes and I would live frictionless lives; money would pour in, slide around.

But our little band was only a little bit famous in our little town. At our peak we opened for mediocre locals in sticky, black-windowed dive bars. We'd drive to Abilene or Lubbock and perform for a dozen diehards mixed with rowdy, impatient drunks. Julie could convert anyone in minutes, hush the room like a church. We were giddy, waiting for some record label to scout us, some exec to chase us out to the parking lot with a crisp recording contract. This is how I know for certain that talent isn't enough. It is one of the great, unfair mysteries that Julie didn't break through, dazzle the world with her transcendent beauty. When I realized the band wasn't an escape hatch, I cut out and tried to convince myself I had my own ambitions, separate from playing the bass and from the Universe. I decided to go to college, major in music. "You pave the way," Julie said, giving me her blessing. She said when she finished high school, maybe she'd join me.

Eager as I was to get away, I was still too chickenshit to apply out of state. My grades were nothing special—I didn't get into schools in Austin or Denton, places with strong fine arts programs in cities with big music scenes. Who did I think I was? Then a single, mediocre miracle: I was offered a spot off the wait list at a bloated university known for its hospitality program. The school was in Pivot, close enough to drive to the Dallas bars but four hundred miles away from Wink. A new path seemed to shine for me. Even being too poor to afford tuition didn't matter—I was instantly approved for a fuck-ton of fed loans I'd never, ever be able to pay back. Pivot would do!

Pete and I sit on a flat rock and guzzle water. I have this new thing I'm doing where I take a dozen sips in a row. This is something Jad has been encouraging me to do. It's part of his Healthier Kit initiative, like forcing me to walk, or lie about walking, the requisite ten thousand steps a day.

The leaves of a nearby tree flip up to show their bright undersides, and three separate birds are singing their songs. At home I'm completely plant-blind, bird-deaf.

Along with his beard, Pete's hair has grown out shaggy. He says it's a record of his pain, but it suits him. He looks great on this hillside in hiking boots and a flannel shirt, though he moves like someone pulled from wreckage, like it hurts to turn his head.

Why do we so often look our best when we feel our worst? Freshman year, I fell into a deep depression. I didn't miss Wink, but I missed home—for me home was You Are the Universe and Julie. I was racked with guilt—racked!—for leaving her with Mom. I couldn't imagine what they talked about, what that house was like without me in it.

I'd go too long between showers, the feel of the water piercing, painful. Oddly, my always-problematic skin cleared up. Eating seemed absurd—chewing felt as natural as shoving a sandwich into my armpit. I grew out what I hadn't realized was an unflattering haircut. Homesick for a town that took me years to claw my way out of, I'd made a stupid, expensive mistake. I hardly did any work, but I still went to my classes out of loneliness, to break up my days. This was the worst I'd felt in my short, idiotic life, and, conveniently, this was the same semester I discovered ketamine. I'd trawl the big, flat campus between classes, walking and rewalking the sorrowful slate paths, toggling through the intervals: buzzy numbness and choking despair. Zombied from the K, I kicked off my shoes and sat on the lip of a marble fountain in the quad, pulled up my skirt to wet my dead legs.

"Kit—hi." My music theory professor caught me there one afternoon, gently touched my elbow. "Pretty day. What are you up to?" she said, and I desperately scanned the menu of human responses.

"*So* pretty," I said, loud. "This day."

She glanced at the clutch of skirt in my hands.

"Oh, this is just what I like to do," I said, looking through the murk at my toes. "On days." Coins were sunk in the depths, but I'd never seen anybody throw one in. "What are *you* up to?"

She shielded her watch from the high sun. "I have a thing I'm late for. A meeting." She shook her watch around on her wrist. She leaned in closer, scanned me. "I've noticed a difference in you, in class."

Tension licked my spine. Did I seem high? Could I parrot this back? *I've noticed a difference in* you *in class.*

But my professor beamed. "You're absolutely glowing!" she said. Her brown hair was tinted lavender in the sunlight. "Whatever you're doing, keep it up!"

The body overcompensates so people don't notice you've tipped into a psychic chasm. I got sexier as my behavior grew increasingly erratic. Without seeing Julie every day, I didn't know who I was. I missed my sister so much. *You think this is bad?* the world taunted. *Just wait.*

Nothing mattered at school. Bad grades were fine. Fuck my mom. Fuck that professor—no, like, literally, actually fuck her, which I did, in her office, not long after the compliment fest at the fountain. Nothing counted. Smoking crack from a lightbulb didn't count. "A taste" was what the crack-giver called it—some guy from Intro to Western Civ that I barely knew—he doled out this reasonable, responsible portion size for my first time. Even crack didn't matter to me, had no real pull. *Meh,* I thought. *What's all the fuss?* The pipe mechanics were interesting, maybe. How had this dude gotten the screw part of the bulb off so cleanly? I didn't know. I was in the back seat of his car with someone else I didn't know. A bartender. A barber? A stranger. Smoking crack.

Later, when Julie died, I'd confuse this period of my life for first grief, like somehow I'd mourned her in advance. By the time I lost her, drugs and risky sex—my kind of mourning—were off the table. By then I had an accidental baby on the way and a sweet, trapped husband, his once-promising life hitched to mine.

I SEEK OUT leaders, people like Pete, Yes, and Jad. People who will choose the restaurant, the movie, be my tour guide. I let myself be pulled—it makes things so much easier. "Never having an opinion is a form of control," Jad says, and he's not wrong.

Pete puts down his canteen and grabs my wrist. He points to a hill in the distance, and it takes me a while to notice a staggered mass of bighorn sheep climbing up the side. He stares in awed silence at first, then quickly loses his mind.

"Take my picture! Jesus!" he hisses, shoving his phone at me. "Oh my god!"

The animals don't mind. I take shot after shot: Pete with hands on his hips, eyes bright. Pete with a sexy finger in his mouth, face tilted down. Like the moon or mountains, sheep underwhelm in photos.

I'd never considered the creatures I might see in a state I hadn't intended to visit, out here big and free. Sometimes at night I think about whales loose in the ocean living their lives, and it upsets me.

Pete informs me that the sheep are eating clover and sedges, willow and sage. He says they can contract pneumonia from us and die, that it's a real problem.

"What the heck is a sedge?" I say. Pete could tell me any sheep thing and I'd believe it—I'm completely at his mercy.

Bizarre as it is, the sight of a fluffy lamb on wobbly legs triggers my letdown. I grab my tits and Pete laughs as my place in the animal kingdom rushes in.

"I'll be quick," I say. I squat and take my breast-pump kit out of my backpack—the nozzles and flanges, the tubes and the reservoir, the special brush I use to clean the parts. I can put this thing together in the dark. I've never owned a gun, but I get it: the feeling of pieces fitting precisely, a series of successful clicks and turns. Holding a well-crafted thing in one hand.

"I'm sorry I have to do this out here," I say. "I'm totally engorged. Is this gross for you?"

He says, "Oh, relax. I don't mind." He swipes at images on his phone—dicks or animals or maybe some of each.

Sometimes Gilda will walk up to me and shove her head under my shirt.

"Quick squirt?" she'll say.

"It's manipulation," Yesenia told me when I confessed this.

"Isn't she too young to manipulate?" I asked.

The thing that kills me about my phone calls with Yes is how silent her kids are in the background, all fucking three of them. Meanwhile Gilda will be throwing herself around in the living room like a demon, shouting, "Help me, Mom! Mom! Why won't you help?" Yes has taught her kids to walk up to her and calmly place their hand on her arm. "They wait to be regarded," she explains. Then, and only then, they politely ask for what they need. On my end Gilda will be screaming, wailing on the carpet, "Can't do it! Can't do a cartwheel or any kind of wheel!"

Yes insists manipulation is like swallowing, something ingrained in even the youngest of our species. Gilda will be four soon, an age that is my supposed cutoff for nursing. It's Yes's hard line anyway, I'm not quite sure what other mothers might think. This isn't something I've talked about with the playground moms. Soon enough, I'll have to stop nursing or start lying about it. I balance this anxiety by hanging out with Pete, who doesn't know or care what's normal. Motherhood itself is abnormal to Pete, which takes the pressure off. I doubt he even remembers how old Gilda is. He came to the birthing center right after she was born, but he barely glanced at her in her clear little tub.

"Good job," he said before snapping chopsticks for me, cracking open the platter of elaborate sushi he'd brought for dinner. He barely looked at Jad either, and I'm ashamed to say how much I love this about Pete, how when I'm around it's like he can barely tolerate anybody else. If you keep everyone you care about separate, you'll always have their undivided attention.

When I tell Pete about the endearing things Gilda does, he nods politely and glazes over. Maybe when she's older, they can talk about animals together. We live on this planet with a ridiculous goddamn number of them. Joke animals like the blobfish and the duck-billed platypus. What are they for? Right now on a savanna there is a giraffe wrapping its black tongue around the highest leaf. Why? It's psychedelic, this world, kids will remind you. You get to a certain age and you don't think about the micro-kangaroo traveling pouch-bound along its mom's hairy body. You don't think about marsupials at all. Who has time for wombats when you're trying to get laid or pay a parking ticket or get to work or whatever?

Gilda keeps one of our bathroom drawers filled with acorns. Nutspace, she calls it. You get used to it: a drawer full of a hundred acorns that shift and spin and rattle around every time you open the drawer. There's no reason to even open that drawer anymore because the only thing in it is acorns, you should know by now, but you remember the former drawer when it had floss or hair ties or whatever useful thing—you remember your childless former life, or your body does. It's a reflex, how your hand goes out to open it, a drawer that was once of use. The body is stupid every day—it doesn't know until it's too late: acorns.

"Where's the floss?" I'll ask Jad, and he'll say, "Under the nuts."

"My nature!" Gilda screamed the one time we tried to throw them out.

But I love that part most of all, the weird wildness she brings to our house. Dinosaurs are very important in our daily lives. I've missed so much new information. The dinosaurs I learned about as a child, they've been updated—that one they taught us had two brains, for example, that one is called something else now, and the two brains are a myth. It's all changed.

Certain things are so loaded in youth, forgotten about later. Dinosaurs and planets and quicksand in your childhood, hayrides and hand jobs in your adolescence. I used to spend a lot of time contemplating the Bermuda Triangle and the Loch Ness monster. The big mysteries of the universe. Why don't they just fly into the triangle and test it? I wondered. Why don't they drain the loch? It's not because we don't have the technology—it's because once you grow up no one has the curiosity or wherewithal to spend time contemplating those things. You're like, *Eh, there's a lot we don't know.*

Pete bought cigarettes at the airport, and he lights one now. "Brian hates when I smoke," he says, taking a deep drag. I love it, how he waves the cigarette around like we're in a bar, pristine nature as the backdrop. The smoker is old Pete—this health-conscious sheep lover is some different person. He coughs and hacks, his clean, well-adjusted lungs screaming. He beats on his chest, tight and fit from Pilates.

While I pump, I tell Pete I'm thinking about starting a jogging routine like Jad's—why should he get to hog all the endorphins—but the only time to fit it in would be before the sun comes up, when Gilda is still asleep.

"It's probably dangerous," I say. "Still dark out then."

"You're worried you'll trip? Nah," he says, "the pavement around your place seems pretty okay."

I didn't say, *No, babe, I'm worried I'll get murdered and minced and shoved into a garbage bag.* Imagine being able to leave your house at any hour, be free in the world, your biggest concern a sprained ankle.

Pumping gives me instant relief, though I don't empty myself—it'll take too long. I get a few pulls out and the tingling stops. Pete turns to the sun to give me a little privacy. I dump the collected milk in the dirt, something I wouldn't have dreamed of doing a few years ago, back when every drop seemed like liquid gold. I have no way to refrigerate this yield, and even if I did, it's too complicated to fly it home with me. Plus it's probably poisoned by the gorilla pill, plus Gilda doesn't actually need it anymore.

The bighorn sheep are still there glancing at us, hopping staggered up the mountainside, but Pete seems less impressed now.

"I love the word *engorged*," he says.

I WENT TO college and Julie stayed behind, and for a while, when she was seventeen, she tried to make a different kind of life out of music. She'd always been awkward around children, but a friend recommended her for an after-school job teaching piano lessons to rich kids in Midland. The timing was perfect. You Are the Universe was dead, and Anna Jean's, the diner where Julie waited tables, had briefly closed with a health code violation—maggots, went the rumor. Piano money was good, and nobody knew Julie was completely unqualified to teach. She played by ear, any song on any instrument she wanted, but this didn't exactly translate to instruction. She bought a beginner's book, thinking she could learn along with the kids. The first mother Julie worked for was friendly and delusional, an alcoholic salt heiress. She answered the door beaming, poured herself a huge glass of wine, and later called her mom friends to give Julie stellar, drunken reviews. The mom friends beamed and poured wine and invited Julie into their homes too. These parents mostly wanted a break—so long as Julie occupied their child, everybody was happy.

A standard lesson was fifty minutes, and Julie often showed up a few minutes late. If the children's fingernails were too long, which they usually were, Julie would insist they needed a trim before they could begin. This meant she'd leave the child on the piano bench and go in search of clippers or tiny scissors. In a messy bathroom drawer she'd find decent lipsticks, barely used, in universally flattering shades. She'd find money, coins mostly, but sometimes bills crumpled among the mess. There were loose pills, over-the-counter painkillers, but also good stuff, stamped with promising letters and numerals she'd look up at home. She never took the nail-cutting premise far enough to venture upstairs, where there might be a medicine cabinet with a whole prescription bottle. Some mom was likely to be lying down on her bed up there or else pacing the halls, talking on the phone.

Once Julie found the clippers, she'd walk back to the piano bench, where the kid was waiting for her, bored, looking out the window. She'd carefully clip each nail, something that was very stressful, she said: the fidgeting, sullen child—the tiny, rubbery fingers. Later, on the screened-in porch with a huge goblet of her own wine, she'd dump out her pockets and among the stolen cash and makeup and broken pills, there they'd be—the clipped fingernails, sharp little crescents. Once the nails were done, there were only forty minutes left. Julie would slowly return the clippers to where she'd found them, slowly walk back to the bench and the waiting child. Thirty-five minutes.

She never used the music book, but she'd open it, set it on the stand for show, then teach all the children the same song she knew by heart, something she had taught herself on our water-warped upright. Before Mom was a hoarder, before she was a pack rat even, she was a refurbisher, dragging unappreciated things into our house, shining them up. She glued and sanded the broken keys herself and had the thing professionally tuned, but Julie never loved the piano like she loved the guitar—she played songs on it like she was mopping or dusting, a chore she did around the house because it needed to be done.

"Do what I do," Julie would say to those little kids, playing the low end while they played high.

She'd leave the bench again to pour herself a glass of water, filtered and cold from a dispenser in the refrigerator door. Never in the history of children has a child refused a snack, so she'd offer one. She and the child would sit at the kitchen table together—maybe she'd help peel an orange and then both of them would need to wash their hands. Back to the piano bench, twenty-five minutes left, a line or two of the song, a bathroom break, fifteen minutes, back to the song. She could start packing up her things a few minutes early, the slow-motion closing of the unconsulted lesson book, the pushing in of the piano bench, the careful tying of the shoes she was always directed to remove at the front door. Sometimes a mother—often in a sports bra and yoga pants, often gorgeous and not all that much older than Julie— would come down to ask about the child's progress. Julie would look at this woman's bright mouth, her swank dentistry, and tell her about the great strides her child was making.

When Anna Jean's opened up again, Julie quit giving music lessons, but she didn't quit the pills. I wasn't concerned about her, not then. We were both dabblers, or so I thought, just playing around. After freshman year I came home for the summer and she got me a job waiting tables with her. This made so much more sense to me than school—taking orders on the soft pad, walking plates of greasy food the few feet from the counter to the tables, refilling saltshakers. The sound of bacon frying and the grimy din of conversation, the stir and clink of spotty coffee spoons. Every day a crystalline repetition. Julie and I worked different shifts but sometimes we overlapped, helping each other with closing duties in the back, marrying ketchups and wrapping silver, silent and efficient. The cooks couldn't be bothered to learn my name, even though I worked as much as Julie did. They called me the Other One, or they called me Sis. Sometimes they called me Julie, knowing that it wasn't my name but that I'd answer to it anyway.

THERE'S A PARKING LOT by the trail that leads to the Boiling River, which is weird to me. The idea of driving right up to nature, I guess. It hadn't occurred to me that we could have taken the rental here, saved ourselves a bunch of time. The lot is full of teenagers standing around their cars: girls in sweatpants with words written on the butts, shirtless boys.

One dude is saying in his deep new voice, "Absolutely. Oh yeah, absolutely. Absolutely!"

My response to these young, well-rested people is something like rage. A girl in a hot-pink bikini guzzles Fireball in the back of a pickup truck. She can't be more than fourteen. I want to slap someone. I want to call her mother.

"Keep it classy, Montana," Pete says, but these kids are so enthralled with one another they barely notice us.

Pete takes my hand, leads me away from a shattered bottle—more Fireball—on the asphalt.

We leave the teens to their liquor and head down the trail. Pete points out oak or maybe ivy, something poisonous I'm not supposed to tromp through. The landscape is lunar, craters and steaming cracks, deep pools of orange and blue. A sign warns us of dangerous ground. It's a drawing of a kid being consumed by fire while some other kid—the smarter one who stayed on the path—points and stares.

Vapor rises from the ground, curls and floats.

"Steam is a fractal," Pete says. "Smoke, too." He makes his fingers flit in the air. "Did you know that?"

"Oh, I know about fractals," I say. I don't really, but I've seen chemical ones dancing on the backs of my eyelids. Pete thinks he knows fractals, but he only knows the *science* of fractals, not the experience. He goes on about recursion, ruining the sexiness of the sweeping, majestic shapes.

We see more rising steam long before the dip in the land, the wide water, the people down there in it, lounging on the rocks.

"There she is," Pete says. "Our lodestar."

He explains the boilingness to me, how there's an underground cascade that flows from a hydrothermal vent. "This is a fault-fed river," he says. What gushes out is more than a hundred degrees, but where it blends with the cold river, it makes for a very hot bath. "This place is, like, a cauldron of nutrients. There's this special worm in the riverbed? You can't find it anywhere else on earth."

"You're a special worm in the riverbed," I say, putting my pack down next to Pete's. He takes off his boots, unbuttons his shirt, and strips off his pants. He's been wearing swim trunks this whole time. I work at a knot on one of my sneakers.

"Aren't you wearing a swimsuit?" he says, folding and neatly tucking his clothes into his bag.

"Fuck no," I say. "Never again."

I wade into the water in my running pants. There's a sports bra under my T-shirt, over my still-engorged, ridiculous tits. My teats. Even before Gilda I had giant ones, crypto-boobs I could hide in clothes, cleverly conceal with the right cut of jacket. Now they're out of control, feral in anything I wear.

The current is fast and the rocks we're wading over are sharp and slippery, bright green with moss. I tiptoe in, hands in the air, let the water come up to my waist. The confluence is bizarre—half of me freezing while the other half simmers.

People in the Boiling River don't talk to each other. They sit there silent, watching as Pete and I walk downriver. They gather in groups of two or three, in deep pools where they soak up to their necks. Our slow-mo migration leads us to a rocky little alcove, and we try to ease into it, but there's already an older couple inside. They firmly tell us the water is better downriver.

"Go many, many feet that way," the male half of the couple says, stern.

"*Many,* many," Pete repeats, and we laugh at these river pricks and hold on to each other and keep moving.

We finally find a spot where we can float in deep water, just the two of us.

"A nice, light scald," Pete says as we settle in.

Occasionally the water gets too hot or cold, like someone is messing with the tap, but mainly it's bliss. The river is delicious the way a wildfire is delicious, doing its thing, indifferent to the life in its path. It's a rolling pleasure, waves so intense we have to stop speaking to appreciate them. To moan.

"Remember this feeling?" I say to Pete in between rushes, and he says, "Mmmmhhhh."

We are quiet while we go to similar druggy places in our pasts.

SOME OF THESE PLACES are shared, identical: Pete and I doing bumps in the walk-in freezer at Easy Cheesy, then pinging between the three good gay bars in Dallas until last call. The Ecstasy we took that Fourth of July, how the fireworks show we'd gone to see was fine, but it had nothing on the texture of the picnic blanket Pete had laid out for us, or the casual way he'd reached over and scrubbed lipstick off my front tooth.

Or junior year at that vegan campus house—not a fraternity, everyone who lived there kept insisting, a *collective*—where they had the best parties. This was the night Pete and I first met Jad, back when he used to wear all black, only black, like a stagehand or a priest. Some drunk guy was bloviating in the kitchen, telling party people that suffering was transmitted in meat, that a steak was blood and shit and fear and pain. "Come on, man," Jad said, "nobody wants to hear that." At this, the guy got even louder, questioned Jad's commitment to the cause. "I've never even tasted flesh!" Jad said, and Pete, his back to them, said, "Congratulations, you're both annoying," so only I could hear. But I wasn't annoyed—I was intrigued.

Tall enough to have had any kind of face, Jad didn't need the strong jaw, the high, open cheekbones, or that one deep dimple. He's too pretty for me, honestly, but his brow is permanently furrowed, his resting expression like there's something terrible in his sight line, concern aimed somewhere just over your head. It's odd—a little unnerving. I wanted him immediately.

At this party, there was a "secret" pile of coke on a black dinner plate in the cabinet above the toilet. So many of us knew about that plate and were trying to play it cool, just using the bathroom a lot. It all went fast. Pete got good and high and left early—"too many straight herbivores," he'd said—so I sat on a couch alone, drinking as quickly as possible, which is the only way I used to drink. I realized Jad lived in the house when I watched him walk around behind people, tossing their empties into a garbage bag. I kept beaming at him, then looking away. He'd been sipping the same beer all night, but I was messed up enough for two people. Back then I could not, for better or worse, do anything to blot out my desires. I had no subtlety when I was neon minded like that.

I don't understand what the different moons mean, besides the lunatic one everybody knows, but I couldn't see anything celestial from Jad's bedroom window that night. If you're a woman who gets off on danger, all you have to do is get drunk around a man you don't know very well. But Jad was so careful, sitting next to me on his bed, not making a move. He went on and on about his dual design/biology major, how one day he hoped to illustrate science texts.

"Hasn't everything been drawn already?" I said, such an asshole, but he laughed and said the science was always changing. There were all sorts of things he could do, he said, all sorts of directions he could go. He was so kind and earnest and I was so high, wanting him to keep talking and keep talking and then, without warning, wanting him to shut the fuck up. Keep-talking to shut-the-fuck-up is the narrative of every coke experience of my life. I kissed him so I wouldn't have to listen to his five-year plan, then kneeled in front of him and took my shirt off, a proposal, in my way.

He looked worried. "I want us to be present," he said.

"Oh I am," I said, closing one eye so I could see his face better. "I'm omnipresent." Somebody was puking in the adjoining bathroom, their retching theatrical.

Jad again handed me the glass of water by the bed, again watched me drink some. He kissed my forehead and demurred, which is a word I don't use, but it is precisely what he did, with pink lips and lowered lashes, like a girl in a Renaissance painting.

I took off the rest of my clothes, lay on my stomach on his bed, and waited.

"What are you doing?" I asked him, nervous in his silence.

"Taking inventory," he finally said. I flipped over, watched him slowly scan me.

"What, you usually like girls with clavicles?"

"Not at all," he said, too quickly maybe, but I was so confident then, nobody could have convinced me otherwise.

"I *have* clavicles," I said, grabbing at the soft plane where the bones were buried. "I just keep 'em to myself." I turned to my side, ran my hand over the high slope of my hips.

"Okay," he said then, signing a deal with himself. "But let's not do all the things." If this was a trick to make me want him more, it worked.

He got into bed with me and we twisted up together, did most of the things. I got him to make these little moans. These were carnal sounds, and I thought of words like that: *carnal* and *carnage* and *carne asada*—something about the way they came out of the vegan convinced me only a chosen few had pulled that sort of lust from him.

He touched my face and looked at me, this time not over my head but directly into my eyes, that furrow in his brow still there, but instead of worry, his face was full of wonder. Like, *Who the hell* are *you?* That look, I keep it handy, even now, pull it out from time to time.

He used his boxer shorts to wipe off my neck and the sticky splat on my jawbone, but he did this tenderly, with reverence. He pulled me close and went to sleep right away, like he'd been waiting for me for nights and nights, restless. I was wired, drunk but with so much powder in my blood. My swallowing mechanism was fucked—my eyes seemed to move independently, like a lizard's. I took in the features of his room: framed photos of dark-haired people with his same face. The ubiquitous Hitchcock posters, his clean laundry folded neatly in a pile.

The puker in the bathroom was at it again, classic heaves, really playing to the back rows. The way Jad slept made me certain he didn't know about the secret coke plate. He didn't hear me crashing around his room as I dressed to leave. My pants were a cruel puzzle. I never did find my bra.

Outside, there was still no moon. The vegan house was on a hill near the computer science building, its gleaming black glass and metal so different from the drab liberal arts buildings where Pete and I spent our time. I walked past the blood bus in the parking lot, closed for the night, where students donated fluids and bragged about it, coming out with their gigantic free T-shirts and little paper cones of fruit punch. Up ahead, I could see the viaduct I'd have to cross to get back to my dorm, the long neck of it spanning old and new, connecting the shimmering cube to the dumpy carcass of the quad, the funded parts of the university to the failing ones.

"It's a little stabby" was the joke we made about campus that year, a joke because a student had been knifed in the chest but survived. Later she admitted to slashing herself, and by then we'd all become experts on hesitation wounds, the many ways her story didn't add up. That semester the campus police patrolled in the evenings, handing out glow sticks—which we found hilarious—and encouraging us to stay in groups. But that night, campus was empty, no rent-a-cop to light my way or see me home. The fear was cold and electric, sharpened by the coke, a charged cloud of static I moved through.

I called Pete as I came to the viaduct. He was awake and speeding too, but he would have answered my call no matter the time.

"Talk to me while I maybe get stabbed," I told him.

"Did you fuck the vegan?" he asked, his TV loud in the background.

I thought of Jad's skin, how it was softer than the skin of any girl I'd been with, and how I'd never seen so many tattoos on one person, so much vibrant, fresh ink.

"They're new," he'd confessed when I ran my hands over the detailed scenes. "I'm making big changes in my life."

There was an ocean on his back: A herd of leaping narwhals, an open-mouthed siren. Deep in the water was a pinup girl and some geometric designs, script I'd later learn was Arabic, a skyline I'd learn was Ankara. I wanted to know: wasn't he afraid the hand and neck tats might preclude him from, I don't know, getting a dumb job later?

"That's exactly why I did it," he'd said. "So I'll never have to work a dumb job."

Oh, sweet, stupid Jad! If only that had turned out to be true!

People in Wink didn't have tattoos like that. I touched the vivid colors, unbelievable velvet under my fingers. I don't know what I was expecting, maybe that the skin had been marred. Instead, it was like he'd been tenderized.

Then I saw it: above a spaceman on his rib cage were the words *Try not to get too attached*. This was something our mother used to say. "And you'll never be disappointed" was the second half, though that part was implied and, later, left out. What Mom meant was for Julie and me not to get attached to material things, hopes, dreams, ideas of what we might do the next day. She was saying it to herself, I'd realize later, because she—with her eventual clutches on free catalogs and outgrown clothes and ruined appliances—needed to hear it most of all. She said it when Julie and I asked why she'd broken some promise, why she didn't take us to the movies like she'd said she would, or why she'd pick out the little boot figurine in Monopoly and then wander off, never taking her turn. She said it when we hugged her, put our sticky hands on her face, tried to sleep with her in her bed. Jad's spaceman settled something for me, a message that I should let him in, this guy I didn't know yet. He'd made his body a living collage, no loyalty to any style or theme, no real narrative, just a seamless, shimmering cloak.

"Oh, we fucked," I told Pete on the phone, spewing lurid half-truths. I didn't know how to talk about Jad yet, so I leaned into the big dick and the *Vertigo* poster, details I catered to Pete's interests.

I was walking fast, and though I was talking to Pete, my heart thumped wildly and a backlit trash can looked, for a second, like a crouching killer. As I bragged and lied to Pete, I thought in a loop, *Please don't let me die on a viaduct.* Of all the places one could be murdered, how embarrassing, no black water to be thrown into afterward, no current to sweep you out, just corpse to concrete, splattered in front of the shiny computer-sci building. I thought about tragic news of me traveling down I-20, reaching Julie.

There's Julie, on the periphery of every memory.

I didn't call her that night, though she would have answered the phone too. She would have played a role similar to Pete's—would have made me feel safer, would not have judged, would have inquired too about the dick, the drugs I did, the fun I was having. Talking about my life in Pivot—a life that did not involve her—felt like gloating. Once Julie graduated from high school, it became clear that she would not be joining me in college—that she wouldn't be going anywhere at all. My homesickness had long been replaced by guilt. What was she doing every night? I thought of her alone in our room, how my empty bed drove her out to the screened-in porch with Mom and even further, to the worst parties and drug houses, to the meth trailers out in Nayleen and Moffet, towns you'd be stupid to even stop and piss in. I was living a life while Julie wallowed in Wink, wasting her last years. It seemed I'd served as some sort of guardrail for her. Once I was gone, she careened.

This part in the recollection—it's my snag.

"BIOFILM IS SO important," Pete says, cupping handfuls of river.

How can he know so much about everything? When does he have the time to learn? When we met, it seemed we were in a similar place, intellectually, but now he's leaps and bounds ahead of me, writing plays, reading books, and watching documentaries while my brain shrinks and smooths from motherhood.

"For sure," I say, like I have a clue. I know he'll explain biofilm anyway, and he does, but I don't really follow. I gather that the stuff is a type of beneficial scum. We simmer in the river, and I break that word apart: bio-film. A sticky, living movie, mineral pornography.

"The microbial community here is insane," he murmurs. "Microbial or antimicrobial?" he argues with himself, his science shaky.

"Whichever is the good one," I offer.

"Microbial," he decides, letting his confidence carry him away from his own question.

He takes my hand and flips it over, kisses and releases it.

"Baby," he says, like I've just bobbed up next to him. "How are you?"

"I'm good," I say. "This is so nice."

He nods and stares at me. "I mean, you're enjoying this?"

"Definitely," I say.

"You're feeling relaxed?" There is something under his question I don't care for. It's the tone I'd take as a waitress. Happy customers camping out at one of my tables, smiling at me, saying how much they loved the food, a shitty 2 percent tip resting on top of the check.

"Y'all enjoyed it?" I'd ask, too cheerful, lifting the bill tray to look dramatically under and around, smiling deranged at a grimy pile of coins.

"Hundred percent," I say to Pete. "This is great."

I don't say, *I'm fucking relaxed, Pete.* Maybe I haven't thanked him enough for this river and nature's bounty and all the money it took to get us here. Or maybe it's that I haven't asked enough about Brian, haven't been holding up my end of things.

A hot rush passes over our feet, a fresh influx of drugs.

"You feel that?" I ask.

"Lord," Pete says, and closes his eyes.

I stare into my palm. I think of them, the microbial community, dancing and screwing and multiplying on my pink skin, organic gunk in the water, good for us. I really do feel high. I am in the river with Pete, but I am also seventeen, with Julie and Yes and Big Large in the softest, strangest place. I'm in the water but I'm not. I'm remembering something long forgotten, some neural pathway newly lit.

Part Three

THE

PINK

RUG

LIKE A DREAM, THIS HAPPENS IN THE PRESENT TENSE, is still happening. They tell you not to look in the mirror when you trip, so of course that's what I want to do. Big Large and Yes and Julie warn against it, but I'm stubborn and nobody can tell me a thing. My logic: if I can see myself reflected clearly, I might love me.

This is a totally different kind of trip than any we've ever done—a different drug altogether, not mushrooms or LSD. We're at Big Large's house, only Julie has stopped calling him Big Large and instead calls him his true name, Pablo.

Anyone could look at Julie with him, the way she tilts her head and stares up at him, how she bounces on her toes when they talk, and you know right away why he's such a draw. It's not just Big Large's age or size, it's the slow way he gets out of his truck, how direct sunlight makes him sneeze. His flannel shirts and his cute beer gut and the piney-smelling stuff he rubs into his mustache. His mustache, for Christ's sake. Big Large is our dad if our dad were a sweetheart, a reliable, good person.

His trailer's out on a big piece of inherited land. This spot is actually pretty, with sloping hills and all sorts of weird rocks and wild succulents. It feels like Texas out here, the mythic, storybook version, not so much like a dusty pit of hell. Big Large splits the bills with his mother by doing electric for the county. He drives a truck with a crane stuck to it, a big bucket stuck to the end of the crane. His job is to stand inside and use his little joysticks to lift himself up, do whatever needs to be done to Wink's power lines. Bigger than everybody, Big Large is used to seeing the world from on high already, and he likes the view, all the concealed things he gleans behind people's fences: normal yard stuff like sandboxes and doghouses and bleached-out patio furniture, but also things he isn't supposed to see. An illegal fire pit. A dozen white crosses all in a row—dead pets, he hopes. An old nudist squatting, balls sagging, tending to a koi pond. That's how Big Large finds the San Pedro cactus in the first place—he lifts himself up in his plastic bucket and sees somebody's secret: a psychedelic beast growing up against the house, swollen and ancient, non-native, transplanted on purpose. Big Large knows exactly what the cactus is, has been reading about it forever. He thinks of hopping the fence quick and cutting off a hunk but worries about shotguns and the demeanor of a snorting Doberman. Instead, he knocks on the front door with a lie ready, some pretense of getting access to a meter. The old guy who answers is wearing a tie-dye caftan and sandals with thick socks. Feeling safe, Big Large forgets about soft codes and flat-out asks if the guy knows what he has. "Hey there, sir," Big Large says. "What's the story with that magic cactus you got?"

The tie-dye man sells San Pedro by the foot, it turns out, and Big Large uses his saw to take off a limb right then. He loads it into his truck and drives home, fearless under the midday sun.

"Well, girls," he says, thrilled, his tailgate down to show it off. "Got us nine feet of drugs." He starts the long process of drawing the magic out, hacking the amputated arm into smaller pieces on his porch. He does the math, calculates however many inches of cactus per kilogram of us. The psychoactive bit lives right under the dark green skin, Big Large explains. He pulls it off in long curling strips while Julie, Yes, and I watch. Nothing looks suspicious—the sheriff could drive by and we'd just wave—but the process is slow. We girls get bored. We live our lives around Big Large's plan. We leave his trailer and go home and come back—Big Large cuts and cooks and cooks and drains, and finally, after a few days, it's time.

It's noon on a Sunday when we down our cups of muck, our chunky cactus tea. Nothing happens for a long while. Then it does. My hands get weak, tingly. That feeling of coming up is second only to the feeling right before you actually eat a drug: glittery, so full of possibility.

I look at Big Large and try to see what Julie sees. He is so big, but has he always had this sweet smile, those precious chubby hands? We're on our backs in the living room. Julie's and Yes's eyes have gone huge and inky black—their hair is alive and determined, sowing roots into the beloved pink shearling rug. The carpet under the rug is mauve, the couches are a muted orange pastel. Tapestries and crochet owls line the walls. Big Large's mom has style.

But I need a mirror now, most of all. "I'm doing it," I say. "I want to see me."

Yes and Julie stay sprawled out on the rug while I gallop off—and I do mean gallop, like a crazed, fresh-born fawn—to the bathroom. Big Large says, "She can handle it," meaning me, I guess. This is a different sort of trip, he reminds them, spiritual and sacred. He is up and stomping around as he speaks, not mad, just big. I hear him asking Julie and Yes if they're cool enough, if they're too cold, if they're thirsty. Should he close the shades or open them, maybe flip the record?

On the vanity in the bathroom is an abalone bowl full of bobby pins. Big Large's mom does wedding hair for a living. Weekends, she travels as far as Houston to tease and spray and tuck baby's breath into updos. I need a second to prepare myself for the mirror, so I sidestep it, curl up in the garden tub. I've never been in a bathroom so nice, the porcelain a glossy lavender, same shade as the custom toilet. The wallpaper is a seascape, and there's no soap scum like at our house, no hairy, sweet-smelling drain to look down. Yes's mother regards Julie and me with suspicion—she hates how noisy our practices are in her garage, how we leave sticky plates and candy wrappers and cords and instruments strewn around, cigarette butts scattered all over—but Big Large's mom is kind to us when she's home. In her tub, I feel a sudden longing for her soapy body. So few are safe from me, my ridiculous crushes. It smells like a rich girl's neck in this bathroom, like suntan lotion, but there's a top note of air freshener, and I imagine it smells the way a toilet on a yacht might smell. Though she doesn't have much money, Big Large's mom has taken the time to create a polished, personalized space, something I've never known an adult to do. Among the staged seashells and pretty shampoo bottles is a full-length lighted mirror, the kind you'd find in a fitting room.

I unfold out of the tub, ready to see myself. The girl on the wall unfolds. I walk toward her. She is someone's sister, friend, daughter. Under those ill-fitting jeans she has short, hard muscles. Her skeleton is a wonder, doing its work. Her wispy hair is adorable. I take off my clothes to see more of her, the gorgeous curve of her soft stomach. Big Large's voice booms from the living room: "Who needs a pillow? Who needs two pillows?" His footfalls are heavy, a huge reverberating space between the trailer and the dirt it sits on.

The mirror girl is laughing out loud, remembering how when Julie and I were really little, we climbed up on the sink in Mom's bathroom, naked. We squatted and stared at our areas in the bathroom mirror. Our mother left anatomy at work, where she helped patients empty their bladders and move their bowels. We kept our bodies vague—we didn't say *vagina* in our house. Certainly not *vulva*. Our areas were so different! The coloring, the shape. How had we inherited such different features from the same two parents? "My area looks like Mom's," Julie had said, and I could see she was right. Mom would stand in the laundry room and strip her scrubs off after work. She'd toss them into the washer and pull on her tatty teal robe, which was always gaping as she lounged on the couch, legs open. "Maybe I got Dad's area," I'd said, and this sort of detached, comfortable observation seemed totally reasonable. Innocent and earnest, searching, this statement wouldn't be bizarre for a few more years, the notion that I'd inherited my father's pussy.

In the mirror, the soft, short girl looks at her naked knees. They're perfect. I always feel so bad about this part of me. Too saggy, turned slightly inward—little-kid knees. I wear jeans and long dresses to cover them, knee socks with skirts, tights in the winter, even though it is always too hot for that in Wink. The mirror girl thinks, *Why should anyone feel bad about a knee?* It's like feeling bad about a lightbulb, a perfectly useful, blameless thing. A knee is a hinge that moves a leg. Without knees, we would slither around on the floor. "Any knee is a gift," the mirror girl says.

"You okay?" Big Large knocks soft, asks from beyond the door.

"She's okay," I say.

I love the way this mirror girl moves, how hunched her shoulders are, her gigantic pupils. Eyes so dark they look black, chin too pointy maybe, but if you want those cheekbones you have to take it. You have to take the high forehead if you want to get that tiny nose, to get those huge saucer eyes. She is glowing, alien, a sight to behold. Greenish and strange and a miracle. A lovable person: me.

Life says: You have nothing smart to say, no talent or gifts—you should starve and cut and hate yourself, throw yourself away. The cactus disagrees. My teen self falls apart as I examine her. The fractures are not only understood but felt, and I get it all at once: the world opens for me, incrementally evolves, skews, and finally, beautifully, splits apart.

Big Large is looming outside the bathroom door, huge and concerned.

"She's fine, Pablo," Julie says.

She's totally fine, the girl in the mirror. I'm fine, a human being doing the best she can in her bodyshell, so lucky to be alive. I commit to dialing up this feeling for the rest of my life, to considering my dissected self useful. One day there will be wrinkles in my neck and I won't be upset. I've been using this neck the whole time! A neck is just a hose that moves your head—it's bound to bend and kink. Who can be mad at a hose?

I pull my clothes back on and leave the bathroom. The four of us go outside to wander around in the hot sun, Big Large pointing out the mountain laurel that's everywhere, how it smells like grape Kool-Aid and grows all around, never mind that there are no mountains near. We skip and run, follow each other down hard-packed paths, so light on our feet. "This is official frolicking," Julie says, and it's the first time I've felt this free. We come to a blooming meadow, with shade and lizards and lush greenery. It's an oasis in the red dirt, and there's no way it's real. We lie on our backs with cold stones on our chests, we roll around together in the tall, damp grass. The cactus has got us now, is showing all its tricks.

By the time we get back to the living room, the pink rug is celestial, calling to us. We pour ourselves onto it.

"Pinky," I say, or someone says. "Piiiiinkkk."

We push our hands all the way into the plush. Elbow deep, deeper even. We are kittens, kneading our paws in pink. The rug is a portal, an animal we're riding, the soft spot on a baby's skull. The rug is a she. She's herself but also all she attracts—microscopic bits of Big Large and his mom, layered flecks of their skin and twisted-up strands of their hair, and the dust of us too, mixed in, plus everybody's sock lint and silty dirt from outside, anything that clings to our feet. Always pink, she deepens and swells and blots: rose to carnation to fuchsia, then a shifting spectrum of colors I experience fully but have no names for. Pinky is fur and chemicals and stardust. She's vapor or she's soft and tacky as chewed bubblegum. She changes and we change too, our sweaty hands clutching her mane.

Big Large is in charge, hosting like he does. He's flat on his back on Pinky, but part of him is keeping track of the lights and the temperature and the song that's playing, ready to jump up and make a change if need be, trying always to keep one foot grounded in the rug. Yes is smiling, fingers tap-tapping on her thighs, steady as a clock.

"Kitty," Julie says. She's got a gray dot in the bow of her lip, a graphite beauty mark where I poked her once with a mechanical pencil. I have a similar mark on my thigh from her, same fight. Look around in your life and you'll see these everywhere, leaden moles on all walks of people, battle scars from childhood. Like mine, Julie's dot is perfect, part of her now, and we forgive each other everything.

"Kitty," she says, again. "Kit-Kat." We make eye contact over the heads of Big Large and Yes, who are beautiful but distant. The four of us are together on the rug, but only Julie and I are *in* the rug. With her inside voice she says, *I'm going to tell you something, okay?*

Her face is open and serene and the way Julie talks to me—it happens outside of sound, outside of time. It is a rising and drifting vocabulary, a message that floats from her skull like smoke, spreads apart, and dissipates. What is it that she says to me?

"Hey," Yes says. I'm sitting up now, Yes stroking my hair. "Hey, what's this about?"

"That's what I was trying to tell you," Big Large says in a quiet voice. "Kit's crying." He crawls over to a window and yanks a shade, floods the room with light. "Should we worry?"

It seemed to me the wetness was coming from Pinky, but no. I don't know what Julie said, what I was crying about, only that it's over now. Why can't I remember what she said?

"She's okay," Julie says in her real, everyday voice. She wipes under my eyes with her thumbs. "You're okay," Julie says. She uses the hem of her skirt to dab at my cheeks.

"I'm okay," I agree, and I'm no longer wrecked, no longer weeping. It's the relief of waking up from a forgotten nightmare, safe in my small bed.

Julie and Big Large and Yes are talking to each other, and the sounds they make are prickly and green, holding me close. The narrative of every psychedelic trip I've taken: wonder, terror, comfort.

I don't know if Julie's dress is shifting its hue or if Pinky is, but the two of them are identical now: a bright coral. "She's gone camo," Yes says, and points, picking up on my thought. Now Julie is just a floating pretty head and soft hands, long bare legs and feet, pieces of her resting sweetly on the rug.

We look like sleepy children: repositioning and clearing our throats, stretching, yawning, drinking small sips of water. The sun moves. A record ends, and Big Large gets up to flip it. We are coming down—trying to settle on a band name, once and for all. The idea of a band is brand-new, a concept Julie, Yes, and I have started entertaining. We play together because it's fun, but Julie doesn't need anyone to make songs. She records every stitch herself, layer upon layer, but when she decides to perform in front of an audience, which we hope one day she will, she'll need backup. I can sing the parts she gives me—I can play my little bass lines once she shows me what they are. She makes, I mimic. On the rare occasion when I have an idea of my own, she'll patiently listen. "What if you turned up the guitar right there?" I'll say. "What if we add a little something after the chorus?" She'll look at me, serene and kind, thinking. Then she'll say, "Or what if we do this?" and she'll turn a knob or switch the key and everything shines, light busting through.

Julie's voice sustains everything. Yes has rhythm and knows the basics, her kit borrowed from a cousin. I saved and bought a left-handed Sawtooth from the Pecos Walmart. Julie makes up our assignments, our containers, the space to hold her sounds. Sometimes she turns and gives Yes a look if she's dragging. She calls out my dropped notes or a part I let get pitchy, but Yes and I are nothing if not enthusiastic. We feel chosen, both of us trying to keep up, the act physical, like factory workers assembling Julie's designs. We struggle to stay in it, pound it out, pull it into the room. It's the same feeling I used to get when we were kids, me chasing after slippery Julie on our wet lawn, my body knowing, *Oh my god, she's too fast. I'll never catch her.* In Yes's garage, practice after practice, somehow we make it through—we make some songs.

"The Fontanels," Yes tries again, and everyone groans.

We are in a heap on the pink shearling rug, deciding who we should be.

"You Are the Universe," Big Large says, after we tell him We Are

Stardust is too stupid, We Are the Universe too self-centered. Julie, Yes, and I look at each other. We like You Are the Universe, and we love Big Large. We don't know or care that he has accidentally stolen the name from a new age paperback on the shelf in front of the rug, right in his line of sight. Everything feels predestined, beautiful, and planned. Big Large asks if he can be a part of our band—of our universe—and we say no. No way. Sorry. A rare moment of girls denying a man access, but the cactus has stripped us of niceties. "Absolutely not," we say, and Big Large understands, his hands up like, *Sorry, sorry for even asking.* Still, we take his name and we feel brilliant, Julie's hand resting heavy on my head, all of us in a pile on the pink rug. The band is a fantasy, a wish, a dream we dream together. It doesn't exist and then it does.

Tomorrow, we will make merch, we decide. "You Are the Universe" on a ringer tee, tiny holes pinpricked in the fabric to look like stars. The wearer's chest will come through. *You* are the universe—get it, your skin! Maybe it isn't the best band name, we think later, but we're committed. A name is a name, and if you had the chance to change yours, wouldn't you just as soon go with the one your mother gave you?

The universe hands you something. You take it.

Part Four

THE

BOILING
RIVER

ETE SIGHS, DEEP AND SHUDDERING. THE WATER CUTS him at his neck and wrists, his submerged body pale and green-ish, an odd contrast to the healthy tan of his face, his golden hands moving in his beard.

"I'm remembering things wrong," Pete says. "Or I'm, like, forget-ting things I thought were unforgettable. Brian takes his coffee like a dipshit—four fucking Splendas—but I can't remember the first time he said he loved me. I remember when *I* said it to him. Too soon, and he didn't say it back. I said, 'I love you, you know,' and he said, 'Aw, Deet, thanks for telling me.' All the pet names we called each other—I don't know where they came from. He was Bird and Birdie and later he was Kicks, because he had so many damn shoes. He called me Kicks too—somehow at the end we were both Kicks. But where did Deet come from? Just the rhyme, or was it something else?"

Pete's hand snakes in and out of the water as he talks, takes the pale green cast on and off like a glove.

The current rushes too hot, hotter than it's been, uncomfortable. I want to make the joke about slow-boiled frogs when I notice Pete's eyes are brimming. For a second I think he might cry, something I've never seen, and I'm not sure how I'll handle it. Then he sneezes, loud and terrifying.

"I told you he's deathly afraid of blind people? No, I didn't, because he specifically asked me not to. Irrational and totally inappropriate.

He traced it back to getting shampoo in his eyes. I said, 'That's a fear of *going* blind, Bird, not *the* blind.' What a monster. Four Splendas, and if he has even a *sip* of coffee, he immediately has to take a shit. Even in a restaurant! And his shit smells like chemicals—like a perm. I mean shit smells how it smells, but his is *beyond*."

Pete is talking so loud, the older couple upriver squint and glare at us. "I'd watch him take that first hot sip and picture his ass popping open like a spigot. I'd see his coffee mug in the cabinet and retch." I lose it, laughing. Pete waves at the river jerks. He splashes his face with water, slicks back his hair.

"Fucking Brian," he says. "That's all I'm going to say." He relaxes his shoulders, tilts his head from side to side to pop his neck. He reaches for my underwater hand and we lace our fingers together.

I'm feeling less high, less druggy, but there is still a sense of calm at my core, a keen relaxation. My cheapo therapist would be proud of me, that I even have a core, that I can feel it, that I'm sitting in my body for once. I want to be present for Pete.

So often I'm adrift, a brain in a jar. I used to try to pour myself into other people's bodies. Entering a person, being entered, it stops time, bends it. It's a collapsar, an event horizon. This sounds like hippie shit, but that sensation lasts longer, goes deeper with psychedelics—the total dissolution of the personal body, the safety of being swallowed by a pure, universal one.

It seems to me these lost pastimes—being a psychonaut and being slutty—are connected. Maybe because they're two things I enjoyed being that I'm not allowed to be anymore. Identities that induced a feeling of security, false as it might have been. My old coping mechanisms have become incompatible with my life choices. "It's just growing up," Yes says. "Easier for some of us than others."

Water, too, has been made dangerous since Gilda. You imagine them choking, blue, fished from some dark bottom. I'm so happy she's not here to turn this place into something treacherous. But I'm not used to sitting around doing nothing for so long, and looking at

Pete's peaceful face, I feel that pang of sunset boredom, when you're ready to turn your back on the sky and get on with your night, but some loved one lingers, entranced by mutating pastels.

"This feels very nice," I say, and it's true. Nice, but not Meaningful.

I thought getting pregnant might bring me to the corporeal, but no. Instead, I felt the body *within* my body—Gilda flipping around, a life inside the weird, loose sock of me. There's this inspirational quote, vaguely religious, that Yes is always saying. It's cloying and not particularly catchy. She intones: "They know us better than anyone, for our children have heard our hearts beating from the inside." Sometimes she shortens it, which makes it stranger and less corny, oddly more affecting. "They've been on the inside," she'll say to me, knowingly, and I'll picture a bunch of mug-shot fetuses in orange jumpsuits, doing time in the space of whooshing guts. "They're insiders," she says, and I see unborn stock market babies, trading futures from the womb. It's a nice expression, concept, idea or whatever, but I don't believe it, abridged or not. If anything, I felt more removed from the flesh when I was pregnant with Gilda. Even now, in all my mammalian, milk-spewing glory, it's pretty easy to ignore every inch of my body that isn't my tits.

When I got pregnant, I wasn't as devastated as I maybe should have been. Jad stepped up, assured me he was ready to be a parent if I was. He was a truly good person, better than I deserved. I revised our story—transformed our broken condom from a mistake into a blessing. It was senior year and I'd changed majors yet again, this time to printmaking. I'd already tried painting, sculpture, and photography by then, failed at each of them in turn.

My favorite artist is known for pixelating gruesome crime photos, synthesizing and cropping them, blowing them apart. After processing, he'd paint over the gridded blood spatter and bent bodies with bright, glossy washes, turn them into something joyful. Then the artist had a kid, and it killed his work. What came after that baby was embarrassing. Gone were the awful images made dazzling. Now the artist took close-up photos of his daughter—the enlarged pout of her young lip, her tiny nail beds—to use as his base. He felt new shame for centering violence in his work, and this was violence twice over, the artist argued, people killed and then re-killed, exploited by him. But to me, the new pieces were more exploitative—if the artist had been communing with the dead before, giving them vibrant voices, now he was stealing from his daughter, holding her down, drawing her outline in chalk. The new work was boring and safe, all chaste pastels. Sentimentality is the coward's shortcut.

Even before I had Gilda, every song I've ever tried to write, every project I've touched, it's all been sentimental—no real voice or edge. Knowing where a trap is doesn't mean you know how to avoid it. Knowing what's beautiful doesn't mean you can make it yourself. Having access to genius—growing up with it sleeping in the twin bed next to you—it crystallizes your shortcomings. There's always been a tremendous gulf between my taste, which is excellent, and my ability, which is nonexistent.

Jad wouldn't let me say I was dropping out—he still won't—he's got this idea that I'll go back and finish when Gilda goes to school herself. It'll never happen. When I got knocked up, all I felt was relief. Finally, here was something perfect only I could make.

I wasn't scared off by the idea of motherhood. Julie and I mothered ourselves and each other for years, because we had to. Mama tried, like the song says. She had her moments. She loved our problems, our unbearable teenage sadness. Of the teacher who singled me out for chewing gum in class: "Fuck her," Mom said. "No law against gum."

I'd been so embarrassed, my name written on the chalkboard.

"Who cares!" she said. "The custodian's gonna erase it tonight. The sooner you forget about it, the sooner it's gone."

Julie, dumped by her first boyfriend: "Fuck him," Mom snapped. "He has no chin. In a hundred years we'll all be dead."

Girls who were mean to us: "They should all be murdered," said Mom, the same thing she said when the gas pumps were occupied, if there was a line at the Dairy Queen. Murdered, all. We ran to her, lambs, desperate for her to make everything okay, but we weren't touchers in our family. If I wanted to touch Julie, I'd have to tackle her and do some kind of exaggerated ironic squeeze. If she wanted to touch me, she'd make it a joke—I'd be standing and she'd sit near my feet and wrap her arms around my legs. I'd drag her down the hall like that. If my mom wanted to touch either of us, she instead touched the kitchen table where we were sitting, the arm of the couch we were sprawled on. We touched each other's clothes, adjusted them, but touching the warm body itself—that was rare.

"Want to make somebody love you?" I said to Julie when we were in high school. "I know how."

I was talking about a girl in my class, the first person outside of my family who loved me back. "You just have to hold them." I had a method. This girl and I would not have called ourselves queer. We called what we were doing "preparing." We prepared for all of ninth grade, half of tenth. We were very, very prepared.

A lot of teenagers—with their bad skin and reeking armpits— wanted to be touched. A lot of them, like us, weren't well mothered, or if they were, it was something they still longed for. "It's so easy," I told Julie, cocky and stupid. The idea was that you couldn't go wrong holding someone, as a mother holds a child, cradling them, even the boys—especially the boys. If you could get close enough to hold them truly, like you meant it, and you had to really mean it, you could pin them back to that early, perfect motherlove, your body a kind of time machine.

Being touched, touching, holding my girlfriend afterward, the two of us on our backs in a yellow field, or later with a different girl in somebody's back seat, or with some boy in his goaty-smelling bed. Touch: it progresses, it's forward-moving, impossible to walk back. Once we've been inside each other, we're permeable, we're mesh, forever. All that touch you miss out on once you get too grown to cuddle—you crave it. A connection that frees you from yourself.

When Julie and I were young, before touching got weird, we'd lie in Mom's bed with her. That's when the Little Walker would come out, just two fingers walking around on somebody's back. There was no better feeling than the gentle, unpredictable path of the Little Walker. Mom made us walk her back first and then she'd fall asleep, never returning the favor. Julie and I had to be Little Walkers for each other. Sometimes we tried to wake Mom up when it was our turn. "It's not fair," we'd whine. "We don't care if you're tired." We clapped near her ears when we were feeling mean. We laughed when she'd startle.

"Whatever you two try to do to me, I get worse fifty hours a week," she said.

Before her job at the memory care place, Mom worked in a psychiatric hospital. We worried one of her patients would show up some night and kill us all, but Mom said they loved her because she knew how to talk to them. One guy crapped in his sneakers and she acted like she saw it all the time, "We all have our bad days," she told this shoe shitter. Somebody would come in screaming about Satan and she'd touch their shoulder and say, "Set the devil aside—let's talk about *you*."

At home she was different. "I've been taking care of assholes all day," she'd hiss at us, patience gone. "I'm off duty." She'd say the same thing if one of us got scared, if we needed a drink of water in the middle of the night.

"I'm not taking care of nobody no more," Mom would say, as if this weren't obvious. When I got pregnant, I promised myself I'd be a better mother, home and available, no job or addiction to take me away. Julie crying, "I need you, Mama," at Mom's locked bedroom door. I want to go back in time as me now, scoop her up.

As I sit in the river, the watery sense of calm is gone, replaced with the chaos of the past. Here I am, shuffling through Julie's T-shirts in my mind, a fat stack of them, dressing her like a doll. The ratty shorts, the pajama sets, the holey socks, the baby onesies Mom used to let me snap. The bib I put on her when I wanted to feed her. In the hot water, I am tingling, traversing her changing tastes over the years. Florals, stripes, tie-dye, shades of pink and plum and finally coral, her favorite. Everything flame retardant, cheap, discounted, pilled. Pete is next to me but so is Julie, a prismatic blur. She is out of order, all the ages she'll ever be.

"About how much longer do you expect we'll be here?" I say to Pete. I'm not restless anymore, I'm irritated. My skin feels too tight, itchy. "Like ten minutes? Fifteen?" I say.

"Let's not think in minutes," Pete says. He tips his head back, strokes my underwater hand. "Let's not rush. I want us to really soak it in. I'm giving you permission to sit here and soak, baby. Be with me, right here."

"Okay, great," I say. I want the inverse of a soak, the precise opposite, but what would that be? To desiccate. I wonder if Pete is thinking about Brian or if he's having to shove thoughts of Brian away. Probably Pete is *healing*, right before my eyes.

I try to pull myself from where I am, maybe think about Bad Dad's perfect ass in duck pants, the way Celadon's lips were cracked, bitten, almost bloody. But I can't do this with Pete around—I can only soak.

"Soak it in," I say. "Soak. It. In." I chop at the river with each word. Pete blinks at me, lets his ears slip under and fill.

A woman with a deflated stomach wades past and stands downstream in the rushing water, her bathing suit bright coral and baggy at the ass. Julie's exact color, Living Coral, according to Pantone. I look for the child who stretched and remade this woman's body, but she's alone. Maybe I'm projecting, maybe the stomach is genetic, I don't know, but the longer I look at the coral woman, the more I appreciate her unusual silhouette, how she flaunts it.

Before it got too painful, I used to keep my valves open for Julie. I'd listen for her, look for her everywhere. That guy who sells oranges near the highway with a little black dog balanced on his head—the dog reminded me of Planchette, the dirty teacup poodle Julie had at the end. Shivering and neurotic, Planchette was stinky and ridiculously small—Julie loved that goddamn thing.

Or our corner drunk, Bea—or is it B or Bee? I've never seen it written—a mystery in her many layered ski masks. I once heard her sing the chorus of a song Julie covered, a cover of a cover by the time it got to us, a song about a girl who wants to walk naked down the street. Was this a message? Had Julie somehow slid inside this odd woman who was always in full winter gear, no matter the heat? Bea would grab her stomach and laugh, loud and pure, like a child. I never could see her mouth. Once, in the early and vulnerable lochia-leaking days, Gilda a newborn grub strapped to my chest, I followed too closely behind Bea, listening for clues. She stopped short, turned, and screamed at me, "Somebody's gonna eat that baby!" Her eyes, wet behind her gray ski mask and her other gray ski mask, seemed so certain. Drenched in cortisol, I was terrified. Bea was dangerous, ruined. A stranger once full of promise—full of Julie—forced out of my life. Now I walk Gilda down a different street.

There was the incident at the hair salon by my house. A client was talking about her scar. I was a client too, in the next chair, but I couldn't turn my head to look directly at the talking woman.

"It's so terrible," the woman told her stylist. "I'm sorry you have to look at it every time I'm here."

I searched for what was wrong with the woman's reflection, found nothing.

Her stylist said, "Hon, you can't even see it."

"Oh, that's kind," the woman said. "You're kind. But you don't have to say that."

How upset her father was when it happened, the scarred woman went on, her mother, thank god, long dead. I listened around the silvery sound of my stylist's scissors, desperate to know more.

"It was so stupid," the woman said. "I never should have had it done."

Had it done! A botched plastic surgery? But what if this woman had a little brand on her skin, like Julie's, twinkling at me from beyond? Julie burned a tiny star behind her ear—one of her cranked-out ideas. She did it at home in the kitchen, scorched the shape herself with a bent paper clip, red-hot.

The woman stood and her stylist shepherded her behind my chair, deeper into the salon. When my cut was finished, I paid and quickly walked her same path to the back, my pretense a lost jacket.

"Did you come in with one?" my stylist said, trailing me.

The woman was there under a dryer, her head encased in the dark globe, towel around her neck, a smock covering the rest of her. I wanted to drag her out of the chair and strip her, inspect her inch by inch.

PETE'S RIVER HAS disturbed me, kicked up the muck at my dark bottom. My good-enough therapist says grief is multifaceted. Crying is cathartic but I almost never do it. I can force myself to pain, but the trigger is always wrong. I'll be doing dishes, singing along to the stereo, a song with no real memory attached to it, nothing concretely Julie, just a moving verse. A word cracked in half. The brokenhearted folk singer—he knows where to find his lost love. She's in somebody else's room, she's moved on. He goes to her and breaks down—he can change, he swears. The desperation in his voice belies the facts. The listener knows, the singer knows, the woman he's singing to—we all know the same thing: He can't change. Won't. No matter the catch in his voice.

Pete follows my gaze to the coral woman. "Hey," he says. "You okay?"

For fuck's sake, worry about yourself, I think at him. "Getting too hot," I say. What comes next does not pour from some cracked seam in my brain, softened by the water. The truth is this thought is not a next thought at all. It's constant, an always thought, a warped jingle.

It overwhelms me as it sometimes does, that's all: *I don't want to do any of this without you.* Julie should be twenty and twenty-one and twenty-two, ad infinitum, on a tour bus and a stage, in a studio. Or not even that, she doesn't even need to be flourishing or accomplished, she could be exactly the way she was at the end—addicted, annoying, a warm slurring voice on the telephone.

"Wanna do some breath work?" Pete says, and it is the last thing I want to do, breathe with Pete. He knows me so well, that I'm trying to be in the moment with him, but that most of me is with the coral woman downriver.

"Do what I do," he says, heaving deep. I try but I'm doing it wrong, so he explains the technique—how you make four walls, a ceiling, and a floor with your metered inhalation, forceful exhalation.

"Breathe a box," he tells me.

I do this with him. In, out.

"Then what?" I say, my box built, something roiling in me.

The end, again. If I'm pressed, if I'm really cornered, I tell people Julie died in her sleep. I say a thing and say a thing until the truth backs down.

A dreamy death, peaceful, is what I want for her. Still, even strangers can't always leave this alone.

"Wasn't she so young?" they ask. "What happened to her?"

I say she was nineteen years old—that part is true. She'd worked a double at Anna Jean's, also true. I leave out the wine, the light pole. Probably she was asleep. Truly. I can't make sense of the plot, so I cling to patterns. She'd drifted off behind the wheel before, once with me in the car and once with Mom. It happens to lots of people—it had almost happened to me too, driving between Dallas and Wink, my exhausted brain trying to tell me all that highway braille on the shoulders was meant to let you rest, that this was the precise purpose of it, so you could sleep and coast, keep on driving. Both times Julie had overcorrected, jerked the car across to the other lane, then glided back to safety. She turned up the AC, said, "Oops."

With each periodic infusion of new hot water, there is a rising smell, more petrichor than sulfur, not unpleasant but strong, spewing from the broken rocks. Euphoria comes in waves, same as grief. I match my breathing to Pete's again, if only to get him to leave me alone. I don't want to distract him from our purpose. All the money he spent, how much he needs my support. He must be so mired in his own thoughts, so desperate to feel better. I need to make an effort. I close my eyes, shut off the Living Coral woman.

On the continuum of wellness, this experience falls somewhere between the time I visited Pete's acupuncturist and the discount yoga class where I fell asleep in corpse pose. Like the worry rock in my pocket or dollar store aromatherapy candles, it's a nice distraction, never making a dent. I'm always full of needles, floating in a tank, on my back on a sun-dappled couch, simmering in distant water. And none of it is as fun or effective as sex with a total stranger, most drugs, a cold pull of freezer gin. Montana is one of many expensive, useless attempts at healing. Processing. There have been dozens of boiling rivers already. There will be more, a hundred unsuccessful analogues, well-meaning people dragging me around. I'll be boiling forever. I'll never get out of here, never get the scum off.

Then there's splashing and phones blasting dumb music. Pete and I turn toward the motion of flashy swimsuits and bleached hair, shades of toned, tanned flesh. The teens in pairs and trios, holding hands, clomping into the water. Some of them are blowing whistles, some are wearing Day-Glo plastic jewelry.

"Woo!" one girl keeps shrieking.

They're shoving and tugging at each other, taking selfies, swigging from their bottles. I don't mind teenagers—truly I still feel like I'm one of them, but any party you're not invited to seems like it's full of assholes. We peaceful river folk are outnumbered.

"What do we do?" I say.

"Free country," Pete says, and closes his eyes again, unbothered.

It's not the teens, it's me. When my mother went through menopause, I asked her what hot flashes felt like. "Like rage," she said. "Like you want to peel your own self off like pantyhose." That's what I'm feeling, brimful of shame, flooded with warm fury. I have come to the not-so-sudden conclusion that sitting in this river is the absolute worst thing for me right now. When I am walking around in my life, I can shove things away. Here, soaking in the slick muck, I'm porous.

I stand up and steam rises from me, floats off in that magical shape.

"Too much," I say to Pete. "Be right back." He opens one eye and watches me leave. He looks like he wants to say something to me.

I wade against the bright parade of youth. They sway in strings of two and three, hands linked against the current. Invisible and unconsidered until I am right in front of them, I take each strand by surprise, when physics will simply not allow us to occupy the same space. "Sorry, sorry," I say to them, and I am deeply, molecularly sorry for existing. They look at me, shocked, then drop hands, annoyed, splitting to let me through.

"ARE YOU LETTING IT get away from you?" was a question I asked Julie, a question she asked me too. It was a joke to us, something we parroted from Mom.

Everything was permitted in our house, all was allowed. Even during her Jesus years, Mom would say, "Have a good time," never asking where we were going, when we were coming back. We thought this was great. "Don't need the details," she'd say. "You girls have fun. Have *the most* fun," she'd rasp, drunk or high herself, waving from the porch. When she was feeling particularly parental she might add, "Don't let it get away from you," or "Don't let it be a crutch," and we would crack up.

"Is it a crutch, Julie?" I'd ask and ask, a joke until the very end. Even over the phone from school, I could always tell by the hollowed-out sound of her voice that something was working on her, pulling her under.

"Kit," she'd say, "it's a motherfucking electric wheelchair," and we'd crack up.

Julie and I had a congenital disregard for our safety, right from the start. I loved drugs, truly, but addiction was never my problem. I could use something and quit it, I don't know why. Start and stop, this and that, everything I was offered, everything I came across. I could do something once or twice, a dozen times, then leave it. But Julie did a thing and did a thing until there was nothing left.

"Everything in moderation, even moderation," she'd say, beaming.

She did not care what happened to her, and I could not force her to. The sheen of sweat on her lip, the damp rings in the pits of her dark floral dress. I'd seen shades of carelessness deepening in her for years. It was the reason people liked watching her sing. There was no illusion they were there to see the rest of us: Steady, reliable Yes with her taped-up drums. Me, stiff in profile, terrified. An audience of thrashing young people, truckers, old regulars, kids with black X's on their hands. Tough-looking girls, boys who hadn't showered in weeks. Watching someone walk away from themselves, fearless—even I had to admit—it was thrilling to see.

"It's fine, Kitty, I'm fine," she'd say. "Let's talk about something else."

You can check in with your addict, you can disapprove or approve or toggle between approvals. You can aid or abet or refuse. You can recognize the problem or be on top of the problem or ignore the problem or be a part of the problem, but the problem is there waiting, sealed up, ruthless, no matter what you do. The problem is the person. The destruction is a race between the person and themselves. You know, part of you does, there's nothing you can do to stop it. You can hold it off, but there comes a time when you have to rest, enlist others to help. You don't want it to happen on your watch, but worse, you don't want it to happen off your watch. Not happening at all is not an option. It's coming, you've known for years. The most you can hope for is that you'll be the one calling to tell the others—you'll be vigilant enough to witness the crescendo. You hope to at least be on the inside of the bad news, be the one making the terrible phone call, not receiving it. The call is coming either way.

I MAKE IT back to land. The air feels freezing by comparison. I shiver and realize there's not a towel in my pack—I rifle through Pete's stuff, wrap myself up in one of his.

There's a couple straggler teens, separate from the mass. A scrawny boy in swim trunks and a backward cap, the Fireball girl from the parking lot in a bikini top and micro shorts. She has a small, heart-shaped face. The two of them are kicking off their shoes, only the girl's sandal is giving her trouble. She squats in the soft dirt, almost tips over, rights herself. She tugs and tugs at the leather strap. Her head lists to the side. Her struggle is a hook that sinks in me. So many things are difficult for this girl. Once her shoe is solved, she's having drawstring issues, her tiny shorts bunched around her ass. She sits on the ground and sticks her legs straight out for the boy, who is happy to help. Her phone falls from her pocket and she lets it, leaves it there on the ground. She stands up, proud as a girl popping out of a cake. The boy takes her hand and holds it up high, spins her around slow.

She stumbles, catches herself, or no, *he* catches her, and she smiles at me as she is revolved, dead-eyed and breathing heavy, in front of the boy. Her chest is sunburned, pink and peeling.

Another girl in the water waves to the couple, an accumulation of plastic concert bracelets on her wrist. She's one of many bobbing heads that turn and look back. "Kayla—so messy!" she yells, and the other heads titter.

"Goddamn," the boy says, and the girl—Kayla—her eyes are closed as she spins for him. She's new to shaving or just bad at it—there are razor nicks around her knobby knees, a gummy and disintegrating Band-Aid on her ankle. Her jaw is slack.

The boy wants to get Kayla into the water, but this is a problem because Kayla does not seem to be a person who walks anymore. She can run, she can tilt and stagger and dance, but staying a course is not what Kayla is about. This isn't such a problem for the boy, who wants to appear strong and strapping. He's happy to take control. He piggy-backs Kayla and she goes limp. He gropes hard at her thighs, keeps her from falling off. From where I'm sitting on this riverbank, from where I am sitting in my life, this all seems to be a very bad idea.

"Hey," I say.

Kayla is likely not a person who swims anymore—it's possible she's not even a person who floats. They trudge toward the mossy, slippery rocks, where the hot river will hide the boy's grabby hands and hard little dick.

"Hey," I yell, and jump up. "Hey!" I'm waving with both hands, loud enough that most of the rivergoers, including the mean old couple, including the coral woman and Pete, turn to look at me.

"It's Kayla, right?" I shout.

Kayla reanimates at the sound of her name, swivels her head to see me.

"Kayla! It's just—I'm sorry, guys. Kayla—Kayla, can you come here for a sec?"

"Huh?" the boy says.

"Wait," Kayla says, twisting back. "Wait."

From the labored way the boy turns, I can tell she's not so easy to haul off, tiny as she is. They make their slow way toward me.

"You know her?" he says to Kayla, looking at me.

"Maybe?" she says, squinting.

What Kayla needs is a safe, hulking presence in her life, someone like Big Large to step in and keep her safe. But for now she's got me.

"You don't," I say, teeth chattering. I tuck Pete's towel tight around me and talk across the boy, beyond him, my focus his shitfaced passenger. "Know me, I mean. It's just that I'm away from my kid and my phone, it's dead, Kayla," I say, waving it at her. I'm giving her the hard sell, channeling the fiercest playground moms, the no-bullshit tone Nancy gets when she launches into her essential oil tirade. What is it about the sound of your own name that's supposed to make you pliable? "I need a phone and, Kayla, I saw you dropped yours here," I say. "I gotta call home, check on my kid. Can I use it? I'll be so quick."

Downriver, Pete waves and I wave back. *Look how totally normal I'm being.*

"I don't know," the boy is saying. He stands back, looming. Kayla is chipper, happy to help. She looks at the ground, sees her phone, and is delighted, like I've performed a magic trick.

"Sure," she says. "Sure, yeah. I want down, Luke," she says.

The boy—Luke—stares at me, suspicious as Kayla squirms.

"Down," she says.

"You don't have to, K," Luke says. He looks at my wet clothes and dirty feet like I'm a derelict, like I've come directly from the depths, a swamp woman. "Can't you find somebody else?"

"Pummy down!" Kayla says, and it's the rising whine of a melodramatic teen girl, nonnegotiable. Luke does what he's told. Kayla slides off his back and staggers over to me, arms out, eyes half-closed.

She bends down to retrieve her phone, but this, too, is difficult. She takes a knee and paws it from the grass.

"Thank you," I say. "My daughter, she's three. Almost four."

"Listen," she says, and shakes her head like there's some ultimate understanding between us, like I don't have to explain myself at all. She's too trusting, unshelled and vulnerable in the harsh world. It takes her two tries but she enters her passcode, then tosses the phone to me. "I got you. Here."

WHEN THE CALL CAME, I was on the outside of it, all the way in fucking Pivot. I was twenty-one and pregnant as hell, fixing to become a parent. Jad and I were doing Sunday things. Laundry, marinating tofu, Jad holding up different ends of the couch so I could stick rubber bits under the feet. Mom called and I let her go to voicemail.

Jad vacuumed and I dusted, all while my mom called and called. Then I got a call from Julie's phone, and I ignored that too. "I can't handle them today," I said to Jad while we meal planned, grocery shopped, loaded up the car.

The calls alternated: Mom, Julie, Julie, Mom. I just knew they were on the screened-in porch, trashed, the mess of them together, irritating me. I rode high in my regular, boring life, and each time I rejected a call, my shit felt more together. That night I was about to run myself a bath when Julie called again. Sometimes the only way to get them unstuck was to just answer, let them slur whatever drunken message or looping story and be done with them. I took the call. "What is it?" I snapped, but nobody spoke. It was the sound of the screened-in porch, the sound of Wink, tiny and quiet and windblown, but nobody was talking. "Jesus Christ, what?" It was my mom's voice and I thought, *Fuck, wasn't that Julie's number?* I felt tricked. But then it wasn't Mom's voice either. That sound, how to describe it? Was it even a person? *It's that cat* was an actual thought I had as I grabbed a fresh, fluffy bath towel and walked down the hall. It sounded like Yoko, the old white shorthair, the original Friend. Mom had Yoko and Julie had Planchette the support poodle. That was the bizarre family they'd created, two wine-soaked women and their little shadow animals.

I twisted the tap, let water beat into the tub. The sound on the phone was a high cry, a wail. It was possible they were *that* drunk—this was something they might find funny, my mom and Julie together, putting a cat on the phone to call me, squeezing it to make it talk. I was about to hang up, fuck them, when I heard the words.

Accidental overdose was what I'd predicted, worried some late night would spin too fast, that Julie would showboat a heroic dose and blow her heart up on the front porch, Mom useless, standing by, watching her froth and foam. Or worse, that she'd do it alone, supernova her sweet brain in our childhood bedroom, nobody around to see. Or violence: the chance she'd get shot knocking on the wrong trailer door, buying from or selling to some black cloud, some hurt and broken person who would see the shine—her undeniable glow—and want to crush it.

Instead it happened on a highway with nothing in her system but wine, not even that much of it. It was late, early, almost morning. She went out to Flip's for cigarettes and scratch-offs, same as she always did. The sun was coming up. She wasn't speeding, from what the highway patrol said. She just . . . drifted. The car wasn't even totaled—she and Mom never liked seat belts, nobody I knew growing up seemed to wear one. Everybody in Wink wanted to be thrown clear, that's what they said, tossed from the wreckage onto the soft asphalt. I had to relearn basic safety later in life, pin myself tight to the project of my own self-preservation. The light pole survived. The Buick survived—that turd of a car, a big brown brick with a little dent and a shattered windshield.

I don't remember the trip to Wink, only that Jad insisted on driving, that I insisted he wait in the car at the hospital. My mother had been there for hours, sobbing to the chaplain, then signing all those awful papers. She met me in the lobby, and an elevator took us under the building. Next comes the thought that can't be thought, the thought that must be thought, the sick chorus: how Julie looked on the slab. Someone kind had washed her hair, knowing we were coming. Picked out the glass, touched her cold hands, arranged her bony shoulder under the blanket. Mom made that animal sound again, or I did, both of us.

You have to get through the worst thought fast, so you can be done with it. The final note, the bleak tail end. Julie's open mouth: it wouldn't—my mother and I both tried—it wouldn't close.

KAYLA STAYS DOWN, her palms flat on the dirt. She spits, and a slick thread glistens and stretches to the ground.

"Takin' a break," she says, spits again.

"Good idea," I say.

Luke won't leave us, but he has turned away, toward the amplified shouts and laughter of his friends. I scroll through Kayla's contacts. Under M, I find it, like I knew I would: Mama Cell. This is the right thing to do. A tired-sounding woman picks up on the third ring.

"Hey, Kay," she says around a mouthful of something. She sucks her teeth.

I pace, cup the phone. "Do you have any idea where your daughter is?"

The woman breathes in and out, jostles the phone around. "Hello?"

"I'm calling . . . in regard of Kayla," I say, suddenly nervous. "With regards to . . . ," I try.

"I'm sorry, what?" she says.

"Her *inebriation*—your daughter's. Are you aware that she's in danger, at the river?"

"Who is this?" she says, voice tight.

"She's been drinking."

"Kayla?" she says, fear creeping in.

"Yes! Your kid! She's drunk!"

"Who is this? Where's Kayla?"

"Kayla's safe," I say. "But where are *you*? That's my question."

"Hey," Luke says. "Who's on the phone?"

He's not mad yet, just confused. He's too scrawny to be menacing. He's taller than me, but who isn't?

"This was an almost-drowning," I rush on. "And you should be thanking me! Kayla, honey," I yell. "It's your mom."

"Ohhh," Kayla says, confused.

"Hey!" Luke says, his voice cracking.

"Fuck off, Luke," I whisper-scream. "Do you know Luke, Kayla's Mom? Do you know any of her friends?" Luke doesn't come closer. He looks at Kayla, then looks around for help.

"Put Kayla on! Who is this?" Kayla's mom is shouting.

"I'm a concerned citizen of the world," I say. I hold the phone out to Luke, then let it fall softly on the grass, a coward's mic drop. I throw Pete's towel in a heap and dip back into the river. Pete's watching, he's seen it all. "It's okay," I'm saying to him, though he's much too far away to hear. Heart knocking, I tromp through the stinging water, wet to my waist. I wade past all the drunk teenage heads, not that they notice me anyway. "Sometimes slow is the fastest way to get where you want to be," my cut-rate therapist says. The water gets deeper, to my tits and beyond. I dog-paddle to Pete, and he hooks his leg around me, keeps me from drifting. I slip into my same spot.

"What was all that?" he says.

"What?" I say.

I look back at the riverbank. Kayla's still on the phone, and Luke is shielding his eyes, staring out. They won't come after me. He's afraid—they both are.

"You were talking to those kids."

"Who?" I say. "No."

He tilts his head, blinks fast. "I'm sorry, what?" he says. "You were. You definitely were."

"I wasn't."

"You weren't," he says, his pitch rising. Both of us are looking at the shore now, Kayla and Luke looking back at us. "You weren't just talking to those two kids who are staring at you right now."

I wring water out of my hair. "Okay," I backtrack. "I was. They're drunk and stupid. Being disrespectful."

Pete puts his hand on his chest, cringes. "Yeah," he says, "but what did you *say*? Or did you—" he starts. "Did you *do* something?"

The water rushes again, so hot, and I reencounter myself, my circumstance. It *is* beautiful here—it's stunning and undeniable, and this generates a new kind of fury. Julie should see this river and the supernatural smattering of clouds that curve above us. She should be the one in this water, breathing this air. What I feel is bafflement, anger. I cannot fucking believe she's not here, that she's not anywhere.

"What could I have possibly done, Pete?" This comes out so tinged with hate it seems to shock both of us.

"I have no idea," he says, hurt. "That's why I'm asking."

I take a deep breath, reel myself back in. "I didn't *do* anything," I say like it's all a big joke. "*Obviously.* Shut up and enjoy your microbes and your river worms and your whatever-the-fucks."

Pete's not laughing. "Maybe we should go," he says. "It seems like you've . . . hit your limit."

"Whenever," I say. "No rush." Pete and I don't fight often, but when we do, this is our way—everything left unsaid. "Take your time."

Pete gives me a long look. He shakes his head and clears his throat.

I'm in a red place now—turns out, I can ruin anywhere. I want the underwater vents to go wild. I want real lava. Isn't that what this whole deal is getting at? *Shoot your shot, pussy,* I command the river. I want everyone to cook—meat falling clean off bones, all of these ridiculous, alive people. I would trade every last one of them for Julie. Even Pete. Even me—especially me.

BEHIND THE QUEERHUNTER bar is a pool of natural water, piped in from a hot spring. It looks like any other swimming pool, but the bartender sets us straight. The water is eighty-six degrees and rich with minerals. We walked all the way from the Boiling River, and it's like the same water has been following us, flowing under us this whole time. One wall of the bar is all window, and from where Pete and I sit with our drinks, we can see every kind of body bobbing around out there.

I haven't had a drink in so long, I'm tipsy after a few sips. I don't remember what the labels mean, but we're drinking whiskey, the best color they serve. Vacation seems like a time for rum, but Pete's choice tastes like moss and gasoline, delicious.

It's getting dark outside now, spotlights shining for the night swimmers. I stare at one bulb until it blinks and fritzes, a wink. *Hello again,* I think. Huge mountain moths gang up and flap around in the beams. Pete's a round ahead of me. I know him so well, I can tell he's drunk even before he can, how his vowels turn real Texas and his eyes go squinty. He's letting me stroke his perfect ears. It's dim in the bar and his hair is so shaggy I'm mostly working by feel, loving them from memory. We were wrong about this place—the bartender is certainly gay, attentive to both of us but focused on Pete, anticipating his needs, pouring him the boldest pours.

"By the time I'm home, my breast milk will be totally fine," I say, not that Pete asked. I'm feeling judged, though Pete isn't judging.

"Pumping and dumping is a myth," I tell him. "It takes hours for the alcohol to enter your supply." I tell Pete that actually, the perfect time to have a drink is at the precise moment you're breastfeeding, kid on your tit. I learned this from Yes, but I've never done it. My brand of maternal paranoia means Child Protective Services hovers around every corner, waiting to pounce, which is hilarious, considering all those long, motherless weekends Julie and I endured when we were small, not a whiff of government intervention anywhere.

"Gets you the biggest window. You can get a buzz, then sober up before the next feeding."

"It's like drinking and driving," Pete says. "Gotta drink while you're driving *to* the party." He mimes a steering wheel with one hand, holds up his whiskey in the other. His face changes and he drops the bit, looks down at the bar.

"Jesus," he says.

It's a kind of relief, that Julie's accident has rushed into Pete's mind too, like a fever I spread to him through the water. Does he also feel that she is somehow with us? Outside in the pool, caught in a light beam, in a bug or bird, or maybe that she's here, sitting inside some stranger down the bar.

"You're fine," I say, laughing. "It's funny."

"It's not," he groans.

I put my bad straw hat on his head. He poses in the gold-flecked mirror behind the rows of bottles. A song I usually hate comes on. The lyrics are as juvenile as the performer—*singer* is too generous a word—but this is a carefully manufactured hit, meant to infect. I sing along and it's the perfect soundtrack for this night, the smell of old beer all around. Even Pete sings. The last time we had this much fun was pre-Gilda, at the feminist strip club where all the girls have choppy bangs and glasses and tattoos. It was my birthday and Pete bankrolled me. We threw money—Brian's, I guess—onto the stage, and after each song the dancers would get on their knees and swoop their cash into this little trapdoor.

My need for a cigarette is never stronger than in the interval that follows my first drink. Pete would of course give me one of his, he'd buy me my own pack, but I'd feel too guilty, the Smoking Mom. Instead, we take not-so-secret drags of his vape, the generous bartender pretending not to notice the periodic bowing of our heads, how we exhale into the empty sleeve of Pete's jean jacket, which is vintage and cool looking even draped over his barstool. Vaping Mom—I can live with that.

It was such a good idea to come here, a perfect opportunity to get trashed in this very specific, Gilda-free circumstance. The video poker machines blink and flash next to me. One is called the Cherry Master and one is the Creator. I intone these names over and over in different voices. "They're like jewels in my mouf," I tell Pete.

If there's anything better than sitting in comfortable silence in a loud bar with your best friend, I don't know what it is. In the melting light, with the metallic clank of a pinball machine and bad music buzzing from bad speakers, being drunk feels a bit like being okay. If you squint, this could pass for a Meaningful Experience, no nature needed.

"Hey," Pete says then, and turns to me, speaking in a way that seems serious, the grain of his tone running counter to the room, the circumstance, the fun I'm finally allowing myself to have. Our yawning, adorable bartender replaces the soggy coasters under our drinks. Pete goes quiet until he moves on, down the bar and away from us.

"Can I say something?" Pete says.

I brace myself for more river accusations, or worse, a Brian discussion—these are not the conversations I want to have right now, but it's fine. I'm not so giddy I can't tilt back into sobriety if Pete needs me to. He says how important this trip has been, and I force myself to stick my head out of this warmth for a second. I hope we can get through this quick, that I can let him bitch, reassure him, then tug his hand to get us both back to this glorious sleeping bag of a feeling.

The bartender shakes the shaker over his head, strains a drink for another customer, smiles back at Pete. Pete looks at him with wet eyes, like he'd rather be on the other side of the bar. "Okay," I say then. I know what this is about. This can be a meat trip if Pete needs it to be. He can fuck Brian out of his system with this bartender tonight. I can call a car for myself, can go back to the hotel and take a bath, stream some porn, go to sleep early. This makes total sense, and I feel dumb for not realizing it sooner.

Pete pulls secretly at the secret vape, exhausts into the sleeve.

I'm wondering if he'll pay for the car back. I won't ask him to, but if I do it myself, I'll need to put it on a credit card. I'm trying to figure out which one to use, if it's better to do the one with lower interest that's almost maxed out or the one with more room but a shitty rate, when Pete says, "You looked *so* crazy today. You scared the shit out of those kids." He laughs a little, shakes his head. "They were like, who is this lunatic? You swam up on them like—" He mimes my terrifying dog paddle, the maniacal look on my face. "I love you, but you have to get yourself together. It's what Julie would have wanted. I'm sorry, but it's time."

He's officially wasted, that much is clear, and I try to take this into consideration before I reply.

"And it's time for you to go ahead and fuck all the way off," I say, like I'm kidding. What does Pete know about Julie, someone he never even met?

"Babe," he says, hand on my shoulder. "Jad won't just come out and say it, but I will. It's like you're not *you* lately. Listen." He touches his beard, looks away. "I wasn't supposed to say anything, but we thought this trip might help to—Jad thought it could be really impactful."

"You always tell me *impactful* isn't a word," I say, and then the gist of what he's said hits me, sinister and disarming, like when you see a clump of mystery hair blowing down the sidewalk. "Did you say 'Jad thought'? You talked to Jad?"

"Yeah!" Pete says. "Because you've been so *off* lately. We thought it could be really impactful—sorry, *meaningful*—to get you out of this spiral."

I'm in a spiral? "I'm confused," I say, not at all confused. I'm pissed.

"Jad told me about the panic attacks. And that dream last night? That was scary as hell. We've been really worried."

My god, have they been whispering on the phone? They haven't been in the same room in years—and I'm somehow so nuts I've brought the two of them together? Imagining the collusion and planning wrecks me. Were there secret texts? An email with statistics and serious links?

"I'm sorry my night terror was so traumatic for you," I say. "And that hasn't happened in years, by the way."

"Wait, are you mad?" Pete says. "Why are you mad?"

Betrayal is all about reconstructing the cleave: what you knew then versus what you know now. The idea that Jad and Pete could ever be a "we." The thought of the two of them putting aside a legacy of annoyance to scheme together. They've disrupted their lives, dropped everything for me.

"I didn't realize you two were in touch," I say. Something is catching in me, smoldering.

"I mean," Pete says, "we're really not. Just about you. You've said so yourself—you've been *so* weird. I didn't think you'd be mad?"

"You don't talk to anybody," Pete continues. "You're so up here." He points to his head. "All that interiority . . . it can affect your life."

My interiority is *my life,* I don't say, and this is as mad as I can get, so mad I am vibrating inches above myself. If I get any madder, I won't be able to fit back in my body.

"There's all these new medications—if medication is even the right thing. There are people who can help you," he says. He can't be serious. These Big Pharma pimps have gotten to him.

"I see a therapist," I say. "I'm being therapied."

The gracious bartender drops off a fresh round. When he reaches for my empty glass, I shake my head and say, "Leave it," like he's a dog trying to gobble a chicken bone off the street. He puts up both hands, smiles, backs away.

"No, yeah, totally," Pete says. "I wasn't sure if you liked him, but that's great. That's good to hear." There is pity in his face. "And he's pretty good?"

Only I can talk shit about my shitty therapist.

"He's actually *very* good," I say. "Just because I can afford him doesn't mean he's bad."

"Jesus." Pete laughs. "I didn't say that. Look, I just want to do everything I can to support you. Jad and I both do. We thought this trip might be a step in the right direction."

"I feel so misled," I say. "I thought all this was for you."

"Babe, of course it is," Pete says, but he won't make eye contact. I need a new best friend, somebody who knows nothing about me. "It's for both of us. Look, don't be mad. And don't tell Jad I said anything. He already hates me."

"He doesn't *hate* you," I say. Nobody can hate Pete. "But I won't say anything. And you'd better not either."

"I won't," he says. "I swear on Brian's life." He slurps his drink.

"Seriously," I say.

"Promise." Pete sweeps the lank curtain of hair out of my eyes, holds my hands in his, brings my fingers to his lips.

"You're so nasty," I say. "Fingers are the grossest thing to kiss."

I'm fine. It's fine. The body takes over. It tells Pete how grateful it is, how helpful this trip has been, how special.

Out in the dark, bighorn sheep walk straight up a mountain face. Buffalo curl up over hot spots in the ground, and moose—are there moose in Montana?—are out there hulking. Frothing and scabby, diseased—every one.

"I love you," the body is saying. It orders a shot of Jägermeister, because the body is so stupid. It's eating honey roasted peanuts from a little dish on the bar, to hell with the germs, the piss particulate and spray from drunken sneezes—the body thinks they're delicious: contaminated snack for the ages.

The body squeezes its best friend's hand. "This has all been tremendously helpful," it says.

Drinking: if you let it, it will grease up every strained moment.

The adorable bartender appears, again and again. He is maybe starting to regret being too nice to us, too loose with his pours, but then a guy comes in who is much worse off than we are. He can barely stand, won't let go of one tall table until he's touching the next. We watch him monkey-bar the room like that, staggering along until he's right beside me. Pete gives me a look like, *Do not engage.*

The drunk asks for a shot of menthol, which of course isn't a thing, and the charming, patient bartender tries to sort it out. "Do you mean crème de menthe? Or maybe peppermint schnapps?" he asks.

"Yes, for christsakes," the drunk says. "Peppermint schnapps. Two shots. A double. Two doubles. *Dos.*"

It's getting late—they've shut down the natural-pool part of the bar. Somebody opens a valve and the water seeps back into the ground, like draining a giant bathtub.

"From whence it came," Pete says. "From whence!" We watch the level lower until the swimmers are standing half out of the water, arms crossed and shivering.

"Be back," I say, and stumble as I get off the stool. Pete grabs my elbow to steady me.

Someone in scarlet lipstick has kissed the mirror in this revolting bathroom, over and over, her lust brightest at the center, fading with each new smack. It's not Julie. If these mouths were coral, maybe I'd know. This is not her color, not her small, thin mouth—frog lips, we used to call them. These kisses are lush, a full display—just the work of some drunk girl. I stand at the sink and take out my phone, take a picture of the wasted lips, me reflected behind them.

It's probably too late, but I text Yes.

Remember rug? I say. I shouldn't have to say anything else. It's been so long since we've talked about it, but I need her to come to it on her own. My fingers twitch. Maybe my memory of that night is out of scale. She's typing, but there's no message yet. What if it didn't matter as much to Yes, or worse, it didn't happen at all? Julie's gone. Big Large—Pablo—is gone in a milder way, moved to Waco, last I heard, but we lost touch a while ago.

My phone jumps with Yes's text. *Pinky!* she says. *Ruggggg*

This is precisely the correct response, such a relief.

I wanna buy one, I say.

Can't, Yes says, *only one Rug.*

I wish we were there, on that lustrous pink pelt, in the soft blur of that safe house.

How's Montana? she asks.

These motherfuckers, I say, and I unload about Pete and Jad and their collusion, tell her everything in a dozen typo-filled messages.

Can you believe they went behind my back?

She writes, *I can believe they really love you a lot.*

Infuriating.

Love you, I text. *Gotta go.*

I front-kick a stall door and it flies open, claps back, and slams in my face, my fault. I kick it again, gentler. The female half of a country song floats in from the jukebox, her male counterpart lost to my rushing piss. The woman sounds so much louder than her partner, but I know it's all perception.

I flush but stay on the toilet and call Jad. He answers before the first ring finishes, whispers, "Hey, you."

"Hi," I say, and my irritation dissolves at the sound of his sleepy voice, happy to hear from me. "I didn't wake her up, did I?"

"Nope," he says. "She's totally out. I'm watching a western."

"Good," I say. "Watch all the westerns while I'm gone. How is she?"

"She's fine. She went down easy."

This I find hard to believe.

"Does she even miss me?"

"Oh, man," Jad says. "What do you think? Where are you? It's loud. Is everything okay?"

"S'okay," I say. "Hiiiiii."

"Are you . . . ," Jad says. "You're drinking?"

"I may have been . . . ," I say. I try again. "I maybe might be currently being overserved. *Currently.*"

"Of course Pete gets you drunk," he says, but I can tell he's not mad.

"Nobody gets anybody anything," I say.

"Where are y'all?"

I say, "Can you hear the song that's playing?"

It's a singer Julie and I loved, a guy whose voice keeps getting deeper and deeper as he ages, as we aged, Julie and I, until she stopped and the singer and I kept going. There isn't love without obstacle, he sings, and I think, *I'm on the toilet and my husband's in Texas,* and this could be, should be, a new verse to this song.

"Watch this part," I say, which is something I always say about music when I'm listening, nothing to see. I want to grab Jad, jerk him through the phone. The violin swells around the chorus. Love is found in the difficult places—the bramble, the brush. Love is in the fuckup.

"This song's about me," I say.

Jad says, "You're not driving, right?"

"Nope," I say, and there it is, a tiny ember of rage, a reminder. "Just drinking."

I hang up then, don't even say our customary "Bye-bye," the way Gilda does when we've asked her to do something she doesn't want to do. "Can you please stop standing on the table?" I'll say, and she'll say, "Can you please go bye-bye so I can keep doing it? Bye-bye!"

Jad calls back and I tap him away. I sit and wait for a sign, something electric or animal, a wild stranger knocking on the door. I run my fingers over some promising graffiti—a cursive *Love* inside a heart, the phrase *Yr doing great*—they're so kind, Montana's toilet vandals.

DURING MY KETAMINE SEMESTER, I was still calling Julie almost every day. She told me she was having black thoughts, that she couldn't hold her stupid ren faire wine goblet without thinking about cracking off the base and stabbing the ragged stem into her thigh.

This was during a period of time when it seemed Julie was never not holding that goblet, never not drinking, never not wanting to stab herself a little and then tell me about it. This goblet thought, she assured me, was not altogether unpleasant. It wasn't even particularly dangerous, she said, more like the feeling you get when you see someone wearing hoop earrings, how for a second you flash on the idea of pulling metal—painlessly, you imagine—right through the soft lobes. A long golden hair coming out of a mole, a brimming whitehead on a stranger's cheek—it was better to soak in such thoughts, Julie said. Let them project like light across your face in a dark room. In your mind you could safely pull the hoop, tug the hair, pop the zit. The crack of the goblet, the shimmering end, the stem into the thigh—think it and let it be over. The sooner you gave in to the worst, the sooner the worst could do its work and be gone.

It had become impossible for Julie to split the thought from the wine itself, and so the two acts were twined—not negatively, she claimed—from the second she and Mom opened a bottle of wine. When Julie and Mom opened a bottle of wine, what they were doing was opening a box of wine, pulling a little foil sticker off a spout.

Hurry up, Julie would think, tugging at the plastic valve, before she'd even had the goblet thought. *Hurry up and have the thought.*

Then *I* started to have the thought of Julie having the thought. Afternoons, she and I drank on the phone together. I'd sip from a coffee mug in my dorm room, back turned to my first roommate—a mathlete from Wichita Falls who pretended not to listen to my conversations—or else I'd leave with a spiked Gatorade bottle, pace the flat, industrial campus: the library, the statue of a giant red jack, the viaduct. Julie drank on the screened-in porch with Mom, and the drunker she got, the harder it was to hear her, the connection between us fraying. I had to have the thought of Julie having the goblet thought. Then she'd have it for real and she'd admit that she'd had it and then she could be done with it and I could be done too, knowing her thighs were safe, that I could enjoy my drink wherever I was drinking it. Away from her.

"Do you have goblet thoughts?" she asked me once.

"I've had roof thoughts," I said. "Tall-building thoughts. It's human nature."

"Yeah, I bet everybody has roof thoughts," she said, satisfied.

I believed, still believe, Julie was the last person in the world who would hurt herself on purpose. The people you have to worry about are the ones who swear they've never had wrong thoughts. I believe she braced herself against that line of thinking so often, was so practiced, that her safety was reinforced. She never told anyone else about these thoughts. She never told Mom. Maybe I should have. She never told her tweaker boyfriend or the old, online men who would take her away for a weekend and then fall out of her life.

Other students came home on weekends to do laundry, but I'd make the five-hour drive to be sure Mom and Julie were eating, to sweep and mop as best I could in a house that never felt clean. This wasn't exactly hoarding—that came after Julie—but the kitchen sink was already mostly unfit for use, the dishes and rotting food and things that had nothing to do with a kitchen at all—antifreeze, hemorrhoid cream—beginning, even then, to pile up. Always an asshole, I'd narrate as I cleaned. "I'm mopping now," I shouted. "I'm wiping *black spatter* off the wall. Something *dead* is in the trash. This bathroom smells like *menstrual blood*. Like *pickles*." I'd get madder and madder the longer I worked, Julie and Mom ignoring me, drinking and smoking on the screened-in porch.

I was no angel. I'd bag up the trash, pour myself a huge glass, and sit between them. We'd scrape scratch-offs, watch strange cars drive up at all hours, Julie sprinting off the porch to lean into rolled-down windows, walking back to us with a goofy smile, saying, "What? That's just my friend," some gleeful radiance starlighting her worst decisions.

Mom had got on disability for her carpal tunnel—wrist grist, she called it—and she and Julie had teamed up and become awful together, their love intolerable. Julie forgave Mom for years of under-parenting, just like that—plus sick old people have the best prescriptions. The two of them had a gaping, wide-open secret. Julie didn't even put the tops back on the pill bottles Mom kept out on the stove, and Mom had access to everything: stuff to help her wake up, to sleep, for pain, for taking a shit. The two of them had always looked alike, and they'd started dressing in Mom's old scrubs, padding around in grippy hospital socks, patients in their own home. They had the same glasses and haircut. They spent every second they could out on the porch: Julie with that emotional support poodle at her side, Mom with her three fat lap cats—proto Friends. The two of them would smoke, play cards. Julie didn't sing anymore—she barely even listened to music. She stagnated.

"You're stagnating," I told her.

"How so?" she'd say, beading a necklace so long it ran down her lap, coiled on the floor.

I knew there was a real problem when Julie told me about the sigils, one night on the phone. She didn't call them sigils, though I'd later learn that's what they were, her skewed version. She called them wads.

"A wad is a wad," she explained.

Big Large had moved by then, and Yes was married with a kid. Julie'd started hanging around this group of druggy ghouls, dating the king tweaker from the town over. I'd met him once, at a field party years before, and I never liked him. He was a blond dyed black, and the part in his long hair seemed to get wider and creepier as the color grew out. He had a handgun he was always showing everybody, but it turned out he was also into astrology and angel cards. "He's well-rounded," Julie claimed. He was the one who taught her about wads: these small pieces of paper, places to fold up what you wanted.

"You can't just write the wish out in words, that's not how wads work," Julie went on one night. I was in my dorm room, about to go to sleep.

Wads were both more complicated and simpler than that, Julie insisted. You had to reduce a big wish down to a specific wish, and you had to make a symbol for your wish. She got that part right, but later I found out she was doing the rest all wrong. You're supposed to destroy a sigil, and the destruction releases the power, sends the request out into the universe. Some people burn or bury them, but Julie liked to keep her wads. She'd crumple them into hard little nuggets or roll them into tiny scrolls. She chewed them into balls of pulp and spit them out like kernels. She wanted fame and a fresh pack of cigarettes, she said. She wanted another fancy eight-channel mixer because the one King Tweaker gave her—stolen, I guessed—got left in the Buick with the windows open and the rain ruined it, right in the box.

Her jaw was always working at this point, wads or not, and she talked wetly into the phone.

"Let's say you want money," she said. "You can't write a dollar sign on a scrap and call it a day. You have to decide you want money on the double you're about to work. It has to be, like, based in the possible. It's witch shit, not magic! You think about upselling, right? Add some bacon to burgers, get a better tip. Bacon feels right—bringing home the bacon, you know? So get your bacon ideas together, fit a shape to them. Maybe you try like a frying-panny thing and it won't feel right. Maybe like a, like a, pig's snout? A circle with two circles inside—but nope, that's not it. A curly tail? No. When you find the real bacon shape, you know. You just know. It's three wavy lines—that's it. A slice of bacon." I could hear her breathing fast, scratching manic on a pad of paper.

"You squint and those wavy lines look like the dollar sign you've been after all along. Feels right! You can't fake it! Same thing with, like, a luxury good. If you want jewelry, you'd do the shape of a emerald or something. You do a . . . like a fucking, I don't know, whatever shape of emerald you want, however many sides it has. Do that shape. You can't fake out the wad. There's no shortcut. It's all gut, you know?"

"What the fuck are y'all doing out there?" I said. "Put Mom on the phone."

"What, you gonna tell on me?" she said, a bitter laugh. "She's right here—has been the whole time."

It was finals week, but I made the drive out to Wink anyway, where Julie's work pants were cinched around her waist and she was swimming in her apron. *Gaunt* was the word. *Grim.* She wrapped me in her bony grip and kissed both my cheeks, told me I looked beautiful, all the while her eyes darting, upcast, like she expected us to be hit by something falling. She said she was late for her shift and stepped off the porch, head bobbing like a chicken's.

Mom and I watched her drive away in the big Buick. "What the fuck are y'all doing out here?" My voice eerie calm, my mother put-

ting out her cigarette, gathering up her wine and watercolors, some
maniacal paint-by-numbers scene she was working on.

"You know I can't do nothing with that girl," Mom said to me on
the porch, in the hallway, backed into a corner of the kitchen, where I
thought about slapping her. "Y'all don't mind me. Never did."

Julie's wads were everywhere, in ashtrays or at the bottom of her
wine goblet or on whatever plate she'd been pretending to eat from,
but they were also on the coffee table and the arm of the couch,
flicked on the piano, tossed on the floor. They stuck to everybody's
bare feet: Julie's wet, pulpy wishes tracked all over. I tried to read
them—I wasn't sure if that was allowed but I did it anyway—and I
couldn't make sense of any of her shapes. Whatever she wanted was
warped, illegible and dissolved, turned to nothing in her mouth.

I LEAVE THE STALL, look again at the scarlet lip prints while I scald
my hands. Nothing keeps happening—Julie's not coming. They make
me sick, these lips, how dewy and alive they are, how they're layered
all over my reflected face and neck, no escape. I retch into the sink,
but it's dry, no relief.

Don't let anybody see the full picture. Break yourself into pieces,
scatter the loss over time and space. Divide your heartache. Sure,
death is one thing people will let you open your jaws and scream
about for a while, especially when someone dies young—it isn't fair,
I'll never get over it, etc.—but what nobody admits is how incredibly dull grief is to witness. It's boring, like hearing about somebody's
toothache, all-consuming but completely personal, nontransferable.
Shut up about your sorrow—take that grief and tamp it down. The
people who love you need you to hurry and clean yourself up, blow
your nose and fix your hair, come back from the brink.

I lurch to the door and my foot knocks a squatty metal waste bin
in the corner, which seems alive somehow, and innocent, pleading
with me. I kick the shit out of it. Soaked cotton goes flying, rank and

tangy, old blood and older blood, new blood too. I stomp and stomp, and it's harder than you might imagine to warp the lid, to dent and crush the small body, but that's exactly what I do.

I front-kick the bathroom door open SWAT-style, but nobody is around to notice my dramatic exit. I tilt through the bar and crash-land into my seat, knocking Pete's knee. He's got his shoe off, foot up on a stool. The bartender works on something with Chartreuse while Pete talks about the Boiling River, how special it was, and about the blisters he got from hiking in his new boots.

"My heels are like bubble wrap," he says, feeling around in his sock.

"Oh, no," the bartender is saying, smiling at Pete. "Ouch."

"Worth it," Pete says, crunching his ice. "She's back," he says to me, holds his drink in the air. He's shouting a little.

"I did some violence in the bathroom," I say, while at the same time Pete says, "Don't you feel energized?"

We take a second to pull apart our overlapping speech. "Gross," Pete says, laughing.

"Small violence," I say.

"Yeah, I get it," Pete says, not getting it. "Disgusting. But don't you feel revitigized?" He's trashed.

I don't want to be a downer, so I say, "I do. Really. Literally yes." I tuck into the fresh new drink.

The minty drunk is still close to us. To outshine Pete's blistered feet, this guy is telling the bartender about his nasty job, something to do with manufacturing these little valves and plugs and everythings that go up inside people's bodies, all of them resistant to bacteria. He says Pete's word then, *biofilm,* which is apparently not only in rivers but also on medical devices, in bloodstreams, anywhere wet and secret. I run my hands over my arms. Biofilm—the slime of it, we've brought it into the bar with us. What are the chances of this word, this gunk, showing up again so soon? Before I let this overwhelm me, the drunk's on to the next thing, telling the bartender about all the cars of his life, the ones he's refurbished or wrecked or gotten rid of. "Classics, art on wheels," he says. He lost some to rust, one in a divorce. He has an SUV now, no style at all, no time in his schedule or space in his garage to tinker.

"Kids. Car seats and so on. The boy does lacrosse, so there you go. Daughter's orchestra. She picked the double bass. It was cute when she was small for it, but now it's a pain. We have to belt it in the back seat."

"Tomorrow, we're healed," Pete is saying, but I'm compelled by the drunk's mention of an instrument. I want to linger on a little girl's hands choking out notes, but the drunk zooms to another car from his past, a gunmetal MGB. He tells the bartender about the night he drove it from Twin Falls to Reno, top down the whole time, how he hit a deer out in the desert. "It just burst," the drunk says. His nose is running, and he keeps taking long swipes at it with the side of his hand. "It detonated-ed." The drunk says he had to check into his fancy hotel with blood and fur all over his suit.

Pete is saying how happy we feel. He's so proud of himself, relieved to have done his duty, completed the task of fixing me. He is drunk, refreshed, renewed. Revitigized. Positive about the future, finally, about the rest of our lives. He's going to fall in love again. He's going to write a play about a guy who falls in love again.

I'm trying to split apart so I can listen to Pete but still hear the drunk, too.

Pete says in the Boiling River he came out of his body, ascended. "Did it happen to you too? I was above," he says, "looking down."

"Blood and fur!" the drunk is saying to the bartender. "Fur and blood!"

One of these plots is more meaningful to me. I can't help it.

I turn to the drunk. "Where do you feel this story you're telling?" I ask him. I'm having trouble staying steady on my stool.

"What?" he says. "What?" The drunk gives me a dark look. I've interrupted him.

"About the deer. Where do you feel it in your body?"

"On my suit," he says, annoyed. "All over it."

Pete puts a hand on my forearm. *Do not engage.*

The drunk glares at me and wipes spit from his chin. I've crossed some line. He looks down at his rumpled shirtfront like I've doused him with something. He's incensed. He stands, tips back his head. He opens his arms wide to show me what I've done.

ASTRONOMICALLY HUNGOVER ON the plane ride home, Pete and I sit behind a funeral director and a pilot in training, strangers to each other. I can't believe our good fortune, this caliber of eavesdroppable material.

"Put this in your play," I say, but Pete shushes me, says his brain is throbbing. I listen as the baby pilot tells the undertaker that airplanes are all about redundancy.

"Two engines," he says. "Two wings . . ." He trails off. *What else?* I think. Two instances of two does not a pattern make.

Pete roots around in his carry-on. "Did I show you this?" he says. He unfolds a silk scarf and spreads it on his lap. "Brian's," he says. "Mine now." He shows me the label, a brand I've never heard of.

"Is that supposed to mean something to me?" I say. Rich people and their coded worlds.

"Guess not," he says, stroking the thing.

"Why don't you just tell me how much it cost if you want me to know?"

"Forget it," he says, letting my dig roll off him. He pulls down his sleep mask, puts his head on my shoulder.

Headphones on, I listen to an old shoegaze record, sour and hypermelodic. My head is fine, but I'm nauseous, the airsick bag open in my lap. I pinch the webbing between my finger and thumb, a trick Jad taught me. I look out the window and wonder if I'll know when we're flying over home. I want solid lines between states, clear indicators.

Sometimes I hate where I'm from, but the shape of Texas on a map—
I can't explain it—it chokes me up.

Pete and I split a ride from the airport. "What do you got going
on today?" I ask.

"Sleep," he says. "Eggs and a Bloody Mary later."

"Fuck your brunch life," I say, and he knows I'm not quite kidding.

The car drops Pete off first and we kiss goodbye. We're only three
highway exits apart, but weeks could pass before we see each other
again. I'm back on planet Gilda.

It's her nap time, so Jad and I orchestrate my arrival, text back and
forth as I get closer in the car.

I take my shoes off on the stoop. Jad clicks the door open, sound-
lessly shoulders my hot-green bag. We look at each other and I feel
exposed, judged, mad at him all over again. But he looks tired, beat to
shit by Gilda, and I swallow my irritation down.

I fall into him, a rare real hug. He whispers everything I need to
know: that she is asleep, that we have a half hour of freedom. He walks
his fingers across his palm, relays tactical information. The plan is
the living room couch, a quickie, maybe a conversation. I'm bending
down to peel off my socks when Gilda wails from the bedroom.

"Fuck me," Jad whispers. "It's like she can smell you."

Of course Gilda can smell me. Little Gildimal, Gildabear. My
nipples tingle at the sound of her—classic mammal. The alcohol—it's
bound to be out of my system by now. I rush to give her a quick squirt
of good-good, erase some of the guilt.

Part Five

CELADON

I GO TO THERAPY AND LIE ABOUT BEING REFRESHED AND revitalized.

I'm in my sliding-scale therapist's office, on his big brown sofa, not telling him about the grocery store. I'm also not telling him about Pete and Jad's betrayal, the drunken Tampax massacre, Kayla and Kayla's mom, the Living Coral woman, the Water Witch. I'm telling him how relaxing Montana was, how meaningful to be in nature.

"Fantastic," he says. "I'm pleased to hear it."

He looks pleased, proud of me, so much so that I feel guilty and tell him a true enough story about my morning. It's revised and edited, condensed a bit, but the beats and themes are real.

"Gilda woke up at four a.m. to use the bathroom," I tell him. "I should have been happy because she's still getting the hang of potty training, especially overnight. But four is crazy, and once she's awake, she's awake. I was a little frustrated."

It was so much worse than that.

She flushed the toilet over and over. "I'm flushing!" she shrieked, then bounded back to bed, full volume. "I flushed!"

"Baby?" I said. "The sun is still sleeping."

Jad was a useless faker, a pillow over his face.

"If you ever miss your Animalmash buddies, you can still wear Pull-Ups at night," I'll sometimes try, reminding her about the deranged gang of cartoon hybrids printed on the ass of her former diapers. "So you don't have to get up to use the potty? That would be okay with me."

"Not okay," she says, shaking her head. "Because I wear undies now, because I'm big." The hype I've used on her for months—she throws it right back in my face.

I don't tell my sliding-scale therapist any of that, or that I fumed in bed until five, refusing to begin my day before then, though my day had obviously already begun. I let Gilda nurse—if only to keep her still—but even that didn't last long.

"I need mouth food, not good-good," she said, as though her mouth had nothing at all to do with the milk. "Is it wake-up time?" she asked. She pulled up my eyelids, poked my cheeks. "Are you awake yet?"

"Nobody likes that," I said.

"I'm hungry! My stomach hurts!" she said—pain gets a response every time, she knows this—until finally a super-pissed Jad bounded out of bed and said, "Come on, bud, I'll take you." He didn't say anything to me—though stating aloud that he would take Gilda was certainly *for* me—but it seemed we both felt, no, we knew, this was a responsibility I was shirking. This was confirmed when moments later, before they'd even reached the end of the hall, Gilda broke free from him and said, "Noooo, Mom is the one. I want Mommy to do it!" and she ran back to me and screeched in my ear, "Mommy, come!" In quiet fury, the only kind I'm allowed to have in my own home, I threw back the covers while Gilda screamed gleefully, "Yes! Pick meee!" I hobbled down the hall with her on my hip and I didn't say, *Fuck this fucking bullshit life,* but I sure thought it. Jad sidestepped us in the hall on his way to take one of his famous half-hour shits, and it was plain that I was living my destiny, that order had been restored. Mommy was home.

I don't say any of this to my beleaguered, barely paid therapist, but when he looks at me kindly with his greenish, brownish, bluish eyes—pig-shit eyes, my mother calls this type, a little bit of everything mixed in—I try something new.

"Say more about that," he says when I make the shaky transition from talking about my lack of sleep to the hypothetical weight that certain objects, words, *colors,* seem to have in my life—in *one's* life, hypothetically. It's the same tone I used to take in school, trembling at the back of some lecture hall, my embarrassing preamble. *Sorry. Not that I'm asking this, but if I were going to?* I'd say. *Possibly, if I were to about to say something—not that I am!—my question might possibly sound like this? Does that make sense?*

"You mean déjà vu?" he says. He's small and tidy in his button-down shirt—it's French-tucked to look casual but I'm certain he labored over it. I'm wearing my therapy dress: black, sleeveless, a poly blend that doesn't wrinkle, that looks better than it feels. I haven't dry cleaned it in a while, but it only ever comes here, to sit on this couch with me once a week.

"Not exactly?" I say. I cock my head, fake a yawn. "Sort of, though?"

"Déjà vu is healthy. It's how the brain fact-checks information. It makes sense that you might get that feeling more when you haven't slept well. Was there a particular experience you wanted to discuss? Have you had déjà vu today?"

"No," I say. "Not today." I listen to the forced air coming through the vents. "Or what is it when it's more, like, repetition?" I say, careful. "Like you learn a word and then the word is everywhere? I'm just curious," I say. So curious!

"Could you give me an example?" he says, stirring cream into his coffee. Steam rises from the slick white surface.

"Biofilm," I blurt, thinking of the Boiling River, its slime. Biofilm is safe, it's not a Julie-item, though it is, perhaps, Julie-item adjacent.

"Biofilm," he says, and then he says nothing, giving me space to slowly explain the cauldron of nutrients Pete and I simmered in, this new term arriving twice in one day, with two separate contexts.

"Isn't that a little unusual?" I say. "Within hours." I fake another yawn but it's overdone, more like I'm cupping my hand over my mouth to keep from puking.

My affordable therapist is not alarmed. "Ah," he says, "you're talking about the reticular activating system."

"Reticular," I say.

"Activating system. It's here," he says, turning his head and tapping where his close-cropped hair meets the back of his neck. "You learn about something and it seems to keep coming up. Say I discover Tuvan throat singers—my husband and I watched a documentary last night—when next I hear the term, there can be the sensation of linkage."

"The *sensation* of linkage or linkage?"

"Sensation, I suppose. It's not that there are more throat singers. Only now—"

"The world seems choked with them," I say.

"Funny," he says.

"Yeah," I say.

We don't smile. He puts down his coffee mug, turns the handle until he's satisfied. I touch the place on the back of my head where I suspect my reticular activating system lives, under a knot in my hair. "Should I be writing this down? Reticular . . ."

"Activating system," my sliding-scale therapist says. "RAS. You can remember RAS." He gets up, goes to the watercooler, glugs out a glass. He splits our sessions between coffee and water. He always offers me both, but I feel I should leave the perks for his real patients. I know once we've gotten to water, the end is near. Jad and Gilda are probably circling the block now, waiting for me to be finished.

"Maybe that'll be my next one," I say. "Instead of biofilm, it'll be RAS. I wonder if that's ever been anybody's? That'd be funny." My voice is too loud in the room, the knot in my hair is two knots, fused. I'm running my fingers through and through, between them. I try to ground myself.

"I'm listening," he says, his back to me.

"I've got to make self-care a priority," I say. My sliding-scale therapist, like the rest of the world, is very big on self-care. "That's what this trip showed me. Maybe more exercise."

"You mean besides running?" he says. "You're still training, yes?"

"Oh," I say. "Yeah."

"Could be good, so long as you don't overdo it," he says. "Yoga? Something low-impact. Mind your joints."

"Right," I say. "Maybe outside. Being in nature was really beneficial to me. Seeing animals. That sort of thing."

He sits back down. I want to tell him how Julie is everywhere, that since I don't know where to find her, she's boundless. She's out of order, young and grown. Montana has unleashed a thousand Julies, a bunch of different hairstyles and heights, gaps in her teeth. She is the newborn my mom won't let me hold, she is a screaming silhouette onstage in a dirty little club, she is moonfaced, wine-soaked, cranked out of her mind.

Instead, I go ahead with a safe version of the trip—the bighorn sheep and the wildflowers, a version where Pete and I bonded, where I paid attention and listened and was a good friend. I don't lose it, don't unreel—I'm never in danger of unreeling here, in my sliding-scale therapist's office. This is the last place I'd unreel.

"All sounds good," he says. "Beneficial." But he's distracted, turning something over in his mind. He closes his eyes and tilts his head, consults whatever odd internal clock therapists have.

"I wanted to stop early today if we might, because I need to speak with you about something," he says. He adjusts the cuffs of his beautiful shirt, sits up straighter. "Probably best that I be direct," he says. I've said too much weird stuff, exposed myself. Biofilm! It was a bridge too far.

But my pretty-okay therapist smiles, and it's his real smile, not his tight professional one. "We've made tremendous progress," he says. "Which is to say, *you've* made tremendous progress. To see you staying in your body, to watch you become so seeded and sighted."

Maybe he says "seated and sided." I can't know.

"I believe we've reached the end of our experience," he says, like this is a roller-coaster ride or a haunted house.

I blink at him, pin the words to their meaning. His face throws me off, how open and honest, friendly. He's just a guy talking to me, finally.

"I'm in a position to give back to the community," he says, "and I love being able to do that. But I can only do so much, and I'd like to open a slot for others, people more in need."

"You're breaking up with me," I say, and my tone is perfect, like this is hilarious. I think of all the batshit things I could say to make him keep me.

He smiles again, a real smile. "I'm needed elsewhere," he says. "I've inseminated you with—"

"It's not me, it's you," I deadpan.

"It's neither of us!" he says, toothy and fond of me. I look at the frame on his desk for the last time, a shot of him beaming next to his husband, the two of them life-jacketed in a boat. My shit-for-brains therapist is only real in the photograph, he's left the room.

"We've come to the end of all time," he says, though surely that's wrong—he must have said, "We've come to the end of *our* time," which is what he always says when we've finished a session.

"This has all been so great," I say. "Tremendously helpful. Truly." I'm still working at the knot in my hair, but it's getting tighter, closer to the scalp.

"You've met every milestone," he says, looking at his notebook, flipping back over our months. I know it's all for show. A prop. His grocery lists, doodles.

"Well, you're very good at this," I say. "At your job."

"I appreciate that," he says. I tug the knot out by the roots—I can hear the rip—and then I roll the rat between my fingers, secretly slide it down between his couch cushions. If I were alone in this room, I would hold it up to the light, put it in my mouth.

My ex-therapist stands, waits for me to stand too. He waits for me to gather my tote bag, to feel around in there for the car keys, to realize I don't have or need them because Jad dropped me off. He herds me toward the door and puts out his hand. This is brand-new, something he's never done. We shake, and it's the first time I've touched him, or maybe not, maybe we shook when we met, but if we did I don't remember. His hand is tiny and hot and dry, his grasp firm. Normally he's delicate, asking me about every action before he does it—it's a bit drafty, how would I feel if he sat at his desk instead of on the chair in front of me? Would I mind if he sucked on a mint or tilted the blinds a bit?—but now he pats me on the shoulder with his other hand, steps close to me.

"It's been wonderful seeing how far you've come," he says. "Grief is never easy, but you've met the challenge with aplomb. I wish you all the best." He says that—*aplomb*. The finality of his message is not up for discussion. He's done with me.

"Have a nice life," I say, and this makes him crack, a little snort as the mask fully slips, character broken. It's the best reward ever, making a therapist lose it, the loftiest, truest goal, better even than making a hot stranger laugh. We're friends now, one completely normal person and another completely normal person. This is what I've been working toward all this time, this exact feeling, all these months of lies leading me here. I won therapy. I can't wait to text Pete and tell him. Then I remember he's on the wrong side of history, an enemy who will only misinterpret my dazzling triumph.

"Tremendously," I say, backing out of the room. "Truly."

Jad's in our car in the parking lot, Gilda strapped in the back. This is his lunch hour he's sacrificing, every week when I have therapy it's this complicated rigamarole, balancing transportation and childcare, setting Gilda up with snacks and entertainment. Today she's got a yogurt cup, puffy unicorn stickers, and construction paper—"one slice of pink paper, please," she said. All of this to distract her from our small separation.

When I get in the car, Gilda is loudly singing the song I loathe about the finger family, each member more annoying than the last—daddy finger and mommy finger, this disgusting family fist—and I tell Jad what's going on, that I've had my last session.

"So what happens now?" he asks. I could confront him about the trip, start a big fight, tell him everything. I don't.

"Nothing happens," I say to his worried face. "That's it. I'm graduated. Finished. Solved, whatever. I'm cured."

THERE'S A COMMOTION at the playground gate. Some amateur wheels a wagon onto the grounds and all the kids dogpile it. I watch the other parents. Let one of them solve it, somebody else make a move.

"Something to make our lives difficult," Celadon says.

She's appeared next to me like a miracle, same time of day, same bench where we first met. I'm so happy to see her, and I want to tell her about Montana, how pissed I am at everyone. Instead, I see her dangling green charm and let my eyes close for a beat, think about the things she's been doing to me in my mind. I've conjured her. She glares at the wagon, the chaos it's causing.

"Exactly," I say. I want to put my palm on her chest, feel her heart pump. She's wearing a calico dress the color of a fresh bruise, billowing linen with big front pockets, hem so long it drags the ground. She's got sandals with a black leather strap across the toes, her feet filthy, but the toenails painted opalescent, crustacean colored. She could be wandering in the desert or coming up from dark water in that dress, a glory. I'm embarrassed to be back in my marlin-assed overalls.

A boy a little older than Gilda is up to no good at the fence. "Absolutely not!" his mother cries. She marches him to the bench where Celadon and I are sitting. The mom doesn't look at me, but she frowns at Celadon.

"Stay here," she says to her son. She strides out of the park.

"What'd you do?" Celadon asks.

"I kicked Simon's ball away from Simon!" the boy says, exuberant, swinging his feet. "I kicked it over the fence and out of the world!"

"Ah," Celadon says. "Nice one." She zips her charm back and forth along her chain.

"I'm real bad," he says.

His mother comes back into the playground with the ball. She glares at Celadon now, grabs her kid by the wrist. "We have to apologize," she says to him.

Like all the other kids, Simon has been sucked into the wagon situation, his ball forgotten. But this woman has tipped into a teaching moment, real anger in her jaw.

What I'm thinking, and what I suspect Celadon is thinking, is this: rage can be a gift. Public loss of control, whether from a child or a caregiver, is a magical thing to behold. I try to remember this myself, when Gilda is thrashing on the floor at the grocery store while some other mother points at produce, saying, "'A' is for asparagus!" to the child she's got strapped in her cart. Gilda's jerking seizure is a public service, her insane tantrum making the asparagus kid angelic by comparison. Asparagus Mom can file this feeling of superiority away, can recall it later, when her precious angel is thwacking his feet on the seat of the passenger in front of them on a transatlantic flight.

Right now, Gilda is well-behaved, smiling shyly at the wagon kids, and the bad boy's mom is doing the mirroring thing every parent has to do, big frowny face, education through exaggeration. "IT MAKES MOMMY SO SAD WHEN YOU ARE NOT KIND TO OTHERS," she's saying, infecting herself with overblown emotion. They say smiling for no reason makes you happy—the opposite must be true. When Gilda goes limp and won't let me put socks on her feet, I dredge up all sorts of overwhelming disapproval. *Who cares?* my brain is thinking underneath my furious face. *It's fucking socks.*

The inverse of this works too: you can inject performative joy right into your veins. "YOU MAKE MOMMY SO HAPPY WHEN YOU

EAT ALL YOUR OATMEAL" was something I said just this morning, ecstatic.

Celadon leans back on her hands, knocks her shoulder into mine, and says, "These motherfuckers are mad for that wagon."

It's her prim accent that gets me. My real laugh is a loud, low gulp, air sucking in.

She stands again, and the fabric of her dress is so voluminous, I wonder if she's sweaty under there. Something about how the dress fits—or rather how it doesn't, how it absolutely swallows her—gets to me. I'm doing the glance-don't-stare, taking a sip of my coffee with my eyes lowered, looking up through my lashes, which lately Gilda has been trying to pull out, now that I've taught her about wishes.

"Ow!" I say, swatting her little hand away. "Even if it worked like that—which it doesn't—it would be my wish to make, not yours!"

Gilda moves toward the throng. The wagon bringer realizes her error, looks helplessly at the children clawing their way into the bed, tumbling out the sides. "This is not for sharing," the woman says to the swarm.

"Is she going to handle this?" Celadon says. "Should we—?"

"Probably," I say, standing up too.

"No thank you, Gilda," I shout, careful to keep a kind lilt in my voice. Celadon and I clap our hands, loud startling cracks, the way you'd scatter raccoons eating trash. A mother who cares more than we do goes over and speaks to the wagon bringer. Together, they manage to extricate the thing, to flip it over and push it under a park bench. The children lose interest, disperse to their different corners. Some maul a nanny waving a bubble wand. Celadon and I sit again.

The muggy breeze picks up her hair and it streaks across her face. There is the smell of old cigarettes and something else. A familiar solvent, a spent firework. I want to pull her into my lungs. I've paid less attention to people I've fucked.

"Which one's yours?" she asks, looking out at the children.

She has a tattoo on the web between her thumb and forefinger. It looks homemade, a stick-poke, and the ink has seeped and bled. An ankh maybe, a cross. It's neat, something I can maybe ask her about later. I'm already thinking about a later, a point in time beyond this playground. At her house on her stylish couch, a glass of red wine in her hand, the view of the looping highways, the low concrete buildings behind her. Our kids: nowhere.

"I've got five," she says, and yawns. I'm so focused on the tattoo, I think she's read my mind, that she means she has five of them. But no, my god, she means children. "No idea where they are," she says, gesturing to the park.

Five! This is crushing. Must all my favorite women have so many kids? In order to see Celadon I would have to be around *six* children. I dash the thought of a playdate. I look at the crowd and wonder which little ones are hers.

"All boys," she adds.

Oh, hell no. Empathy kicks in. This must have been some mistake. My grandma Emma—maternal side, we called her Gummy—had twelve kids. Why so many? "Didn't ask for any of them," Gummy told us. "But I was beautifully blessed by god each time." I doubt Celadon has been beautifully blessed. Maybe her husband has a weird, malformed dick and the condoms keep breaking, or the pill makes her puke her guts out, or she's been cursed with quintuplets.

"You?" she asks.

My blood rushes at the thought of five screaming mouths, all the tiny teeth, so many needs. I let the space between Celadon's question and my answer grow and skew. There's a horrible thrill in between my breaths—not panic, not at all.

What if I'm not me? What if the exhaustion I feel is from staying up last night, shouting and smoking, dancing in a dark bar? What if this morning I woke up alone in my studio apartment, played back a bleary recording of a wine-soaked half song, not half bad? There's an exposed brick wall in my mind, a secondhand velvet couch. Water taps into a slop sink, keeping time, and on a chipped countertop there's a stack of my sticky, unwashed cereal bowls, no urgency to clean my own mess. The scooped-out feeling I have isn't from dealing with Gilda's bottomless need, it's from sitting on the floor too long with a guitar in my lap, the kink in my neck from listening, tilting one ear to the hollow body. What if this is my life: watching sunlight pour through the cracked shade, creep across hardwood, drain and fade and come again the next day.

"Oh, I'm not a mom," I say, and this pours out in a dark rush, too easy.

"Oh!" she says, "Sorry, I thought—"

"No, yeah. I mean, I know how it seems."

Just like that, I counteract Celadon's many babies. I undo Gilda and Jad, my marriage, motherhood.

"I'm babysitting," I say, so casual. I'm doubling down. Tripling. "That little girl in the leotard?" I say. "She's almost four."

I haven't eliminated Gilda—I've only reassigned her. With no reason not to trust me, Celadon accepts this fact. She nods and says, "She's darling."

"My niece," I say. There's a ripple of guilt, my true purpose stated aloud. "My sister's kid. Her husband works a lot and she's a little bit . . . unfit." I'm not a monster—there's Jad, back on the scene.

"Oh, that's hard," Celadon says. She touches her namesake charm and it catches the light, sends sparks across her chest.

"Hospitalized," I say in a low voice, all in.

"That's *so* hard. But so lovely that you can help them."

I watch the delicate throb of her throat as she swallows. Gilda waves to me.

"Such black hair!" Celadon says.

"Yeah," I say, automatically touching the fine down at the nape of my neck. "She takes after her dad."

Usually this type of talk makes me bristle. "Actually, we look alike in pictures," I'll tell people. "The nose, for example, not the shape of it, but the proportions? The way it connects to the mouth? What's the word for it? A flume? That flume is all me."

But Celadon's observation doesn't faze Julie. "My sister got her ass kicked in the Punnett square," I say, precisely the type of dorky joke Julie would make.

"And the dad is from . . ." Celadon trails off.

"Turkey," I say. "I mean, he's not. He's Turkish. His family."

This is another question that usually irritates me. "And where is it you're from?" is how people phrase it. "From here," Jad will say. "I'm from right here."

"Well, she's gorgeous," Celadon says, and I look at Gilda fresh, like someone seeing her for the first time.

The fact that I've made myself crazy—unfit!—has nothing on this new, hot rush of the divine: in the smallest, stupidest way, I've brought Julie back.

"And you're reading . . . ," she says, looking at the book in my lap.

"Oh, I'm learning on the job," I say. "A parenting book." I flash the cover. "Free-range stuff."

"For or against?" she says.

"Oh, for," I say. "Definitely for."

"That's the right answer," she says, and there's my real laugh again, a honk.

"My sister does the no-range thing," I say. "The stick-to-me method. But I'm not sure it's the best thing." My phone buzzes with a call and I glance at the screen. "Her husband," I say, sending Jad to voicemail.

"You want to take it?" Celadon asks.

"Definitely not," I say. "He's always checking up on me. To be fair, I haven't been doing that great so far. With the parenting. Hard enough to even find time to read the book."

"Well," she says. "Not only have I got one book today, I've two. Ridiculous."

She reaches into her bag, pulls her hand out fast. "Oh," she says, like she's been bitten. "I've brought the wrong one." She shows me—inside the tote bag it's just more tote bags. I've made a similar move before, left the house in a daze, grabbed something useless as I ran out the door. Her brain must be absolute mash with all those kids to look after.

She sniffs, puts the bag of bags between her feet. "I can tell you what your book says," she says. "It says watching them every second doesn't keep them safe, so you might as well let them run."

"She's with me constantly," I say. "Because of the . . . situation with my sister. I want her to have stability, obviously with . . ." I make a fluttery gesture to indicate how crazy everything is in my life, in *Kit's* life. "But this is way too hard," I say, not a lie. "I need to move from attachment to something else."

"You want to *de*tach," Celadon says.

"I do," I say.

"Check out benevolent neglect," she says. "It's a method that could be very valuable for your niece. Another one is dignity of risk. You have to let them make mistakes. These are all teachings from the School of Drift," she says.

"Drift," I say. I take out my pen and click it, jot the terms in the back of the free-range book. "And you're reading . . . ," I say, glancing at her lap.

"Oh, something pretend," she says. "A prop." She flips her book over so I can't see the cover, slides it under her thigh.

A teenage girl is trapped at the gate, clanking around, yelling into her phone. "I'm like *right here,*" she's saying. "I came from the wrong side." Getting into Hidden Wonder makes perfect sense, but something about the latch is so simple that people struggle to get out.

"You have to—" Celadon says, and she mimes huge lifting, curving gestures, an exaggerated version of how to get free. The girl glances coldly at her, whispers into her phone.

Gilda screams, her voice outshining everything. I shield my eyes and see she's stuck on the monkey bars, dangling.

"Hold on. I should—" I say, and jump up, break into a trot.

Rescuing Gilda is easy—unnecessary, really, she could have just dropped. Now I'm trapped, stuck while she shows me trick after underwhelming trick. "Nice," I say. "Nice one." Detachment—how to begin?

My mother once told me her memory care patients hated being spoon-fed most of all, even more than getting shots or enemas. She told me how stressful it was for them.

"But why are they like that?" I'd asked. "You're trying to help."

"Their brains are all tangled with plaque," she said, but I couldn't leave it alone.

Did they forget they were hungry? Was the rising spoon scary? Did they think the sudden food was some mean trick their mouth was playing?

"It irritates them," she snapped, irritated with me. Maybe the patients wanted some small feeling of control.

When you are little and you can't do something simple the grown-ups can do—use a key in a door, pour the milk—you realize how contained you are, how trapped.

"Me do it," Gilda used to say in her high chair, wrenching the spoon from me.

"I'm going back to sit on the bench now," I say to her, firm.

"Okay," she says, and takes a happy leap to the ground. I wait for backlash but there isn't any. Progress! I want to joke with Celadon, tell her how just hearing her terms has helped me, *helped my niece*, but back at the bench her things are gone and she's gone too, slipped away again.

PIVOT WANTS ITS pedestrians to die. The walk-signal buttons don't work, the sidewalks are skinny or broken or they disappear into wide, busy roadways. I have to skitter along next to traffic, be prepared to dart across a street because nobody will stop for me. It's so hot out it's absurd, Montana's flowers a distant golden dream. The Toads were doing the beam when I left, so there's still the froggy hop and the rest of it.

Pivot's a connector, an artery between actual cities. It's six-lane highways, fast food, and hot concrete. Whole blocks seem to get razed and rebuilt from scratch for no reason. One strip mall is replaced with a newer, uglier strip mall, different stores all selling the same things. Maybe it's because I'm without Gilda, or because I'm barefoot, holding my sandals in one hand, but men in cars keep honking at me, truckers leering, all of them looking like they want to drag me into some venereal web. Lately I'd been thinking it was too hot to gawk, or that the city had changed, classed up, but no.

The Burger Crown and Pivot Baptist share a font and the same imitation-stucco façade. The church's marquee is empty and unlocked, a pile of letters on the yellow grass. What an opportunity! I hope some teens find this and go to town. The drive-thru is backed up; the tail end of it pokes into the church parking lot. I haven't eaten there in years, but I always appreciate the particular aromatic discharge of a Burger Crown. *Flame-broiled-savior, flame-broiled savior,* my feet slap as I walk past. Sometimes you've got to let your toes breathe.

When Julie was thirteen and I was fifteen, Mom made us go to the megachurch in Odessa. We hated everything about that place except for the live music, a rock band called the Revelations. The bassist was amazing, but the greasy front man kept blocking the view, bleating soullessly, flashing his televangelist teeth.

During the service, Julie stared down at her open palm like there was a scandal unfolding on it, interesting and deeply personal. There were so many people, a zillion cars baking in the parking lot outside, so much hair spray choking the air, so much offbeat clapping. Because we were new to the church or because Mom was beautiful or both, people came at us from all sides of the pew during the huggy, hand-shakey part of the service. I was on high alert with those believers. These people did not leave room for the Holy Ghost as they embraced us. I locked my arms, kept them a Bible-length away. The nearest to the spirit I've ever felt was when I was quaking next to Julie, both of us trying not to laugh at somebody's terrible singing or ridiculous hat.

One afternoon we stopped for gas on the way back home. Mom dozed in the car while Julie pumped the gas, and I went inside to pay. I was barefoot and sleepy, rubbing my eyes—my church shoes had lacerated my heels. All the old guys milling around the station looked at us and perked up, like, *Well, well, we got ourselves a couple runaways!* Never have men been so helpful, so menacing, one of them escorting me down the aisle, chatting to me about the weather, the local football team, asking, was I in high school myself? And what about my pretty friend?

"Tell you what," the cashier said in his slow drawl. "State says I can't sell you a bottle on Sundays, but for you I'll make a exception, don't even need no ID." He sniffed, licked his lips. "Or you want something else? Lotta drugs out here. Come in from everywhere. Easy to get." Mom stayed sleeping while one guy scraped bugs off our windshield, another circled a rag on our headlights, leering at Julie. They worked as a team, seemed collectively disappointed to learn we were not drug addicted, not looking for quick cash.

In the car we told Mom what happened and she said she was proud of us—we were women now, and politely refusing men was what being a woman was all about. She said we should try to remember that this kind of attention was a good thing, that the men who wanted to fuck us could keep us safe from the men who wanted to hurt us. That statement explained so much about my mother and her relationships, the way she saw herself in the world. *What if they're the exact same men?* I wanted to ask.

The sunlight hits one of Pivot's many squat, mirrored buildings, and I go a little blind. A guy in a turquoise pickup drives by me again, slower this time. I try to remember the way Julie walked.

.   .   .

SPLITS IS IN caffeine mode, the DJ booth empty, disco ball unlit.

There's a new, baby-faced girl at the counter instead of Christian. I order an iced coffee.

"Leave some room?" she says, and I nod. She scans my bitten fingernails. I stand on one leg and scratch at my dirty foot, now forced back into its sandal.

"It's been a weird week," I say. "You ever have a weird week?" The girl nods politely, ringing me up. "My therapist let me go," I say. "I mean, I wasn't paying him that much. He needs to see other people." Maybe this is a story better told to Christian—too much to get into here with a totally new person. One of the girl's muscular arms is bare but the other is beautifully tattooed—a wonder arm. "I'm just tired," I say. "Looking forward to coffee. You know when you're so sleepy your eyes aren't awake? Like, I keep thinking my hair is dogs. Blond dogs coming at me."

She marks barista shorthand on my clear cup, sets it on the counter.

"Sorry?" she says, looking at me. Her face has changed.

"Like big golden retrievers," I say. I make my hands lunge at the sides of my head.

She's concerned now, a mix of fear and pity.

"I don't actually see dogs," I say. "It's just a jokey thing I'm saying." She won't meet my eyes. I don't blame her—there are people like that around here. She's got to brace herself for anybody in town who can scrounge up five bucks. Bea the ski mask lady shouting at families, or the infamous ball-sack guy from down the block.

That's when I realize I don't have any money, that I've left everything—phone, keys, wallet—at the gymnastics place.

"Hey." I lean forward, lower my voice. "I'm so sorry, but I left all my shit at Tiny Toads," I say. The new girl blinks at me. "I don't have any money. I mean I have money but not on me."

"It's fine," she says, snapping up my cup, underhanding it into a trash can.

She's finished with me, looking at the next guy in line because it's his turn or to end my embarrassment, put me out of my misery.

"Please," she says, "can you step aside?"

"I'll come back later," I say, but she's already taking the guy's order, talking over my head, all business. Christian comes from the back, drying his hands on his apron.

"Where's Little Bit?" he asks, and I say I left her at Tiny Toads, that I left my wallet too.

"I got you," he says.

"No, it's okay—"

"It's not a problem."

He saves me, starts making my drink. The new girl finishes up with the customer, clocking us. Christian motions me to the end of the counter, and the new girl walks behind, touches his forearm, flushes pink.

"Sorry," she says, "I didn't know we knew her," and then, for my benefit, "I didn't know we knew you."

"Not a problem," he says again, and I wonder if she feels exactly like a problem, same as me. "Her first day," he says to me. "Give this to Bitty." He puts a chocolate wafer into a glassine bag for Gilda.

"I will," I say. "It's okay," I say to the new girl, and I mean it. I'll come back later and put all the cash I have in her tip jar. I sit at the table that faces the window, my back to both of them so they can forget about me, get on with their day. A lady ties up a giant black poodle outside, perfect. It's groomed in the classic style—those big poufs on the hips—and it stands there, still and regal.

When I was super pregnant, a few weeks after Julie died, I came here and ordered coffee from Christian. I'd always liked him because he was smart and funny, played good music, and I knew from our small talk that his wife was pregnant too, a month or so ahead of me. While he made my latte, I asked him if she'd had the baby yet.

"Yep," he said, carefully placing my cup on a saucer. He'd made some pretty design in the foam like the good ones do, a leaf maybe, a heart.

"Congratulations!" I said.

"A little girl," he said.

He smiled and looked at his hands.

"You getting any sleep?" I asked.

He said, "Yep, we're doing okay." The cashier rang me up—a different cute, crop-topped woman—and I noticed she looked pale and stricken, like she was suddenly very sick. I tossed money into the tip jar, moved through the line, and didn't think much about it. I went into labor the next day, and I was back at Splits a week later, Gilda strapped to my chest. At the counter, I turned so Christian could see her face. He touched the soft whorl of her dark hair.

"She's out," I said.

"She's perfect," he said, and I felt the way you do when a friend meets your new love for the first time, so much pride at showing her off like that.

"How's your daughter?" I asked. "How's your wife?"

Christian stopped steaming milk and leaned around his silver machine.

"I'm so sorry, but I lied to you," he said softly. "Our daughter, she passed, seconds after she was born. Her lungs," he said, and swallowed. "I'm so sorry for lying before, but I didn't want you to be thinking about that during the birth."

I was undone by his kindness, the way he swallowed his grief and let me drink my coffee, a cheerful idiot. I don't remember what I said—apologies tumbled. The formerly stricken crop-top cashier was mercifully out of earshot, glowing and healthy in a yellow dress. I was aware then of the heavy heat of the morning and the exertion of my walk. I was still wearing that glorious mesh hospital underwear they give you, my thick pad soaked and syrupy where Gilda had blown my church doors wide open, as my mother put it. I grabbed the edge of the counter and sobbed. Gilda, eyes pinched shut, began to wail too, smelling and boldly broadcasting my misery. Christian rushed to grab me a tissue, stepped out from his station, and put his hand on my back.

"I was afraid this might be upsetting," he said, and I didn't correct him, didn't tell him about Julie.

"I'm just so sorry," I said.

I've never been a person with much real-time access to my emotions—I come to them much later, vomiting them up in private—but I blame my reeking hormones that day, the beginnings of sleep deprivation, the impossible truth of Julie sinking in. *Never again,* I swore to myself.

I WISH I WAS one of those people who can tell time by the sun. When the poodle lady comes out and unties her dog, I leave Splits too, follow them down the street. For a while I think we're headed to the dog park, but the poodle turns the woman down an alley, takes her through a parking lot. I hang back but stay with them for blocks, past the check-cashing place and the jerk-chicken hut, past the used car lot and the elementary school. We cross a street and walk into a gated apartment community: first the poodle, then the woman, then me. The poodle, from what I can tell, is spirited and smart, well-behaved. The woman keeps looking over her shoulder at me. When they turn a corner and run up a set of stairs, into one of the units, I decide it's time to give up.

It takes me a while to figure my way back to something I recognize, and it takes me longer still to get to the dog park, where I'm disappointed to see not a single dog playing. It's oppressively hot and people aren't stupid; they bring their pups in the morning before it heats up, or they wait to take them after work.

Dogs or not, I sit in a plastic chair under a measly bit of shade. I walk past all the time, but this is one place in the neighborhood

I'd never take Gilda. Imagining her here brings me to the emergency room of my mind. The snap of a wet snout, sirens, stitches. Layers of pinkish gauze.

When I was in college, Julie only visited me twice.

Sophomore year, a girl in my oral communications class saw a You Are the Universe sticker on my notebook. Yesenia had designed this one, a close-up of the Witch Head Nebula with a thought bubble that said *Space Junkies*. This was, regrettably, the title of our one and only EP. This girl, who wore children's barrettes in her frizzy bangs, reached for my notebook, touched the shiny blue star that made the witch's ear. I felt a little jolt, like she was touching me.

"I love them," Barrettes said, eyes huge in her skinny face.

"That's my sister's band," I said slowly. "I mean I'm in it too. Was."

"Oh my god," she said, near hysterics. "Jules is your sister."

Barrettes was, amazingly, one of our dozen die-hard fans. Oral comm was pass-fail, a joke class. We had to give these little speeches, perfect them over the course of the semester. I don't remember mine, but Barrettes presented the mysterious, magnetic properties of the theremin—"the only instrument you can play without touching," she stammered—her knees shaking every time she stood in front of the room.

"Oh my god," she said again. "Are y'all still together?" She asked if we'd consider playing in the Student Life Center. "You know first Saturdays in the quad? It's stupid, I know. But my boyfriend's director of student life? He's the events guy?"

Boyfriend. Obviously.

"We can pay y'all," she said.

Yes was two kids deep at that point, there was no way she'd go for it. "Let me ask Jules," I said, because I didn't know how to get into it, to explain that Jules was a different person, a third person Julie and I had lost track of.

The Julie who drove over from Wink was not only not Jules, she wasn't the Julie I was expecting. She wasn't waifish and greasy haired with a smile that could crack the world apart. She'd switched from the speedy drugs to the slo-mo kind. Her lower jaw was no longer frantic, no wishes in her mouth. She was bloated and nervous, taking deep, shuddery sighs. I was worried in a whole new way, unsure if this puffy, sedate Julie was a step up or down from the skeletal, gnawing, skin-picking Julie. She'd dumped or been dumped by King Tweaker—I never got the full story—and she'd started bringing Planchette every-where for emotional support. In my dorm room, she unzipped him from his special mesh bag.

"You can't let a dog loose in here," I said.

"Sure I can," she said.

We'd already told Barrettes we'd be doing a DJ set, nothing live. Julie wasn't interested in playing anymore. We weren't You Are the Universe without Yes, Julie said, and this was the excuse people had been buying for a while by then. There were other reasons Julie didn't want to play, like being completely unable to hold a guitar in her swol-len, shaky hands, or hold a note, or, I don't know, stand fully upright. Barrettes handled everything, was thrilled with whatever small scrap of Julie she could get.

Julie sat at my desk, touched my pencils and textbooks, my graph-ing calculator.

"Don't you want to get dressed?" I asked.

"This is dressed," she said, looking down at her plaid pajama pants and stained plasma-donation T-shirt. She took the pillows off my bed and made a nest for Planchette.

"He's staying here?" I said.

"We can't bring him to the show," she said. "He'll be scared. He'll get all stepped on."

At the student center, we each got an envelope with twenty bucks inside. Barrettes kept handing us energy drinks spiked with vodka. We played tracks we liked—dark wave, minimal electro. Julie swayed where she stood, head drifting. She swerved, started grabbing records so ambient they sounded like nothing, like maybe she forgot to cue up the next track. Nobody was dancing because it wasn't music to dance to. These songs were the sound of shoes tumbling in the dryer—the sound of your upstairs neighbor living their life. Then we were arguing, reaching over each other, spilling our drinks. Barrettes was wasted and disappointed with the turnout. She thought Julie—Jules—was a genius. The small crowd stood around looking bored. They gazed at their phones, went outside to smoke. "Dance, you fuckin' quadriplegics!" Barrettes screamed into the mic. We stared at her, mortified. Her wise boyfriend disappeared out a side door.

Then the set was over. It was winter and we walked the fifteen freezing minutes back—across the quad, the long neck of the viaduct, past the fountain and the statue of the big red jack. I could smell my dorm room from the hallway: dog shit. Not only dog shit, but Planchette had gotten into the trash and shredded the bloody toilet paper from my German roommate's epic nosebleed. Alcohol-fueled and overcaffeinated, I lost my mind—my room was ruined, how would I unsee all this blood and shit? Julie's Texas came out. "Don't you disrespect my dawg!" she yelled, cuddling the trembling Planchette. She gently scolded the tiny dog, "Nuh-uh, nu-uh, no, sir," but she made no move to clean up the mess. Her eyes were rolling. She kept bringing an invisible cigarette to her mouth.

"What the fuck are you on?" I yelled, but she didn't answer. I did something I hadn't done in a decade—pinned her down because I was older and stronger. I pressed her into the bed and made her slap herself in the face. Planchette yipped. Julie was laughing and then she wasn't. I knew how bad this was but I couldn't stop. I rationalized, thinking about years of context, how this kind of slapping was something she used to do to me too. I also felt justified, like a mother fox nipping at her young, little fuckup of a fox, trying to teach it how to be better at life.

We heard my roommate's key in the lock, turned our heads to watch. She opened the door, took in the room, the tableau of frenzied dog, fighting sisters, blood, and shit. She backed out without a word, shutting the door.

I let go of Julie and she smacked me in the mouth. She shoved her keys into her pocket and slammed out of my dorm without her overnight bag, without Planchette. She started the long drive back to Wink in the Buick. She later told me she woke to sparks, her bumper zipping against the guardrails, glitzing like sparklers. She made it home, preheated the oven for a frozen pizza without realizing Mom had been using it as a place to store shoes. Julie melted a bunch of pumps and started a small fire, then doused everything and decided to deal with the mess in the morning. Mom was pill fucked in bed, oblivious. Julie went to our room, where she had mashed our two beds together so she could sleep diagonal.

The second time she visited was three days later, when she came to pick up Planchette, who had been sleeping in my closet, a trembling secret my roommate and I were relieved to finish keeping. Julie knocked on the door, sheepish, with another mesh bag. She picked up her shivering dog, held him to her chest.

"Sorry I'm a dipshit," she said, and I said, "I'm sorry you are too." The fight fell away.

She put the bag on my bed and unzipped it. Inside was a slightly bigger poodle, black fur just like Planchette. A toy, up from a teacup.

"What the hell?" I said, looking back and forth at the Planchettes.

"I can't go without one, so I'm borrowing him," she said. "He's a loaner."

She zipped the two dogs up together, slung the empty bag on her shoulder, grabbed her backpack. We said goodbye and she left. Later, I got stoned with my imperturbable German roommate and I thought, what if Julie kept coming back, each time with a bigger black poodle? Teacup to toy to standard to huge to gigantic to monstrous? Bigger and bigger mesh dog bags, then Julie inside the bag, some massive dog dragging her along.

.   .   .

I SHOULD HAVE kept Planchette. He'd been with Julie in the car like always. A neighbor found him wandering their property a few days after the accident and brought him home, and Mom and I stared at the little guy, shocked because we'd completely forgotten he existed. He looked fine, as far as we could tell. Without Julie, he walked from room to room in the house, bereft. He sat in her chair on the screened-in porch, slept in a pile of her dirty diner aprons.

In the blankness immediately following the accident, those bleak arranging days, Mom was catatonic, Yes kept trying to make everyone eat, and I was tasked with getting the news out. Julie's phone was recovered from the scene, somehow still functional, and inside it was her life, users and dealers and the hundred or so acquaintances she cherished, alphabetized contacts but also people filed under names like Cowboy Robb and Jingle Dog and Wheres Your Willpower. I couldn't bring myself to speak to anyone—texting was easier. We'd lost touch with Big Large—Julie incinerated every bridge when I left for school, plus he'd moved by then—but still I wrote to him first, the true message, heartfelt. He was in her phone under Pablo. I went through the rest of her contacts one by one, copied and pasted identical texts to everyone else, even King Tweaker, because I knew Julie would have wanted him to know. I mentioned the sunrise memorial, no church, obviously, though a sunrise ceremony felt tacky too. Mom and I considered a moon remembrance, but every choice was the wrong choice, the event itself profoundly wrong for having to happen at all. I texted everyone and then, big and pregnant, I passed out in my old twin bed, Jad on a pallet on the floor because sleeping in Julie's bed felt wrong. She and Jad had a complicated relationship.

"You have no edge," she'd joke, and he'd clap back, "You're all edge."

"Exactly," I'd say to both of them. "That's exactly why I love you." Admittedly, I might have been the reason they never got close—I kept them apart, though not intentionally. I never knew where to focus my energy when they were both in the room. No matter where I turned, I felt divided, disloyal.

In the morning, I saw Big Large's reply. *Thanks for letting me know,* he said, like I'd told him his dry cleaning was ready. This was an act of love, I realized later, because I could not have handled one more person's pain right then.

He came to the memorial and stood near our dad—two guys bawling, heaving, and choking in similar button-down shirts, identical aviator sunglasses. The service, like the sunrise, said nothing about Julie. It was only illegible grief, sunflowers in baskets, people sitting stunned in the folding chairs Yes had dragged out to the dirt.

Mom had the three cats and her own problems, so I found a poodle rescue in Midland. Jad thought we might keep Planchette, bring him back with us to Pivot, but I'd made my decision. The woman at the shelter looked at the tiny, trembling dog, at my miserable, puffy face, my huge belly. "Oh, sweetheart," she said. "You've got a lot on your plate."

Weeks later, I saw a woman with Julie's hair and a different face walking a big black Planchette. This woman ran the dog down our street, threw a Frisbee for it in the green space near the highway. I'd come outside and see the dog tied to the bike racks by the library or resting under the tree by the liquor store. Sometimes the woman had a different face and different hair, sometimes she was older or much younger, once or twice she was a man. Planchette would get smaller or bigger, sometimes he wasn't black so much as gray, sometimes he was apricot or a color one could consider white. I've always wanted to come here, to this dog park, in hopes of seeing him, but I've never been able to with Gilda around.

There are no poodles today, no dogs at all, but I feel compelled to stay here, waiting. A couple has a loud conversation near the fence. They're wearing blue lanyards around their necks from the drugstore. Coworkers, but the heat in their talk tells me they're more to each other. The woman is ripping into the guy, who's saying there used to be a speed bump in the road. "Not a bump but one of those—" He stretches his arms wide.

"The big ones? A hump? You think a hump used to be here, and it magically disappeared."

"Not magically," he says. "Removed. City took it."

"They *took* it? When, in the night?"

"It was right here." He steps off the curb and stands in the middle of the street, spins in a circle. It's peaceful, no cars. "Maybe they scraped it?" he says. "With a big . . . with a machine."

"With a *machine*?" she says. "You think they aged the cement too?" She says "see-ment." This is Pete's peeve, people confusing concrete with cement. "Nobody cares, Pete!" I say to him, but Pete has time to care about these things. "You think they ran some oil where it was and stuck on some gum and tar?" the woman says.

The man takes his hat off, wipes sweat off his slick head. "Don't matter," he says.

"No," she says. "But you'd rather be crazy than wrong."

The woman walks off, leaves the guy staring at the ground. I ask through chain link if he knows what time it is. He seems put out, annoyed to even turn his wrist for me. I remind myself that men sometimes feel grossed out around mothers, feeling like every mother is *their* mother. Sure, *MILF* is the most frequently searched-for porn term, but this doesn't seem to carry over into the light of day. Besides, Gilda's not with me now.

I'm late, according to Professor Street Hump. I bust out of the dog park and down the street. I try to look like a jogger but I'm fooling nobody. I run past Splits and the doughnut place and the nail place, past some flawed strip mall signage Julie would love— UNDERGROUND HOOKA RÉSUMÉS—same font, same line. Gilda's stroller is still outside Tiny Toads, right where I parked it—nobody wants that piece of shit. I push through the glass door, bell clanging, and see Jazzy kneeling in front of Gilda, holding her little hands. Everybody else is gone.

"There you are," Jazzy says, standing up, brushing off her breathtaking knees. "We called you but . . ."

She gestures to my phone on a folding chair, next to my wallet, my keys. What a thrill, to see everything exactly where I left it.

"I'm here," I say.

"No worries," she says, though if her face is any indication, worries have been had.

I glance at the time on my phone. "I'm eleven minutes late," I say, defensive. It's the truth.

"It's all good," Jazzy says, but I've ruined her forever, or she's ruined herself, killed my fantasy with her judgment. *You ridiculous person,* I think, looking at her leg warmers. *It's ninety-nine degrees.*

I pick up Gilda, put her on my hip, and we walk outside. "How was it?" I ask, strapping her into the stroller.

She frowns, considers me. "Why are you all blotchy?"

"I was exercising," I say. On my phone there are two missed calls from Jazzy, a text from Jad saying *hows ur day?*, and a photo Pete took of some wheat-paste graffiti in his neighborhood. It's two snow monkeys in a hot spring.

You + me, Pete's accompanying text says—perhaps he's sensing that I am still salty about Montana. Pete's been making us "look for beauty in the world" and send images back and forth. Our exchange is lopsided—I don't get a lot of interesting stuff in the tight radius where I'm shackled. *Security guard with a great ass,* he'll text. *Crepe myrtles in bloom.* Mine are all *Macaroni and cheese* and *Gilda eating macaroni and cheese.*

I put my phone in my overalls and push Gilda through the parking lot. "You're really red," she says, looking up at me. "You're all the way late." This is some bullshit, but I know this will be the first thing she mentions when Jad comes home. Eleven minutes! She'll bring it up for weeks and weeks, and just when I think she's forgotten about it she'll bring it up again. It will sear, become part of our family lore. "Remember the time Mama forgot all about me?"

GILDA IS QUIET in the stroller. Her tights are off and balled up in the basket underneath, her bare legs slicked now with sunscreen. I wish I were a little kid so I could do that too, take off this damp denim and walk home in Jad's ratty white T-shirt and my bad under-wear. We take the short way home, snaking to keep in the shade. What I said to Celadon—I pretend it's true, that I'm off in an asylum somewhere, one of the nice ones, I hope, maybe a Pete-funded facil-ity. It's the least he could do, truly, after agitating me like this, spring for a nice place, not the kind where screamers roam the halls in shit-spattered gowns. I'm locked up in a day spa and Julie is the one walk-ing past the go-kart track and the chicken-fingers place, gasoline and canola oil twisting beautifully in the air. Julie's the one breathing deep, looking at the pretty way the sunlight zips down Gilda's sharp little shins.

"A kid to me was so, so mean at Toads," she says. "And do you know why? Because there's sad on the bottom of his heart."

"You're absolutely right," I say, and swallow hard. "What did he say to you?" I ask, and she doesn't answer, too upset or ashamed, secre-tive like a teenager already.

"What do those wires do?" she says, changing the subject. She looks up at the power lines as we walk under them. She asks me this all the time, and she's never satisfied with my answer.

"Hold electricity," I say.

"Power?"

"Yes."

"What does electricity look like? It's blue, isn't that right?"

"We can't see it," I say. "It's a current. It might be blue."

What flows inside is a scream, a stutter and pulse.

"What if we cut the wires open? With really big scissors?" Does she think of huge hands in the sky, coming down?

"Nope," I say. "You'll never be able to see it. But it's in there, moving around."

"It's like god," she says, not a question.

I don't know how she's come to the idea of god—my mother probably, who is still very much a fan of the guy. I don't care for the cloying Hallmark tone Gilda gets when she brings him up. Even at this age, it's like she already knows how to rebel against what I believe—what I don't.

"No," I say. "Not exactly."

At home, the table lamps don't twinkle or fritz when I turn them on. We listen to Julie's favorite ambient record and there's no interrupting static or buzz. It's soothing, peaceful, fit for a hair salon or hospice. It's one long track that shifts keys slowly, imperceptibly—a wash of faded colors sliding over and over themselves, intensifying, canceling each other out.

In my lap at dinner Gilda says, "I think I'd like to go to the cemetery sometime."

"Why's that?" I ask, my voice steady.

"Oh, I don't know," she says, looking at her grilled cheese sandwich, smiling. Then, in singsong: "Because guess who lives in the cemetery? Dead Julie!"

It's not entirely surprising to hear this, and the phrasing makes me laugh. Certain concepts seem to lodge darkly in Gilda. She calls shadows wall bruises. She sometimes asks if the crows are bats, and hearing the want in her voice, I'll say, "Yes, yep, those are day bats, baby." Dead Julie is a band name Julie would love.

"She's not in a cemetery, though, Gil," I say. "She's at Mimi's, in an urn. A container like that," I say, pointing to the vaguely Asian vase Pete gave us, the nicest thing in our whole house. *She's in a cardboard box actually*, I don't say, *under a stack of rotting magazines drenched in cat piss.*

"I can hold her?" she says, excited. "In my hands?"

"Sure," I say. "If that's something you'd like to do."

While I run her bath, she hums an eerie tune. She puts her hot hand on top of my head.

"Mama," she says. "Are you haunted?"

Oh, buddy, I want to say, *you have no idea.*

In the tub, she plays with a waterwheel my mom has sent her, a prismatic hunk of plastic that spins under the rushing faucet. It's trippy and beautiful, the way the colors whorl. We watch it for a while, then Gilda asks me how tongues "happen." She says, "How did they become in our mouths?" This is truly psychedelic, something somebody on a pink rug might ask, high as fuck on cactus.

I have a picture in my mind of Julie, her face half buried in shag fur, eyes closed—I wish there was some way to lift it out of my brain and frame it, show it to Gilda.

"Nobody can be certain," I finally say, a safe answer.

"People don't really know a lot," Gilda says.

When kids aren't being incredibly creepy, they're being adorable, telling absolute truths.

"Mimi is so nice for this," Gilda says, holding up the dripping toy. "Isn't she so nice?"

"She has her moments," I say.

FOR A WHILE, Mom made an effort. She wasn't sober, but she'd stopped buying boxed wine—no jugs either, she bragged to me, bottles were plenty—and she'd started hiding her pills, sometimes calling Julie out if any went missing. This was the summer before my senior year, and I was living at home again, saving money, working at the diner. Jad and I were getting serious, and I was lovesick, whispering into the phone, annoyed to be back in Wink instead of on campus with him.

When Julie wasn't waiting tables, she sat around in her faded coral bathrobe, depressed, Planchette curled in her lap.

"Nobody asked you to be my babysitter," she whined from her bed, but it wasn't true—Mom had specifically asked me to do just that.

"She's so pissed at us," Mom said, and I said, "Good—she'll get over it."

I tried to play good cop, let Mom swallow most of Julie's ire. In the middle of the night, she'd slink out of our room to rifle through drawers and cabinets, and I'd pretend not to notice, just like I never drew attention to how many times she repeated herself or refilled her enormous goblet. In the fall I'd go back to school, and Mom and Julie would likely go back to business as usual.

The sound bath was Mom's idea. She'd seen it featured on a news show, and it compelled her. She'd been talking it up—how beautiful she'd heard the space was, how holy—begging Julie to go with her for weeks.

"How 'bout tomorrow?" Mom busted into our room one night to ask.

"Not interested," Julie said, sullen, propped up in bed. She claimed sugar was the only thing that helped with her sour stomach, and she'd just inhaled a honey bun from Flip's. The crushed and glazed wrapper rested on her chest, and Planchette licked and licked at her hand, a sopping oval of dog spit dampening the tatty comforter.

"It's supposed to be really good," Mom said, sweeping her hands across our vanity. She picked up the boar-bristle hairbrush Julie and I shared, sniffed it, put it gently back down. "Peaceful."

"No thanks," Julie said.

We listened to the sticky rhythm of Planchette's moist little tongue.

"I'll go," I said finally, and both of them turned, slack-jawed, to stare at me. Mom and I never did anything just the two of us, no Julie as a buffer.

"What?" I said. "It sounds neat."

"Oh," Mom said, waving me off. "You don't need to bother."

"I know it," I said. "I want to."

I hadn't been the best daughter myself that summer. I'd fully regressed—an adult brat, ungrateful in my old bedroom, sleeping next to my full-grown, bratty sister. I knew this would piss Julie off, Mom and me doing something together.

"You sure?" Mom said.

"You want a ride or not?"

The sound bath was in the scrubby desert two hours south of us. Mom might have been suspicious of my company, but she needed me—road trips made her nervous.

The next day we set off together, Julie still asleep. We would drive all morning to get there, then we'd take a sound bath for an hour— "You don't *take* a sound bath," my mother insisted, "you experience it"—then we'd turn right around and come home. The place we were headed to was an acoustically perfect tabernacle. In the car, my mom kept saying that phrase, "acoustically perfect tabernacle," and with her tone and repetition, the words took on a twinkling significance. Acoustically perfect—such a rare quality in a tabernacle!

Because I hadn't planned things well or at all, early in the drive I realized it was not in fact my day off from work, that I'd have to call the restaurant. I pulled over on a wide shoulder of the highway and stepped out of the car. Fire ants crawled on the asphalt, swarmed my sneakers.

I hoped another waitress would answer and pass the message on, but Anna Jean herself picked up, owner and namesake. She wasn't happy to hear from me—no server calls their restaurant just to say hello.

"I'm having a family situation," I told her, hoping this was vague enough to avoid further questions, that the sound of the rushing semis would strengthen my case.

It was freezer day, she reminded me, and she was already in a bad mood, annoyed at having to throw out ruined, unsold food.

"It's my mom. She's fine, we're all fine," I said, knowing Julie would be showing up for her shift later, that my family situation was Julie's family situation too. "She asked me to do something important with her. I'm not coming in today," I said, firm, and Anna Jean, who had a mother too, let me slide.

I don't know how acoustical perfection is ranked, but the tabernacle was stunning, a giant egg atop desert sand, gleaming. There was a short line outside, like a ride at an amusement park. A sign instructed us to walk through the gates to the silent grounds. The cashier somberly pointed to a No Talking sign, a drawing of a big finger to big lips, shushing us. We paid for two tickets.

Oddly, there was a tiki bar outside, which yanked at my mother. Silent drinking is strange—the crack of our Bud Lights was so loud. Mom was animated, raising her eyebrows and nodding her head at me, her thumbs up. There were misters cooling us off, lizards skittering around. Young, beautiful people took selfies, the tabernacle looming in the background: Austin types in sundresses and cowboy boots, girls with spray tans. Mom drained her beer, ordered another round. A man in a flowing white muumuu came and pressed his hands together, wordlessly indicating that our group should follow him. I've never been able to down a beer, so my mother helped me out. On the walk across the dry, sandy path, she swayed, grabbed my arm.

Inside the egg it was breathtaking, the ceiling a wonder of inlaid tile, curved and kaleidoscopic, impossibly detailed, like a mosque, a cathedral, a spaceship. Intricate patterns swelled and repeated, the colors building and changing, the iterations moving toward the very center, which was glowing, made of opalescent stones. It was like walking into someone's dream. If it was true that humans had made that place, I wanted to kiss them. I wanted to live there, climb a ladder and start licking the dome.

The mismatched yoga mats and tattered blankets on the floor clashed with the marvel above. My mom barely glanced at the ceiling, mad because they made us take off our shoes. "These don't come off," she said to the whole room. She stood there staring as everyone filed in and did as they were told. "I didn't plan on this," she whispered to me, and relented, kicking off her flats. She covered one foot with the other, embarrassed by her corns and yellow toenails.

The muumuu man directed us to our numbered stations. Mom shuffled to her spot next to me but seemed annoyed by the idea of lying down. Certain personality types hate getting on the floor. She asked the muumuu man loudly for help. Was there a chair she could sit in instead? How about a stool? He pointed to his mouth and shook his head, pressed his hands together in prayer. She talked slower, louder, told him she was sore from the car. "Bad bones," she groaned, pointing to her hips, her knees. As she haggled for a pillow, a man wearing a teal leotard came in and sat in front of a huge steel drum. His hair was dyed pastel pink, eyebrows too. He said nothing, gave the room a hot smirk. I saw my mother reconsider the whole situation. "Mom," I whispered, "lie down. Do what you're supposed to do."

Nobody explained how the tabernacle worked—nobody had to. We were all silent, flat on our backs. The drummer started playing and sound washed over us. The steel drum was the shape of the tabernacle itself. Inside that drum there was another drum, I imagined, a mouse playing it for a room full of lying-down mice, a beetle drum inside that one for a beetle crowd, and so on, down to the molecular. Reverberating octaves shimmered, rising up from the drum and falling back through us, past us, into the earth.

Acoustically perfect.

The ceiling was like one of those trippy posters at the mall, how you let your eyes go slack with the promise of some new image, planes shifting, realigning, colors melting. I was overwhelmed. I felt like I might cry. It was something about the intricacy of the pattern, the same way certain orchestral swells seem tied to the tear ducts.

Then something in the room ran alongside that transcendent feeling, overtaking it. It was another sound, and it was coming from my mother. At first I thought she was choking, that she was right all along, lying on the floor can be a dangerous thing. But no, she was sobbing.

I felt it too—something different from what was being pumped into this room, what we'd all paid for. It was something personal and specific to my mother, to me. Desolation. Some murky fate, waiting for us. My ears filled and the sound went soggy, aquatic.

It was too much, my mom was over-the-top with her big, wet snarfles. She reeked of beer, her mouth was open, snot streamed down her face. The beautiful young people started to shift on their mats, clear their throats. I rolled on my side. I tapped her with my foot. "You okay?" I whispered. The pastel drummer was entranced, unbothered. Mom was pissed.

"I want to go," she whined. She sat up. "Let's just go."

In the car she pouted, aimed the air conditioner vent at her face.

"Satanists," she said. "Ungodly. Stank like a fart in there."

Later, when I told Julie what happened, she forgot she was mad at me long enough to double over at the thought. "Can you imagine Mom in a place like that?" I said. We were cracking up. "You should have been there!" I told her, and in less than a year I would feel this acutely and forever, a sensation my mom and I somehow felt in advance: Julie gone.

EMOTIONALLY LUBED BY the memory of the sound bath, when my mom calls I answer, first ring. It's a good thing I do. Lightning set the field behind her house on fire, and she's been obsessed all day, glued to her window, waiting to be engulfed.

"Why didn't you call sooner?" I say, and she says, "What are you gonna do about it from there?"

She'll leave a dozen voicemails about my cousin's Lap-Band surgery, how they cut him open and roped his stomach like a calf, but put her in actual danger and she goes dark.

"Gary's out there solving it now," she says. She tells me he's circling the blaze with his tractor as we speak, racing around to contain it with a clean line, everything inside allowed to burn.

"He mowed my lawn last week," my mom says. "Didn't ask him to, but I guess he decided."

"That's nice of him," I say.

"Not that nice. He's got one of those ride-on deals," she says. "He just zoomed over it."

How did he manage to circumvent the rusted tackle boxes my mom stacks in towers—how did he deal with the toilet tanks in the flower bed? My mom's beauty is the unforgettable, searing type that makes men do her dirty work decades later.

"One less thing for you to worry about," I say.

"Well, I don't know," she says. "I wasn't worried."

Gilda is sitting inside the wicker basket of stuffed animals we keep in the living room. She's frustrated and whining because she can't find the panda she wants to sleep with.

"Hush, Gilda," I say. "Get out of the basket so you can see what's *in* the basket."

"He probably did it because he feels guilty. Did you hear the house didn't pass?" Mom says. "They red-tagged it."

"How would I hear about that when you haven't told me? What does that mean?" I say. "Red-tagged?"

"Means I have to clean it up," she says. "That it's a little bit unfit. They made some threats. But I have time. They're giving me eleven days. No, ten."

In the past, DNS has only ever given her a warning and time to pay some teenage grocery bagger fifty bucks to drag the biggest stuff to the dump. Somebody in a county truck shows up and drives real slow past her house, nods, and tips two fingers from the steering wheel. All is forgiven, order restored, and soon the mess festers again. Not this time.

"Oh my god, Mom. How will you clean all that up?"

"Maybe Gary'll do it," she said. "If he cares so much." She sighs. "It'll get done." She sips something from a straw. "If I can't clean it up," she says, "I'll just let it go."

"What do you mean 'let it go'?" I say.

"People walk away from houses all the time," she says.

Where, exactly, does she plan to walk?

"Oh my god," I say, "I can't deal with this right now."

"Dramatic," she says. "I'm not worried about it." I don't say, *Well, maybe you should be.*

"Gilly," I say, walking away from this conversation. "Come say hi to your mimi."

Gilda stops whining, grabs the phone, shouts into it, presses some buttons. "It's me, Mimi!" she says.

She pulls out her usual performances, her jokes and songs. Then the phone is upside down, and she's losing interest, nodding her head in response to the questions my mom is asking.

She holds the phone out to me. "Mimi's gone," she says.

I'll get that feeling sometimes, same as anybody, that I need my mother. At the end of a bad day, when I'm aching for Julie in a way that feels dangerous, I think, *Who of all people might understand?* I need my mother, but I can't make myself reach out.

Is it possible to remember what your mother said to you before you knew a language? I mean the primordial, prelingual—her lilt, her timbre. Her warm breath—I swear I miss it. The way it felt to be held by her, my head on her chest, no vocabulary to tie to the loving nonsense that fell all over me.

GILDA IS BATHED and clean, but I'm in no rush to put her to sleep, no rush to be alone with the bright red tag in my brain. I let her stay up and play.

Jad calls the baby monitors walkie-talkies—Gilda calls them

tonkey-wonkeys. They were a baby shower gift, useless, like so many other things we thought we needed. Because Gilda has always slept and napped with us, our tonkey-wonkeys are just toys, her favorite thing to play with.

I'm folding laundry at the kitchen table, a tonkey next to me. "Stay here," she commands, then runs into our room and yells back through the speaker. "It's me!" she says. "It's Gilda!"

"Hi, Gil," I say, but she can't hear my reply. I've seen fancier versions where sound travels both ways, where a parent can murmur assurances to a restless child, or, I imagine, bribe and beg. Ours is the basic model. Some of the newer ones have cameras too, so you can fully commune with the creepy green baby staring out from the crib. Some are even full color, the green baby a gorgeous, rich baby, sleeping in high definition.

Now Gilda wants to be the one receiving the sound. Instead of putting her off, pointing to the mound of unfolded dish towels, I play. She takes my place at the table and bosses me to my bedroom.

"Gilly," I say into the receiver, shoving away the thought of all the things I should be cleaning. "Come back, Gil."

There's her shouted response—"It's me!"—from the living room, not the speaker.

"It's you!" I say, into the tonkey. "Copy that." I play different people for a while, do the voice of a monster and an old man. I'm Trish the Wall Woman, the woman made of garbage who lives in our walls. Trish features prominently in our bedtime stories. Gilda invented her, but I have my suspicions about Trish's shadowy origins. Babies are spies, and by the time you realize they can understand what you're saying, it's too late. Trish isn't scary—"She just likes to slide around in there," Gilda says—and her adventures mostly involve stealing things from the house and sticking them inside her big garbage-bag body.

Unlike Trish, it isn't greed that drives my mother. Once, on my way out to Wink to visit, I picked up a sandwich for her, one of those sealed plastic wedges. It must have sat in her fridge for six months, though she tried to play it off like it was a different one every time I came back.

"That's where I keep my sandwiches," she said, like she just happened to have a consistent rotation of gas station tuna. Later, when I was forced to show her the expiration date, which I cited as evidence of a real problem, she finally said, "You gave it to me, I couldn't just eat it." She threw it on the floor and it ruptured, released its noxious gas.

I do Trish's voice now, a high pitch and a low pitch—I speak very slowly, then very fast. Gilda commands me back.

"I wanna hear me be somewhere else," she says. I return to my folding and she runs into the bedroom and shouts into the plastic box, "It's me!" She runs as fast as she can back to the kitchen table, trying to hear herself. She does it again and again, shouting louder, running faster each time.

"It's me!"

I watch this circuit while I pair socks. Gilda's not getting frustrated. She's elated.

"I can't do it!" she says, breathless, streaking past. "I can't hear me!"

THE SUMMER BEFORE my senior year in high school, You Are the Universe recorded *Space Junkies* at Yes's house. Julie was drunk, slurring her way through the verses, sliding up the notes.

Oh, thank god, her voice seemed to say when she got to the chorus, like here was something familiar, a wall she could hold on to in a dark hallway.

She poked her head out of the closet we'd soundproofed, disappointed. "I want to be with you guys," she said. "It's so lonely in here." Yes checked the playback and it was slippery and sleepy and perfect.

"Amazing," she said.

"I guess," Julie said. "It's so dead in there. It's like jerking off into a cup."

Playing live was trickier. Julie would walk the stage while we played the opening bars in a loop. Her cue would come and she'd be nowhere near the mic. She might be dangling her legs off the side of the stage looking at the audience, dazed. Her cue would come around again and I'd start to get pissed. I'd catch Yes's eyes, and she'd be steady, powering through. What were we supposed to do? How long could we wait? I'd wonder if she was going to sing at all, if this would be the night when she'd finally lose it, that I'd look for her and she'd be off-stage, at the bar maybe, on her way out the back door to the parking lot. I stood there afraid, playing my four dumb notes, a fuzzy thrum. Just when Yes and I had started to think about giving up on her, she'd stride across the stage. *No way she's making this,* we'd think, but she did. The crowd wasn't bored—they were begging.

I GET GILDA settled in our bed, turn on a twinkle lamp, the humidi-fier, and the sound machine. "White nose machine," she solemnly calls it, this normal device made magic.

Children are like mushrooms—I read that somewhere: the deepest sleep cultivated in rooms that are cold, dark, slightly damp. I lie next to her in our bed with my shirt pulled open, skin crawling, psyching myself up to nurse.

I'm singing a Julie song, a Universe song, the one about a pinhole in the shoebox for looking at the sun. It's been so long, and I miss most of the words to the second verse, but I remember my part and Julie's too. Gilda's looking up at me, watching. "I like when you sing mouth songs," she says when I'm finished, and at first I don't know what she means by that; isn't every song a mouth song? But she's used to me singing quietly along with the radio in the car, never with a melody coming straight from me. "A cappella," I say, and she says, "Again." This has been the worst day but singing helps. Gilda is relaxed, quiet. She doesn't even nurse, just falls right to sleep beside me.

I'm alone with my thoughts, suddenly overcome with longing for

Gilda, missing her even as she's lying here. I look at pictures of her on my phone, an awake Gilda earlier today, jumping on this bed. I fold time again and see her on this same day one year ago, two years ago. Gilda on the floor with her fist in her mouth. Gilda with her hands pressed against a window. Gilda in utero, coiled and ready.

Despite the timing, I never once thought Gilda was Julie coming back again, though I sometimes imagined fetal identities spinning around in there, my baby cranking the slot machine of traits and habits and facial tics, flipping combinations right up until the second she was born. None of those babies were Julie—I just knew. The second Gilda was born, I pulled her to my chest. "There you are," I said. She was Gilda and Gilda only. Completely familiar but brand-new.

When I was giving birth in the subpar birthing center at the subpar hospital, my very good but out-of-network, out-of-pocket midwife gazing through the window at the parking lot, what I thought was: *I am so, so glad I've done acid.* Nothing prepares you for childbirth more. The violent weirdness, how LSD lasts and lasts. You're done with it long before it's done with you. Just like labor.

You've seen the gravy ceiling, you've watched a procession of tiny, ancient people ripple across your palm, you've touched a wall you're certain is made of ostrich skin. The peak comes and it's too much, the carpet gnomes swirl around your threaded fingers. The word *swirl* itself, so overused in psychedelic accounts, so stupid, a cut-rate word for what is happening everywhere you look. Beats and movement come through every surface. Synesthesia gets boring—so what if this guitar solo tastes like grape cough syrup? Too many miracles! There's a hard edge to it, so many messages per second, so much noise. You're finished. *That was amazing, sweetie, okay?* you tell your brain. *But let's get some rest now.*

You crawl into bed and close your eyes to watch a vivid, involuntary movie. The duration and speed will not be of your choosing. The subject matter will range from odd to disturbing. You will see a girl feeding lemons to reindeer. You will see a man carefully, slowly unhooking his ears. This is just dreaming, you think, this is being asleep. It is like that, but you're awake. This is terror: images coming unbidden. Bed is bad—it's the worst.

But you have to go deeper in. You have to confront things, stay awake, carry on. No choice. "I wanna come down right now," sings my favorite glitter-rock singer in my favorite glitter-rock song. Well, you can't.

Psychedelics prepare you for the craziest thing imaginable on this earth: a new human tunneling through an older human's body. Somehow, my extensive recreational drug use led me to a completely unmedicated delivery. I turned out to be one of those women who refuse the epidural, who call contractions "rushes," who insist pain isn't painful. Trips taught me how to sit with discomfort. You can't leave, so you might as well soak in it. In many ways, I found labor to be even easier than LSD because in between the rushes—contractions, whatever—you are returned essentially to your pain-free, unlaboring self, a massive distinction from an acid trip, when you are very much never normal. Unlike psychedelics, where the blanket is tossed off whole cloth, in labor the scrim lifts and lowers, lifts and lowers. Labor is actually pretty boring when it isn't completely insane. My midwife gazing out that window, Jad standing off to the side, failing to quietly eat a bag of Doritos.

JAD COMES HOME from a long run, whistling. I hear him digging around in the fridge for leftovers, cheerful and calm, like the after-church rush in the restaurants of my life, serene heaps of people tearing into their hot bread, draining their iced teas.

Instead of ambushing him with my mom's troubling red-tag news, I decide to give him some peace, let his endorphins run laps for a while. I'm unstuck from time in here, Gilda breathing next to me. Is this meditation or doing nothing? Pete calls and I slip out from under Gilda, step into the bathroom, and answer.

"Are you still mad at me?" he says. "Because if you are, then I don't need to tell you about my three-way, but if you aren't . . ."

"I was never mad."

"She says *furiously*," he says.

"Okay, I was but not anymore. You sure you wouldn't rather tell your best friend Jad *all* about this three-way?"

"I'd rather set myself on fire," he says.

"Fine," I say. "Are you gonna make me beg?"

"Well, it hasn't happened yet," he says.

"Never mind, I'm mad again," I say.

"I'm texting you something," he says. "What do you think?"

He sends a picture of two guys in a car. They're in the front seat but they're turned around, glaring at the camera. They look younger than we are, but they have dark circles under their eyes, dour expressions.

"These are them? Are they fuck-app people?" I say. I look closer. "Jesus, that's grim. They look like cartoon robbers."

"Good bone structure on the one guy, though," he says.

"You can admire his jawline while he cuts out your kidney. And who took this picture?" I say.

"I don't know," Pete says, laughing. "Somebody in the back seat."

"It's from such a low angle," I say. "It's from the floorboard!"

Out in the living room I hear the theme song from the show about competitive fishermen. Tunashow, we call it. Sometimes when we say Tunashow we mean sex—I'm not sure how this happened. "Wanna watch Tunashow?" Jad will say, eyebrows raised. Other times it's definitely just a show about tuna. Some nights after I get Gilda to sleep, I slip into the bathroom with my phone. I'll stream young, elastic people doing horrible, amazing things and I'll text Jad from there, *What are you doing right now?* He'll text back, *Am watching tunaguys.* I won't know if that's code or not. This is sex in marriage: confused euphemisms, reality TV.

"I can't believe this is the picture they chose to charm you!" I say. "This is their best effort. They're already coming, aren't they?"

"Yeah," he admits. "In like twenty minutes."

"Is the floorboard friend joining too?" I say.

"We can only hope," he says.

He tells me Brian came over to pick up some mail. "It wasn't bad," he says, "just different. My new thing is pretending to be over him until I'm over him," he says.

I hear Jad cleaning the kitchen, loading the dishwasher. Pete says he needs to get ready for his company.

"Have fun," I say. "They seem not at all like murderers."

"I'm gonna put out some snacks," he says.

Pete getting laid makes me want to get laid. I slip out of our bedroom to see what sort of Tunashow is happening.

Every light is on in our house, all the windows open. This is how Jad likes it.

"The whole world can see us. Anybody could come in here," I tell him.

"You think glass is going to stop them?" he says. "Anybody can do anything."

We have prowler lights but they point at our house, not at the prowlers, which seems like a flaw to me.

In the hallway I run into a foil balloon. Leaking helium, it's a giant heart with eyes, hovering at crotch height. Gilda loves these things, begged me to buy it. I slap it away.

"Goddamn," I say, to Jad in the living room. "That balloon scared me. I thought it was a little man."

"I know," he says. "I walked past it earlier and it followed me. We should just poke it," he says.

"Nah," I say. "It's on its way out."

A caught bluefin is dragged onscreen, gasping and pulling. Jad's put Gilda's stuffed animals back in the basket, their faces turned to look at us. There is the faint scent of Windex, a sparkling coffee table. If I weren't already planning to fuck him, this would do the trick.

I sit close to Jad on the couch. I won't say anything about my mother's mess, the countdown. Not tonight. Instead, I turn to him and flash my tits.

"Well, well," he says, pausing, but not turning off the tunaguys.

I can hear the dishwasher's soft, wet sloshing, no sexier sound.

He kisses me but I bird-peck him, pull away. "I should brush my teeth," I say.

"It's okay," he says, and we kiss for real. I realize how long it's been—this is something we forget to do.

I unzip his pants and pull them down with his boxers stuck inside. I kneel on the floor between his thighs. This is the most relaxing act, a surefire way to keep my thoughts from whirring.

"You like that," Jad says, not a question.

He knows I do—it's my favorite. He's in my mouth and I'm in that hot white space of every erotic thought I've ever had, the slow flip of the cards. A jumble of teachers and exes and friends. Jad himself, that first time. How he kissed the backs of my knees. We didn't love each other yet, but our bodies knew something we didn't. This wasn't revealed in the before-moments—anybody can do that, be attentive and tender in the frenzy—it was what happened in the after. How do you go back to the world once you've been perfectly fucked? Who would want to? I'd been dismantled. Dazzled. He led me back to real life, gently, still stunned. Jad, but a different Jad, from another time, entangled in a bed with some other me.

He stands me up and strips me down, pulls me on top of him.

This is good, this is so good. How lucky that we've always had this. I forget sometimes, how many people don't.

"I love your cocks," I say into his ear.

We both pause at that and then he sucks on my shoulder, buries his face in my chest. There's a sound from the baby monitor but it's nothing, just Gilda turning in our bed. Still, we pause and wait to make sure. You develop this skill, the ability to cleave from sex when necessary, then get right back to it. He picks me up, turns me around like I'm nothing—the discrepancy in our sizes is bliss.

"Did you say—" he says behind me. "Did you say 'cocks'?"

"I think so," I say. This will be hilarious later, something we'll scream about, but right now I'm concentrating. I'm so close. I think of the word *tube*. I don't know if I'm the tube or Jad's the tube—if we're inside a tube.

"You didn't come," he says, after he does. "I thought you were going to."

"I was," I say. "But then I didn't."

This is true intimacy—admitting you didn't get off, taking care of yourself while your patient partner watches, then goes to make a snack while you clean yourself up.

In the kitchen, Jad scoops vegan ice cream, and I get a glass of water and pick up a mushy avocado. "Again?" I say. "We have to be faster."

"This household doesn't deserve avocados," Jad says sadly.

He rinses off the ice cream scoop and puts it back in the wrong drawer. I say, "Hey, why are you cramming stuff in my drawer?"

"That's *your* drawer?" he says, and I realize I do think of that drawer as mine, only I've never said so out loud. There's nothing in this drawer that belongs specifically to me—it's just the salad bowls, the colander, the tongs. But it's true that I feel possessive about it, that I hold it above all the drawers in this kitchen, in this house, in my life. And this is how sorrow comes for me—the frank understanding that Julie won't ever turn a can opener again, won't twist a plastic tray to pop up ice cubes.

I set out the coffee mugs for tomorrow. Gilda likes to put the foil capsule into the machine, push the lever, press the button.

Julie gapes at all of it—this kitchen, this life.

Jad and I eat salted caramel from the same bowl, same spoon. I put my head in his lap. Tunashow ends and he clicks over to Dragonshow, which I sleep through. Then it's time for bed.

I flip off Jad's thousand lights, darkening the house. When we turn the corner into the hallway, the aluminum foil balloon floats into us.

"Fuck off," I whisper-scream, heart pounding as Jad tries not to crack up.

In bed, Jad and Gilda sleep and I lie there perfectly awake. I make the drive to my mother's house in my mind. Two left turns, a right, a straight shot down I-20. When I get there, it's years ago, and nobody's home. The place is as it was when I was little: loved, cluttered, but not a disaster, not condemned. I walk from room to room, opening doors and cabinets, looking out windows. Certain places are baked right in, unshakable. We store our childhood homes in our bodies—we know just where on the wall to feel for a light switch, which of the floorboards creak. What else do we hold on to?

I give in to insomnia, get out my phone. I need a distraction. I also need to make sure Pete is unmurdered, kidneys intact. I text him about Jad's cocks.

A girl can dream, he replies.

I ask about his adventure—*All you hoped for?*

Neutral to fair, he reports. *Five out of ten.*

FIRST THING in the morning, I call my mother.

"Hello? Hello? What's wrong!" she says. "Y'all okay?"

"We're okay, Mom," I say. "Everybody's fine."

"Lord, you never call."

I hope this will be the most annoying part of this conversation, though I doubt it.

"Felt like it," I say. "I've been thinking about the house. Is there anybody able to help you?"

"Maybe Tobe. He came by and hauled away two of the deep freezes. His daddy sent some hamburgers with him."

Tobe's dad, like all the men in Wink and Kermit and Midland and beyond, remembers Mom. Before her fish tanks and her cat trees, she used the car wash on Orbison as her stage. Julie and I watched from the back seat while she slid damp quarters into the machines. Truckers and oil guys and men eating at the front windows at Anna Jean's would cross the street to help lather and scrub our car. Mom loved halter tops and press-on fingernails. She kept a beer cooler full of costume jewelry—didn't matter that it was fake, only that it sparkled. She said it was because she had no shine in her childhood. Gummy and Grandad were peanut farmers. She'd had an old glove for a baby doll.

"And it wasn't even a color," she told us, stroking our Barbie's hair, sitting on the floor with us. "It was a non-color."

"What sort of non-color?" we wanted to know.

"Dingy," she said. "Grayish, tannish. The color of grime. His name was even Grime," she told us.

"No!" we said.

"Okay, no," she admitted. "All but that last part."

She had a bunch of wigs in a pile in her closet. She wanted to be a woman who wore wigs in public, but she wasn't. She had hats, too. She called them her Go-to-Hell Hats, and she didn't wear those out either. These were home things, secret accessories that appeared on her head after some wine or a few rum and Dr Peppers. She tried to sell Avon but kept all the makeup for herself. On Friday nights she'd spread out her stash on the coffee table in front of Julie and me—her tubes and orbs and hinged compacts—and whore us up while we watched TV. Between bites of popcorn, she'd draw different lips over our lips, jab at us with her mascara wand. "It's not fair! Beauty's wasted on kids," she'd say when she was finished, looking at us in the animated glow. "No pores nowhere."

Before we rebelled, Julie and I were her responsible little downers, shy girls with limp braids. Once, a beefy guy invited Mom to go tubing on the Pecos with him and a bunch of his loud, young friends. She took us along because where else could we go, our dad a deadbeat down the road, not answering his phone. These people were probably her same age, but they didn't have kids of their own yet, and when Mom mixed in with them, it was like she didn't have us either. The river cut through private family land, but the beefy guy said he didn't need to ask permission.

"If you don't ask, nobody can say no," he said, smiling at Mom.

We went out there in a long caravan, Julie and me in the bed of the truck Mom was riding in. We hiked to the bend in the river and everybody set their inflatables on the water and climbed in, linked to each other with an arm or leg swung out to make a train. Mom was somewhere in the middle, but Julie and I rode caboose—the beefy guy lifted us into the booze tube next to the crushed ice and Bud Light.

The Pecos is clear as glass, jammed with spotted gar, catfish, perch, bluegill, and carp, iridescent crabs dancing on the sandy bottom. We knew fish names from Dad, but we'd only ever seen them bleeding on a beach towel, scales scraped off with his do-everything knife. I pointed them out to impress the girl in charge of tugging us, some freckle-chested wonder in a white bikini. When the girl's slick legs came unhooked from us in the froth, everybody—even Mom—screamed, "The beer!" Julie told me later she didn't want to be saved. "I wish they'd just let us float off," she said. But the beefy hero dove in, looped his thick arm through our tube, swam us back to the end of the line. Everybody clapped.

JULIE WAS NEVER shy about her mistakes—she seemed almost comforted by how many people it took to get her through her day. She never hesitated to lean on Mom or me or Yes or her many shady friends. She needed twenty bucks—no, fifty bucks. She needed me to print something out and mail it to her: a job application, coupons for dog food. She needed Yes to pick up some weird guy and drive him to some other weird guy's house. She needed someone to call in her many prescriptions: stuff she could sell or abuse, but also legitimate glop for her recurrent yeast infections and these absolute bullshit tinctures for supposed adrenal support. "Maybe it's that my glands are

shot," she said. *Maybe it's meth!* I didn't say. She needed the keys to
Mom's car, but she also needed gas money. She needed me to drive
out from Pivot and help her touch up her roots, which started to go
gray and wiry when she was only sixteen. Her hands shook too much
to sign a check, could I pay a bill online for her and she'd get me back?
It rubbed me wrong, what I took for shamelessness, though I see now
it was more complicated than that. She was sick, and she needed help.
Who better to ask than those who loved her?

And so, it's in this spirit that I hang up with Mom and immediately call Yes. I ask her to do me a favor.

"She's not going to let you come inside," I say.

"Oh, I know," Yes says. "She doesn't even let me on the porch anymore. She talks to me through the screen."

Yes lives two miles from my mom, in the house she's lived in since
we were kids, her mother's house. Only now Yes is the mom, and her
mom is a tiny abuela living in the suite Yes's husband built over their
garage.

"Same same" is something Yes says a lot. That's what we are, no
matter what. In elementary school we treated Julie like a doll, dressing her up and carrying her around, demanding her silence. In high
school we plucked her eyebrows all to hell and got her very, very high.
Julie and Yes briefly formed a band without me called the Smoking
Llamas, just to be mean. We were all in the same movie theater when
Yes gave her first blow job. Long periods of quiet anger about this
or that, Julie or Yes or me out in the car waiting, honking, mad at
the other two. Girls combining and recombining, alliances shifting,
forgiving each other everything. Not quite a sister, but still sister-
adjacent—Yes is adored.

When Julie had lit her life on fire, done everything she could to
push everyone away, she showed up one night to pound on Yes's door
at dinnertime.

"We have a doorbell, you know," Yes said, opening the door.

"Let's go out," Julie begged on the porch. "Let's do something crazy." She felt around on the door frame, found the bell, rang it.

"Stop it," Yes said. "What are you doing?"

"I'm just playing," Julie said.

"I don't have a sitter," Yes said, a baby on her hip, toddler in a high chair behind her.

"Get What's-his-nuts to do it," Julie said, and waved at Joe there behind Yes, sitting at the dinner table with Yes's mom, wondering when they should come to the door and help.

"So that's not gonna happen," Yes said.

Julie rang the bell again, made the baby cry.

"Seriously," Yes said, knocking her hand away. "Stop it."

Julie swayed in the doorway. "How come you never ask me to babysit?" she said, her face shiny, a wine stain on her shirt.

"You want me to hang out with you or you want to be my nanny?" Yes asked.

"Neither!" Julie said. She rang the bell three more times, stumbled off the porch. She and Yes didn't talk for months.

"Can you help me?" I ask Yes now. "Can you go over there and tell me how bad it is?"

"Absolutely," she says, no hesitation, no talk about how she'll wrangle her kids, reroute her day to help me with my messed-up life. Dependable Yes, keeping everything together, a drummer through and through.

A FEW DAYS later at Hidden Wonder, Celadon sits next to me on the bench, our bench, as I've come to think of it. She bends down to adjust the zipper on one of her leather booties, which are of course stylish and expensive looking, broken in beautifully, the color and texture of an elephant's hide. It seems to me she's only wearing one sock—she scratches her calf and a trim of pink fishnet edges out. Maybe this is a fashion statement, a nice mix of fetish model and mental patient, something cool people know how to do. Or maybe the other bootie swallowed its sock, maybe the anklet was too loose and it slipped out of place, got sucked down deep into the dark body of the boot.

Gilda is climbing on the spider mesh, her face red. She gets to the top and waves at me.

"Hi, Gilly," I shout, addressing her first, worried she'll call me Mama, though I've already thought of an elegant solution to that problem. "My sister and I look so much alike," I'll say to Celadon. "We think it must, in some small way," I'll say gently, "bring my niece comfort."

"You want water?" I shout across the park. "Gilda? Wawa?" I wave her unicorn water bottle in the air. She doesn't respond, doesn't even look at me. "Hydration," I say to nobody. There's a heat wave coming—a bunch of people expected to drop dead by noon, lots of dogs getting cooked in cars. I'm a good babysitter, one who will not let her sister's kid sear in the sun, will not return her niece shriveled as a husk.

Celadon is wearing the same stretched-out, tied-up T-shirt again, but this time she's got on flowing capri pants, possibly silk. I'm disappointed to see a custard-colored bra strap peeking out at her shoulder. Even worse, she's wearing only a slim chain around her neck, her charm gone, maybe tucked somewhere I can't see. It's unsettling. I'm sort of half listening, scanning her body for the pale green curve.

A baby wails from a nearby stroller and Celadon and I tense up, whip our heads to look at the source. It's a newborn cry, animal anguish. The baby is invisible, hidden under the stroller's sunshade, but it must have been there all along, sleeping, secret, parked only a few feet from us. The sound is arresting, something that must be dealt with. Celadon and I instinctively look for our kids.

Gilda runs to the one patch of actual grass in the park. She squats and stares at the ground, her bright swimsuit showing through her faded dress. Celadon scans the playground. I look for five handsome, black-haired boys, messy maybe, but stylishly dressed. They'd have long slender necks, like her. Good posture, though all little kids have good posture. Would they look comfortable in the world like she does? She digs in her bag and puts on sunglasses. They're too big for her, gold rimmed, mirrored, and they look cheap but probably aren't. All the while, furious at being awake, at existing at all, the unseen baby screeches.

"Not our job," Celadon says, and I like her so much. Still, neither of us is capable of continuing our conversation against that noise. Celadon turns her book over, flips through the pages. I study my hands. Julie's nails were always black, so last night, during yet another stretch of red-tag insomnia, I—*she*—painted them. I've never made much of an effort in this area. It turns out, no matter how sloppy the job, excess polish comes off the next time you get your hands wet. A Julie lesson: shotgun yourself to the knuckles, then wash dishes or take a shower and your manicure will turn out fine. *Was that so hard?* Julie wonders. *Isn't it nice to look down and see something pretty?*

Finally, Bad Dad strides over to the screaming stroller. He's in no hurry, scrolling on his phone as he walks. He doesn't see me, but having him so close to Celadon is confusing, a collision of fantasies. I didn't know his wife had already had the baby. Celadon clears her throat and gives me a look over the top of her glasses.

Jad is an attentive father, and I trust him implicitly to take care of Gilda. It's not that men are terrible at this—we're all terrible at this. Still, it would make things a lot easier if the dads would stop being so obvious about it. Play the game. Look alive. The secret baby's cry is an iridescent thread. At the other end is Bad Dad's wife, indoors, tending to her new, wounded body, spewing milk in her brief freedom, trying to wash her hair or eat a goddamn sandwich.

Bad Dad lifts the sunshade and grimly looks into the stroller. The crying is louder, more intense. He doesn't untether his newborn. I don't pretend to know what the different cries mean, but even I know this kid wants to be held. Bad Dad lowers the shade.

He finally sees me watching him. "Hey, you," he says, too loud because he's wearing earbuds, likely listening to some douchey podcast. He usually gets me right in the gut, makes me feel fluttery, teenage, ready to laugh at something he hasn't even said yet. Today it's different. His patchy hair is damp with sweat, his head a bit misshapen. *Who is this little potato-looking motherfucker?* Julie thinks. *This is the guy?*

In a beat, I follow this situation to its end. What are Bad Dad and I going to do? Plan to meet in a hotel room? Have stupid day sex and go guiltily home to the families we've ruined? That's the best-case scenario: discretion, semiregular fucking with an almost-stranger, different until it gets boring or you get caught, lives destroyed all around.

He taps the white kernels in his ears, waits for me to walk over to him. His baby is still screaming. I give him a tight smile, shake my head. I remember the time I saw him through the front window of the Mexican place, eating tacos alone. He was chewing with his mouth open, wearing sunglasses inside, and when I walked by, he waved excitedly at me, a long piece of confetti lettuce dangling from his nose. Back then I brushed off my gut feeling, but now it's different. Bad Dad has been deflated—how strange. Julie, no great judge of character, is immune to his charms. Bad Dad has lost his hold.

He takes the brakes off the stroller—at least he knows to do that—then whistles for his older son. "See ya," he says as he gingerly wheels the stroller baby away, out of Hidden Wonder.

"Well," Celadon says. We smile at each other. She's cut her bangs since I last saw her, too short for her face but still cute. There is a snag in her beautiful pants—a loose thread trails down her strong calf.

Gilda is riding the fiberglass rabbit, one hand in the air like a cowboy.

Celadon scoots closer to me, conspiratorial. I notice she's wearing a black fingerless glove on one hand. Did she just put that on? At first I think it's a cast, maybe a carpal tunnel brace, but no. It's dainty, made of satin, an odd choice. It's so warm outside. I'm anticipating more menstrual talk, maybe gossip about one of the kids. I'm game. She's talking low, a soft monotone. She's got a hand cupped around her mouth.

There's a smell like sour milk—I tilt my head down to make sure it's not me. It's mildew—laundry sitting in a washer too long. We all have our bad days. That's when she says, "Ever done Ecstasy?"

"Sorry?" I say.

"Molly, I guess they call it now," she says. "I don't know why." She shakes her head. "We had a poodle called Molly."

Reticular whatever, I think.

"You've done it? Molly?"

She's breaking a rule—moms talk about wine, about how long it is until happy hour, but they don't typically talk about hard drugs, past or present. Gilda is sitting near the slide, scooping dust with her hands. Where the fuck are her shoes? She's totally fine, just dirty.

Something fizzes in my chest, a thrill. Why does Celadon think it's okay to ask me this? Because she thinks I'm not a mom? I made an effort to dress like a young person today, in yoga pants and a T-shirt, my hair twisted in a topknot. Still, I'm sweating like a hog, Gilda's EpiPen in my pocket.

Nancy comes through the gate with her stroller, Riley standing on the back, the seat full of healthy snacks—she's always got the kale chips, seaweed disks, organic blueberries; a diaper bag, fully stocked, no doubt; a half-dozen Little Golden Books; some lovingly crafted wooden toys the kids will beat each other with later. She hasn't seen me yet. *Stay the fuck away, Nancy. Don't you dare come over here.*

"Yep, I've done it," I say to Celadon. I'm answering as Julie. This doesn't feel like a trap.

She nods. "It's so fun," she says. "All but the grinding." She opens her mouth, circles her lower jaw. She's got her eyes on the monkey bars. Gilda is running with a pack of kids now, screaming at squirrels. I gather Celadon's children are not among them—she doesn't track this crew as they streak by.

"Is it your favorite?" she asks. I've waited years to have a playground conversation like this. Should I still answer as Julie? As myself? Nancy spots me and waves. I nod but don't wave back. I try to pin her to the other side of the park with my mind.

"Psychedelics are my favorite," I say. "They were. I mean, it's been a while."

"Of course!" she says. "You're helping take care of a child! You're dealing with your . . ." She trails off. "I mean, who has the time?" she says. "The comedown alone."

"Exactly," I say. "That's exactly right."

We could be talking about what brand of laundry detergent we use, the best natural foods store in the neighborhood. Part of me wants to follow Celadon to this dangerous place, but another, smaller part worries I'm being recorded or tricked, that my words will be used against me somehow.

"I rather like psychedelics too," she says. "Quite a lot. But I like the other more. Molly," she says, nearly singing the word. A redhead in a dirty T-shirt looks at her glumly. A ginger, I guess she'd call him. He's too old for the park, honestly.

"That one's yours?" I ask.

"Not mine," she says.

Soon I notice a woman who must be the boy's mother, her hair an identical shade of copper. It's so easy to match them.

There is a sinking feeling. Something off about the kid, who is still staring at us, something the matter with his face.

"Molly, Molly!" Celadon says. She looks off in the distance like she's remembering something, and I can't know if it's the dog or the drug or both. "But time can go so strange on acid. Once, years ago, something so odd happened," she says. Her shoulder is touching mine and she's got her hand in front of her mouth, like she's thwarting a lip-reader somewhere across the park. There's a chunky acrylic bracelet on her wrist, crystal clear. "I mean, *bizarre*." She turns to me, but because of her sunglasses, I don't see her eyes. I only see myself. Listening.

"We would do this thing, my friends and I would, where we would dash across the rooftops. Literally, I mean. You'd get a running start and then fly. One to the next to the next. Now, this is London, so the buildings can be cramped quite close. Still—dangerous."

"That's insane," I say. And impossible—there's no way. She's got a scabbed-over puncture on her forearm, a pink ring around it. A spider bite maybe. She should have that checked out—looks infected.

"How are any of us still alive?" she asks.

"I don't know," I say, honestly. Plenty of us aren't. Nancy waves again, calling me over. "That woman," I say, talking through my smile. "She's the worst."

"All of these women are the worst," Celadon snaps, hate in her voice. There is a black speck, pepper maybe, between her front teeth. The playground isn't crowded today. I know most of these kids. I look for five boys together, five boys anywhere. Celadon is lit up, fucked up in London, living her best life in her head. Her hands are out like a little platter, catching the story. Then her two fingers are legs, streaking down her forearm to show me how she ran.

"I was dashing from roof to roof when I came to it—a dome. It was a church or mosque, maybe something else. Green glass." She talks and I can see the dome, see everything, the expression on her young face, the way she's moving so fast, murdering the skyline, how she doesn't want to stop on account of this thing in her path.

"It had a *hum,*" she says. "It was so loud, a sound just for me. My friends were laughing, watching me skip around from a few buildings over. I wanted to impress them, obviously," she says, "and so, though I wasn't sure I could do it, I decided to leap. Oh, and I should mention," she says, gripping my elbow, hard, "before I get to the bizarre part, this was before I'd even taken anything. I still had it in my pocket, you know," she says.

"Oh, yes," I say. I'm dizzy, remembering a night ride in the bed of a pickup truck, catching air with every bump, choking on fumes. I swallow and my voice comes out strange. "Sometimes that's even better."

Gilda is somewhere. She's fine. She can't open the gate—she wouldn't.

Celadon bobs her head. "Right," she says. "Right! I decide to jump. I'm preparing myself. I want to be graceful—I want to have style. My friends are watching. I was a dancer once," she says. "When I was young, I was a dancer." She frowns, pouts. I think we're going down some other path, the dancing path, but no. "I was in these shoes. Heels." She laughs too loud, spreads her finger and thumb apart to show me how high.

"Utterly stupid," she says. "But I do it, no hesitation." Anxiety comes from not knowing how a story ends. Obviously, Celadon is here, not dead, not scarred or maimed in any way I can see. But the smell of her—it's strong.

"It's the one fear we're born with—falling—but I was like, *No, fuck you, fear!* I leap, and I make it look pretty, but I don't clear that fucker. I fall right on top of it." Celadon's accent—it's nowhere.

In the reflection of her glasses I see my confused face, the bags under my eyes. It's me, only me. She grabs my arm and I pull it back, a reflex. There's spit in the corners of her mouth. "And as I look down, people are under the dome looking up. A crowd! Looking up through the green glass," she says. "They were not at all surprised to see me. Not at all. They'd been waiting. It was a gallery and they were there to look, ready to be moved by something beautiful. They'd come to view the art. *I* was the art!"

Heart beating, ragged breath. Could I lie on the ground and close my eyes? Could I curl up under this bench?

Celadon pushes her sunglasses into her hair. Her bangs are more than choppy, they're deranged. She tracks the change in my face and pauses, studies me, slows down. "I mean I was fine," she says. "The glass cracked, but it held me. I walked away bleeding from my knees. Can you imagine if it broke?" she says.

Celadon's eyes—where are her irises? "You live around here, right?"

I ask then, desperate to normalize her, to know where she's come from. Why have I never thought to ask this before?

"Over there," she says. She sweeps her hand through the air, along the stacked highways, the hot sprawl.

The ginger kid—the redhead—stands with his feet wide apart, staring at us. His mother has been attracted by the frantic pitch of Celadon's story, and she comes to her son, envelops him, turns him from us. I stand up and scan the playground for Gilda, panicked.

Nancy, I think. *Look over here, Nancy. I need you, Nancy!*

Gilda's there, under the slide. She's fine, but how could I have lost track of her? Something has shattered, and I should pick up the shards, be careful not to cut my hands. Why am I so slow to move through these levels: intrigued, entranced, and finally, fucking finally, afraid. What made me think, *No, this isn't danger, this is something else?*

Finally, Nancy sees my wild waving and walks over.

"So, for you, I could do fifty," Celadon says fast, to get this out before Nancy gets here. She gently pounds her thighs with her fists, agitated.

"What?" I say.

"Fifty bucks," she barks. She's talking so fast, looking at Nancy's curious face as she walks toward us. "I could do fifty," Celadon says. "Nothing less. But it's Molly, not the other."

First of all, that's way too much money. Second, what the fuck? Would Julie talk her down, make a trade, figure out how to close the deal? I think about how much cash I have on me, how there's more on Jad's dresser. I could ask Nancy to watch Gilda, slip out of the park before she even notices. I could go home and turn my house—my life—into something different.

I don't know if it's me or Julie who firmly refuses. It's both of us.

"Hi, Kit," Nancy says. She's wearing her overalls again, and I wish I were wearing mine. I want to be on Team Normal, Team Mom. "Hey," she says to Celadon. "I'm sorry, we haven't been properly—"

"No," Celadon snaps. "We haven't."

Gilda rushes up, limping. She's tearful. "Mama, I have a—I have a—in my foot I have a—"

"Calm down, baby," I say, kneeling to her. "What's wrong?"

"In the palmb of my foot," she says. *This is why we wear our motherfucking shoes.* I try to remember her most recent vaccines, try not to panic. What is there, tetanus? Ptomaine? One of the hepatitises? She won't show me what's the matter.

"Let me see, baby," I say. "Let me see. Did something sting you?"

Wasp, I think, but I can't say the word. My hands shake. I pat around in my pants for the EpiPen, scour the park for yellow jackets.

"Did you get stung?" I say, my voice rising.

"Nobody stung me," Gilda says, annoyed. "But it's bad. It's *inside.*" She grabs her limp little foot and twists it at me.

"A wood tooth," she whines, "in my palmb."

It's only a splinter, but it's big, fully sunk into the meat of her heel.

She's crying freely now. We sit down in the dirt together. "Good-good," she whimpers, and I pull my T-shirt up and my enormous bra down, bring her to my chest. She melts into me, long and pliant.

"I'm here," I say into her hair. "You're okay." Celadon is gaping at me, Nancy too. "Stop staring!" I hiss at them. Nancy sniffs and looks into her diaper bag.

After a few seconds Gilda jerks, hands out to brace, same as when you catch yourself falling asleep. Her eyes flip open. Hidden Wonder is all around us, harsh—the loud, real world. She pulls away, gathers herself like she's pushing a stiff pour back across a sticky bar. "No more for me," she says, wiping her mouth with her hand, done with this, finally.

Celadon is still staring. "Can I help you?" I say. She's not so scary anymore, just a liar like me. She closes her mouth and shakes her head, then stands up and stretches. She hugs herself and scratches her arms, leaves long, red tracks. Nancy and I watch as she grabs her bag, pulls her sunglasses down, slowly walks to the gate. She leaves, alone.

"It's *so* strange," Nancy says, handing me a Band-Aid. "That woman's here all the time and not once have I seen her with a kid. Have you?"

AT HOME, Gilda won't let me get near her foot with the tweezers. I'm afraid to do it anyway. Jad's the one with steady hands in this house. If we don't get it out, Dr. Google tells me, a granuloma will form— a perfect circle of white blood cells and granular tissue will make its way around the wood. I remember a trick my mom taught me: you can push a glass down over the splinter, press, and twist, and the suction will pull it out.

I try, but it doesn't work.

"Does it hurt?" I ask.

"No," Gilda says. I try again, press harder, but the splinter stays buried.

Maybe the glass needs to be shallower or deeper? I'm doing it wrong. I suck in a big, shuddery breath. I call my mother.

"You again," she says.

"Funny," I say. "I need some quick advice." I tell her about Gilda's foot, the glass.

"That poor baby," she says. "You forgot the fire."

"Huh?" I say.

"Did you light a match first? You light a match inside the glass, put it out, and *then* you press it on the splinter."

"I forgot the fire," I say.

"It's science," she says, proud.

"Guess we're gonna try this trick," I say.

Gilda's always begging me to let her play with matches, so she sits there rapt, fascinated by the scrape of the strike, the way the spark catches. My mom's method works, maybe too well. I'm surprised by how strong the suction is, how much blood comes up with the little wooden fang.

"Get it off!" Gilda screams. "My blood!" But she's happier with the splinter gone. I pluck it from her heel, put it in the glass to show Jad later. I smear some antibiotic cream into the tiny wound, then stick on the Band-Aid Nancy gave me. I put Gilda in a pair of red socks.

"I can bleed in these, right?" she asks.

"You can," I say, "but you won't."

We curl up together on the bed and fall asleep. I dream a flock of birds swarms us: flamingos, the sky a coral fire. I dream the dream everybody has from time to time—that there's been this whole other room in our house all along. These aren't Julie's dreams—they're all mine. I dream I'm looking down at something in my hands, something black I have been eating, feeding to Gilda too. It's licorice at first, some type of candy, but it starts to stretch apart. Legs—hundreds of them, thousands—feather and unfurl at the sides. Why didn't I notice this at the first bite? What convinced me this thing was edible to begin with?

I wake up, and Gilda thrashes and jerks, still asleep. I lie next to her and look up the School of Drift on my phone. It absolutely does not exist. I look up dignity of risk, benevolent neglect. They're real, sort of. Celadon's gotten *benevolent* a little wrong. It's *benign* neglect, which means pretty much the same thing—that it's okay to ignore your kid—but I prefer her term. Less cancerous, more like a fairy godmother. *Maybe it's the British version,* I think, and then I remember Celadon isn't really British, that she doesn't have children to ignore.

I could call the police. *I've been convinced of something,* I imagine saying.

Fraud is illegal, but is misrepresentation? Is lying? There's nobody to tell. *I've been a little creeped out by a hot, inconsequential stranger. I'd like to press charges, Officer.*

In her sleep, Gilda says, "Foot."

·   ·   ·

YES CALLS WITH a report about my mom.

"I'm sorry it's so late," she says. "My day was just . . ."

"No, it's fine," I say. "We're up, watching TV. Thank you so much for going out there." Tunashow is on, but Jad's got it muted, is flagrantly eavesdropping as I pace and talk.

"Thank you for calling," I say. "Thanks for taking the time."

I'm treating Yes like a doctor with my test results, too formal, impatient but afraid to press her. I'm relieved when she gets down to business quickly. On my mom's lawn, Yes says, there are a bunch of these wooden cutouts of ladies' asses. Granny Fannies, they're called, and they were a huge trend at one point in Wink, which says a lot about our town. Big asses in colorful bloomers, the shape of ladies bent over. To what? Smell my mom's nonexistent roses? She has no flowers at all, no lawn even, just trash.

"Go on," I say.

"The screened-in porch is clean," she says. "A coffee can full of cigarettes and some magazines, but that's it." She says Julie's chair is still there, pristine, and the front steps are swept and there's a perfect herb garden Mom's been tending.

"Some parts of her house stay healthy," I say. "I can't explain it."

"Sure you can," Yes says.

"Your mom?" Jad mouths from the couch. I nod.

"What about inside?" I ask.

"I knocked, and when she didn't answer, I used my key."

Every time I touch that front door I imagine Julie inside, listening for the lock. I picture her in the living room at the piano, puking in the bathroom, hungover in her bed. You'd think my brain would protect itself against that kind of thing, but no, it happens every time. I wonder if it happens to Yes too.

"I tried to open the door, but it stopped halfway," she says. "I heard stuff falling over. Tammy came rushing to shut me out. She was screaming, 'Go around! This isn't a door that opens!'"

"How did she look?" I ask.

"She looked okay," Yes says. "She was wearing scrubs and a bunch of necklaces, lots of lipstick."

Of course she was.

"But, Kit," Yes says. "I looked in the windows and it was . . . overwhelming. Joe and I are going back in his truck tomorrow to haul off some of the bigger stuff, but beyond that . . . it's outside the scope of what I can do."

I completely understand. Yes's scope is huge. She is the best mother I know, a marvel of boundaries and adult behavior. Knowing where you're really needed is a life skill. This isn't her responsibility.

"No, that's so helpful," I say. "That's all I need to know." I make a unilateral decision, right there on the phone. "I'm going out there this weekend," I say, like that's been the plan all along. "There's still time. I'm gonna take care of everything."

Jad is listening to my side of things, piecing the story together. He is nodding his head at me, supporting me fast and hard from the couch.

MY MOTHER'S MESS comes out of me easy, in a rush. Jad and I sit at the kitchen table folding laundry and talking logistics—where we'll stay when we get out to Wink, how many days we have, what the county requires. This situation is awful, but it's not unfamiliar, a severe version of something we've dealt with before.

"Whatever she needs," he says, "we'll figure it out. You could have told me sooner, you know."

"I know," I say. "I wasn't ready." I'm folding Gilda's little T-shirts, not meeting Jad's eyes. "There's something else," I say carefully.

It's shame that keeps me from telling him the full story. I've been made a fool of, maybe, but more embarrassing is the fact that it bothers me so much, that I'm still shaking from the park when nothing really happened.

Big Large once fell for an ATM scam—he came to Yes's garage where we were practicing and told us he'd been held up in Orla. Who would rob a guy like Big Large? We hugged him and sat him down. We offered to call the constable, but he refused. Later, Big Large tearfully admitted there had been no gun, only a wheelchair. The guy hadn't even threatened him—he'd needed help to cash a check, said he was having a problem. If Big Large pulled a hundred bucks out of the ATM, this guy would write him a check for two hundred.

"He seemed so nice!" Big Large said.

"Oh man," we said. "Dude! Dude, no."

Later still, when Big Large was retelling the story to some of our other friends, he revealed the guy had been on crutches.

"What the fuck?" Julie and I said in our bedroom that night, cracking up, trying to fall asleep. "No gun *and* no wheelchair!"

But I knew why he'd said it. A stranger used words to separate Big Large from his cash. It was his lucky day—he was about to make a hundred bucks just for being a nice person. Big Large didn't poke holes in the stranger's promise, just watched as the dream of it fell apart. Then he ran to us, dropped a gun in his story, and we made him some tea.

Celadon's accent was mostly gone the second time I saw her—it's possible it even slipped that first time, the vowels all wrong, midwestern as fuck. Five sons? Come on. No gun, no wheelchair, probably no crutches either. A thousand clues willfully ignored.

Moving from shame to humiliation—it's not easy. Shame is private, but humiliation is out where everybody sees.

I don't mention her broad shoulders, her long neck, her green charm. What I say is that I met a crazy woman in the park—it's reductive, rude, but this is my approach. She was odd, something was off about her, her clothes, she stank, everything was wrong is how I tell it.

"You know me," I say. "I'm a magnet for those types."

I tell him this woman started talking to me, what a curse it is to be so approachable. I was minding my own business!

"I was, you know, busy with Gilda, obviously—"

Enthralled, I think about saying, though that's too much. Entranced? No.

"—when this woman starts saying all this crazy stuff to me," I say.

"Like what?" Jad asks. He's picking through socks, looking for matches. Socks are his domain—he hates the way I pair them, shoving one into the other and rolling them in a lump. "This is the way I was raised to do it," I always say. "It's ingrained." He's shown me how to fold them nice, tuck the toes in neatly, but it's something I can't learn, no matter how hard I try—some kind of profound laundry block.

"It's hard to explain," I say. "Like, it made no sense."

He scratches the soles of his feet. "Give me an example."

"Just nonsense, but dramatic. I don't even know," I say.

"Huh," he says. I've left out too much.

How do you convey fear to someone like Jad? I could describe Celadon's necklace, how it was there and then it wasn't, the black speck in her teeth. I don't know how to insert danger into this story because I don't quite know what the danger is.

"And then, get this, she tried to sell me Molly," I say. I'm folding Gilda's little shorts in half, making a stack.

"She what?" he says slowly.

"Isn't that crazy?" I say.

"Like, how?" he asks. "How did she try?" Maybe now I've put in too much.

"She just tried," I say.

He stops and stares at me, a tiny mateless sock in his hand. "You should call the cops," he says. "You should report this."

"I should?" I say.

"It's a drug dealer in a kids' park!" he says, laughing a little. "Listen, I love you, but you scare the shit out of me."

.   .   .

ON OUR WAY to bed, I trip on the mat by the front door, then bend down to straighten it. I stop and look. Jad looks at me, looking at the mat.

The dishes have been put away, floors mopped, counters sanitized. I touch a corner of the mat.

"It's new?" I say.

"No way. We've had it."

"It's new."

"It's not. Look."

We crouch together.

"We've always had *a* mat here. But this one is somehow different," I say. "Sinister."

"Sinister?" Jad says. "Did you say sinister?"

"Or, I don't know, it's just negative. Not negative. Different."

It's navy blue, a waffle weave. I put my fingers underneath, touch the rubber backing. It looks like something we might buy.

Jad stands and checks the peephole, then opens the door.

"Why'd you look out the peephole?"

"Just in case," he says ominously.

He steps on the porch and stands on our outside mat, which is red and vibrant and remembered.

"Does this one have a better attitude?" he asks.

We look at each other. Jad's just kidding, this isn't the type of thing that will derange him, not even a little bit. He is quite possibly underangeable, a good quality in a partner. He closes the door, turns the dead bolt.

Later, lights out, Gilda is good and asleep on my chest, and Jad is drifting off too, his hot hand on my thigh.

"We were in a fight," I say. "Julie and me."

Jad stirs, turns on his pillow to face me.

"At the end, I mean," I say. She could be so cruel. We both could. We knew exactly what to say to cut. "She called me wanting something—money, a favor, I forget what. You know how she was. I always said yes to her, but I was so tired of it, so this time, whatever she'd asked for—I said no. Even before she finished asking, I told her, 'Definitely not, I've had it with you.' She lost her mind."

I kiss Gilda's head, close my eyes.

"She was screaming into the phone, saying I was using my pregnancy as an excuse, that I was selfish, that I'd be a terrible mother—worse than Mom even. 'Trash makes trash makes trash' was what she said. Bringing Gilda into it like that—she was just looking for a reaction."

Jad strokes my arm.

"I don't know why I did it, why I gave her one," I say. "I told her the best gift I could give my kid was a life without her in it, that she'd be a toxic aunt, that there was no way in hell she'd ever meet my daughter—no way I'd bring a baby around her. I could hear the shift in her breathing, hear the hurt through the phone. I said what I said, and she hung up. We didn't speak after that—now we won't ever. And what I said came true—those awful words are still booming around in the universe."

"Kit," Jad says. "There's no booming. You can't make something happen by saying it."

"I think we disagree," I say. "About the booming. I know it's not my fault, it's just—I put a dark notion into the world. I did that. It was the last thing I said to her. She had my voice in her head that day, that night, the next morning, in the car. She died with it."

Jad puts his big hand on top of my head. "She knew you didn't mean it," he says.

I don't tell him that I did mean it—in that moment, I really did. I imagined an easier life without her. Julie was a mess, an impossible person. She was going to keep getting worse, and she was pulling me down with her. I'd already pushed her into the past tense: Julie was, Julie was, she was.

"She knew you," Jad says. I swallow hard, nuzzle Gilda. Exactly. She knew me, so she knew a part of me meant it.

"She was so fucked up for so long and I was so tired of it. It was exhausting. But I never did anything about it. Why didn't Mom and Yes and Big Large and I gang up, put her in therapy, stage an intervention, take her on a trip?"

"It's hard to know how to help," Jad says softly.

I turn my face to him.

"I know what you and Pete did," I whisper then. "I know you guys sent me to Montana to get better."

Jad breathes in deep, through the nose, the way men do when they don't want to talk but know that so much talking is about to happen.

"I'm not mad," I say. "I know why you did it. Because you love me. Because I've been in a place where nobody can reach me."

Talking to Jad about the unreachable place, saying those words out loud, I'm keenly aware of two distinct locations: the place where I was, suspended in static, utterly alone, and here, now, where I want to be. Grief isolates, makes you feel unknowable, unknown.

"I want to be here with y'all," I say, and Jad cups my face, kisses my forehead.

"I want that too," he says.

Outside in our cul-de-sac, a car revs its engine.

"Seriously?" I say, covering Gilda's ears, but she's unbothered, deeply asleep.

The revving goes on and on, but eventually the car leaves, its tires screeching and screaming as it turns in the street, peels away. For a split second our dark bedroom is ablaze, shot full of light.

TOMORROW WE LEAVE for Wink, but today Gilda and I take a walk to meet Pete. A "walk-walk," Gilda says now, since for the past few days we've been leaving the stroller at home. I never realized how much of a buffer it was between Gilda and the world. Inside it, she's an observer, a baby—without it she's emboldened, a real participant. It's nice to have her walking next to me, holding my hand, but now every social interaction is awkward, potentially disastrous.

"Wow," she'll say to a stranger, "your baby's eyes are really far apart."

To some frazzled mom, burdened with grocery bags in a driveway: "What foods did you buy? Can you show me them?"

"Is that cat alive or dead in there?" she'll ask, peering into somebody's pet carrier. Today she shouts, "What's going on with your legs, guy?" to the limping man in front of us.

"Hello there," I call out as we pass, tugging her along. "Have a great day!"

Gilda sings while we walk, swinging my hand. How have I never noticed this before? That she's a little jukebox, that she can sing—really sing—on key and on cue, any song she hears. When Julie and I were young, we thought everybody could sing, same as learning to walk or tie your shoes. It wasn't until we went to school and got around other kids that we realized what we had.

"Gilda, do 'Colors and the Kids,' or 'Rock Bottom Riser,'" I say. "Do 'What Is the Light.'" And she does, she does.

Celadon's gone, but I keep catching myself looking for her, not wanting to see her. She's on to another grift, or maybe she's just found a different place to sit in the afternoons, some other lost person to glom on to. Without her, I'm not Julie anymore. I'm just me—Gilda's mom.

"There's Hair!" Gilda screams. I wonder how he'll react, seeing her loose in the world, unstrollered. She runs straight for him. "Hair!"

I think for a second he might dodge her, take a big step to the left, but no, he doesn't. He bends down and waits for her, opens his arms.

.   .   .

"TODAY WE CLEAR a path," I say to my mother. "That's it. Just a path."

I'm home in Wink, digging her out of this mess as fast as I can.

"But I mean, why?" she says. "What for?"

Egress! I scream in my head. She says her only trouble is with the overflow, all the stuff that's in the yard out where everyone can see.

"It's not *for* you," I say. "It's for me." Jad and Gilda are in the car, circling the farm roads, my mother's house unfit for a child, unfit for any being with an olfactory system.

"I think if you're going to pay for a house, which, I mean, I've paid for this one, then you should be able to use the space as you, the owner, see fit."

"I see what you mean," I say. This is the tone I adopt when Gilda insists she can't get into bed because there is already an invisible boy sleeping there. "The boy needs company, right?" I'll try. "Or should we kick him out? Here, I'll turn down the covers and he can leave. Or no, why don't you lie down directly on top of the invisible boy? Wouldn't that be fun! To be inside an invisible boy, sleeping while he sleeps?" Which one of these alternatives brings us more quickly to the sleeping portion of the night, Gilda?

"Poor use of space," says my mother, suddenly an architect, a designer, a flow specialist. "I never go into that bedroom or the other bedroom or the office or the hallway or the guest bathroom. I have ways to go where I go."

"*I* need a path, though, right? I'm coming down the hall, I trip on this . . ." I lean over and pick up a chipped plate, an orgy of deer painted on it. "I trip on this . . . art, I fall into this pile of—"

"That's wood for woodworking. Those are good dowels. Dowel rods."

"Right, I step on a dowel, and I break my leg. Like, a compound type deal. Bone sticking out."

"Far-fetched," she says.

As she watches me wade through the hallway, she narrates, in great detail, a distant aunt's medical issue. "Did you hear? Her throat's closing. It's full of scar tissue so it's doing this." She wrings her hands in the air. "The doctors have to do expanding sessions every two weeks. They have to drill it out," she says, conspiratorial. "Every week they stick these plastic hot dogs into her canal." She gives me a look, says "Die-lators," like it's the filthiest of words. "Her esophageal stuff's gone all gray."

"Excuse me," I say. "Gray? Oh my god. What causes that?"

"Nobody knows, nobody knows," she says. "Throats close for all kinds of reasons."

"Somebody knows!" I say.

I push things against the sides of the hall. Shoeboxes, cookware. "Tell me everything you do before you do it," my mom says, suspicious.

"Blanket statement," I say. "So you know. I'm moving *all* this stuff. Only to the sides. Relocating, not removing."

"Fine," she says. "But, just so *you* know, everything's cataloged. There's underlying principles."

She shoves open the door to my old bedroom.

The problem—the disease—started here. Keeping Julie's stuff was something I understood, a mother wanting to hold on to that. But now Julie's bed is stinking under dirty bath towels, Dr Pepper signage, a plastic bag bloated with other plastic bags.

Once this room was full of loved things, stuffed animals and artwork and posters. Things we saved up to buy, things we didn't pay for. We started by stealing candy, like all kids do, chocolate bars in our pockets, cans of Coke yanked up into our sleeves. We rolled magazines into tubes and slid them between my early, already enormous tits. Julie liked useful things from the hardware aisle at Flip's—a doorstop, a sewing kit, a roll of Scotch tape. "Who would steal a sink plug?" she planned on saying to Kenny Flip if she ever got caught.

The most rewarding theft is the kind you pull off boldly, in broad daylight. Julie walking a plunger right past the front counter, me waiting for her in the parking lot with a big box of kids' cereal under my arm. We brought Yes into our world of petty crime and she was the best of us, calmly gliding out of the Pecos Walmart in stiff roller skates, her old sneakers tied together, dangling over her shoulder. We didn't need or want half of what we chose—these were just tokens of courage we could bring home, take out later to touch.

Yes's mom caught on quick. She made Yes confess and backtrack, drove her all over the county to apologize, hand over things nobody even knew they were missing. Yes wanted no part in our game after that. Our mom noticed too, the junk food and hair dye and thumb-tacks she didn't pay for, but trouble wasn't something we could get into at our house.

Now I don't recognize anything special in this room. There might be empty deodorant canisters or a bucket brimming with nails. Might be a tub of potpourri or a cat skull in here. Definitely a cat skull. It's unsettling how few Friends I actually see, but their evidence is every-where: their litter boxes and their claw marks, so much loose fur. They don't trust me—disrupter of their safe space. They scatter as I move through. I catch quick flicks of their mangy tails, flashes of their slick sides as they skid between hiding places. Being in my mom's house is like walking around in her mind—the armadillo room, the lotion hall, the cat trees, the good glass. Julie underneath everything.

Inside a broken wardrobe I find a stack of old, rancid newspapers.

"Surely this can go," I say.

"I need to pick through. Some of them I haven't read." Her infor-mation, she calls it.

The thing about a hoard is that it takes on a new, singular quality, like a stew. It's not a hundred wet egg cartons rotting in the corner. It's a color and a smell. The guest bathroom is brownish, a fester, valu-able items mixed into gradients of rot. I find a leather box in an open drawer of damp pennies. Inside is Mom's wedding ring and a picture of Julie's third birthday party. I'm in the background full of cake envy, rage in my face.

I sit down on the closed toilet—which is sparkling clean, somehow—and cry. I text Pete about my aunt's shrinking gray esophagus.

Oh my Christ, he says. *I'd cut my fucking head off.*

My mom keeps the shower clean and one hallway vacuumed. Goat paths, the internet calls these areas. Acquisition is what they call it when Mom drags a smashed kiddie pool from somebody's garbage into her living room. Contemplation is Mom stroking the doll clothes and stacks of receipts, the jumbo bag of rubber bands and the beach sandals she got from the dollar store.

"I know what's here because I put it here. Everything is chosen," she says, reaching down to pet a pile of dirty laundry.

If preppers are pessimists readying themselves for calamity, hoarders are downright chipper by comparison, crafty and optimistic, full of possibility and pride. My mom picks up a disposable, waterlogged coaster and tells me she saved it because look how cute the bar logo is—a bear cub drinking a beer. She happens to have a postcard of a dog in a Budweiser shirt sitting at a table, so she makes sure to put those two things together.

"And do what with them?" I ask.

"Wait for a third thing to come along and make sense," she says.

Together, we make slow, steady work of her house, all of this in preparation for the team who will meet us here tomorrow. The words *certified professional organizer,* in any order, together or apart, make my mom feel attacked. But she's trying.

"If you think about it, what we're doing is showcasing," I say, and my mother's mood lifts. "We want to make sure all this wonderful stuff gets the attention it deserves."

Later that night, safe with sleeping Jad and Gilda in a Monahans motel room, Julie comes through in the drone of the air-conditioning, soft footfalls from the ceiling. She's with me spiritually, genetically, metaphorically. She's awkward at the little stationery desk, creaking in a wooden chair. She paces, clicks around in the minifridge, bored.

The sun is coming up and there is so much work to do at Mom's today.

Pinned by Gilda in the gray light, Jad snoring next to me, I know with absolute certainty, brain to brain, that Julie is ready, that she wants to go. She can't move on until I let her rest, put her down. It's all up to me.

If there's one advantage to being gone, cut loose from space and time and energy and light, it's the freedom to land anywhere. I know just the place for her.

Part Six

YOU ARE
 THE
UNIVERSE

W E GO UP AND OPEN THE BIG WHITE POT TO LET the steam out. It smells like green beans, institutional green beans from day care when Kit and I were little. I never ate mine, though. I always gave them to Kit.

"Remember those beans?" I ask her. "Remember the milk in those plastic cups?"

"Day care milk was in cartons," she says. "You're thinking of the pizza place." Kit is right and I'm wrong, everything I remember replaced by what she's saying. I can see those red cups now, a row of them stacked wetly on a table. I can feel the texture of them, and I can see how the fatty milk sloshes up and coats the sides when I drink.

"I remember green beans," she says. "Do you remember wacky cake? They served it on Fridays." I remember the name.

"Vaguely," I say, and Yes says, "What was so wacky about it?"

"Raisins," Kit says.

I don't remember raisins at all but it's okay because Kit does. We're each in charge of different parts. Kit keeps the unremembered half of my childhood tucked safe in her brain.

"How much longer, Big Large?" Kit asks, and Pablo says, "Soon, soon," but he cooks and cooks, even overnight when we go home. The pot feels like this living thing we have to take care of. Pablo burns a pizza and twice is late for work, but he is so good at the big white pot. The water boils but doesn't boil over, and it never stops boiling, either.

Stuff rises in the pot, and Pablo takes off his pearl-snap shirt and uses it to strain off the crud for our tea. It's beyond gross if you think about it, him wearing that shirt for three days at least, getting all sweaty while he works, going to sleep damp and waking up dry and getting sweaty all over again. He boils and strains and boils and strains and our crud reserve grows. It's nasty but I don't mind, because I like Pablo so much, and I hope there is a part of him that will go into all three of us. I bet he loves that, this idea of three girls getting high from the cactus but also high from him. Who wouldn't want to fuck somebody up like that? Twice I've called the cactus "San Pablo" by mistake and everybody thinks I'm making a joke.

"You won't be able to tell what's me and what's the Pedro," he says. It's like the time he had a big blister on his thumb from a bad firework. I asked him to hand me my guitar and when he did, the blister burst itself all over and I sort of gagged, even though I knew it hurt his feelings.

"It's just water!" he said, and I said, "True, but it's *your* water."

Nobody should have to touch something that belongs inside another person, not unless they've both agreed to it. In this case, in the cactus case, we do want it, we've agreed to want Pablo's water, or maybe *want* is a strong word but we don't mind it, not at all.

We're supposed to let the crud drain and filter and boil and drain and filter and boil for at least five days, according to Pablo's cactus book. We go to school and work and home and when we come back, Pablo is still taking care of the big white pot. We argue about what "at least" means. Can we drink it at the end of the fifth day or the beginning? Or is it the morning of the sixth day? Pablo says the cactus will tell us what it needs. He says there are no mistakes with the cactuses. The time comes, or we think it does, and Pablo takes the thick tea and pours it into a carafe. It's like terrible, muddy apple juice, but nothing is wrong with it, Pablo says, this is exactly right. We sit in his living room and look at each other and sip our drinks. We pull down the shades. I'm watching to see what Kit does, how much she drinks. I take a sip every time she sips. I put my finger in my glass—I don't know why. We are all expecting to get the shits and we've agreed we won't make a big deal about it. Yes is a reluctant vomiter, but she says she will embrace the heaving if it comes.

Pablo's cactus book says you have to set intentions, and so we are saying what we want out of today and what we want to have happen to us. We are already listening in a new way, more careful with each other than we usually are. I am thinking that what I want is to play like a little kid, to be free and curious and not fucked up. I tell everybody, "Don't let me drink or smoke weed on this, okay? I want to feel only this." I think about going into the trip with a problem, a song I want to write, like maybe I could focus on that and solve it. It's not a particular song that is bothering me, though—it's a feeling like I need to get out of my own way. Sometimes I want to write a song and then I can't and I realize it must be because I didn't really want to after all.

I ask, if you can ask a cactus for something, for it to make me brave. What happens to me sometimes is I change my mind right after I dose. I always get scared. Yes is scared too, and she is sipping her tea slow. Kit takes the last bit of sludge in a shot, so I take mine like that too. Kit's never scared. She disappears into the bathroom, and Yes and I start a life with Pablo on the pink carpet.

Being on the edge of this feels scary but thrilling, like that time at Yes's when the Ouija board spelled out "HAS A SCAR" when we asked our ghost to describe himself. I don't know why, when we're deep in pink rug, Pablo is talking about scorpions, but he says telson is what you call the tippy-tip of a scorpion's tail, and the sound of that word, how pointy it is, it pokes into me. A telson, so great! The rest of this trip—the rest of my life—will have the word *telson* in it.

Then Pablo is gone and we're scared again because we think we've lost him, but then we see he is on the porch with a machete hacking up more of the San Pedro arm.

Kit is back from the bathroom, staring out the screen door. "Is this going to take a gruesome turn?" she asks, but Pablo is a big panda man, here to hug. He puts four of the hacked-up stumps in his backpack and says we should get our shoes on. It's a plant like any plant, Pablo says. We can grow more. We decide to walk around outside and let the cactus parts tell us where they want to be planted. Is this mescaline behavior? We can't tell yet.

We tromp through the scrub and brush Pablo's trailer sits on, side-stepping all these different cactuses: horse cripplers, barrels, tasajillos. We're supposed to tell Pablo when we get the feeling we are in the right place.

"Do cactuses like to be around other cactuses?" Kit asks. "Or will they fight?"

"Why fight?" Pablo says. "Maybe they'll kiss."

We single-file with Kit in the lead, like she's been here before, like she knows the land better than Pablo. And, I don't know, she's pretty convincing. When we come to different rocks or bushes or holes, she says, "Look at this rock and this bush and this hole," and even though she's definitely never been out here, her confidence is giving us a tour. It's all in her tone. What is knowing the land but knowing one rock over here looks like a table and over there is a dick-shaped tree and look at all these lizards who are all named Carl.

"I have some ideas," she says, like she's redecorating, Carls streaming out around her feet, and we all want to walk through her dream with her, we have all agreed to do it, and this, I think, is the cactus finally working. We are little kids, preschoolers in safety vests, how they all hold the same bright rope when they walk down the street. Kit is the teacher, the leader, but she's a child too. We let our stumps talk to us. We trot around until we get a feeling and a place feels right. It's a puzzle we do with our bodies. As soon as the stumps pick their spots, we put them down and they melt into the landscape. The second we stop touching them we can't see where we've planted them or else they disappear or else we're too high to see them. No matter what, they are gone. We look and look but we can't find them and we know they are messing with us. Then we stop looking because it seems like the game is getting boring to the stumps, like they want us to leave them alone.

This is the most sober we've ever felt, we all agree. This is an anti-trip, how it feels to come back home.

Kit leads us to this sunken patch of grass like it was our destination all along. The grass is so green and we lie on our backs and Yes and I put big flat rocks on our chests like it's the most natural thing and when Kit asks I say, "Oh, because of magnets," and nobody calls me on this and I'm so relieved. And then everybody but Pablo has a rock on their chest, and we are lying down, Kit on a log and the rest of us below her, on the ground. She's our queen, no doubt. I always know this but it's nice to be reminded.

A thought of my mother claws through me, her alone in our house down the road. I kick the thought away, get rid of it, but first I hold it, make peace with it. Our mother is beautiful. Sometimes when she leaves us, we paw through her beer cooler jewelry box, secret heart of our house. Inside is a flattened rose and her thin gold wedding band, the hospital bracelets we wore when we got born, a necklace made of shells, our baby teeth all mixed together, locks of our hair, a stoppered jade bottle that smells just like her shoulders.

More thoughts claw, and I make peace with them too. I pick them up, scratch them behind the ears, accept them, let them go. The interruptions are the point, all the best monks say so.

Kit and Pablo and Yes and I are not only sober, we are super-sober, doing this very normal thing people do where they lie like the dead in a glade with rocks on their chests. This place—it isn't possible. A glade! In West Texas. I start to feel anxious and I wonder when it is okay to speak again, to stop looking at the wind. That's what we're watching, the wind, how it shows itself by what it touches, how it takes on the color and shape of every leaf and flower and blade of grass it streams across. When Pablo sits up and says, "This is boring, y'all," we laugh because he's right, it *is* boring, only none of us knew how to break the spell. Is this what it is to be a man in the world?

And then I'm sure there is mescaline involved because I roll over, not once but three, four, five times across the dewy grass, and I get to where my face is right next to Yes's face and she turns to me so close. This is what Kit and I called making a creature when we were little. You put the tip of your nose to somebody else's nose and you see the one-eyed and weirdly beautiful thing you make together. Out loud I say, "We should kiss, we should all kiss." This is the man part of me saying the things I want and believe in, hoping everybody else will give in or agree. I don't want Yes, not like that, but she's my friend and I want to know her. My mouth wants to know her mouth, that's all.

Over there in another part of the glade Kit is straddling Pablo and it's like she's giving him CPR. What she's doing is innocent and life-saving and not at all strange. My mouth learns Yes's mouth and inside there I see her as a child, small and still in a church pew, my tongue on a scab on her knee, my tongue in the socket of her lost tooth, her as a little baby. The hot weight of her, smaller then, she's a nugget in my armpit, tinier, the whole world of Yes on the head of a pin. She lets me leach into her, only I'm not me anymore. I'm the creature that forms when she looks at me. I don't know what she sees now, but I'm confident, assured, unashamed, and this is exactly like skinny-dipping with someone who loves you.

We swap. Pablo to me, Yes to Kit, all of us somehow rolling across and around in the soft grass. Pablo's mouth is perfect too, in a different way: the dead dog that broke his heart, teeth that need flossing. I hate talking about people's vibes because I know how it sounds. I wish people didn't have energy, but they do. Pablo's energy is different from Yes's. He's bigger and stronger and he could snap me in half, could snap all three of us girls, but he won't. There is gentleness, but I will not give him extra credit for not killing us, not holding us down and forcing us. This is an idea I transmit to him. I want him to be aware. And the message I get back from him says he understands, would never hurt us, and the spark of him inside his big bear body is so small, smaller than any of ours even. What I'm giving him is something new, different from what I gave Yes. He keeps saying, "You're helping my feelings," the opposite of hurting feelings. I'm helping his, and I know it's true.

I do more tossing and rolling and flattening of the grass. Look at Kit—she is mine now and always. We get close to each other and it's just "Hey, you." What can you say about your one true person? You would think we wouldn't need to make a creature together, we're so close to being the same creature already, reading each other's thoughts, one of us saying, "Now?" to a question that was not asked aloud. We have shorthand, codes, sisterwords—to tell you any more would be a betrayal. We touch noses and the creature is the one we expect.

Maybe talking about a trip is like telling somebody your dream— they have to love you to care about it. This is the part I've been waiting to say:

Back in Pablo's living room, everything has been set free to vibrate. The pink rug calls us, and we melt into it. We are writhing, floating, surfing on pink foam.

I slip into a different place and I am not afraid. The truth is a rung bell. A thought floats to me and I know it like my name, my birthday, no fear, just a fact, beautifully neutral: I'll die here, in this town, and when I'm young too. I know exactly how it will feel when it happens. I look up, over the heap of Pablo and Yes. I see Kit's shocked face and I know she's heard it too, some version of my end. I rush to her in my mind and talk the way we do, with me saying, *It's okay it's okay.*

I don't want that, she thunders in my brain, but her face is calm, serene in the smoke from Yes's cigarette. *Kitty, it's beautiful, isn't it?* I show her what I know—a flash, a painless snap, me thrown clear of myself, brilliant. She starts to cry. *No no no,* she says without saying, and I get firm with her and command her not to fear. How lucky, how grateful, I am to be cut free from this familiar place, to set off on the journey from home. I can boldly move into the current, perfectly content. *It won't feel bad,* I say to her, *it will feel like this,* and my hands churn in the frothy pink rug.

Kit sobs in my brain and also in the room. I make a quick decision. I gently snatch the truth back, lift it carefully out of my sister's mind. It is a fact that comes out clean with clear borders, no trace left behind. I hold my sister's face and kiss her cheeks and I help quiet her. I see the plot of her lovely life. I don't have to tell her, or you, what's coming. So many nights I've watched her dreaming when I should be asleep. From my bed I see her eyelids start to beat and her hands ball up and I wonder where she is over there, what she's running so fast and far from, what pattern the stars and cells and dancing spots are making, and who, if anybody, is fucking with her. I can toss a pillow or clap my hands, try to scatter the dark things that have huddled. If that doesn't work, I'll wait for a sign, the twitch or shudder that says she still needs me. I'm not afraid to get out of my bed and go over there. I can softly shake her shoulder. I can hold her hand or trace her ear. There are so many ways to change the pattern, realign the stars and cells and dancing spots. It's so easy—this is something I have always been able to do. I'll put my hands on her head, reach right through, and save her.

Acknowledgments

You only get to write your first novel once, and I can't believe how lucky I've been to do that with the support of these incredible people:

Meredith Kaffel Simonoff, your expertise, enthusiasm, and kindness are invaluable to me—thank you for seeing the draft beyond the draft (and the draft beyond that one). Maris Dyer, thank you for your brilliant editorial insights, your humor, and your thoughtful and tireless attention to getting things right. Thank you to the outrageously wonderful teams at Gernert, Knopf, and Atlantic Books: Nora Gonzalez, Rebecca Gardner, Reagan Arthur, Emily Reardon, Micah Kelsey, Emily Murphy, Janet Hansen, Aja Pollock, Kathleen Cook, Kirsty Doole, and Will Roberts. Thank you, James Roxburgh, for words of encouragement when I really needed them and for writing the most wildly charming emails I've ever read in my life. Thank you, Tim O'Connell, for your genius help in shaping the earliest version of this book ("Maybe the past should be in the past tense?" you gently, brilliantly suggested). And thank you, Margaux Weisman, for making my books possible in the first place.

Thank you, Giancarlo DiTrapano—you were the very first reader of the seeds and sparks that would eventually become *We Were the Universe*. Everybody misses you so much.

I am grateful for generous support from Yaddo, the National Book Foundation, Tin House, the Texas Institute of Letters, Hermitage Artist Retreat, Regional Arts and Culture Council, the Oregon Arts Commission, the Literary Arts Booth Emergency Fund, and, especially, the

ACKNOWLEDGMENTS

Tasajillo Residency, where Katherine Johnson and Eric Hayes hosted me (twice!) and where I learned about horse cripplers and barrel cactuses and where I wrote the trippiest parts of this book.

Thank you to my amazing writing group: Carrie Cooperider, Diana Marie Delgado, Caleb Gayle, Mitchell S. Jackson, Cleyvis Natera, Tracy O'Neill, Joseph Riippi, Robb Todd, and Nicole Treska. Some of us have been sharing work for almost fifteen years now, and I never take your friendship, terrific ideas, and attention to the line level for granted.

Thank you to the friends who have nurtured me in all the ways (with your time, your company, your playlists, your text messages and voice memos, your cooking, your extra bedrooms, and your sage advice): Melissa Bellaire, Chelsea Bieker, Alfred Brown IV, Courtney Denelle, Leah Dieterich, Mark Doten, Wendy Flanagan, Kate Garrick, Evelynne Gomes Greenberg, Genevieve Hudson, Chloé Cooper Jones, Scott Korb, Michelle Ruiz Keil, Chad Robert Miller, Jules Ohman, Allie Rowbottom, Karen Russell, Kevin Sampsell, Tom Treanor, Adam Wilson, Hannah Withers, and Cecily Wong. Double thanks to Chad for the soft black nothing, for Kentucky and the best sleep, your brilliant insights, and thirty years of friendship; to Chelsea for spasms of cry-laughter, your impeccable style in language and in life, your wisdom, and for noticing and processing *every damn thing* with me; to Tom for Montana and the river, the bar and the hotel and the bighorn sheep that started it all.

Thank you to my parents for letting me roam and write (and come back home when I need to). Thank you to my in-laws and stepparents; thank you to my brothers and sisters—we miss you, Dan; we miss you, Anna Jean.

Thank you, Ronnie, Julian, and Lev, for being the very best people I know, for knowing me, truly, and for loving me still, and (most of all) for letting me love you. The kids want me to end by thanking our cat, so, thank you, Monkey.

Kimberly King Parsons is the author of *Black Light,* a collection of stories that was long-listed for the National Book Award and the Story Prize. In 2020, she received the National Magazine Award for fiction. Born in Lubbock, Texas, she lives in Portland, Oregon, with her partner and children. *We Were the Universe* is her first novel.

A NOTE ABOUT THE TYPE

This book was set in Adobe Garamond. Designed for the
Adobe Corporation by Robert Slimbach, the fonts are based
on types first cut by Claude Garamond (ca. 1480–1561).
Garamond was a pupil of Geoffroy Tory and is believed to
have followed the Venetian models, although he introduced
a number of important differences, and it is to him that we
owe the letter we now know as "old style." He gave to his
letters a certain elegance and feeling of movement that won
their creator an immediate reputation and the patronage of
Francis I of France.

*Typeset by Scribe,
Philadelphia, Pennsylvania*

*Printed and bound by Berryville Graphics,
Berryville, Virginia*

Designed by Jo Anne Metsch